THE BIG FOOTPRINTS

IS

"Taut and harrowing . . . the top level of literate adventure writing."
—*The Wall Street Journal*

"Solidly crafted . . . satisfying . . . Innes can spin his stories out with the best of them."
—*Baltimore Sun*

"Superior adventure . . . suspense . . . and a darn good story."
—*Library Journal*

The Big Footprints

Hammond Innes

BALLANTINE BOOKS • NEW YORK

Library of Congress Catalog Card Number: 76-43293

ISBN 0-345-27411-3

First American edition published by Alfred A. Knopf, Inc.

Manufactured in the United States of America

First Ballantine Books Edition: October 1978

Contents

Part One

THE WILDLIFE
CONFERENCE

I

IT WAS RAINING, a solid tropical downpour, and the beer was warm. The supply trucks had brought it up with the food from Nairobi over the bomb-scarred gravel road I had glimpsed from the plane as we landed. We were rationed to one can each, the froth and the sweetness cloying, and the water unfit to drink. I looked at my watch. It was after ten and the night black, no chance that he would arrive now.

I lit a cigarette, perched on the crumbling parapet of what had once been a verandah, staring through the rain at the big half-circle of rooms lit by hurricane lamps and candles. The shattered glass of the sliding windows showed walls pockmarked by bullets. Some of the conference delegates were already preparing for bed, shadows in silhouette stripping off their clothes and climbing into the two-tier bunks. Others, like myself, out on the battered verandahs, talking quietly, voices subdued by the atmosphere of the place.

The night was very still, no breeze; only the sound of the rain falling vertically and somewhere the hum of a generator. The organisers had rigged lights in the dining-room and kitchens, but these had been switched off now, the power concentrated on spotlights beamed on the waterhole as though to remind us what the gathering was all about. The big circular pool showed pale and flat through the rain, but nothing moved, not even a bird. Perhaps there really were no animals left.

I had finished my beer and the mood of depression settled deeper on me. I thought of all the tourists who had sat here on this verandah, lolling with ice-cold drinks, watching for elephants and rhinos, and all

2

the small fry that had come like shadows out of the night to drink at the floodlit waterhole. It must have been quite a place then, the Lodge so carefully planned and the waterhole like a stage set. Now the lawn was a jungle growth, the swimming pool cracked and empty, the buildings battered and fallen into decay. It would make a good opening shot, but that was all, and a wildlife conference without wildlife. . . . I stared at my cigarette, listening to the rain. It would be a dead duck, and the only reason I had accepted the assignment, the man I had come here to meet—Cornelius van Delden, who knew the northern frontier— had not arrived yet.

The voices on the next verandah were louder now: *I tell you, it's pointless. The tourists won't come back, and without tourism . . .*

You agree with Kirby-Smith then?

About culling? Yes, if it's properly organised.

And somebody else, strident and angry: *Killing, you mean. Call it by its proper name, for God's sake. Shoot anything that moves, make way for cattle. And you call that culling.*

A heavy rasping Bostonian voice cut in: *Major Kirby-Smith is a businessman, that's all. So let's be practical, gentlemen. Call him what you like, but he's efficient and he's got the Government behind him. So I have to tell you this, the Foundation I represent accepts that this pilot scheme is the best deal we're . . .*

A figure appeared out of the night, dripping wet, his safari hat shielding his camera. "Fabulous!" It was Ken's current word when he had something good. He had been playing around with his Leica, taking stills. "It's the rain and the hurricane lamps, all those bunks, and the bullet holes, reflections in pools of water." He came in under the shelter of the verandah, shaking himself like a dog and smiling his satisfaction. "I was in black and white, of course, but tomorrow, shooting in 7252 colour—could be difficult. The light, I mean." He went through into the room behind me, enthusing again about the pictures he had taken, wiping his camera before he bothered to strip off and towel him-

3

self down. "Our roommates are on their way." His voice was muffled as he rubbed at the dark mass of his hair. "Two CBS men."

"How do you know?"

"Karanja told me. They're coming by truck. He was posting an attendance list on the noticeboard."

"Was van Delden on it?"

He shook his head, towelling vigorously. "There was a Delden representing some American magazines. But the initial was M. There was no Cornelius van Delden."

So he wasn't coming after all. The one man who really knew the Northern Frontier District, the man whose father had opened the route across the Chalbi Desert to Lake Rudolf and published a book of his travels in Afrikaans.

"Have you roughed anything out yet?"

"No." And I stayed there, staring out at the rain, thinking about the script, convinced it wouldn't be any good and the whole thing a waste of time now that Cornelius van Delden wasn't coming.

In the end I went inside and mulled over the agenda and the old tourist maps they had given us, sitting at the broken-legged camp table with the hurricane lamp at my elbow. Tsavo, Serengeti, Arusha, Ngorongoro and its crater, all those national parks and game reserves that had once been household names, and in the north—Meru, Samburu, Marsabit. And further north still, up by Lake Rudolf on the Ethiopian border, the least known, most remote of all—Ileret. At dinner they had been talking about Ileret and unconfirmed reports of game moving up through the Rift Valley to the waters of Lake Rudolf. The only real haven left, they had said. But none of them had known Ileret. To them it was the edge of the unknown, all desert country and lava fields, and across the BP map, glazed to protect its surface against the sweat of tourists' hands, some official had banged his rubber stamp, the single word FORBIDDEN staring at me in violet ink.

The map didn't mark Porr, or the islands, only

4

Loiyangalani and Mt. Kulal—Oasis Fishing Camp, it said. There would be no fishing camp now, and I didn't need to measure the mileage. I knew how far it was, a hell of a long way, and the whole area forbidden territory. I reached for my bag, for the map and the translation of that old book—but what was the point of reading the typescript again? I knew the passages by heart, the map clear in my mind, and who else could take me there in present circumstances? *I am retired now, but if they ask me I will come.* Well, they had asked him and he wasn't here and the Conference was opening in the morning.

I leaned back, staring at the wall opposite, where a gekko flicked its tongue, feet and tail spread flat like a little jewelled brooch—the only sign of life. Ken turned in his bunk, complaining about the light, and I told him to go to hell. I was feeling angry and frustrated, the rain drumming on the roof, gushing from the broken guttering, the persistent sound of it filling the room and a trickle of water seeping in at one corner where the plaster was cracked and stained. It glistened wet in the lamplight and I was thinking of the last time I had seen the kindly, ineffective man who had helped bring me up. Almost a year ago now, and his hand quite steady as he gave me Pieter van Delden's book and the translator's typescript of it headed JOURNEY THROUGH THE CHALBI TO LAKE RUDOLF. Tucked into the typescript I had found the map drawn on heavy parchment paper. Two days later he had been found dead in that same dingy little basement office in Doughty Street.

The gekko moved, darting its long tongue at some insect, and I remembered his words, the sense of failure—*There's nothing else of any value for you here.* Those words had stayed in my mind. Had there been a note of censure in his voice? I couldn't remember now. Probably not. He had been too mild a man, and at the time I had regarded his words as a sort of epitaph to his mismanagement of Southly Tait. When he had taken over from my father it had been quite a thriving little publishing house specialising in travel.

Inflation and a changing world had killed it—and him. Or was it my fault, not his? If I had gone into the business, as they had both hoped . . .

I pushed back my chair and got to my feet. It had been a long twenty-four hours, the night flight to Nairobi, the interminable wait on the cratered tarmac at Wilson Airport—odd how habit had retained that very English name—and now the rain, the bloody everlasting rain, and this damnable dreary battered place. I should have brought some Scotch. I could hear the clink of glasses next door, the sound of voices mellowed by drink. A bottle of Scotch would have cushioned my mind against the morbid thought of his inadequacy and my own selfish determination to go my own way. Ken Stewart was asleep now. I could hear his breathing, soft as a child's and I envied him living for the moment, for the instant exposure of his next shot, his total involvement in camera angles.

I started to undress then, wondering whether I could have breathed some life into the business. The memory of his body laid out in that funeral parlour had haunted me ever since. The rain, my own loneliness, the bleak atmosphere of this Lodge—he had been lonely, too, after my aunt's death, and I had been too busy writing scripts, launching my own company, to help him cope with a run-down business and an alien world. And now here I was in Africa trying to make use of the only thing he had left me—a map that he had asked me to return, knowing he was going to die.

Footsteps sounded on the verandah outside. I was half undressed and I turned to find a soldier holding an umbrella and two men coming in out of the rain. Their plastic macs dripped water on the tiled floor as they introduced themselves. They were both TV men, the taller of the two, Erd Lindstrom, fair-haired, blue-eyed, the other, Abe Finkel, slim, dark, and intensely Jewish. "You're representing the BBC, are you?"

"On assignment only."

"An independent, eh?" He stared at me, then gave a quick shrug. "Well, I guess it has its advantages."

But I knew what he was thinking as they dumped

6

their equipment and stripped off their plastics. "Has anybody given you a forecast? How long is this rain gonna last? It's supposed to be the dry season."

"The little rains didn't materialise, so they think this may be it and the weather out of step again."

"So we film it all against a backdrop of rain. And we were told there was a drought. That's why we trucked up. Thought we might get some shots of elephant carcases, something to give a visual point to all the talk, and the rain caught us as we climbed up out of the Rift. You been out at all since the rain started?"

"No."

"Hear that, Erd? They've been stuck in this dump since the rain started." His voice was in tune with the rain, a flat continuous monotone. "At least we got shots of the truck up to its axles, but I'm sure glad we don't have to market this one. That Karanja says nobody's seen anything since they arrived, not even the elephant who used to go the rounds of the garbage cans each morning at breakfast time. You seen anything?"

"Nothing."

Ken rolled over, blinking his eyes. "I got a quick shot at a warthog, tail up and going like a little train. But the light was bad and we're using 7252—Ektachrome Commercial. If this rain continues we'd do better with EF 7241. You got any of that?"

It was Lindstrom who answered. "No, we're on Kodak 7242, and it's negative, not reversal." They were equipped with a Bolex and a Bach-Auricon. They also had the remains of a bottle of rye, so that by the time I finally climbed into my bunk I was happily insulated against morbid thoughts.

The opening day of what was officially designated the East African Federation's Conference on Wildlife Resources dawned humid and heavy, the air reeking of wet earth. It had stopped raining, but that was about all, the clouds hanging over the Lodge like a damp blanket, moist and menacing. Breakfast was a soup-kitchen affair, tin mugs and platters on the ve-

7

randahs because the dining-room roof had leaked during the night and all the tables were wet. The room toilets and showers didn't work, of course, and the area around the tin-roofed conference latrines was soon a quagmire of reddish mud. There were several women delegates and Ken made the most of their ablutions until he was distracted by the appearance of Karanja in a neat grey suit, an ingratiating grin on his face and his big ears standing out like sails. He was holding a loudhailer as though it were a bazooka.

"Guess the Minister hasn't made it," Abe Finkel said.

Karanja reached the centre of what had once been the lawn, turned to face the half-circle of rooms and put the loudhailer to his lips. "Conference delegates and newspeople please I have to express the regret of our Minister, but due to circumstances of so unusual weather . . ." The Conference, due to open at ten with a speech of welcome to the delegates by Mr. Kimani, Minister for Lands and Resources, was postponed until his aircraft could get through. It was not an auspicious start.

"Pity we can't take off for the Serengeti on our own."

I pointed to the agenda. "That's scheduled for tomorrow. Also a view of the cattle reserve in the Crater."

"It'll be scrubbed," Abe said. "The only thing of any real interest . . ."

A figure squelched on to the verandah. I didn't realise it was a young woman, not immediately, for she was tall and broad-shouldered, dressed like a hardened safari hunter in faded khaki trousers, bush jacket, and worn calf-length boots, a floppy hat on her head with an ostrich feather in it. "Any of you men Colin Tait?" Her voice came deep from the throat, slightly husky.

I got up. "Yes, I'm Colin Tait."

She stared at me, a long, hard, searching look. "I'd like a word with you." And she turned abruptly and stepped down into the trampled grass, standing there, waiting. "I'm Mary Delden," she said as I joined her. "Shall we go down towards the waterhole? I can't talk

8

to you here." She began walking then and she didn't say anything more until we had gone beyond the Lodge buildings, past what had been the VIP suite with its verandah directly facing on to the water. The long stalks of the drought-seared grass were wet with the rain, my trousers soaked by the time we stopped out of earshot. "You wrote to Cornelius van Delden."

"You're related, are you?"

She nodded. "My father." She had a dark, very unusual face, rather long with a wide, thin-lipped mouth and a determined jaw; but it was the nose that was the dominant feature, strong and aquiline. Her eyes, as she faced me, were large and of a deep aquamarine colour, the whites made whiter by the darkness of her skin. "I dropped the 'van' when I went to America. There were political undertones and as a journalist Mary Delden seemed a more appropriate name." She smiled and the smile lit up her whole face, softening the virility of it. "Anyway my mother was Italian, not South African." Then abruptly she said, "What did you want to see him about? You didn't say in your letter, only that you had a copy of *Reis deur Chalbi* and it contains new information about . . ."

"I was expecting to meet him here."

"You don't want to tell me, is that it?" She said it lightly, still smiling, but the jut of the jaw and the frosty look in her eyes betrayed a certain hostility. "Let's walk on."

I hesitated, reminding her that the Conference was due to open as soon as the Minister arrived. She gave a derisive laugh. "Nothing is going to happen today and the Conference won't start until tomorrow."

"Did Karanja tell you that?"

"Of course not. But you've looked at your agenda. Tomorrow we were all going off in the supply trucks to have a look at the Serengeti and the Ngorongoro. The organisers in America insisted on that. Can you imagine what the mood of the Conference would be if the delegates were allowed to see the plains empty, the migrating herds all dead, no predators, not even a vulture, and the Crater full of cattle?" Her voice had risen sharply. "They've been bloody lucky with the weather."

"How do you mean?"

She looked at me as though I were a fool. "It was never intended we should see the Serengeti. They'd have found some reason for the Minister to be delayed. Or the trucks would all have broken down. They'd have explained it in some way. Now they have the weather, a perfect excuse. Have you ever been to East Africa before?" she asked.

"No."

She nodded as though it confirmed the impression she had already formed. And then she began questioning me, not about the reason for my seeking a meeting with her father, but about my background. Clearly she wanted to know what sort of a person I was and I sensed that she was trying to make up her mind about something. Finally she stopped. We were at the far side of the waterhole. "I don't know," she said uncertainly. "We've got time enough, all morning, but . . ." Her mouth tightened. "I think you'd better tell me what it's all about."

"I'm sorry," I said.

"You're not doubting I'm Cornelius van Delden's daughter?"

I shook my head, wondering when she had last seen him.

"Then why won't you tell me? Why the secrecy? Is it something in his past, something that happened up there at Marsabit?" She was staring at me, her eyes puzzled. "No, of course not. That book was written long before. So what makes you think he'd risk his life to take you into the NFD?"

Something swept over my head, the whisper of wings planing, and a stork landed by the water, disturbing a pair of guinea fowl. It was the first sign of life I had seen. "How did you know about my letter? Did you see your father before coming on here?" And when she didn't answer, I said, "Is he still in the Seychelles? That's where he wrote from. It's his home, isn't it?"

10

"Yes, it's his home now. An old planter's house on La Digue that belonged to my mother's family."

"But you've seen him, haven't you?" She must have. How else would she know about my letter? "In his reply to me he said if they asked him, he'd come. I was expecting to meet him. . . ."

"Do you really think they'd let him address a conference like this?" she demanded. "Oh, yes, they asked him. They had to. With an international reputation like his . . . But he has too many enemies here. They'll never forgive him for saying that African cattle are an affront to God, that man should learn from animals how to keep the laws of nature and not plague the world with the product of his loins. Have you read his book *Man's Rage against Nature?*"

"No," I said. "But I've heard about it."

"Then how could you think they'd allow him here, when all they're interested in is grabbing more land for the tribesmen's cattle. Kit Kimani is a hard-liner as far as animals are concerned, absolutely blinkered. I don't know where Karanja stands now—he was with us in the old days at Marsabit—but human greed is what dictates policy and the political pressures of a population explosion which has been going on now . . ." She gave a little shrug as though she thought it a waste of time explaining the problems of Africa to somebody who had never been there before. Then, speaking more slowly and in a quieter tone, "When he landed at Nairobi airport his passport was taken from him. A South African, they said. That was their excuse, though they knew damn well he hadn't been in South Africa since he was a child and for the past three years he'd been living in the Seychelles."

"So he did come."

"Four days ago. He thought he might be able to influence the Government, not Kimani, but some of the others. He knows most of them."

"You saw him in Nairobi then? Is he still there?"

"No, of course not. The security police kept him at the airport until the following night when a flight for

11

the Far East came in. It refuels at Mahé in the Seychelles."

So he had gone back and that was that. No chance now of discovering whether he had ever been to the top of Porr, of trying to persuade him to take me up into that forbidden area.

"Do you speak Afrikaans?" she asked.

I shook my head, still thinking about the documentary I had dreamed of, a new discovery that might have made my name, and perhaps a lot of money.

"But you've read *Reis deur Chalbi na die Rudolfmeer*. That's what you implied in your letter. A map, you said. There was no map in Pieter van Delden's book. Did you invent that?"

I shook my head.

"And it was never published in English, only in Afrikaans—at Pietermaritzburg in 1908. So how could you have read it?"

I didn't know what to say, so I kept my mouth shut.

"I think I'm beginning to understand." She was smiling, but not with her eyes. "There's an English translation, unpublished. Now, what could there possibly be in that translation that is not in the original?" And then suddenly she switched to something else. "You made a TV film on sea pollution. It was you, wasn't it?"

I nodded. It was the only one of my films to make the American market.

"I saw it. A very good production. But no heart."

"It was a documentary on giant tankers and the problems of oil spillage," I said, not following her train of thought. "How can a subject like that engage the emotions?" Except fear, of course. It had frightened the life out of me when I was making it.

"Technological problems. You dealt with those all right. But you didn't follow on to show what happened to the seabirds and the dolphins and the seals." She had suddenly become very tense. "But now you're here. . . . Why do you want to go into the NFD?"

"If I could have talked with your father . . ."

"Why should he take you?" She was staring at me

and again I had the impression she was trying to make up her mind about something. "You're not concerned about Marsabit and what happened to the elephants there. Why didn't you approach Alex Kirby-Smith, who has some influence with this new régime?" She paused, her extraordinary eyes fixed on me. "It's the book, isn't it—something in the translation?"

"It's time we went back," I said. "The Minister will be arriving—"

"Kimani isn't going to arrive till the evening and the Conference won't start before tomorrow." Her mood suddenly changed. "I'm sorry, I shouldn't have said that about your tanker film. Few people care about the sufferings of animals. It's just that I was brought up . . ." She hesitated, the expression on her face gradually changing, a softer, almost appealing look. "Won't you tell me what it is—this information you have?" There was a softness in her voice, too, and her hand touched my arm. "I can contact him, you know."

"How?"

But she only smiled. She was tall, about my own height, and her eyes, staring into mine, had a warmth I hadn't guessed at. "Please tell me." She was suddenly very feminine, all the hardness gone. I couldn't believe a girl could change so completely. Maybe it was the Italian blood in her, but I found her change of mood disturbing and I looked away from her, at the water-hole and the stork standing motionless, the bush running away into an endless vista of Africa, the Lodge remote and nobody near. We were alone and my own blood was responding to her warmth and the touch of her hand on my arm.

"Please," she said again, and I shook my head, not trusting myself to speak, for there was a tightness in my throat. She gave my arm a gentle squeeze, smiling at me with her eyes, her lips parted, conscious of the effect she was having. "You must tell me," she said. "I can't decide unless you tell me."

And because I thought it was just the story she was after, I said something about her taking after her mother, and that seemed to change her mood again, for

13

she let go of my arm. "I wouldn't know. She died when I was still a child." There was a harshness in her voice as she said that. Her lips had tightened, the eyes gone hard again. "So you're not going to tell me."

"No," I said. "But if you know where I can contact your father . . ." I hesitated. "I'm not having this hashed up for an American magazine."

She laughed. "You think I'd do that?" She turned, walking slowly away from me, and the stork rose, a slow flapping of wings as it beat its way across the waterhole, but she didn't look up, her eyes on the ground, deep in thought. Somewhere a dove was droning its somnolent *do-doo-do* call and I could hear the guinea fowl chattering, but nothing else, the heat pressing down and the clouds hanging in the sky with the promise of more rain.

When I looked at her again she had stopped and was bending down; she was watching a beetle rolling a ball of earth much larger than itself out of a hollow. "That's a female dung beetle," she murmured. "The eggs are inside that ball." Her gaze wandered along the edge of the waterhole, searching. "Some animal has been here, otherwise there wouldn't be any dung to hatch the grubs." She moved along the verge until she found what she was looking for, a turd the size of a football glistening with the rain. "Phlump," she said, and laughed. "Elephants have always been phlumps in my childish vocabulary." She stood contemplating the enormous stool with a frown. Then abruptly she turned and faced me. "Can I trust you?" It wasn't a question that required an answer. She was speaking her thoughts aloud. "I think perhaps . . . But I don't even know what it is that makes you want to go to Rudolf. . . . It is Lake Rudolf, isn't it?"

I nodded. "Lake Rudolf and a hill called Porr. Perhaps Kulal."

"Kulal." She said it slowly, rolling the name out as though there were some magic in it. "I've always wanted to go to Kulal. Tembo is one of the very few men who really knows that strange volcanic mass. . . .

Will you promise—" But then she hesitated, shaking her head and smiling. "No, that's no good. I'll have to trust you. Anyway, it's only for two days. On Thursday Alex addresses the Conference, then they'll face it out in front of the cameras and everybody will know." She glanced down at the shoes I was wearing, gave a little shrug, then turned and began walking into the bush. "It's not far," she said over her shoulder. "Half an hour or so, that's all." And after that she didn't talk, walking with an easy swinging stride.

I didn't talk either, for we were almost immediately into an area of shallow swamp and it was as much as I could do not to lose my shoes. Once, waiting for me, she pointed to some tracks. "Warthogs. If nothing else survives, the warthogs will." And she went striding on, brushing past a thicket of thorn and climbing a path through rock outcrops that had probably once been a game trail. And at the top she paused and nodded towards a line of green snaking across a burned-up plain. "Down there," she said. "In that lugga."

"You mean . . ." I hesitated, feeling bewildered, and she nodded, smiling.

"He's a very determined man. When he sets his hand to something . . ." She paused, then said, "He went with the other passengers out to the aircraft, but he didn't board it. He just walked underneath it and out into the night, and nobody stopped him. By morning he was into the Ngong Hills, near an old camp where he had friends." She was staring at me, and the expression on her face was very intense. "It's dangerous for him. You realise that? They might kill him if they knew he was here."

"But if he speaks at the Conference . . ." It didn't make sense. "You said he was determined to speak."

"At the Conference it will be different. He'll have the protection then of the delegates and people like us who report for the media. But out here—" She was looking at me hard. "Out here he's alone and vulnerable. You understand?"

"I shan't tell anyone," I assured her.

She nodded. "No. I wouldn't take you there if I

thought that." She walked off again then, down into the plain where the acacia trees raised umbrellas of dark foliage.

Ten minutes later we were into the green belt, on the soft sand of a long-dried stream bed. There was a trickle of water flowing now, pools of it in the sand hollows, and over everything the glimmering, glowing green of growth renewed by rain. A goliath heron, standing like a sentinel, rose at our approach, its wings labouring at the air, and in a clearing beyond the red earth bank there was the bright flash of what she thought was a malachite kingfisher. The banks of sand were marked by the feet of birds. It was hot and very humid. It was also very quiet, only the soft drone of doves and the insistent bubbling call of a coucal. "The water-bottle bird," she said, and at that moment a figure stepped out from a thicket, dressed in nothing but khaki shorts. His body glistened black and his face under the grizzled greyness of a thick cap of hair was old and wizened. He had a rifle in his hand and he kept it pointed at me, while he talked to the girl in Swahili.

"He says Tembo is following the track of a kudu up the lugga. He doesn't know when he'll be back." She stood talking to the old man a moment, then he nodded, smiling, and disappeared back into the trees. We went across a smooth flat expanse of golden sand. "I'm glad that old rascal is with him. His name is Mukunga."

"A Masai?" I asked. I knew it was all Masai country here.

"No, no. He's of the Kamba people—the Wakamba. He came in last night after a thirty-six-hour trek."

"How did he know your father was back?"

"I told you, he went into the Ngong Hills. The old camp there was a poachers' hide-out. Most of his boys were ex-poachers and he knew some of them would have gone back to their old trade. So the word went out and now he's got three of them with him."

"I thought he hated poachers," I said.

"Oh, for God's sake! What do you expect? Mukun-

16

ga's a hunter. They were all hunters. Killing for the pot, for survival, that's very different from killing for profit—that's what he and Alex fell out over. And at Marsabit—only one man ever tried it at Marsabit. . . ." Her voice had dropped and I thought she gave a sigh, but I couldn't be sure. She was walking a little in front of me, her eyes on the ground. "Tembo. That's what they called him. Tembo and ndovu, it's the same, it means elephant. And they're right. Over the years he's become more and more like a phlump. Sometimes I wonder . . ." She paused, half turning her head. "I suppose you think it odd that I call him Tembo, but with my mother dead I spent most of my early life in bush camps, looked after by men like Mukunga. They called him Bwana Nkubwa, the Big White Chief, when addressing him formally, but among themselves he was always simply Tembo. I just got into the habit." She gave a little laugh. "I think when you meet him—" She turned her head at the croaking of a crow, watching it settle on the dead branch of a tree. "We must be nearly there now." She had slowed her pace and was peering at the bank. "He's moving his camp each day, just in case." There was a chattering sound, a bright flash of brilliant blue. "Damned starlings," she said. "A camp, a carcase, anything at all and they tell you where it is." She was climbing the bank, pushing her way through the undergrowth. I followed her and suddenly something hard was pressed into the small of my back and a voice said in English, "No move." I stood frozen, my skin crawling and the sweat dripping between my shoulder blades.

"It's you, Mtome, is it?" She came back, smiling and her hand held out. The pressure of the gun barrel on my back eased and I turned to find a tall, thin, very black man standing close behind me. The lobes of his ears hung slackly, pierced for ornaments he was not wearing. He was dressed in a sweat-stained shirt and khaki trousers held up by a big leather ammunition belt. He grinned in embarrassment, crinkling a deep scar on the left side of his face and revealing

17

the broken stumps of two front teeth. "Tembo not back?" she asked.

"No, Missamari. Back soon." He glanced at the cheap watch on his wrist. "Tembo gone one hour. You want something?"

"Tea would be nice. Have you got some tea?"

He nodded, smiling broadly now. "Plenty tea, plenty sugar. Not got milk. Tembo gone milk a buffalo." And he chuckled quietly at his own joke as he pushed ahead of us into a little clearing where there was a small tent and the blackened remains of a fire. Two guns lay cradled in the fork of a tree and pieces of meat hung drying in the branches. A starling perched close by, chattering and displaying the white band between its chestnut belly and blue throat.

Mtome squatted before the embers of the fire, blowing them into a glow, while the two of us sprawled on the damp ground. The fat, sleep-inducing drone of doves gave to the heavy humidity the effect of a sound track and the distant call of the water-bottle bird added urgency to my interest in the blackened pot Mtome had placed on the fire. He was talking all the time to Mary Delden in a quick, clicking tongue.

"Mtome says he was cooking for some soldiers on the edge of the Rift Valley and a security patrol came in. That's how he heard Tembo was back." Her voice was soft, almost drowsy. "It must be all of sixteen years since that man was brought in from a northern safari. He'd been half killed by a buff in the Samburu country close under the Mathews Range." And she added, "He's the best cook we ever had. He's also a very good shot."

I remembered the Mathews Range from studying the map. It was above the South Horr track leading to Lake Rudolf. "Does he know the lake?" I asked.

"Of course. He's a Turkana. He was born up there and he's been back to Lake Rudolf many times with my father. Kulal, too. He knows all that country."

"Yet you've never been there."

"No. I was too young. We had a permanent camp on the Olduvai and I was always left there when the

18

safari was a long one. Later, when my father began to specialise in the NFD, the camp was moved up near Isiolo, close under Lolokwe, but by then it was time for me to go to school in Nairobi."

It was a strange life for a girl and I couldn't help comparing her upbringing with my own. And now here I was sitting with her beside a fire on the edge of a dried-up stream bed, four thousand feet up and less than two hundred miles from the equator, waiting for her father, for Cornelius van Delden, the legendary figure who had been dubbed Jumbo van Delden by the popular press. I was wondering what he was really like, this man who belonged to a bygone world of tourist safaris and game parks, who had nursed wounded elephants, lived with them in the wild, and had now walked blithely into the territory of this new black régime, camping here regardless of its security forces. I wished Ken were with me. I hadn't even a camera, no means of recording the scene, and I sat there watching Mtome as the pot boiled and he threw in the tea, thinking of the script I could write if Cornelius van Delden really did make his appearance at the Conference.

She was talking to Mtome again. "Is that Turkana you're talking?" I asked.

"No. A mixture of Samburu and Swahili. I was asking him about the scar on his cheek, which is new since I last saw him. He says he was a camel man with the Army and got shot up in the battle for Kitale."

But it wasn't his war experience that interested me. It was the fact that he had been born near Lake Rudolf. "Ask him whether he has ever climbed a mountain called Porr." And I spelt it out for her, explaining that it was on the east shore of Lake Rudolf and looked like a pyramid.

She sat up, hugging her knees. "I remember now. It's mentioned in Pieter van Delden's book." Mtome handed her a tin mug and she put it down quickly. "Is that why you want to go to Rudolf, to climb Porr?"

I hesitated. But there was no point in being secretive about it now that she had brought me here to meet her father. "It seems there was some sort of city there. Not a city as we understand it, more a huddle of rock dwellings on top of a pyramidical hill." A mug of tea was thrust into my hand and it was so hot I nearly dropped it. "Pieter van Delden thought it must be Porr. But he never got to the top."

"Then how did he know about the rock dwellings?"

"It was on the pottery he found. Broken vases, cooking pots more likely, all very primitive, and this motif of orck structures on top of a pyramid, it was repeated again and again on the shreds he pieced together."

"That's not in his book."

"No." I hesitated, wondering how much to tell her, and at that moment a voice behind me said, "Who's this, Mary?" It was a gentle voice, very deep, almost a rumble, and I turned to find him standing quite still, beside the tree with guns in it. He was watching me intently out of eyes that were pale like moonstones under the thick white brows.

"I'm Colin Tait," I said, scrambling to my feet.

He didn't say anything, nor did I after that. I was too surprised at the size of the man and his appearance, the extraordinary sense of power that emanated from him. I knew from photographs in his elephant book that he was a striking figure, but none of them had been close-ups, so that I wasn't prepared for the huge hatchet face that seemed all nose in a thicket of beard and long white hair. It took me back to my childhood and an illustrated Bible that had a picture of John the Baptist preaching in the desert.

"Colin wrote to you," his daughter said.

He inclined his head very slightly, not taking his eyes off me. "Why did you bring him here? I made it perfectly clear to you—"

"He wouldn't tell me what it was about, and as there was nothing happening at the Lodge—" She gave a little shrug of her shoulders. "After you've had your say at the Conference it would be very difficult to arrange a meeting."

20

His hand went up to his beard, fingering it. "The Conference hasn't opened then?"

"No. It's just as you expected. Kimani has been delayed."

He nodded. "So he's not going to give them a chance of seeing the Serengeti. Pity I couldn't talk to Maina or Ngugi in Nairobi. If I could have talked to them, or spoken on radio—" He stood stroking his beard and staring at me, deep in thought. "You're a TV man, Mr. Tait. I think that's what you said in your letter. I take it you have cameras with you?"

"Back at the Lodge, yes."

"Would it interest you to film the Serengeti instead of the opening of the Conference?" He pulled a pipe from the pocket of his faded bush jacket and came forward, squatting beside me and starting to fill it from a roll pouch made of what looked like leopard skin. "Since you're here . . ." He was watching me, the cold stare of those pale eyes disconcerting.

Mtome was filling a mug from the blackened pot and I didn't say anything, thinking of the security forces out searching for him and how very alone he must feel. He took a long time filling his pipe. His hands were unusually large, strong and heavily veined, and all the time he never took his eyes from my face. Finally he said, "Apparently Mary trusts you, so I suppose I must. But to make sure, I'm offering you the chance of pictures nobody else will get." He put his pipe in his mouth, smiling at me, but the smile never touched his eyes. "Have you got the guts to take a chance and risk getting shot?"

"I've never faced that sort of a choice before."

He gave a laugh that was more like a bark. "At least that's an honest answer." He reached for the mug Mtome was holding out to him and drank it off scalding hot. "That's better." He set it down and began lighting his pipe, looking across at his daughter, not at me. "I went about two miles up the lugga, then struck out across country. Hard going and the air heavy."

"Did you find the kudu?" she asked.

21

"I found the carcase, or what was left of it. The noose that strangled it was still hanging from a sapling and there were the remains of a fire. Somebody else trying to live off the land. Did you see any signs of life?"

"The tracks of a warthog, also elephant droppings, about two days old."

He nodded. "That elephant will die. They're all doomed, those that haven't got out. But the warthogs, they have survival quality. Giraffe, too, I think. I caught a glimpse of two adults and a young one, but I couldn't get near them. What's left of the game in this area knows it's being hunted. Everything's very shy now. Have you seen Mukunga yet?" And when she told him how he had emerged out of the trees, he smiled and nodded. "Mukunga was at our old camp on the Olduvai when Alex began his slaughter. That's how I know what happened down there on the edge of the Serengeti. It was over a year ago, just before the start of the migration. Has Alex arrived?"

"No. Karanja says he'll be coming in with Kimani."

"I ought to have a talk with that boy."

"Karanja? It wouldn't do any good."

"No, I suppose not. He'll be changed now, like everything else. He always did enjoy the limelight. Remember when he went in after that lion? Crazy show-off little bastard." There was a note of affection in his voice, the words almost an endearment. "You see him now as a public-relations man," he said, looking at me, "but when he was with me he finished up as a better shot than any of us." He shook his head and I sensed a nostalgic yearning for days that were gone. Then, turning to his daughter again, he said, "So you haven't seen Alex yet. When you do, ask him what happened on the Olduvai a year ago. Mukunga says he must have slaughtered at least fifty thousand zebra there and as many wildebeest."

"It was wartime and he had the Army to feed."

He nodded. "And that freezer plant I told you about. If the Ugandans had been smarter they would have known there'd be a war once that big freezer was com-

22

pleted. Why else would the Government have lent a commercial operator the cash to build such a huge plant? The Serengeti herds were doomed from that moment. No other way he could fill it." He was looking at me again. "The end of that killing was only eight months ago, so the evidence of it will still be there."

"But that was the Army. It wasn't Alex. Mukunga told me that."

He brushed her comment aside, an almost angry movement of his hand as he leaned forward, his pale eyes fixed on me. "That interest you? An ossuary of wildlife, a charnel house of anything up to a quarter of a million beasts."

I nodded uncertainly, not knowing exactly what he expected of me. "My assignment is the Conference," I murmured. "Anyway, I don't see how I can possibly get there." I wasn't sure how far it was, but I knew it was a lot more than a day's journey on foot.

He smiled. "That's why I asked you whether you'd got the guts."

"Tembo, you must be mad." His daughter was leaning forward, her chin on her knees and a bright gleam in her eyes. "The only transport in this area—"

"The first question I'll be asked at the Conference is what proof I have. How do I answer that if I've not seen it with my own eyes? Karanja could tell them."

"Why should he?"

"Because he has a feeling for animals. But he won't, not now, when he has his feet on the rungs of a different ladder. Remember how good he was with the elephant calves?" He turned to me. "At Marsabit he looked after my elephants for me, and elephant calves are difficult to rear. Not as bad as rhino, of course. Once when we were in the South Horr Valley—"

She laughed, tapping him on the arm. "You're up to your old tricks—changing the subject. I want to know how you're going to get hold of a truck."

"And I want to find out what this young man knows about Lake Rudolf that I don't. Now leave it at that,

23

Mary." He turned back to me. "You realise there's nobody knows that area better than I do?"

"I realise that, sir."

He nodded, frowning and sucking his pipe. "I thought I'd been everywhere my father had been." And then he was looking at me again. "Your letter suggested it was something to do with his book. You've read *Reis deur Chalbi na die Rudolfmeer?*"

"Not in the original, only in translation." And I told him about Southly Tait and how the typescript had come into my possession. "I think it had been on my uncle's conscience, that he'd done nothing about the book. It seems he found it among a whole pile of abandoned manuscripts, when he took over after the death of my parents. He only kept it, he said, because of the map, and the fact that the book itself was annotated with marginal inserts and footnotes, also several handwritten sheets stuck in with passe-partout."

"In my father's writing?"

"I presume so. It was all in Afrikaans, anyway. I've checked through the translation. The loose sheet insertions are certainly included, also the footnotes, so I imagine the margin insertions are also in the English text."

"And you brought it with you?"

"Yes, and the map. Xerox copies, of course."

"I always felt there should have been a map in the book, but probably there was no engraver in Pietermaritzburg then, or else they had no means of making a block. Does it mark his route?" And when I described it to him as best I could, he said rather tersely, "It's all in the text. If you know the country you can follow it without a map."

"But not the location of the rock drawings," I said. "Or the old sites where he found the broken pieces of pottery."

"Rock drawings?" He stared at me. "There's nothing about pottery or rock drawings in the book." He took his pipe out of his mouth, regarded it for a moment, then put it back in his mouth again and shook

24

his head slowly. "Not my field, I'm afraid, and anyway, this is hardly the moment—"

"But the drawings," his daughter said. "An early culture, perhaps the earliest." And she passed on to him what I had told her about the motif on the broken sherds.

He listened to her, nodding absently. "I heard something about it. Leakey, I think. Young Richard Leakey —another of his theories. And there was a much earlier expedition, middle 1800s—before Teleki." He turned to me. "Anything is possible up there, but you must realise I have other things on my mind." He wasn't an archaeologist. A very early city dwelling meant nothing to him compared to the slaughter of the wildebeest in the Serengeti or even the sprung noose marking the death of a single kudu.

"Porr I know, of course," he said slowly, as though making an effort to relieve my disappointment. "From Loiyangalani and the El Molo Islands it stands up out of the flat curve of the lake's east shore like a pyramid in the desert. And if the wind gives you the chance of getting over to South Island, then the similarity to an Egyptian pyramid is even more marked. A lot higher, of course—over three thousand feet. It's a trick of the light, I think, for it's only when you get near it that you appreciate its height."

"Have you ever climbed it?"

He shook his head. "No. I've trekked all around it, along the lakeside and by the inland route. But there wouldn't be any life up there on that battered red-rock mass. Somebody has described it as one of nature's most dilapidated monuments, a once-solid mountain shaken to pieces. Hillaby, I think." He gave Mtome his empty mug to refill and said, "I find it strange that this information should have been written into the book only when he was seeking English publication. Is there no letter of explanation?"

"I suppose there must have been originally," I said. "But as it was handed to me there was just the original book, the map and the translation. I did make some attempt to find a letter, but there was such an accumulation of dusty piles of rubbish in that basement office. . . ."

"Very strange," he murmured. "He was an Afrikaner and strongly anti-British. He lived by the Bible and his gun, a great hunter and as bigoted as hell. It's hard to believe he would seek English publication and that he would then include details he had not revealed in the Afrikaans original."

"Didn't he ever talk to you about it?"

He shook his head. "Not that I recall. But then he died just before my eighteenth birthday. He was suffering from malaria and was badly injured by an elephant he failed to bring down with his first shot." He looked at me. "You say the additional material was handwritten and in Afrikaans? And the original from which the translation was made is in your possession? I'd like to see that sometime. Does the writing look at all feminine?" And when I told him it was large and angular, he nodded. "My mother's, probably. He didn't leave her much to live on and English publication wouldn't have worried her, she was half German, half Belgian." He smiled. "I'm a bit of a mongrel, you see." And he didn't say anything after that, sitting there, drinking his tea, apparently deep in thought.

It was Mary who asked me about the map. "Is the writing the same as in the notes?"

But I couldn't answer that because the lettering was all in capitals.

"And the translation, when was that done—in your father's time?"

"No. Much later. My uncle commissioned it in 1971. You remember Richard Leakey's discovery of a skull up by the Ethiopian border that put the origins of man about a million and a half years earlier than his parents' discoveries at Olduvai? It was a very controversial find, a lot of publicity, and Leakey aired a number of theories. One of them was that Lake Rudolf was the cradle of civilisation. According to him, it was there, and not on the Nile, that pottery was first made. In fact, he claimed that Nilotic pottery

26

should be renamed Rudolfic." I turned to Cornelius van Delden. "Leakey also found sherds at his dig on Lake Rudolf and provisionally dated them pre-Nilotic. That was what decided my uncle to commission a translation of the book."

"But he never published it—why?"

"I did find some correspondence that had a bearing on that. It seems almost two years elapsed before the typescript of the English version was finally delivered. I suspect the fee was so small the translator wasn't greatly interested in the work."

"So it was never published."

"No."

"Just as well, perhaps." He said it so quietly that I wasn't sure he intended me to hear. And he added quickly, "No chance now of anyone looking at what he found. It's closed, all that area." He put down his mug and glanced at his watch. "Time you were leaving, if you're to get back for lunch. We can't feed you here. One warthog is all I've been able to bag so far." He indicated the strips of meat hanging in the fire's smoke. "Bush pig and posho, that's not very good eating." He smiled and got to his feet. "Maybe when all this is over and things are normal again . . ." He gave that harsh bark of a laugh and shrugged his shoulders. "When I'm back on La Digue, send it to me. Better still, come and see me. No animals there, but the birds are interesting."

He looked quickly round the camp, nodded to Mtome, and led the way down into the lugga. "Now, about tonight . . ." And as he walked with us across the sandbanks of that rain-washed river bed, he gave us instructions where to wait for the truck. His daughter did her best to find out how he was going to get hold of the vehicle, but all he would say was, "There's no problem there. It's returning it may be a little more difficult." And he added, "I plan to be at Lake Lgarya just about dawn."

He saw us to the point where we had entered the stream bed, the rock hill just visible at the edge of the plain, shimmering in the sweltering heat. "Remember,

27

if you're seen leaving the Lodge area, or challenged by one of the soldiers, then don't come. And a convincing explanation of your absence must be given to those who share your rooms." He glanced up at the sky. "Better bring waterproofs. The rain won't hold off much longer." He patted his daughter on the shoulder. "Don't take any chances, Toto."

"Ndio, Tembo." She was laughing, I think with excitement.

He turned then with a wave of his hand. "See you about two in the morning then." And he went ambling off up the lugga, his head swinging this way and that, alert and watchful. He didn't look back.

We went on then and I said, "He's like a caged lion. He even looks like a lion."

She smiled, shaking her head. "No, not like a lion. Like an elephant. If you get to know him you'll notice he behaves like an elephant, too. He never forgets, never forgives, and nothing ever stops him." And she added, "He's a very large man in every respect, and very exhausting, which is why I make sure there's a lot of ocean between us."

II

THE RAIN STARTED again shortly after lunch, a heavy downpour as though a tap had been turned on. About an hour later a wind sprang up and the tap was turned off. Suddenly the sun was shining and everything steamed in the heat. I was lying on my bunk, but I couldn't sleep, the sound of voices a continuous murmur as delegates talked and argued, moving from one group to another, renewing old contacts, making new ones. Ken said it had been like that all morning, nobody minding very much that the Conference had not opened. I could see them now, out in the bright sunlight, endlessly talking; the newsmen, too, huddled together or moving from group to group, trying for statements from those who were internationally known.

Shortly after four a light plane flew low over the Lodge, and half an hour later the Minister was being photographed with the Conference Chairman, Sir Edmund Willoughby-Blair. Kimani looked very slight beside the big blond Chairman, but what he lacked in height he made up in energy, his movements quick and full of vitality, his broad, rather flat features alive and full of smiles.

It was on this scene that the sunlight faded, snuffed out by an electrical storm that crashed round us for an hour or more. It was night before the rain finally stopped and we sloshed through mud to our evening meal—tinned stew, rice and overcooked vegetables, tea from an urn and a can of beer beside each place. Soldiers moved around the tables, clearing the plates away, their faces glistening black in the light from the naked bulbs, and I watched Mary Delden talking animatedly to a group of men at a nearby table. No sign of nervous tension in that strong brown aquiline face and she didn't even glance in my direction.

A Frenchman at a table by the verandah suddenly called out, "Regardez! Un éléphant," and the dining-room erupted, everybody trooping out into the night. The spots had not yet been switched on, but a young half-moon and some stars showed through ragged clouds and for a moment everybody glimpsed a grey bulk standing motionless on the far side of the waterhole. A cloud shadow passed across it, and when the moon emerged again it was gone. Karanja was calling for the spotlights to be switched on, but it was too late. A big American with a Boston accent standing right beside me claimed excitedly, "An elephant. I saw it with my own eyes." And he added to the group about him, "That just goes to prove what I've been saying. Things aren't as bad as that guy Winthrop would have us believe."

"Moonshine," somebody said, and there was laughter, everybody happier now that they had actually seen something.

A hand touched my arm and I turned. It was Mary Delden. "Twelve-thirty," she said. "Okay? And bring a hand camera, nothing heavy."

I nodded and she continued on past me, heading for her room.

The rest of that evening I spent on the verandah, dozing in the only chair with the Beaulieu news camera in its case beside me. It hadn't been difficult to convince Ken that we should split up in an endeavour to make good the lost excursion to the Serengeti; he would cover the opening of the Conference, using the Bolex electric H16, while I tried for some dawn shots under the guidance of somebody who knew the country. I think he guessed it was Mary Delden, but he wasn't the sort to ask questions.

The spotlights were switched off again at nine and an hour later the Lodge was silent, only a few lamps still glimmering in the dark, the moon cloud-covered, no wind and everything very still. I must have fallen asleep, for the next thing I knew there was a figure beside me and Mary Delden was whispering. "Time to go. Are you ready?" She had a Retina camera slung over her shoulder, a waterproof draped over it, and the pockets of her bush jacket bulging with film.

I nodded and got to my feet, picking up the Beaulieu and my plastic waterproof. She was already moving quietly out into the trampled grass, a dark shadow heading down towards the waterhole. I followed, keeping close behind her, feeling my way in the dark and thinking of that elephant. And if there was an elephant around, why not other beasts—rhino or lion? Wasn't this the time they came down to drink?

A branch broke under my foot. She reached back and took my arm. "Quiet now," she whispered. "There's a patrol stationed on the road a mile south of the Lodge." And she walked on, still holding my arm.

The moon was still hidden by cloud, only a faint luminosity lingering. We skirted the waterhole, leav-

ing it to our left, and struck out into fairly open country. The going was firm, the hard gravelly soil sparsely
covered with a coarse growth of stiff little bushes
about knee height. Trees loomed up, dark shadows
whose shapes seemed imbued with life.

"How do you think he's going to get hold of one of
those Army trucks?" I whispered.

"I don't know."

"Why didn't he tell you when you asked him this
morning?"

"I'm a female, that's why. He's never heard of
Women's Lib."

"But he should have told you. You've a right to
know what you're letting yourself in for."

"He doesn't trust women." She said it flatly, but
there was an undertone of bitterness in her voice as
she added, "We've never been very close, and anyway
he never tells anybody what he's going to do. He's a
man who acts as though there was nobody else in the
world—" She suddenly froze, her grip on my arm
tightening. She was staring past me, at the dark
shadow of a tree that became two trees, one of them
moving. Or was it a trick of the light?

She moved on quickly, then stopped at the sound of
wood striking wood and a thin squeal that might have
been fear or pain, or the cry of some nocturnal bird. It
wasn't repeated. Instead, there was a soft gravelly
sound as though something heavy was being dragged
along the ground.

"He should have put it out of its misery." She was
standing very still, staring after the fading sound. "He
knew what they'd done."

"What was it?" I asked.

"Elephant. The same one." The moon was coming
clear of the cloud now and I saw her face, tight-lipped
and angry. "Bastards!" she murmured. And after that
she was silent until at last we topped a rise in clear
moonlight and saw the road winding down to the lugga.
Nothing stirred, the open plain an opaque emptiness
bounded by rock outcrops. She stopped then, watching
the road. "I think we're clear of the patrol. Karanja

said it was at the top of the slope leading down to the lugga."

We began the descent and halfway down to the lugga something chuckled away to our left. There was a mewing sound, then a soft whoop. I thought it was a night bird, but she had quickened her pace. "They know," she said. "They always know." The whoops faded into the distance, lost behind an outcrop. "I don't like hyena," she murmured, staring towards the black tree shadows where the road forded the lugga, her head cocked, listening. But there was no sound now and nothing moved. Dark clouds were spreading towards us from the west, blacking out all the plain, and in a moment the moon had gone and we were engulfed in darkness. It began to rain as we reached the road and walked down it to the ford where we found a fallen tree growing out into the lugga and sat there waiting.

"Half an hour to go," I said, looking at my watch.

"He'll be ahead of schedule. He always is."

There was the whisper of a breeze here, but apart from the stirring of the leaves and the sound of the rain there was nothing, only silence. I could just see the outline of her features in silhouette and beyond her the pale line of the road climbing to the skyline. She was sitting very still, not tense, but alert, and I sensed an undercurrent of excitement in her. We were alone in the African bush, just the two of us, waiting, and I had time then to consider what I had let myself in for. The man was persona non grata, virtually on the run, and stealing an Army truck. . . . "How far is it to this lake he spoke of?" My voice sounded over-loud in the silence.

"Lake Lgarya? Three or four hours. I'm not sure."

"And how long shall we be there?"

"Long enough for you to get your pictures."

I hadn't been thinking of that, but when I asked her what she thought would happen when we got back, she didn't answer. The silence was oppressive. Nothing in my whole life had prepared me for this and she sat there, remote and outwardly quite calm, as though this were just an ordinary safari. "Those guns," I said. "Where did he get them from?"

"I've no idea."

"He couldn't have brought them with him from the Seychelles."

"Keep quiet, can't you, and listen."

Silence again and the need to talk so urgent I had to keep a tight hold of myself. I could feel my heart thudding. I was scared, and I didn't know how to conceal it from her. Something flickering past my face. "It's all right," she said. "Only a bat." And I realised I had leapt to my feet. "You drive a car, don't you?" She sounded faintly amused. "When you're driving you're like the zebra grazing alongside lions after a kill, you close your eyes to accidents, never admitting you could get killed, too. So stop worrying. You're far safer sitting here in the rain than driving a car along a motorway. Anyway, there isn't much left to be scared of in this area." She turned her head, looking directly at me. "Do you understand what he's trying to do?"

"I think so."

"I wonder if you do." She paused and then said, "Have you talked to the delegates?"

"Some of them."

"Then you'll have realised they're hopelessly divided. They're here at the invitation of the East African Federation. The state of the Lodge, the commissariat, everything, is a reminder that there has been a war here in Africa and many of them are more concerned with the practicalities of the moment than with what effect their actions will have on the future. In wildlife, as in everything else, there is the political element, and unless he can jolt them into concerted action . . . Are you any good with a camera?"

"I'm not a professional like Ken."

She nodded. "I'm not a professional either, but so long as our pictures are good enough to show the world what's been happening out here . . ." She paused, listening again. The rain had almost stopped, the wind increasing and the rustle of the leaves louder. "The mere threat of world revulsion may be sufficient to swing some of them. Otherwise, I'm afraid they may go along with this idea of a pilot conservation scheme. You haven't met Alex Kirby-Smith yet."

"I was told he hadn't arrived."

"He flew in with the Minister. He's seen some of the delegates already, those they know they can rely on. Today he'll be trying to convince others privately." And she added, "He always had quite a different attitude to animals. Even as a child I sensed that. He's a commercial operator. He has the same attitude to animals as a tree-feller has to a forest. They're a natural resource, a crop."

"You know him, then?"

She laughed abruptly. "Of course I know him. He and Tembo were partners. They ran a safari business together. They were both hunters then, operating under licence, fulfilling quotas. For Tembo it was a way of life. It brought him into close contact with the country and the animals. That's all he cared about. With Uncle Alex (I called him Uncle in those days)" —she laughed again, a quick nervous laugh that was almost a girlish giggle—"with him it was different. It was business. He began to build up an organisation. He undertook scientific research for the Government, advising on numbers of lion, elephants, whatever was to be culled. Then he'd go in with refrigerator trucks, the lot. He had all the back-up facilities so that even the hide and the bones, every morsel of the animals he culled, was put to some use. It was all very scientific and he was so bloody persuasive."

"And that was when your father and he parted?"

"No. It was before that. When I was about nine. It was shortly after my mother was killed and I remember I cried and cried."

"You liked him then?"

"Yes. Much more than—my father. Uncle Alex was a great charmer. Still is. And for a little girl—" She sighed. "Tembo, you see, has no graces. He's a tough, driving, hard-bitten man, and absolutely uncompromising."

"And on Thursday he's going to confront Kirby-Smith—"

"Listen!"

For a moment I couldn't hear it. Then, faint above the wind in the trees, I heard the sound of an engine. The skyline up the road became limned in light and a moment later the truck's headlights appeared over the rise. We went out on to the road, the lights blinding us until they were dipped. The engine slowed, the truck braking to a halt right beside us, and both the men in the cab were black. The African at the wheel sat staring at us and I didn't recognise him at first, his face ashen under the dark skin, sweat on his forehead and the whites of his eyes gleaming wildly. It was Karanja.

I thought at first something had gone wrong and he had come out to fetch us back to the Lodge. Then I saw that the other African was Mukunga and he had a rifle in his hands. A voice from the back of the truck said, "All right, Karanja. You can ride in the back now." And Cornelius van Delden climbed out over the tailboard.

"No trouble with the patrol?" his daughter asked.

He gave that barking laugh of his. "They weren't there. The rain—I thought they wouldn't be. But I had Karanja drive just in case." He turned to me. "You ride in the back, Mukunga."

"Ndio, Bwana."

"You go in the back with Karanja. Keep an eye on him."

Karanja was out of the driving seat, standing hesitantly on the road beside me, all the jauntiness he had displayed at the Lodge gone. "Mr. van Delden." His voice was high and nervous. "I think it better I walk back now. You are clear of any soldiers and—"

"You always called me Tembo. Remember?"

"Yes, Tembo. But I shall be missed. And how can I explain to the Minister—"

"Of course you'll be missed." Van Delden's voice was harsh. "Why do you think I brought you along with me?" He put his hand on the man's shoulder. "You've got about ten hours in which to think up a

35

good excuse for driving off with the truck. Besides, I want you to see what your people have done in the Serengeti. You, who were so good with animals. Think of Lucy, and the little toto you named Labda because you weren't sure she'd live. A big cow elephant now, but more likely she'll be dead with a bullet in her guts. That's if she's lucky. Now jump in the back and let's get going."

For a moment I thought Karanja would make a dash for it. I was standing right beside him and I could see the whites of his eyes as he looked round wildly. He was breathing quickly and I think near to panic. Mukunga sensed it too, and slipped the safety catch of his rifle. But van Delden's hand was still on Karanja's shoulder. "Come on, man. Make the best of it." He spoke quietly, as though gentling an animal, and somehow it seemed to get through to him, the tension relaxing, his body sagging in its grey suit. "Okay, Tembo." And he turned and climbed docilely into the back of the truck.

"Give me your camera," van Delden said to me. "It's going to be a rough ride."

I don't know what it was like in front, but it was certainly rough in the back. Van Delden took it slowly through the lugga, but as soon as we had climbed the further slope he put his foot down. The truck was an open one and it was empty, nothing in the back but an old tarpaulin, black with oil and soaking wet. We tried folding it so that we had a cushion to lean against. This made it just bearable so long as we were on hard gravel, but the road worsened as we drove south into what had been Tanzania. The fighting had been heavy here the previous year and there were soft patches, badly rutted, the truck slithering wildly and no weight on the back wheels. In the end there was nothing for it but to stand, gripping the handbar at the back of the cab. I could see where we were going then and brace myself as we skidded and jolted across the rutted sections, but it was hard on the legs, and my eyes streamed. "I am coming here one time," Mukunga

36

shouted to me. "Very bad. Plenty lorries and much dust."

"With Major Kirby-Smith?"

"No. That is Mtome. Me with askari, hunting."

"With the Army?"

"Ndio." He nodded. "Very bad."

"What were you hunting—buffalo?"

"Hapana." He shook his grizzled head, his teeth white in a grin. "No, me hunt men. Me track, askari shoot."

I glanced at Karanja on the other side of me. No wonder he'd decided against making a dash for it. "What were you doing during the war?" I asked him.

"Same I am doing now, public relations." He said it quietly so that Mukunga couldn't hear and I knew he was ashamed. Then the rain started again.

After that we didn't talk. The going got rougher and it was all we could do to hang on. Once van Delden slowed, leaning his head out of the broken window and calling back, "You all right, Tait?" I gritted my teeth and said I was, but when I asked him how much further, he shouted, "Not sure. Thirty, maybe forty miles. We'll be turning right on to a minor track soon. Better hang on then." And he built up speed again, the headlights slashing the night and showing outcrops of red rock, great laval heaps of it. We crossed another lugga and he took it too fast, throwing us off our feet and nearly breaking an axle, the wheels thumping against the mudguards. Eyes blazed at us in the darkness, Mukunga's hand on my arm, his voice shouting, "Fisi." I had a glimpse of the hyena's grey ungainly body shambling clear of us as we thundered past, then we were over a rise and braking sharply as a bomb crater rushed towards us. I could see the dull gleam of water in it as the truck carved its way through low scrub on the verge, rocking wildly.

We slowed for a while, the rain teeming down and more craters. A burned-out scout car, some lorries gaping holes, then we were clear of the battlefield, driving fast again. My hat was rammed down on my head, but the rain poured in under the collar of my waterproof. I was wet to the skin and cold. Mukunga did not seem to mind it, standing beside me, the sodden khaki shirt clinging to his hard frame, water streaming from his tough monkey-like face. Karanja, on the other hand, was shivering with cold, his cheap suit shapeless, his teeth chattering. He was looking at me, looking at my waterproof, and I knew what he was thinking. Then suddenly he let go of the handbar and dived for the tarpaulin. The wheels bucked, spinning, and he was flung against the side, where he lay for a moment as though stunned.

Mukunga suddenly thumped on the cab roof, called out something in Swahili as we slowed, and then the truck swerved, a sharp turn to the right on to a barely defined track, water in ruts gleaming pale in the headlights. The wheels spun as we slithered through mud to the burned-up grass of the flat land bordering the track. We headed across country then, the wheels hammering at unseen holes. "Serengeti," Mukunga shouted to me. "Njia nzuri sasa—road good now."

I looked round and thought for a moment Karanja had been thrown out. There was no sign of him, only the bundle of tarpaulin heaped against the side. He had wrapped it round himself so completely he was cocooned in it. Rock outcrops loomed ahead like islands in a flat lake. The first glimmer of dawn showed behind low cloud. The rain died, visibility improving. We skirted the rock outcrops and they were like pictures I had seen of kopjes in the South African veldt, and as the light strengthened and I could see further and further ahead, the plain we were on seemed endless. The clouds thinned. Ragged gaps appeared. A glimpse of the morning star low down in the west and then the sky began to take fire, the clouds all aflame and constantly changing shape, so that we seemed to be headed into a cauldron of molten lava. Even the plain was red, the wetness of uncropped grass reflecting the volcanic flaming of the sunrise and everything beginning to steam.

It was then that we came to the first of the bones. They were scattered over an area of three or four hectares, a litter of skulls, rib cages, and leg bones, all picked clean and gleaming in that blood-red dawn. I thumped on the cab roof and van Delden slowed, leaning out of the window to tell me he expected larger concentrations of bones near the lake. But as he started to drive on again, I shouted to him that I wanted to film now, while the light was this startling, flaming red.

He slowed, stopping beside a clean-picked carcase, and I jumped out, calling for my camera. "It's colour," I told him. "In this light it will look fantastic." I was excited, my mind already scripting the words, beginning to grasp what could be made of this.

I had him back up the truck, explaining that as soon as I signalled I was ready, I wanted him to drive up to the carcase, then get out and bend over it. "Pick up one of the bones," I said, "and I'll zoom in on you."

He did it just as I had suggested, and seeing him get out of the cab, the plain behind him all misted pink and his strong features picked out in a ruddy glow, even his beard tinged in red, I knew I had a subject that would make every viewer sit up electrified. But when he reached the bones, instead of bending down and picking one up, he turned suddenly, his back to the camera, and called out, "Karanja. Come here."

I nearly took my finger off the trigger, but then I thought I'd never have the light so good again and I kept the camera rolling, gradually zooming in as Karanja clambered out of the back of the truck and walked towards van Delden, who now bent down, picking up a long shin bone, holding it out for the African to see.

I moved in then, walking quickly forward, keeping them in focus and circling until I could close in on their faces. Mukunga was in frame, too, his rifle lying across his shoulder, the wizened face very clear in the growing brilliance of the light. And then, as I zoomed in for a real close-up, Karanja seemed to notice me for the first time. His mouth gaped, a look of intense shock, and suddenly he covered his face in his hands.

Then he bolted, running like a hunted animal back to the truck.

Van Delden turned and looked at me, still holding the bone and staring straight into camera. "You realize what you've done?" He was smiling, and on that strange reflective smile the camera ran out of film and stopped.

"What do you mean?" I asked.

"Print that picture and it's as good as a death warrant."

Mary Delden moved in front of me, her Retina held to her eye for a close-up of her father looking straight into the sunrise. I heard the click of the shutter and she said, "You did it purposely."

He nodded. "Of course. Now he's been filmed here your pictures are safe. His life depends on your cameras not being seized." He turned to me again. "Have you finished now?"

I nodded, still thinking of Karanja running scared with his hands over his face.

"Then let's get on to the lake area. We haven't much time and I want pictures of my own to show the full extent of the slaughter."

We drove on then, and as the sun rose we turned on to a track running west. A few miles further on, trees appeared to the south of us, marking the edge of the Serengeti plain. All this time we were passing scattered areas of bones half hidden in the dried-up grasses and Karanja sat on the floorboards as though in a trance, a dazed expression on his face, which was almost grey. He wouldn't stand up and hold on to the handbar, preferring to be bounced around in the bottom of the truck. It seemed he dared not look at the animal graveyards through which we were driving.

We crossed a track running south and almost immediately the wheels were crunching bone and from my vantage point in the back the plain ahead was marked with circular concentrations of rib cages like great mushroom rings. It was as though an army had fought its last battle here, falling as it stood, regiment by regiment.

40

The sun was already climbing up the sky, all colour gone, and when we finally stopped we were in the middle of the battlefield, the weathered bones of dead regiments of wildebeest all round us. It was such an incredible sight that we just stood there for a moment, staring at it. Then Mary Delden turned to her father. "Who did it? Not Alex. When he culls he does it properly, putting bone, hide, everything to use."

"This was wartime. The last big battle was fought up there on the edge of the plains and with their lines of communication cut—" Van Delden shook his head. "Good thing the Grzimeks can't see this." It was the Grzimeks, father and son, who had pioneered this one-time national park, had written a book I remembered —*Serengeti Shall Not Die*. "Mukunga warned me, but I wouldn't have believed it possible—such an orgy of killing." He was climbing up on to the roof of the cab. He had an old Polaroid camera and as he waited for the first picture to be developed, she said accusingly, "You're going to show these pictures to the delegates and let them think it was Alex."

"He had a contract to supply the Army out of the Serengeti."

"But not like this, not killing everything."

"It got out of hand, that's all. The troops saw how it was done and the lust for killing took over." He took another picture, then turned to her. "That's his business, isn't it—killing? And now he's going north, a new contract, to feed the starving Samburu. War or drought, it's business, and there's that big freezer plant. He's got to fill it with something."

She was silent after that and I slipped another magazine on my camera, changing the lens, and took some panoramic shots, followed by some close-ups of discarded bones that had been piled in a heap.

Talking to van Delden afterwards, I gathered that in their migration the wildebeest subdivided themselves into herds of anything up to two or three hundred beasts. Sometimes the concentrations were smaller, sometimes larger, but round every concentration of these remains we found the tyremarks of ve-

41

hicles that had ringed them in, enclosing them while the men in the trucks had gunned them down. I was endeavouring to film a particularly clear group of tracks to show how the animals had been panicked into a mass when Mary Delden called to me. The urgency in her voice made me turn, and then I saw it, a grey shape, almost a skeleton, covered by mangy fur.

It was a hyena, all belly and hindquarters, and it was moving towards me, the eyes gleaming and a slavering froth on the jaw. It seemed half dead from starvation, it was coming towards me so slowly, and I swung the camera, shouting at it and backing away. "Run, you fool!" she screamed. I ran then and the wretched animal, which had checked at my shouts, loped after me, moving suddenly with surprising speed.

A rifle cracked. Another shot and van Delden called, "All right, Tait." I stood there for a moment, feeling shaken and my legs trembling, then I took a close-up of the emaciated hyena lying dead on its side, and another of van Delden with the rifle to his shoulder. And afterwards, as we wandered through the neighbouring boneyards, we came upon several hyenas slinking among the skeletal remains, their powerful jaws crunching up bone in a desperate attempt to obtain enough sustenance to exist for one more day. It was a depressing, heartbreaking sight, and the Serengeti plain, emerald bright now in the sun, a smiling landscape dotted with rock outcrops. Except for these last few scavenging hyenas there was not a sign of life, not even a bird, the sky empty, a blue glare with the fluffy white of clouds piled up on hills too far away to see.

"Got all you want?" van Delden asked.

I nodded, staring down at the bones spread out in the grass at my feet.

"What you've seen here," he said, "is the work of man at his most destructive. The effects of this slaughter will have been rippling out for the past six months, upsetting the fine balance of nature from the jungle to

42

the sea and as far north as the deserts of Ethiopia and Somaliland." His pale eyes were fixed on me, almost glaring. "Get that into your script. You've got the film. Use it. The migration here was at times about a million strong—zebras, wildebeest, finally the gazelles, Grants and Tommies. Tell people what it means to kill out great herds like that. Make them see how it affects all living things. Lions, hyenas, jackals, the bat-eared foxes, wild dog, too—they all lived off these beasts. Vultures, even eagles, right down to the ants that exist to clean up the last remains. Tell them." He checked himself then. "Karanja!"

Karanja was sitting in the shade of the truck, his head bowed between his knees. He lifted his head slowly. "Yes, Tembo?"

"Have you thought out what you're going to say to the Minister?"

For a moment I thought he had lost himself in a mood of complete dejection. But then he got to his feet and came towards us, smiling and with something of his old jauntiness. "If Mr. Tait agree, and Miss Mary, perhaps I say I take the truck to find them, fearing for their safety."

Van Delden did not say anything, busy with his Polaroid, and Karanja turned to me. "You must say, Mr. Tait, that you and Miss Mary go to get pictures of the dawn, some animals maybe, and then you get lost. Okay?"

I nodded. "So long as they don't take our cameras."

"No. I see to that."

"And what about our film?" It would be so easy for him to have the film seized on some pretext.

"Your film will be safe." But he said it without conviction, his eyes shifting.

Mary Delden was crouched by a litter of rib cages and, still with her eyes to the viewfinder of her camera, she said to her father, "To be on the safe side I'll hand you some of my films." She straightened up and produced two cassettes from the pocket of her bush jacket.

"No need." Van Delden was waiting for the development indicator. "If this comes out all right your camera and films should be safe." He released the developing button and opened the camera. "Clear enough, I think." And he tore out the film and held it up for us to see. It was a clearly identifiable picture of Karanja as he stood talking to me, and behind him was the truck and Mary Delden crouched with her camera before a heap of bones. "Tomorrow I shall be showing the delegates the pictures I have taken this morning. Whether I include this one or not will depend entirely on you." He leaned forward, his face close to Karanja's, tapping him on the chest with his finger. "Just see that neither Mr. Tait nor Miss Mary are in any way harassed for being so stupid as to lose their way. Got it?"

Karanja nodded, his eyes rolling, his tongue licking his lips. "I see they are okay, Tembo."

It was blackmail and I couldn't help feeling sorry for the man, routed out of bed at gunpoint and forced to commandeer one of the Army supply trucks, his position, his whole future, threatened. I looked round at the endless plain, at the bones gleaming white in the hot sun, and a husky voice at my elbow said, "Now perhaps you understand what this Conference is all about—how those who have lived with animals feel." And then, with a sudden warmth that took me by surprise, she put her hand on my arm and added, "Anything I can do to help, when you come to write your script . . ." She left it at that, her gaze wandering over the plain again, and then she turned quickly away. "It's getting late," she said to her father in a tight, controlled voice.

"Yes. Well, we'll just go as far as the lake. Now we're here and have the use of a truck."

We drove on then, down the track that headed south towards the trees, and in ten minutes we had left the plain and were into an area of scrub and acacias. Here we saw our first vultures scavenging at the sodden hide of what appeared to be a recent kill. And then suddenly we were on the edge of the lake and there were flamingoes standing in the shallows, a

44

splash of orange, and water birds swimming around unaffected by the slaughter on the plains.

We stopped then, and on the far side, on the slope above the lake, I saw a line of buildings. Van Delden got out and stood for a moment looking at them through his binoculars. "When I knew this place it had only just been built. Later a lot of people who made their names filming animals in the wild for television used it as their base." He mentioned several of them, names I had vaguely heard of. "It was partly tented, the best position camp for anybody studying the migration. But the man who ran it gave it up in the end—the Tanzanians made it impossible for him. Now . . . See for yourself. It's just a ruin." He handed me up the glasses and I saw that the buildings were roofless shells, the woodwork crumbling. Two had been gutted by fire, and behind the largest, which had the remains of a verandah, a long neck stood up like a thick pole camouflaged in black and yellow, the small head nibbling at the leaves of a tree.

"There's a giraffe," I said.

"Several if you look carefully. And a waterbuck down in the reeds to the right." His voice was very quiet, his eyes blinking, tears running down his cheeks. "It was always a good place for game. The Olduvai River is only just over there." I couldn't believe it, this hard old man weeping for the past, not bothering to hide his emotion as he nodded towards the trees sloping away to the left. "That's where we had our first base camp. All the animals moving between the Ngorongoro Crater and the Serengeti watered in the Olduvai. There were a lot of lion, and cheetah. And on the edge of the plain behind us, in the evening, when the migration was moving through, the trees would be thick with vultures, maribous, eagles—all the scavengers and predators perched there, waiting for the next dawn to pounce on the afterbirth of the night's calving and the remains of baby wildebeest killed in darkness. I used to sit out on that lodge verandah with the sun rising, hartebeest, zebra, and wildebeest grazing within yards of me." He shook his

45

head and sighed, and I thought he was sighing for the animals that were no longer there.

"Things were different then." He glanced at his daughter, blinking his eyes, then reached up for the glasses and climbed quickly back into the cab as though to hide his momentary weakness. And when she suggested driving as far as the lodge to get a picture of the giraffe, he said, "No. We haven't time." He said it gruffly and I guessed he didn't want her to know how the sight of the place had affected him.

"At least let me get a picture of the lodge. You and Mother had your wedding reception in the dining-hall there, didn't you?"

"Yes."

"I've never seen it. I'd like a picture."

"No." His voice sounded oddly abrupt. "The tank's barely a quarter full." He started the engine then and after a moment's hesitation she climbed in again and we drove fast up the winding track, back on to the plain. The going was harder now, the land drying in the sun, and by ten-thirty we were back on the gravel highway. He stopped there and called back to Karanja: "Do you think the Army will send a patrol out looking for you?"

Karanja hesitated, standing there beside me, a worried frown on his face. "Is possible." He shook his head, leaning down over the side of the truck. "I don't think they have the petrol. They fill up at the Nairobi barracks, you see, and only enough for supplies to the Lodge, so they cannot waste it looking for me."

"Good. Then I'll stop just short of the lugga and you can drive on from there."

After that it was all we could do to hang on, for the ruts were hardening and he was driving fast. We saw two tiny little antelope that Mukunga said were dik-dik, also an emaciated jackal, nothing else, only birds, none of them big—no vultures, no eagles, the skies above us empty and low cloud drifting in. From bright sunlight the day grew overcast, and shortly before noon we slowed by an outcrop of red rock, coming to rest at the top of a rise. Ahead of us the road dipped down to the green of trees. Nothing stirred, the air heavy and very still, a sort of brooding quiet. Van Delden got out. "All right, Karanja. You drive them to the Lodge now. And you, Tait—you get into the front with Mary. And remember, you've been lost in the bush all night." He smiled at me as I dropped into the roadway beside him. "You look tired enough, so I think you'll get away with it."

Karanja climbed slowly into the driving seat, his broad flat face tense. I didn't like it. He looked scared. And as I squeezed in beside Mary Delden he was saying, "What I do if the Army arrests them?"

"See your Minister," van Delden snapped. "And stick to your story." And he added, "Remember, I've got a picture of you down there on the Serengeti and if anything happens to them, if their film is seized, then I'll produce that picture tomorrow. You understand?"

"Yes, Tembo."

"D'you know what time Kirby-Smith is due to address the Conference?"

"No." He shook his head. "It will be in the morning, I think."

"Well, find out the exact time and pass it on to Miss Mary. She knows how to contact me." He looked across at her, his big head framed in the window, his white hair blowing in a sudden gust of wind. "See you tomorrow," he said and stood back, telling Karanja to drive on. The last I saw of him he was loping off into the bush, Mukunga behind him carrying his rifle.

"Will he really come to the Conference tomorrow?" I asked.

"Oh, sure," she replied. "It's Alex Kirby-Smith he's gunning for."

"Why?"

She shook her head. We were across the lugga and grinding up the slope behind. "Something that happened between them. That's all."

"When they were partners?"

But all she said was, "A long time ago." She was sitting very stiff and straight, her teeth clamped down

47

on her lower lip, staring straight ahead. She was like that for perhaps a minute and then she added, as though explanation were necessary, "Their attitude to animals is so entirely different, you see. And now . . . I don't know . . ." Another long pause, then she turned to me, smiling. "Well, you've met the great Cornelius van Delden, so what do you think of him?"

I didn't know how to answer her, conscious of the soft pressure of her body against me and her large eyes glinting with laughter. "I've never met anybody like that before," I murmured hesitantly, searching for some word to encapsulate his strange, wild personality. But all I could say was, "He's larger than lifesize."

She nodded, laughing. "You can say that again. He's always been larger than life." The laughter died and she said slowly, "He's a very wild man, always has been, and he'll take chances. . . ." She hesitated, then shook her head. "I don't know any man—I've never met any man—his equal. Once he's made up his mind, nothing will shift him, no argument, no threat, nothing. He sets his mind to something and that's that, whatever the danger to himself or others." She turned to Karanja. "How did you think Tembo was looking?"

He glanced at her, his eyes staring. "Very strong," he said. "Very strong and like a pig's head. He does not think what he is doing to others." He knew what she had been saying and the echo of her words sounded a note of warning. My mouth was suddenly dry, for I knew I had got myself mixed up in something that wouldn't just end with him delivering a speech to the delegates. I sat there, thinking about it, and she was silent now, staring straight ahead again.

"This man Kirby-Smith," I said, trying to distract my thoughts. "You must have known him well. What's he like?"

"I was only a child."

"But you've met him since."

"Once or twice."

"Then what's he like?"

She didn't answer, only shook her head, and at that

48

moment we rounded a bend in the road and a soldier was flagging us down, his rifle at the ready. He wore a cap rather like a kepi with the insignia of a rhinoceros sewn on to the front. "An ex-game scout," she whispered as Karanja greeted him, smiling with obvious relief. "They seem to know each other, which may help." But the man still insisted on calling his corporal, who came out of the little shelter of boughs they had built for themselves grasping a submachine gun.

The talk went on and on. Finally, the corporal nodded, shouted some instruction to his men, and climbed into the back with the soldier. We drove on then and Karanja said, "He will take us to his captain. Those are his orders."

"Did they send out a patrol to search for you?"

"No. But they know you and Mr. Tait are missing."

"So they will not be surprised that you went out looking for us."

"Perhaps. But I am not Army, and to take an Army vehicle . . ." He gave a quick shrug, his voice uneasy. "And there is my Minister. . . . He will be very angry because I'm not here this morning. And tomorrow, when Tembo . . ." He shook his head, looking worried and the sweat shining on his face. "Miss Mary."

"Yes?"

The Lodge was coming into view, the sprawl of buildings brown against brown clouds, the waterhole a pale circle gleaming dully. A hand banged on the cab roof, the corporal shouting instructions in a nervous, excited voice.

"Ndio," Karanja called back.

"What was that about?" I asked, the nervous tension mounting, my hands gripped tight around the camera.

"He wants him to drive straight to the guard post."

"Can't he drop us off first?" I was thinking of the film in my camera, the two reels in the camera case at my feet. But all she said was, "It would only make them suspicious."

And then Karanja was speaking, very fast, his voice

49

high and uncontrolled: "Please. You see Tembo tonight. You tell him is not possible he come to the Conference. He think he has protection of delegates and newspeople. But I cannot guarantee. I know my Minister. Mr. Kimani is political man and very ambitious."

"He daren't have him arrested there, before all the delegates."

"No. No, he cannot do that. But when your father is gone, then he will instruct the Army to act. He will now have the alternative. Please, Miss Mary, you must believe that. Mr. Kimani is a hard man and such action . . . coming to the Conference, speaking to the delegates." He shook his head. "Is most extremely crazy please. Mr. Kimani then has his hand forced and he will act. He has not any alternative. You understand?"

"I understand," she said. "But do you? He'll still have those pictures and he'll use them." I was surprised at the hardness in her voice. "I think you'd better talk to your Minister."

We were already turning into the Lodge driveway, now overgrown and rutted, the welcome board on its timber arch half rotted away, its lettering unreadable.

"He will be stopped," Karanja said obstinately. "They do not let him reach the Lodge. His pictures will be taken. You tell him please."

A hand banged on the tin of the cab roof and we swung left. I was looking at Mary Delden, her lips tight shut and drops of perspiration clinging to the tiny hairs on her upper lip. Her features were tightset, the nostrils below the bony curve of her nose flared slightly. Pressed close together as we were I could feel her tension. The truck stopped and in a tight voice she said. "You can't arrest him. Not with all these delegates here. You tell Mr. Kimani that." The corporal jumped down and disappeared into an outbuilding. "Do you understand, Karanja?"

He didn't say anything, his hands gripping the wheel so tight his knuckles looked almost white.

"Karanja, do you understand?" She spoke in a fierce

50

whisper as though he were a child who had closed his mind to reason.

He shook his head slowly, sweat shining on his face and a look of hopelessness. "He will be stopped. Not arrested, but taken to the airport under guard. I cannot prevent that."

The corporal came out with an officer, a big man, very black, with three pips on his shoulder and a walk that had a sort of swagger to it. He went straight to the far side of the truck and began talking to Karanja. I couldn't understand what was said, but it was obvious that he was subjecting him to an angry cross-examination, and his manner was truculent. The talk went on and on while we sat in the heat of the cab. Finally, Mary Delden leaned across and spoke to the captain in Swahili, her voice angry, almost petulant. Then abruptly she turned to me. "Open the door and let's get out. I'm tired and I want a wash." She picked up her camera, slipping the strap over her head. "Also I'm bloody hungry." The corporal moved to prevent us and she turned on the officer and said in English, "You've no right to keep me here. If you do I shall go straight to the Minister and demand that he gets the American Consul on the R/T." She reached past me, thrusting the door open. "Now, get out, Colin, and push that corporal out of the way. I'm not going to sit here and roast."

I didn't have to push him. The captain barked an order and the corporal stood back. I got out then, and she followed me. "Come on. A wash and lunch, then some sleep." She didn't speak to Karanja or the officer, she just walked straight off towards the main building and I followed her. "You think he understood you?" I asked as we entered the dark cool cavern of what had once been Reception.

"Of course. He understands English perfectly. Not speaking it is a matter of principle." The delegates were already at lunch. We could hear the roar of their voices, the clatter of plates coming from the dining-room. "Better get all your film into safe hands. Not your cameraman's. Somebody else. And if we're interrogated separately, then we went as far as the lugga, fell asleep for a time and finally made it out to the road, where Karanja picked us up just before midday." A flicker of a smile and then she left me, walking with long easy strides towards her room down near the empty shell of the swimming pool.

III

THAT NIGHT I SAW Alex Kirby-Smith for the first time. He was seated a few tables away, talking to a group of Americans, a tall, heavily built man packed with a great deal of energy. His face as he talked was very alive, eyes creased by years of sun glare and a sharp aquiline nose that gave him a predatory look. His hair was long and fair, and it was swept back across his head as though blown flat by a wind. There was no mistaking him in that gathering. Even if I hadn't known it, I think I would have guessed he was a hunter, something in the sharpness of his eyes, the hard, bright gleam as he talked. His hands were in constant motion, emphasising his words, and one of those hands was gloved. It was the left hand and the brown glove was so incongruous in the sultry heat of the dining-room that my eyes were rivetted. It was some moments before the explanation dawned on me. It was an artificial hand.

The men with him at the table were all Americans and he seemed to be trying to convince them of something, leaning forward, his elbows on the table, a cigarette gripped in his right hand, talking energetically. But I couldn't hear what he said because Abe Finkel insisted on giving me his version of what had happened at the Conference. He was a good mimic and his account of the various speeches would have been very entertaining if my mind had not been on other things.

The Kirby-Smith table began to break up. He was still talking as he pushed his chair back and got to his feet. He was very tall, a striking figure in immaculate bush jacket with a red silk scarf at his throat, his heavy, cleanshaven face almost boyish with enthusiasm. And he moved with extraordinary lightness as though constantly poised on the balls of his feet. "It will be a hard trip," I heard him say. "But I think it might be arranged if you really want . . ."

"Don't you think that's great?" Abe Finkel said, tapping me on the arm. "Coming from old Willoughby-Blair. Wildlife is part of the pattern of total life and animals as important to man as man is to animals. Isn't that a laugh?" And he sighed and shook his head at me. "You miss the first day and you don't even listen while I'm giving you the benefit of my brilliant observational faculties. I don't believe you got lost."

"Nor do I," said Ken, grinning at me. "You spend a night out with the only good-looking girl in the place . . ."

"It was raining, my friends." Abe smiled. "Girls don't like having it off in the African bush in the rain, and even if there aren't any lions or rhinos there's still snakes and spiders—" He pretended for a moment he was lying out in the rain with soldier ants crawling over him, wriggling his body, his voice husky and complaining. "That a puff adder you got there?"

"Go to hell," I said, watching Kirby-Smith as he moved from table to table, talking to delegates.

"Not funny, eh?"

"No."

I had a clearer view of him, only two tables away, and there was something about his face—the tight hard mouth, the sharp thin nose, and the eyes alive, almost sparkling. She was right about the charm. He was one of those men with an attractive smile that can be turned on at will and though he was about fifty now he still had the engaging air of a much younger man.

53

I wondered how he had lost the hand. A hunter with only one hand . . .

"You didn't get lost."

"What?" I turned to find Abe Finkel leaning close to me, no glint of humour now in his eyes. "What do you mean?"

"You heard me. It's a load of crap, you and that girl getting lost. You went out on a job and you got something nobody else has got, right?"

"What makes you say that?"

"Do you think we don't check our equipment cases? You slipped three mags into the film carrier while we were at lunch. And what about Karanja? The story is he went out looking for you and got bogged down, that's why he wasn't in Conference this morning to introduce Kit Kimani. But this afternoon he was interrogating you and finally made off with the film from your camera. Why?"

"A precaution, I suppose. I don't know. He said he did it on the orders of his Minister."

"Sure, but why? What did he think you might have got in the can?"

"I don't know."

"You don't know! Jeez, you're a poor liar. And putting the exposed mags in our case. Erd found them there right after lunch, while you were still feeding, and I slipped them into my pocket just in case." He stared at me, smiling. "Well, you going to share your dark secret?"

He was much too sharp and I didn't say anything, only shook my head.

"I might hang on to them."

I didn't know whether he meant it or not, his eyes watching me full of devilment. "I don't think you'll do that," I murmured.

"No? You think a hardened old pro like me has any kindness for new boys, and a limey at that?" He was still smiling, his tone lighthearted, but the dark eyes watching me showed he was serious. "I want to know what you've been up to. Or would you prefer I asked the Delden girl?"

"You'll know tomorrow," I said, and got to my feet. I was feeling tired now and I wanted some sleep.

"Tomorrow—where?"

"At the Conference. When Kirby-Smith speaks." And I added, "You may want to do a deal then, so keep that film safe." His eyes were alight with curiosity, his face shining in the naked glow of the lights, but he didn't ask any more questions, and I knew he wouldn't talk, not with the prospect of a deal. The film was safe with him and I left them and went to my room.

Ken came in as I was stripping off my clothes. "You really got something, Colin?" He was frowning, his expression intent and puzzled. And when I didn't answer, he said, "Karanja took off in that truck shortly after midnight. I got that from one of the guards. I was up at dawn this morning. I was worried about you."

"You needn't have been." I poured some water into the canvas washbasin and began sluicing my face.

"There was a woman journalist wandering about, enquiring about Mary Delden. They share the same room and she was scared something had happened to her." He paused, waiting, while I dried my face on the towel. "Cornelius van Delden," he murmured. "I know something about him now and there's a rumour going around that he's in the country and the Army's looking for him."

"Who told you that?" I threw the towel down and turned to face him. "Have you been asking questions?"

He shrugged. "Not only me, but Abe and several others. We're all of us consumed with curiosity. And you out with that Delden girl. The same name."

"Why the hell start asking questions?" I demanded angrily. "I told you not to worry if I was late back."

"No need to get excited. I'm the only one who knew you were anxious to contact Cornelius van Delden and I kept quiet about that."

"Mary Delden is his daughter." I reached for my pyjamas. "That's all I'm going to tell you at the moment." I was thinking of that camp site down in the lugga and how he had bunks and supplies trucked in,

55

Army guards acting as servants; two entirely different worlds, and tomorrow he would walk into this Lodge —into a trap by the sound of it. "These rumours. What exactly are they saying?" I asked.

"You've seen him, haven't you?" He was standing with his back to the window and at that moment the spots by the waterhole were switched on. His glasses glinted in the light. "All right. If you don't want to talk . . ."

"What are they saying?"

"That he hates Kirby-Smith's guts. That it's Burton and Speke all over again and somehow he'll manage to address the Conference."

"Burton and Speke?"

"It was Abe Finkel used that phrase. I don't know anything about it. All in the African books, he said. I'm not well read like Abe."

I had a vague recollection of some Victorian drama. The source of the Nile—that was it. A duel of words and Speke supposed to have committed suicide. And if the Lodge was buzzing with rumours that van Delden would make an appearance . . . "Who've you been talking to?"

"Just the delegates and the media."

"What about Kirby-Smith? Have you been talking to him?"

"No, but Abe has."

"What did he say?"

"Merely that Cornelius van Delden was a crank and persona non grata with the present Government. He's quite certain they'll see to it he doesn't appear at the Conference."

So the trap was set and tomorrow it would be sprung. A man with a beard like that, so recognisable, couldn't possibly slip into the Lodge unseen. The whole area was closely guarded now, patrols out and sentries posted. I could see them moving down by the water-hole. I ripped a page out of my pad, scribbled a note, and gave it to Ken. "Take that to Mary Delden, will you? Tell her what you've just told me."

He hesitated as though about to ask more questions.

But then he nodded. "Okay, I'll tell her." It was only after he had disappeared into the night that I realised I was still standing quite naked. I slipped into my pyjamas then and climbed into the bunk to lie awake for a time wondering how van Delden thought he could possibly get into the Conference. I was picturing him and Mukunga fighting it out with the Government guards, the sound of rifle fire echoing through the Conference room, and it was on this fantasy that I fell asleep, too dead tired to care what happened.

I heard an elephant trumpeting, high like a squeal, and shouts, and then I was awake, or thought I was, and there were voices whispering in the room, Abe talking softly, no light and shadows moving in the dark. A door closed and there was silence. I thought I must have dreamed about the elephant, that it was only the others coming to bed, and I rolled over and went to sleep again. The next thing I knew it was dawn and I wanted to relieve myself. At night we had been using the room toilet, flushing it out with a bucket of water in the morning. I climbed sleepily down from my bunk and crossed to the bathroom. The door was shut and when I tried the handle it wouldn't budge. Abe's voice behind me said, "Do it outside. The door's locked."

"Why?"

"He's sleeping in the bath."

"Who?"

"For Christ's sake! Who do you think? Go back to bed. It's not six yet." And he pulled the blanket over his head.

I went outside and peed over the edge of the verandah, staring out at the silent Lodge. The mournful note of the mourning dove called down by the waterhole and a stork stood like a sentinel on top of the main building. Dawn was just beginning to break and the air was full of the murmur of insects and the hoarse croaking of frogs. Nobody was about, everything very still, almost breathless, and van Delden asleep in our bathroom. He must have arrived in the early hours, which explained why there had been no light anywhere when I had woken to the whisper of voices.

57

I climbed back into my bunk, but couldn't sleep, thinking about the script and what the climax would be, whether I was qualified to write it. I knew nothing about animals, nothing about Africa. I was London born and bred and all the things I had done so far had been in the UK, except for that one tanker film, and then the crew had all been British. I looked across at Abe Finkel, rolled up tight again in his blanket, at the litter of equipment under Lindstrom's bunk. They were in on it now, and though they had admitted they knew little more than I did about wildlife, they were so much older, so much more experienced.

Ken stirred in the bunk below me. "You awake, Colin?"

"Yes."

"Think we could get a picture of him sleeping in the bath? There's a window at the back."

"Is there enough light?"

"The sun's just rising and the window faces east."

Abe sat up. "You want to get yourselves shot? He's got a Colt strapped to his waist and a guy like that sleeps with one eye open." He swung his legs out of his bunk and slipped to the floor. "We'll set it up before we go to breakfast."

"He may not agree," Ken said.

"Oh, he'll agree. Didn't you hear what he said last night? We keep him here under wraps till Kirby-Smith starts talking and we'll get all the pictures we want. A guy like that, taking the risks he has, needs all the publicity he can get." He went outside to relieve himself and then he began to dress. "Our real problem is how to get the stuff out. I'm going to have a word with the pilot of that plane. I know where he bunks." He looked at me as he pulled on his boots. "How much are you prepared to contribute by way of incentive money?"

"I'm on a tight budget," I murmured.

"Aren't we all." He shrugged. "Never mind, leave it to me. We can settle up later." And he went out, carrying his shaving things as though he were going to the wash house.

He was gone about half an hour and by the time he returned we were all of us up and getting dressed. "He's flying the Minister out this afternoon, leaving about four, and he'll take our film with him."

"How much?" I asked.

"He's one of their mercenaries and he doesn't take risks for nothing. I gave him a cheque on a Swiss bank account for a thousand Swiss francs to be counter-signed by the American Consul on delivery. That okay by you? Your people have no representation."

I didn't know. I was out of my depth, uneasily aware that I hadn't the facilities for this sort of thing. And then Mary Delden appeared on the verandah, looking fresh and neat. "Can I come in?" Her husky voice sounded nervous, her eyes darting around the room as she entered. "Is everything all right?" she asked me, and I realised she wasn't sure of the others.

It was Abe who answered her. "You might have warned us, Mary. Arriving like that in the middle of the night and your boy friend dead to the world—I might have screamed my head off." He was smiling, his dark face alive with the humour of it. "Had me scared."

"I'm sorry." She was smiling herself now, an expression of relief. "Where is he?"

Abe nodded towards the closed door of the bathroom. She went over to it and knocked. "It's Mary. You all right?"

The bolt clicked back and he opened the door, fully clothed, his bulk filling the gap and his eyes taking in the occupants of the room, a swift appraisal. They fastened on Abe Finkel. "Was it you I talked to last night? Good. And you've arranged for the pictures to be flown out."

"We'll need your co-operation."

"Yes, of course. I heard everything you said. What about the tape-recording?"

"That's taken care of." The cassettes will go out with the pictures."

"Excellent." He turned to Mary. "No change in the arrangements, I hope."

59

She shook her head. "Do you have to do it this way, in front of everybody?"

"How else?"

"They'll say it's because—you hate him."

He shrugged. "What does that matter, so long as I stop him." And he added, "So he starts speaking at ten-thirty?"

"About then. The Conference opens at ten as yesterday and there's one delegate to speak first, an ex-senator from Boston named Franklin. Karanja thinks Alex will talk for about half an hour, then after that there will be a discussion, with the Minister winding up just before lunch. In the afternoon we'll be taken to have a look at the area designated for the pilot scheme. Mr. Kimani will be promising us shots of rhinoceros, antelope, possibly lion, too."

"He's got it all fixed, has he?"

"Army scouts will be upwind and the game will be driven."

He gave a harsh laugh. "They've been collecting the poor brutes in bomas for several weeks now. It's one of the things I shall be telling the Conference." He looked at Ken and then at Lindstrom. "You're the cameramen, are you? Well, after I've had my say, see that you've got plenty of film in your cameras. You'll get a shot of an elephant then, and it will be something much more startling than anything Mr. Kimani can offer you."

"Was that what we heard last night?" Abe asked. "There was a lot of squealing and shouting from the barracks area. That's why we were awake when you arrived."

The big lion-like head nodded. "That was an elephant. The one you told me about, Mary."

"And you drove it into the Lodge area, in that condition?" The words trembled in the morning air, a note of anger and her face outraged. "How could you?"

"They posted guards so I had to distract them." And seeing the look of distaste on his daughter's face, he added, "It's doomed anyway. You know that very well, so don't be sentimental about it."

60

But she had turned her head to the window. "Karanja," she said. "I think he's coming here."

Through the window we could see him strutting across from the main building. "You'll come and fetch me, will you?" van Delden said to me. "As soon as he gets on his feet."

I nodded and he disappeared into the bathroom, bolting the door behind him.

Karanja made straight for our verandah. "Good morning, Miss Delden. Mr. Tait, everybody. I hope they do not wake you last night driving those elephants away." He seemed to have recovered some of his cheerful self-confidence.

"Was there more than one?"

"Oh, yes. They come for the garbage, you know." He hesitated, glancing uneasily at the two Americans, and then turning to Mary Delden. "I speak to you privately please. And you, Mr. Tait."

He took us over towards the swimming pool, and when we were out of earshot, he said, "You tell him please he is not to come here. It is no good for him. The officer in charge has guards posted all round the Lodge. After breakfast there will be more soldiers and there is no chance he will be able to slip past them, no chance at all."

"And how do you expect me to tell him?" she asked.

"I think you have some signal arranged. Please tell him. That is all I have to say. Except that my Minister is most anxious he does not make a fool of himself, not here in front of all the delegates."

"I can imagine." She was smiling sourly. "The Army arresting him and the news cameras rolling. That would really put Kimani on the spot."

"Please, Miss Mary. No cameras will be recording. It will happen away from the Lodge. You understand? He will gain nothing."

She nodded. "I understand. But you know him. Once he's set his mind to a thing . . ."

"That is why I ask you, as personal favour please. You must convince him is no good."

"You go and tell him. His camp is down in the

61

lugga." And she told him exactly where. "I couldn't get through the guards, and anyway I have to be at the Conference."

He hesitated, then shook his head, smiling craftily. "I think he has left his camp now, otherwise you don't tell me where it is." And then, assuming the mantle of authority, he said sternly, "You will do as I say please. For his own good. To avoid trouble." And he turned and walked quickly away. He had done what he had been told to do and I had the feeling that his confidence was a thin shell and that underneath he was scared.

"What will they do to him?" I asked as I followed her to the main building.

"He'll be all right," she said. "He's a Kikuyu, and so's Kimani."

"Tribal loyalty?"

She nodded. "They'll both of them blame the Army and Kimani's a clever little man. If that doesn't work—" She gave a shrug. "Well, I guess Africa isn't all that different from Washington or London when it comes to politicians. Their main preoccupation is the same—the pecking order, and survival." She stopped there, glancing back at the waterhole, sniffing the air. "What a wonderful world it would be without politics. I always think of the Garden of Eden as a place devoid of politics. Even here, where we are supposed to be fighting for the survival of wildlife, it's all politics, each delegate with his own bloody axe to grind, his own image to project. Cornelius, he's the same—and Alex. They each have their own viewpoint and they're blind to anybody else's, a mental curtain. . . . Oh well, you coming to breakfast now? I'm ravenous." She smiled and there was a sudden air of forced gaiety about her. "A full belly is the best sedative."

"I haven't shaved yet."

"Okay. I'll see you at the Conference then."

I watched her walk away, wondering what she was really feeling, brought up in a safari camp run by her father and Kirby-Smith, and now the two of them at each other's throat and about to come face to face. I was thinking of my own background, so orderly, so commonplace—and hers so explosive. Had she known what her father would do when she accepted the assignment? Had she realised it would be a confrontation and herself emotionally torn between the two of them? For that's what she seemed to imply—the two of them ruthlessly projecting themselves.

I went back to the room and got my washing case. Abe Finkel was there, neat and shaved, sitting on the verandah. "Ken and Erd are feeding now. We'll go later. Can't risk a guard finding him here before the balloon goes up, h'm?" His curly black hair gleamed and his eyes were alive like coals, a real professional newsman, knowing he'd got a break and keyed up to a pitch of excitement. "The pilot is in room 71. He'll wait for us there."

Right up until ten o'clock there were never less than two of us in the room or on the verandah. But the only guards we saw were out beyond the waterhole, where they had more sentinels posted and a detachment patrolling back and forth. It never seemed to occur to them that Cornelius van Delden might already be in the Lodge area.

Just before ten o'clock we all of us went over to the dining-room. The tables were stashed now, the chairs set out in rows, the room half full already. We found seats at the outer edge of a row and Ken set the Bolex up on its tripod. I had the Beaulieu with me just in case, but my main concern was the recording and I wondered whether I was near enough to the line of chairs and the lectern facing us. But once Sir Edmund Willoughby-Blair was on his feet and I had a playback of his opening words I knew it was all right. His brief résumé of the views expressed by the delegates the previous day was given in a clear strong voice. Concluding, he said, "I think we all recognise the problems facing the Government of the East African Federation. Our concern is the future of wildlife in this area, but anyone who listened to the Minister's speech yesterday and still does not accept that these problems must have a bearing on the animals who at one time occupied so great a part of the Federation's land area is not being realistic."

The Minister nodded and smiled. He was sitting next to the Chairman in a neat, rather too bright blue suit, the gleam of a gold ring against the dark hand resting on his knee.

"The problems, as I see them and as they have emerged in Conference, are threefold: First, the after-effects of an exhausting and protracted war. Second, the aspirations of a people on the move, natural aspirations of land tenure in an area of very high birthrate where population pressures have been increased by a flood of refugees. Whole tribes have been forced to move or expand their territories. Third, the resettlement of nomadic people from the drought-stricken areas of the north and the consequent switch from a pastoral way of life to the more efficient land use of husbandry. Those, gentlemen, are the three basic factors that confront us, and no amount of dedicated, even emotional argument will make them go away. Now today, the last full day of the Conference, we shall be concentrating on the practicalities, with a visit this afternoon to an area which I am told still has a concentration of big game that can, the Minister thinks, be preserved. In other words, a game reserve, or park, that is politically possible."

He glanced down at the neat blue figure beside him. "But we must not forget that Mr. Kimani still has to sell the idea to his Government colleagues and to the Army." He turned to his audience again, speaking slowly and emphatically to give weight to his words. "I would ask you, therefore, not to make it impossible for him by passing resolutions this evening, at our final meeting, that he cannot possibly support. I say this again, and most urgently, we have to think in terms of practicalities, of what is possible, given the circumstances. And to assist in this I have limited this morning's proceedings to two speakers, both practical men. One of them—Alex Kirby-Smith—has lived in the country all his life, is one of the world's scientific authorities on the management of game, both in the

64

wild and in reserves, and, what is more important, because of his services during the recent war, he is acceptable to the present Government of the Federation."

During this part of his speech, the Chairman had been looking across at Kirby-Smith seated by the verandah, where the glare of the sun was like a spotlight on the large, tanned face, emphasising the sharpness of the nose, the keenness of those suncreased eyes. There was applause from a little group sitting near him and he smiled his acknowledgment, a glint of gold teeth in the sunlight, the red scarf at his neck a casual splash of colour against the khaki of his bush jacket.

"But first," Sir Edmund went on, "I'm going to call on George L. Franklin of the Boston Foundation, a practical man in a different sphere—the world of finance. We have to face the fact that any wildlife programme requires money, for administration, management, protection. It cannot be self-supporting as in the old days when tourists came in the thousands. Those days are gone, perhaps for good. So, subsidies will be required. And now I call on George Franklin."

Franklin spoke for just over twenty minutes in that flat grating accent I had heard several times before. I think he was probably an accountant. Certainly there was no sentiment in his speech. He gave a breakdown of costs, facts and figures based on the old parks and updated to current rates of pay for wardens, scouts, roads, transport, and all the complex set-up for effective management of an area of about two hundred square miles. And he concluded by stating that the Foundation he represented was prepared to support such a project to the extent of twenty per cent of the cost for a minimum period of five years.

I glanced at my watch. The time was just ten twenty-five and Franklin was now answering questions. Cameramen were moving unobtrusively towards Kirby-Smith, positioning themselves for the pictures they wanted as he moved to the lectern. Karanja was unrolling a map on the wall. Ken tapped me on the arm. "D'you want a shot of him as he starts speaking?" he whispered.

I shook my head, watching Abe Finkel as he moved quietly to the door. He was against the light then, in silhouette against the shattered windows, Erd Lindstrom beside him, and both of them had cameras. Mary Delden was already out on the verandah. She, too, had her camera, and from there she could see our room and keep an eye on the speaker. "You stay here," I told Ken. The light was too tricky for me to handle it. "I want a close-up of Kirby-Smith's face as he sees van Delden enter." I left the tape-recorder running, picked up the Beaulieu and headed for the door, the voice of Sir Edmund Willoughby-Blair following me as he thanked the speaker for his frank and detailed assessment and the generosity of his Foundation.

"Not yet," Abe said, gripping my arm. He was watching the Chairman. Erd Lindstrom was halfway to our room. "I've sent him to warn the old man. We'll signal him when the moment is right."

The Chairman was already calling on the next speaker and Kirby-Smith was on his feet, the cameras round him rolling and clicking. It was his moment and he made the most of it, even to the point of answering questions as mikes were thrust at him by men bored with the proceedings and in need of something more exciting, more colourful. "You ever ridden a wild elephant, Mr. Smith?"

"No, only rhinoceros." They didn't care that it was just a joke. They lapped it up. And he was cheerful, almost debonair, the charm switched on. He moved to the lectern, the cameramen following him. "There's a rumour you're going north. Is that for the Government?"

"It's in my speech."

He was at the lectern now, facing his audience, smiling, his good-looking features alive and vital, brimming over with confidence, and Abe raised his hands. I saw Lindstrom acknowledge the signal and I watched the room, waiting. Kirby-Smith was talking

66

now, about the war and the part wildlife had been forced to play. "An army on the march takes what it can. It feeds off the land, and in Africa that means game. I know there are people here who think this inexcusable, but 'to expect men to starve so that elephant or rhino or gazelle will survive is to ignore your own nature. There's not one of you, not a single one of you here, however dedicated to the preservation of wildlife, who, put to the test, would starve himself to death when he had the means to kill. Even those of you who think it all right to kill for the pot, in other words subsist off the land, abhor the behaviour of men like Stanley and Teleki, moving through with a vast retinue of porters and killing to keep their men supplied with meat. But they did it to save their expeditions from foundering, as I did it during the recent war to feed an army."

He paused, looking over the sea of faces, assessing the impact of his argument. "Some of you, I know, do not condone my part in it. But what would you have? I will tell you how an army marching on its stomach would have done it. . . ." Abe moved, raising his camera, and I turned, distracted from the speech, to see black guards running and Lindstrom walking backwards, his camera aimed at the leonine figure of Cornelius van Delden striding in battered sandals and dirty shorts towards us. Grey hair showed like a mat in the torn neck of his ragged shirt and there was a revolver strapped to his waist.

Heads turned, distracted by the shouts. The name Cornelius van Delden ran round the room. The newsmen, crouched in front of Kirby-Smith, cameras pointing, took their fingers off the trigger, leapt to their feet, and ran. In a moment the room was in an uproar, delegates crowding to the windows and out on to the verandah. I made a circling gesture to Ken and he panned over the scene outside, the camera closing in on van Delden, over the emptying Conference room, and then he moved in on Kirby-Smith standing speechless and forgotten, on the Minister sitting dazed, and the Chairman banging an ashtray on the desk, and I switched off my tape-recorder and pushed my way out on to the verandah.

The little backwards-moving procession reached the verandah, backed up against the craning delegates, and halted. "How did you get here? . . . We heard you had been deported. . . . Mr. van Delden, will you be speaking?" And a very Germanic voice: "You vill make a stadement please. Ve vant to know vether is true there is nodding of vild animal from 'ere to ze coast." And somebody else, a Scandinavian by his looks—"Ja, we like a statement now."

The guards had halted, uncertain, black faces and khaki uniforms a crowded background to the bearded head of van Delden, and there was nothing they could do. They were faced by a battery of cameras and a solid phalanx of delegates.

"Gentlemen!" Sir Edmund's voice was no longer soft and persuasive. It boomed out like a sergeant-major's. "Gentlemen, your attention please. Will you now go back to your seats. We are listening to a very important speech. Now, please—immediately."

Slowly the scene dissolved as delegates began to resume their seats, but many of them hung around after they had made way for the Chairman, doubtless to see how he would greet this man come out of the bush like some prophet of old. They were not disappointed. Sir Edmund had a great sense of occasion. "Cornelius van Delden." His face beamed, his hand outstretched. "I remember you, back in '73 when half the scientists in the world, myself included, gathered at Lake Rudolf for that eclipse of the sun. Come along in. You were invited, of course, but I gather you were held up." And he turned, his arm round van Delden's shoulders, his bland, frog-like face beaming at the cameras as he said, "You know, we met before that, when I was serving in the KARs—the Mau-Mau troubles."

It wasn't the most tactful thing to say, bearing in mind that the Minister was a Kikuyu, but perhaps he meant it that way, for he must have known how van Delden had been treated at the airport, the search for him that had been mounted. But I don't think Kimani took it in. He had remained seated, his face blank, lower lip sagging and the whites of his eyes showing as though he had seen a ghost.

"The Minister I believe you know. And Alex, of course." And still standing with his arm on van Delden's shoulder, as though afraid if he dropped it he would be out of camera, he faced the room, his voice booming: "Gentlemen! I am sure you will all wish me to welcome the arrival at this Conference of a man who needs no introduction to you, at least as regards his reputation—Cornelius van Delden. He has unfortunately been delayed, circumstances beyond his control, but now that he is here, I know you will wish me to suggest that he gives us the benefit of his long experience—after Alex has finished speaking, that is."

There was applause as he waved van Delden to a seat and then resumed his own. The Minister was conferring urgently with Karanja, but the room gradually settled and Kirby-Smith took up the threads of his speech, not as smoothly as before and not with quite the same control of his audience. Cornelius van Delden was too striking a figure, and the delegates were still craning to look at him. But Kirby-Smith was a good speaker and as soon as he came to his projected trip into the north he had their attention.

"I gather there has been a good deal of talk amongst Conference members about Ileret as a possible alternative to the pilot scheme offered by the Government and I believe most of you know already that I am leaving for the north very shortly to review the game situation on the shores of Lake Rudolf. Federation military aircraft overflying the region have reported considerable concentrations of game—" He turned to the map on the wall behind him. "Particularly in the Horr Valley area." He indicated the gap between the Nyiru and Ol Doinya Mara ranges below the southern end of the lake. "Also, on the slopes of Kulal. In fact, there appear to be above-average concentrations of game all the way up the west side of Rudolf." He came back to the lectern then, not to look at his notes, but because it was the most dominant position, standing there between the Chairman and the Minister.

"Ileret is close to the Ethiopian border. It is now part of the Military Zone and as you will have noticed from your maps all the area you will probably remember better as the Northern Frontier District is designated forbidden territory. I have to tell you that this is not only because the Army regards it as vital to the defence of the Federation's northern flank, but there has, as you well know, been a prolonged drought in that area. It is a pastoral region occupied by nomadic tribes, mainly the Rendile and Samburu. Their herds have been almost wiped out, even their goats and camels have suffered terrible losses. These tribes face starvation and though rain is now expected in the area, this can have no immediate impact. A few days' rain may save the last of their cattle from extinction; it cannot create new herds on which the people can live. The Government—and I am sure you will agree with this on humanitarian grounds—has accepted that this is an area calling for urgent relief. As Sir Edmund has told you, the preservation of wildlife is not something that can be considered in isolation. The people of the country have parallel claims. This, gentlemen, is a disaster area and the concentrations of game reported to be moving into it could destroy the last vestiges of vegetation, thus finally annihilating the Rendile and the Samburu."

The Minister nodded energetically, but a voice from the back called out, "It's their cattle and goats, not the game, that's destroying their environment."

"In the circumstances," Kirby-Smith went on smoothly, "you will appreciate that Ileret as a game reserve is not politically possible at the moment. But —and here I have some hopes for the future—the Government has asked me to undertake an expedition into the area. The objects of this will be twofold: to examine the situation on the ground and to take immediate action to relieve the threat of starvation." He held up his hand as several voices were raised in pro-

70

test. "Before you express your quite understandable reaction, please remember this: here in the comparative comfort of this Lodge you are being fed on tinned rations that the Federation Government, with limited resources, has had to import. The general population, however, has to live off the land. In the north, there is almost nothing left for them to live off, except game moving into their area."

"What game?" It was the same voice from the back.

"I'm talking about elephants mainly. There's other game, of course—"

"Have you any idea how many elephants are left?" And another delegate said, "Can't be many. They've been under pressure for years, the forest burned up for charcoal, trees giving place to shambas and new villages, the herds of cattle multiplying even faster than the population, war, unrestricted poaching, finally drought. And now you want to—"

"Order. Order please, gentlemen." Sir Edmund Willoughby-Blair banged with the glass ashtray he was using as a gavel and nodded to Kirby-Smith.

"As I was saying," he continued, "I fully understand your reaction, but when people are dying, as they are in the north, they will seek any remedy. If it is left to them to take advantage of this extraordinary northward migration there will be wholesale slaughter and much of it will be wasted, the flesh left to rot. I have equipment and men trained for the task at hand. Nothing will be wasted. It will be a scientific cropping of a natural resource and only a proportion of the animals will be killed, sufficient to meet the needs of the moment and tide the people over until their herds begin to increase again. I repeat, it will be scientifically done, the animals cleanly shot, the meat fully used. The result, I hope, will be a resumption of normal life for these tribes and viable units of wildlife preserved—by which I mean that the numbers of each species will be reduced to a level the country can reasonably support. Much of it is near-desert and for the animals, as well as for the people, it is essential that a balance be maintained between the available or potential vegetation and the population it has to support. The result of this operation"—here he turned to the Minister again—"when completed and a proper balance struck will, I believe, be the reestablishment of Ileret as a game reserve. If this proves possible in the circumstances then prevailing, I personally shall feel I have contributed both to this new country of the Federation and also to the cause which is most dear to the hearts of all of us here, the preservation of wildlife in East Africa."

He sat down then and in the silence that followed the Minister rose quickly to confirm that the Government would consider sympathetically the case of Ileret as soon as the present disaster situation had been dealt with.

"I would like to put a question to Mr. Kimani." It was Cornelius van Delden, his voice surprisingly gentle, quite different from his appearance, which contrasted so startlingly with the immaculate khaki of the previous speaker.

The Chairman nodded. "I was about to call on you to give your views on an area you were associated with for so long."

Van Delden was standing now, his head thrust slightly forward. "It is some years since I last visited Lake Rudolf. I cannot, therefore, comment on the situation as reported by Major Kirby-Smith. I can only say I'm relieved to know there is still some game left in East Africa. Here, as you have seen for yourselves—"

"There are many places like Lake Rudolf," the Minister snapped. "Even here, near to the largest battle we fought . . . delegates will have the opportunity of seeing for themselves this afternoon."

Van Delden nodded, turning and facing the body of the room, a big bear of a man in silhouette against the glare from outside. "Yes," he said. "I've no doubt you'll be shown some animals, but they will not be from anywhere near here. If any of you newsmen care to forego your lunch and can arrange to be taken to the area ahead of time, you'll be able to take pictures of the animals before they are released from their bomas."

Kimani leapt to his feet. "That is not true."

Van Delden shrugged. "Then take them. Straight from here. Before you can give Karanja or anyone else instructions to let the beasts go." He smiled, fixing Kimani with his hard pale eyes, staring him down, and it was obvious the Minister was at a loss. Kirby-Smith came to his rescue. "Next, I suppose, you'll accuse me of trapping them for the Government." The expression of amused surprise on his face produced a ripple of laughter. "It's well known, I'm afraid, among the older hands here that van Delden and I never hit it off. He's accused me of all manner of things since we broke up our partnership some fifteen years ago."

"Are you saying you didn't do the capturing? You gave no instructions?"

"Of course I didn't."

"But you don't deny the animals have been trapped?"

"This is ridiculous. You've only just arrived in the country—"

"It's what my scouts say. There's hardly anything left in this area larger than a warthog. The animals on show this afternoon will have been trucked in. And there won't be any elephants, not one, because full-grown elephants are too big to truck." He turned to the Minister again. "Your intention is obvious—clear the land of anything that competes with agriculture and cattle. So perhaps you would tell us now exactly what instructions you, or your Government, have given Kirby-Smith on this expedition to Lake Rudolf. Is it extermination?"

"No." Kimani banged his hand on the table, his eyes almost bursting from his head. "Of course it is not extermination. I have instructed Mr. Kirby-Smith personally and my instructions are exactly what he has told the Conference."

"Then another question. Did you personally instruct on the cropping to be done in the Serengeti during what is now I believe called the War of Federation?"

73

"No. The Government then was military."

"It was the Army that instructed me," Kirby-Smith said quietly. "Why?"

But van Delden ignored him, still facing Kimani. "But now that you are Minister of Lands and Resources, you can't be totally ignorant of what happened." He turned to the room, facing the delegates. "Major Kirby-Smith had the job of feeding the Army. Just as he now has the job of feeding the nomads in the Northern Region. Scientifically. It will all be done scientifically, he says. Do you know what the word scientifically means to him? It means extermination."

"Nonsense." Kirby-Smith's face was flushed, the smile and the charm gone. "You've accused me of all sorts of things. I've already said that. All of them without foundation. But to accuse me of exterminating wildlife, this is the most—"

"Then ask Kimani why he arrives so late that the opening of the Conference is delayed a day and the visit to the Serengeti cancelled. If delegates had gone to the Serengeti . . ."

"I take you tomorrow," Kimani said quickly, still on his feet. "Any delegate or newsman who wishes—"

"To Lake Lgarya?"

The man stood there, his mouth still open. Then he looked at Kirby-Smith and promptly sat down.

"No," van Delden said. "Nobody will be taken there, for if any of you saw it there would be such an outcry—"

"You know nothing about it." Kirby-Smith was no longer looking at the delegates. He had eyes only for van Delden, the two of them facing each other across the room. "Of course, animals were killed—"

"All the wildebeest, all the zebra, all the gazelles, the whole lot wiped out in a senseless orgy of killing."

"You exaggerate, Cornelius. You were in the Seychelles. You've no idea of what the war was like here. All the area south of here was a battlefield. The troops had to be fed—"

"A million animals slaughtered." Van Delden's

harsh voice rattled round the room. "Wholesale, indiscriminate slaughter. Killing for killing's sake."

Kimani leapt to his feet again, ignoring the room to face van Delden as he shouted, "It is a lie. It was economic killing. Sufficient for the Army, no more." And he added, his voice high and very loud, "I know why you make these accusations. You are disappointed that the authorities do not let you stay, and since you refused to accept the air passage for return to your home, you have been hiding somewhere, so you know nothing about it."

"I have seen it." Cornelius van Delden stared round at the delegates. "I have seen what you will never be allowed to see—the graveyard of a million splendid beasts, trucks encircling droves of terrified animals, guns mowing them down as they milled in helpless masses, packed so close their bones lie heaped on top of one another."

"You lie," Kimani screamed. "I will have you arrested as the agent of the South African whites determined to destroy my country."

"I lie, do I?" Van Delden pulled a bundle of prints from his pocket and moving quickly along the rows of chairs distributed them to the delegates. "Pass them round, please. A man can lie, but not the camera. These were taken yesterday morning, using a Polaroid. They're not as clear as the human eye. They do not convey the vastness, the totality of his destruction of what used to be known as the Serengeti migration. You look at them. Just look at these pictures. That's what happens when there are no game laws and men are allowed to let their lust for killing run away with them. Extermination," he thundered. "And you sit there and let this man fool you into thinking it will be just a token culling. He has a contract and a freezer plant and you are condemning the last remaining herds of elephants to total extinction."

There was a stunned silence as delegates passed the pictures from hand to hand. One of them got up and asked Kimani if they could be taken to Lake Lgarya tomorrow "to see for ourselves," and the Minister shouted, "No. It is a damn lie. A trick."

There was a ground swell of talking, the cameras panning from delegate to delegate, and I saw Karanja watching Kimani and smiling quietly as though enjoying his Minister's discomfiture. Kirby-Smith stood up again, said something about conditions being different now. "In the Serengeti it was war." But nobody was listening, the delegates all talking among themselves. Sir Edmund banged the ashtray. "Order please, gentlemen. I suggest we adjourn now. Conference will open again after a quarter of an hour, in I trust a calmer atmosphere."

Chairs scraped. The newsmen closed round van Delden, grabbing at the pictures, thrusting them into his hand and taking close-ups of them as he held them. Pandemonium reigned and Mary Delden at my elbow said in a trembling voice, "He shouldn't have done it. Twisting it like that so they blame Alex . . ." She stopped there as Kimani thrust his way out on to the verandah, waving wildly at the guards leaning on their rifles. "Oh God! They've got him cornered now."

"Where's Karanja?" I thought Karanja might be able to help.

The corners of her mouth turned down. "He's no help. He's scared stiff, poor devil."

"No," I said. "He's enjoying it."

But she didn't hear me, drawing herself up, as though bracing herself. "I'll go and have a word with Alex. There's nobody else can stop them." And she walked quickly across the room, pushing her way through the crowd until she was standing at Kirby-Smith's elbow. He was talking to Sir Edmund and I saw him turn and bend his head to listen to her above the din of voices. It made me realise how tall he was, for she was my height, yet her eyes were only level with his chin.

Ken grabbed hold of my arm. "Can you get me some more film? I'm nearly out, and if you want good coverage when they grab him . . ." But it was too late already. Kimani had the captain with him now. He

76

was shouting orders and guards were running to him from their positions around the Lodge. A shot cracked out, a flat whiplash of sound that silenced everybody for an instant. I thought for a moment it was some trigger-happy soldier, but there were shouts now from beyond the circle of buildings. "Ndovu, ndovu." Another shot, followed by a squeal, and a grey shape swayed into view from behind the last of the rooms. It crashed against the VIP verandah, scattering tiles and moving forward again, dragging one leg, its trunk raised. It stopped at the sight of us all gathered outside the dining-hall, the trunk waving as it searched for our scent, its ears spread like sails.

Suddenly I saw its eyes, small and sunken in great hollows behind the uplifted tusks. They were big tusks and the body behind the grey skull was all bone. I had just time to realise that the wretched beast was almost starved to the point of death when it trumpeted, the trumpet note ending in a squeal of fear, and then it was coming towards us again, its head and trunk swinging from side to side as though it did not know which way to turn.

That somebody wasn't trampled was due to Kirby-Smith's presence of mind. While we stood rooted to the spot, too surprised to move, he ran forward, grabbed a rifle from one of the guards, then, moving out ahead of us into the path of the elephant, he raised the gun to his shoulder, balancing it loosely on his gloved hand, waited a moment and then fired. The grey mass of bone came on without a check, then suddenly sagged at the knees, pitching forward head lowered, tusks digging into the ground, scoring great furrows in the turf as it came to a stop and slowly keeled over on its side.

There was a great yell from the soldiers and in an instant they had fallen on it, knives appearing like magic in their hands, others using their bayonets as they hacked in a frenzy at the carcase, grabbing the meat they had been starved of for so long. The tall captain was in there too and it was Kirby-Smith who finally forced them to some semblance of order, shouting for men who had once been game scouts and arranging for the orderly dismembering of the carcase. Then he called to the delegates, gathering them about him and pointing to the left hind leg, which had a length of thick wire imbedded in the flesh. The whole foot was rotten, all swollen up and thick with flies, the smell of putrefaction hanging on the air. "That's what happens in Africa when the disposal of big game is left to men without rifles, men who are hungry for meat and have no feeling for the animals they prey upon."

I looked round for van Delden, wondering what his reply to this would be. But he was nowhere to be seen. "In the old days," Kirby-Smith went on, "this would be the work of poachers. But now there is no such thing as poaching. Anybody can kill. . . ." He hesitated, then went on quickly, "This is a wily old bull who knows about humans and is not afraid to visit the waterhole here. Last night he was going over the garbage bins. He's probably the same beast the tourists used to photograph. But he put his foot into a wire noose attached to a log, an old poacher's trick, and a slow, painful death. Much better to deal with the problem cleanly with a rifle."

I saw Mary Delden standing irresolute, her eyes searching the crowd, and I went over to her. "Where is he?"

She shook her head, frowning, her mouth set in a thin line and tears in her eyes.

"What's the matter?" I asked.

She stared at me. "Don't you understand?"

"What?"

"Christ!" she breathed. "I told him about it. I told him there was an elephant around the waterhole, dragging a great log. Don't you remember? The dung beetle, the droppings. The rain had obliterated the marks, but in the night, that squeal we heard, the dragging sound. He used it to get into the Lodge and now he's used it to get out, the boys driving it here, a sacrificial offering and the diversion he needed. Christ Almighty! the callousness of it!"

I understood then. Not just how he had planned to

78

get away, but how everybody, however much they were committed to the preservation of wildlife, still made use of animals for their own ends—van Delden to make his escape, Kirby-Smith to support his business, Kimani to increase his political standing, and the delegates, committed and dedicated men who had come from the ends of the earth, all here because animals were a part of the position they held in life.

"While they're all bathing their heads in gore," she said hoarsely, "and disputing the rights of man and beast to live perpetually in a state of war, let's raid the kitchens and grab some beer. I want to get drunk. I want to get so drunk I don't have to think any more." She grabbed hold of my arm and turned in a stumbling run, crying silently in a blind rage against humanity.

Part Two

THE SOUTH
HORR GAP

I

IT WAS SUNDAY before we finally got back to Nairobi, and like the rest, I was utterly exhausted, for the Conference had been extended a day, with disastrous results. Realising that the visit to the site of the proposed game reserve would be an anti-climax after the events of the morning, Kimani had insisted on personally conducting the delegates over the nearest battlefield, which was the one we had driven through on our way to the Serengeti. There he had lectured us in the pouring rain on the problems of an army fighting without lines of communication to any port and entirely dependent on the country for its food.

It had rained all that night and it was still raining on the Friday morning when we were huddled into wet hides for our promised view of wildlife in the reserve area. The animals had looked wet and bewildered, but by then the discomfort of our existence was such that nobody seemed much concerned about how we were able to see such a representative selection. Predictably, the Conference voted later that day in favour of the pilot scheme.

We had left that same evening, everybody glad to get away from the leaking misery of the Lodge. But by then the roads were almost impassable and it had taken us almost two days to reach Nairobi, trucks bogged axle-deep, floods in the Rift Valley and our food exhausted. The rain had not let up until our vehicles were struggling into the outskirts of Nairobi and by then I was so thankful to tumble into a dry bed that left to myself I should have gone home with the rest. Even here there was muddle and uncertainty.

Flight schedules had been posted at Reception, all of them subject to confirmation, and on the Monday the place seethed with rumours of cancellations and delays.

We had been booked into the Norfolk Hotel, which was not the most convenient for finding out what was going on. It was away from the centre of town, nicely secluded in its own grounds, which was probably why it was the only hotel still open to visitors, all the others having been taken over by the Government either as offices or Army barracks. But the war had left its mark, a bomb crater gaping full of water in the middle of the central lawn, the glass of the surrounding windows all shattered and the phones in every room ripped out. With no taxis available, the only means of communication were the phones in Reception, and for these the newsmen had queued half the night only to find themselves cut off as soon as they tried to transmit copy that was considered in any way detrimental to the régime. All mention of Cornelius van Delden and the pictures he had taken in the Serengeti was banned.

The mood on that Monday morning was angry, particularly among the delegates. They were no longer guests of the Federation, meals were at black-market rates and the price of accommodation exorbitant. And with the first flight cancellation a rumour circulated that we would be billed for the extra night we had spent at the Lodge. For the media this was acceptable as being part of the pattern of a disorganised country in the aftermath of war. Men like Abe Finkel were accustomed to it, but for the delegates, conscious that their expenses had to be found from funds raised by voluntary subscriptions, it came as a shock. And there was no certainty how long they would have to wait. Only the Americans were sure of getting away that night. They had chartered a plane. For the rest of us it was a day of uncertainty, of waiting.

I spent most of it working on my script. I wanted to get it all down in outline while it was still vivid in my mind. Ken and I had been allocated one of the chalet rooms. Originally it had had big sliding glass windows opening on to the lawn, but now the glass was all gone and when darkness came the night pressed in on us, insects battering against the naked light bulb and an orchestra of sound, cicadas in the grass and frogs in the bomb crater. The first draft of the outline finished, I joined Ken in the entrance foyer, which was crowded with delegates and their baggage.

"Is Abe back yet?" I asked. He had set out to walk into the city centre immediately after breakfast.

He shook his head. "Erd's getting worried he'll miss his plane." And he added, "There's a rumour that we may get away tonight. A flight's due in from Tokyo around two A.M. and there may be seats."

My eyes searched the crowd. Now that I'd licked my script into some sort of shape there were questions I wanted answered.

"If you're looking for Mary Delden, I haven't seen her either."

"Was she here for lunch?"

"I didn't see her. But she may have had sandwiches in her room, same as you did."

The woman who had shared her room at the Lodge was talking to Franklin and I pushed my way through the crowd. But she hadn't seen Mary either. "We were booked in together, room 109, but I never saw her after we'd had dinner together on the terrace. I don't know what the hell she's up to, but she didn't sleep in the hotel last night."

"Have you asked at the desk?"

"They say she checked out about nine-thirty this morning, paid her bill and took her baggage. And it was an Army truck came for her." She stared at me, her eyes bright with curiosity. "I sure would like to know what she's up to."

I went in search of Erd Lindstrom then, but his only concern was for Abe. "I don't trust that pilot. He's one of their boys, a mercenary, and now he's got his money. . . ."

"You think they may have arrested him?"

"I don't know. Abe's pretty smart, but anything's possible in this crazy country."

83

There was a movement in the crowd, a surge towards the baggage piled by the door. Over their heads I saw a coach drawing up in the roadway outside. It was painted camouflage green and brown, the windows empty of glass. "Your transport's here."

He nodded uncertainly. "Looks like it."

The Americans were trooping out now and Karanja was there. "Please you take your place in Government bus for airport all people on flight to New York. You show receipted bills for hotel before boarding please."

"What are you going to do?" I asked.

"Last Abe said to me was not to worry and get on the flight. So——" He shrugged and moved into the tail of the crowd, collecting his grip and his camera equipment as he reached the door. "He's done this on me before. Something's cropped up, I guess. His gear's still in the room, and I've left him the small camera with all the unexposed film. Tell him, will you. And I hope he doesn't get held up too long. The same goes for you. This is no place to have authority breathing down your neck." He was frowning as he turned and followed the others out to the coach. And after that they just sat waiting with the doors closed, Karanja leaning against the side of the bus with a sheet of paper in his hand and two soldiers standing guard.

There was tension in the warm night air and it crossed my mind that if Abe had been arrested, Mary Delden might be in trouble, too. After what had happened they might arrest all of us. I was wishing I could take Abe's place on the flight—New York, anywhere, so long as there was an end to this uncertainty of waiting. "Sont-ils certains de trouver un avion à l'aéroport?" It was the *Paris-Match* correspondent voicing all our thoughts and Karanja was talking to Erd now, questioning him. "S'ils ne veulent pas que nous écrivons ce que c'est passé . . ." Marcel Ricaud left it at that, his words hanging in the air and an icy chill running through the group left standing on the terrace, every one of us conscious of our vulnerability. We had been given a glimpse of the ugly side of war. We had been told things that the Government did not want known, witnesses to their failure to prevent van Delden speaking his mind, and so long as we were here the world outside could be kept in ignorance.

"What's the hold-up, Mr. Karanja?" It was Sir Edmund, his voice bland and reassuring.

Karanja didn't answer. He was still talking to Erd Lindstrom through one of the glassless windows.

"Mr. Karanja." The tone of command had its effect. Karanja turned. "I asked what the hold-up was."

"An American is not present." And Karanja called out, "Anybody know where is Mr. Finkel representing CBS please?" His eyes rolled white in the lights and then fastened on me. He came over. "You are with Mr. Finkel at the Lodge. Where is he now?" His head was thrust forward, his manner slightly truculent, and I could smell the beer on his breath.

"I've no idea," I said. "And there's Miss Delden. She's missing, too."

"Miss Mary I know about. Is Finkel I am looking for."

"Where is she?" I demanded. "What have your people done with her? Is she under arrest?"

"No, is not under arrest." He looked surprised, almost offended.

"Then what's happened? Where is she?"

"She don't tell you?" He hesitated, then said, "Is gone with Major Kirby-Smith."

I stared at him. "With Kirby-Smith? Are you sure?"

He nodded. "Miss Mary okay. Now you tell me—"

"But why?" I couldn't believe it. "Why should she go with Kirby-Smith of all people?"

"Miss Mary good journalist, that's why. Now you tell me where is this man Finkel. All Americans present, only Mr. Finkel missing. You tell me where he is please."

"I don't know."

"Then find him. He is not in his room and the bus cannot leave till he is found."

"But he's been gone since before lunch."

"I think," Sir Edmund cut in, "you had best let the

85

coach go while you telephone the authorities. The Ministry will probably know where he is."

"Is too late for the Ministry now."

"Then phone the security police. Tell them to pick him up. He's probably in one of the bars. You might even try the old Muthaiga Club. But get those Americans away to their plane, now, before I ring Kimani myself."

I don't know whether it was Kimani's name or simply the long habit of obedience, but Karanja went back to the coach without argument and gave orders to the driver to proceed to the airport. The rest of us watched in silence as the coach drove off. I think, like me, they were all feeling a sense of abandonment as it disappeared down the heavily treed road, for the Americans had been by far the largest group at the Conference. There was a general movement towards Karanja, who was suddenly engulfed, a sea of anxious faces deluging him with questions about flights and departure times, and all he could say to pacify them was, "I will telephone."

It was Sir Edmund who rescued him, taking him by the arm and leading him through the flap of the reception desk into the manager's office behind. When they emerged again Karanja was smiling. "Everything arranged now," he announced. "You all leave by Government bus for the airport at twenty-three hundred." And Sir Edmund added, "I'm told there are two flights coming through during the night, one of them, a jumbo, is half empty, so there will be seats for all of you." The jumbo was bound for London via Naples, the other, a 707, for Frankfurt.

"Let's go and have a drink," Ken said. Everybody was moving towards the bar at the end of the terrace, a sense of relief showing in their faces, in the suddenly increased volume of conversation.

"You go ahead," I told him.

"Still worrying about her?"

I shook my head, feeling confused and not certain why it mattered to me that she had gone off with Kirby-Smith. A good journalist, Karanja had said. But it had to be something more than that. "I'll join you in a minute." And I went back through the foyer, climbing the stairs to room 109. But it was just as the woman had said, one bed still unmade, the other not slept in, nothing of hers left there, the wardrobe, the drawers, everything bare, including the bathroom. I stood there for a moment thinking about where she would be now, remembering the last time I had seen her, at the Lodge, lushed up on beer, her face puffed and shining with sweat, her dark eyes reflecting the violence of her feelings. She had looked older then, and I remembered how she had said, "He's always been like that—ruthless, egotistical, always disappearing into the bush. I never had a proper father." The tears had been streaming down her face. "How can I love a man like that? I hate him." And she had turned suddenly and left me, staggering blindly out into the rain, the beer not strong enough to drown the tide of her emotions.

And now she was with Kirby-Smith, who was everything her father was not, a commercial hunter. Where would she be now, at his house in Karen? Abe had said he had one of the old settlers' houses out on Miotoni Road. Or would she be camped somewhere on the road to the north?

I closed the door and went back down the stairs, wondering why I had bothered to check her room. It didn't matter to me what she was doing. Tomorrow I would be back in London, the whole episode nothing but material for a script. And yet. . .

I was still thinking about her, about the extraordinary love-hate relationship she had with her father, when I reached my room. But I didn't stay there. I went out on to the lawn, where the night was like velvet, all diamond-studded, and the older building, beyond the crater, a white blur in the starlight. I could see the balcony of Abe's room, but there was no light there, the whole building dark. So he hadn't returned and again I had that sense of uneasiness, the feeling that Africa hadn't finished with me yet.

A light beamed out from one of the chalet rooms, a

man standing there, dark in silhouette. It was a moment before I registered that the light was in my own room. The figure moved, stepping through the glassless windows out on to the lawn. "That you, Colin?" It was Abe's voice. And he added, coming towards me, "Ken said you were somewhere around." His tone was quiet and relaxed, no trace of tension in it.

"Where the hell have you been?" He didn't seem to realize the trouble his absence had caused. "Karanja was going to hold the coach for you, but then Sir Edmund—"

"It doesn't matter."

"You should be on your way out to the airport with the others. Where have you been?"

"Checking on your film, for one thing." He took hold of my arm. "Come on, we'll go back to your room. We can talk there. And I've got myself a bottle of the real stuff. Maybe that'll quiet your nerves." I started to protest that there was nothing wrong with my nerves, but his grip on my arm tightened. "Wait till I tell you what I've arranged."

"The thing you've got to arrange is transport out to the airport," I told him, my mind still on the problem of getting safely clear of Africa. "That charter plane is waiting there and if you don't get moving—"

"I'm not leaving with the others."

"What do you mean?"

"I'm staying on here. And so are you—if you want to. Now come on back to your room and I'll fill you up with something better than local firewater."

He wouldn't answer any of my questions until I was seated on my bed with a tooth glass half full of neat whisky. "Where did you get this?" I asked him. "It's bourbon, isn't it?"

"Right. A present from the American Consul." He lit a cigarette and flopped into the only chair, leaning back, his eyes half closed. "It's been a long day," he murmured, sipping at his drink. "That was the first thing I did, checked at the Consulate to see that the pilot had delivered your film safely. He had and the Consul countersigned my check." He stared out into the night, rubbing his hand over his eyes. He looked tired. "They picked me up as I came out of the building."

"Who did? The police?"

"Police, Army—I don't know. They weren't in uniform, just dark trousers and white open-necked shirts. They didn't ask me what I'd been doing at the Consulate, they just hustled me into an old Peugeot, gave me a thorough going over in the back of the car, and when they didn't find what they were after they drove me into town. I thought I'd land up in some goddam prison or maybe an Army barracks. They wouldn't talk. They wouldn't answer any of my questions. And they weren't interested in my press pass or the fact that I was an American TV man. And when I insisted on their taking me to the Ministry, the guy sitting beside me in the back just gave me a broad smile and said, 'You'll be well cared for, Mr. Finkel.' I figured that was a threat and I was in real trouble, but instead of landing up in jail, I found myself on Ngong Road on the first floor of a fancy black-market restaurant that turned out to be the old Nairobi Club. The windows were open on to a balcony and Kimani was sitting there in the sunshine with a drink in his hand, the pilot opposite him and another African, a man named Gethenji or something like that, a director of the new Federation Bank." He knocked back the rest of his drink and reached for the bottle. "Are you ready for another?"

I shook my head. "What did they want?"

"The film, of course. Kimani's no fool and he'd figured out what you'd got and how you'd got it. And by then, of course, I knew it was political dynamite. The Federation is pressing hard for full diplomatic recognition from the States. They want an American Embassy here, not just a Consulate. That's why they agreed to the Wildlife Conference. So in the end I did a deal with him." He smiled at me. "It was the least I could do after such an excellent lunch and those gorillas waiting for me downstairs."

I was thinking of that night drive through the rain,

the incredible blazing dawn in the boneyard of the Serengeti. "What sort of deal?" I asked bleakly.

"You want to get to Lake Rudolf, don't you?"

"If I could have persuaded van Delden to take me, yes. Where is he? Did they tell you?"

"They don't know. At least, that's what Kimani said, and I think he'd have told me if they'd picked him up. He said he thought he was probably working his way down to the coast and would get out that way, back to the Seychelles. Now, do you still want to go to Rudolf, or don't you?"

I shook my head, feeling Africa closing round me, scared of what he might have arranged. "Didn't they offer you money?"

"Oh yes. That's why the bank director was there. I have the impression Kimani's position isn't all that secure. What he had in mind was a straight cash deal through the bank's representative in Zurich."

"Then why didn't you take it?"

"It wasn't my film, and knowing you wanted to get up north . . ."

"There are two planes coming through tonight," I said. "All I want is to be on one of them, out of here."

He laughed and I knew by the sound of it he had had too much. "So now van Delden's gone and the girl, too, you've lost your nerve." He thrust the bottle into my hand.

It was half empty. "You know about Mary Delden then. Did Kimani tell you?"

He nodded. "Clever girl, tagging along with Kirby-Smith."

"How do you mean?" The bottle rattled against the glass as I poured.

"She knows where there's a good story—drought, starvation, a culling operation. And Kimani wants it told. Savior of the starving multitude. That's political stuff in the Third World. So I guess does Kirby-Smith, provided it justifies him."

I slammed the bottle down. "So that's it. You're afraid you're missing out on a story. You trade my film of van Delden in the Serengeti for the chance of -

90

meeting up with Kirby-Smith and getting something for your own network."

He shook his head. "I had no choice. Just think for a moment how that film of yours could be intercut with the shots of van Delden's intervention at the Conference. Actual pictures of him standing on the Serengeti plain viewing the carnage. It could be damning for a man in Kimani's position, knowing the President was bent on full American recognition. Anyway, that's my reading of the situation, and it fits in with Kimani's willingness to do a deal. He wants the world to know they have a problem up there in the north. So you get your trip to Rudolf. That's what you wanted, isn't it?"

He was twisting it, trying to make it appear he had done me a favour. "You're not interested in Lake Rudolf," I said.

"No, but you are. Would you care to tell me?"

"No."

"Okay, but you have a reason." He reached for the bottle, pouring himself another drink as he said, "So do I. Not a spef—specific reason and I'm not after a story. It's not that at all." He put the bottle carefully down on the floor. "I'm a New Yorker, right? I was born and brought up in the Bronx, on the Grand Concourse. I'm a denizen of the concretest jungle in the world, and though I've been to a hell of a lot of countries, it's been mostly cities, or with mobs of people around—camps, mines, oilfields, anywhere there's a news story to cover. Driving out to that Lodge, the feel of Africa, the immensity, the solitude, and yesterday, coming back we saw a lion—a wild lion on the prowl for food." His voice had become a little slurred. "It was so thin and emaciated the ribs stuck out like a wicker basket and it stood there looking at us from the other side of the flood water where we'd bogged down. I'd never seen a lion in the wild before, only well-fed beasts in cages. So I figured just once in my life I'd cut loose, do something I wanted—not for money, not as an assignment, just for kicks. D'you understand?" He shook his head. "No, of course you

91

don't. You're too young to have started worrying about what you've made of your life. But I'm close to fifty now, and seeing van Delden, his absolute commitment, his complete disregard of self—and the extraordinary impression he made . . ."

He paused there, staring down at his empty glass, his eyes half closed and a strangely sad look on his face. "Most of us, we live our lives not believing in anything very much. But men like van Delden, they walk through life with God at their side, sure in the knowledge that they are here for a purpose." He put his hands up over his face, leaning forward as though in prayer. "Jesus! I envy them, now, when it's too late. I'm just a spectator. That's all I've ever been, all I wanted to be. Not involved, not committed. A spectator." He spat the word out, contemptuous and sneering. "I've read a lot. Biographies mainly. A substitute for the real thing." He let his hands fall, staring at me with his dark eyes. "D'you know why van Delden went to the Seychelles?"

"He retired," I said. "His wife's family had a house there. . . ."

"Balls! He's not the sort of man to retire of his own accord. He was run out of Kenya—deported."

I didn't know whether to believe him or not. "How do you know?" I asked.

"The Nation. After I left Kimani I had a look through the back numbers. It was about a year before the war. A man named Enderby disappeared up near Marsabit in territory van Delden had acquired as a sanctuary. He was a white hunter collecting for zoos and safari parks and specialising in baby elephants. The mortality rate was appalling. But he didn't care, nor did the Government. Like the tourist traffic, it brought in foreign currency. Only van Delden cared, and when Enderby started moving in on his territory, he warned him—not privately, but in front of the African game warden at a meeting in the warden's office in Marsabit. He told him he didn't care whether he had a Government permit or not, if he started using guns and thunderflashes on his land he'd shoot

92

him." Abe nodded. "I talked to the reporter who interviewed that game warden. He's still working for *The Nation* and he told me the warden was quite certain van Delden had meant what he said. He also told me it was common knowledge Enderby was involved in the ivory trade, and Marsabit was known for its big tuskers."

"You think van Delden shot him then?" I was remembering that wild old man in the blazing Serengeti dawn, the cold anger in his pale eyes.

Abe shrugged. "A man like that, with his moral standards and his love of elephants—it wouldn't seem like murder now, would it?"

"What about the reporter you spoke to, what did he think?"

"Served that bastard right, that was his comment. He said everybody knew van Delden killed the man."

"Then why wasn't he put on trial?"

"No body, no witnesses, and anyway they didn't dare. Think what he'd have made of it with some of the most prominent people in the country making fortunes out of ivory." He sloshed some more whisky into his glass. "Where do you reckon he is now?"

I shook my head, wondering whether there was any truth in it. And Abe's voice adding, "He's always been an elephant man, and with their reconnaissance boys reporting herds of elephant moving north through the Mathews Range and the Ndoto . . ." He was staring at me, his eyes glassy bright. "There's a military post at Marsabit on the highway north into Ethiopia and they report elephant for the first time in over a year. Not much fodder for them there now, I'm told, and the springs where the Rendile once watered their cattle all dried up, but I've a feeling . . ." He shook his head, laughing at himself, a sound that reminded me of the giggle of a hyena. "It's just the way I'm made, I guess, but Marsabit was van Delden's stamping ground."

"You think he's trekking north, not heading for the coast?"

He shrugged. "How the hell do I know? It's just a feeling. What would you do in his place, knowing ele-

93

phants the way he does? At *The Nation* they had the old 1965 survey maps. To the north of Rudolf there's the Molo River, all swamp and thick bush. Marsabit Mountain is over four thousand feet high, and to the west, overlooking the lake, there's Kulal, over seven thousand; two oases of virtual rain forest before the long desert march to the Molo and survival." And he added, "The Tsavo now—Tsavo East and Tsavo West. Before the Africans started fighting each other, those were the two largest parks, and some of the best elephant country left. Now I'm told they're almost empty of game. What the Tanzanian Army didn't kill, the Africans bordering these parks finished off. But not the elephants surely. Rhinos, yes, and buffalo, but I don't reckon elephants would just passively stay there to be slaughtered. Do you?" He stared at me as though expecting me to say they would, his eyes gleaming belligerently. "All I ever read about elephants . . . And game wardens. I've talked to some of them, interviews. . . . It all adds up to this—elephants live so long, always in family groups—they have this percip . . . they have the intelligence to differentiate between areas of safety and areas of danger. You understand? So, a family group may have safe-area knowledge going back two hundred years or more. Could be, even as far south as Tsavo, some wandering bull passed the word about van Delden's sanctuary. Too fanciful? Maybe. I don't know. So many hunters' stories, legends . . . difficult to tell what's fact and what's fiction." He downed his drink and got carefully to his feet, scooping up the almost empty bottle as he rose. "Well, I'm off to bed now. There'll be a truck here to pick us up about eight in the morning, and I've got Karanja acting as guide. If you want to go north—"

"You've got Karanja?"

That's right. And I didn't ask for him. The Minister simply said Karanja would fix it and he'd send him with us."

"From what you told me I'd have thought his public-relations man is the last person he'd let you have."

94

"Maybe he wants to get rid of him. I don't know. Could be Karanja's not his man. If you'd seen as much of politics as I have . . ." He held the bottle up to the light, squinting at it and shaking his head sadly. "Don't reckon politics out here is much different from what it is back in New York. Just as rough, just as crooked, probably more so. Anyway, if you want to get to Lake Rudolf . . ."

"Marsabit is a long way east of Rudolf," I said.

He turned, the door half open. "Marsabit, Kulal, Rudolf—it's all one to me. So long as I meet up with some elephants."

"The Army will have killed them by the time we get there." I was thinking of what they had done in the Serengeti.

"I don't think so. They're not professional hunters like Kirby-Smith. And Marsabit is the most northerly outpost, less than a dozen men." He was standing there, swaying slightly, a sardonic smile on his face. "You think I've been talking a lot of crap, don't you? That I'm just a newshound on to another story. But you're wrong there." He shook his head. "It's not van Delden or Kirby-Smith I'm interested in. It's elephants . . . and Africa. The thought of all that space, the goddam frightful emptiness of it." He focussed his eyes on me, holding on to the door. "You can come with me or not, just as you please. I don't care. Like the elephants, I'm following some strange compulsive urge of my own." And he added, "I don't expect you to understand. I don't understand myself." He nodded, smiling. "For once in my life I'm going to see what I want to see, film what I want to film. Goo'night."

He staggered out, closing the door behind him, and I was suddenly alone—alone and feeling scared. I was sorry then that he had taken the bottle. I could have done with another drink, remembering what I had read of Lake Rudolf in that faded typescript, the desiccated lava landscape, the volcanic cones and the hot winds whistling down from Kulal. Was it worth risking my life chasing an archaeological will-o'-the-wisp of that Godforsaken country? And Abe Finkel—

trading my Serengeti film for the sight of a few herds of elephants—God damn the man!

I moved to the chair he had vacated, sitting staring into the velvet darkness, my mind numb and the frogs croaking in the crater. Some strange compulsive urge, he had called it. Was I expected to share the problems of a man approaching fifty? I thought of London, trying to balance the life I knew against his offer of the unknown, the opportunity like a yawning void, a journey into space. Forbidden territory! I got the map out of my case and switched the light on, staring at it, trying to visualise what it meant, physically. I was hot and tired, exhausted after a day's work on my script, and I couldn't get van Delden out of my mind. Had he really killed that ivory hunter, or had Abe Finkel's imagination run away with him? An elephant man, and so sure they were being doomed to extinction. I remember his words, the way he had faced the delegates, and then arranging for that poor beast to be driven into the Lodge area as into an arena so that he could slip away. And the tears standing in his daughter's eyes, her anger, her blazing anger at the callousness of it.

I was still sitting there, the map draped over my knees, when Ken came to tell me the bus had arrived. I didn't say anything, thinking of the aircraft flying through the night, back to England and normality, knowing I wouldn't be on it.

"You'd better get moving, we're on the first flight." And I heard myself say, "I'm not coming. I'm staying here." And I told him about the opportunity to visit Lake Rudolf, trying to keep my voice casual as I arranged what he should take and what he should leave for me—the Beaulieu, all the spare film, and what cash we had left. It wasn't easy to convince him that I really meant it, but in the end he said, "Okay, if that's what you want. But rather you than me." And he began gathering up his things. It only took a moment, and then he was at the door, lingering there as though he half expected me to change my mind. "What shall I tell John?"

I had almost forgotten about John Crabtree and the BBC. I handed him the scribbled pages of the script. "Have that typed and give it to him, together with the film. He'll have to make what he can of it."

"And you'll be back—when?"

"How the hell do I know? Tell him I'm working on something else, outside of our assignment. I'll see him as soon as I reach London."

Ken nodded, standing there loaded with gear, waiting. "I'll tell him," he said finally. He wished me luck and then he was gone, the door shut and the room suddenly bleak and empty. I was alone again with Pieter van Delden's book and the old map, the frogs booming and my mind reaching out to the north, imagination running riot, my thoughts chaotic.

I must have gone to sleep there in the chair, for the next thing I knew I was shivering, a damp wind blowing into the room and the time almost one-thirty in the morning. I undressed slowly and crawled into bed, asleep almost as soon as my head touched the pillow.

Dawn woke me, the harsh cry of birds, and I lay watching the almost instant blaze of the sun, the shade lines darkening. None of the softness here of the English countryside, the birdsong, everything harsher, the grass coarse and the sun's heat not a life-giving warmth, but something to be afraid of. I looked at my watch. It was almost seven o'clock. If he had been on the first plane Ken would be landing at Heathrow inside of an hour, and I was still in Africa, committed to something for which my life had not equipped me. But at this hour of the day there was a freshness in the air, a sparkle, and suddenly I didn't care. Rudolf, the northern frontier, a new world . . . I threw off the bedclothes, stripped and showered, the tingle of my body matching the change of mood. And then Abe came in, looking bright as a bird and full of energy.

"You're still here then." He was dressed in khaki shorts and bush shirt, and he had all his gear with him. He smiled. "Just thought I'd check on my way to breakfast. I'll be out on the terrace."

I nodded, wrapping my towel round me. "I'll join

you as soon as I've shaved. Order for me, will you? Has the truck arrived?"

"Not yet. But Karanja's here."

"You think they're really going to give us a truck?"

"If they don't, then your film remains at the Consulate." He turned to go, but then paused. "There's news of van Delden, by the way. A Land-Rover has been hijacked from a military post at Narok."

"How do they know it's van Delden?"

"You better ask Karanja. He's joining us for breakfast. Eggs and bacon okay for you? It may be the last decent meal we get for some time."

Ten minutes later I dumped my kit in the foyer and went out into the bright sunlight of the terrace. It was almost empty now that the Conference delegates had gone, a few Africans drinking coffee and Abe sitting at a table shaded by a thatched arbour. He was the only white man there and Karanja was sitting opposite him, dressed in a faded blue shirt and khaki trousers, a map spread out on the table between them. "Jambo," he said as I took the chair beside him. "You have good breakfast now, then we go."

"What's this about van Delden taking a Land-Rover?" I asked.

"The information come to Army Headquarters yesterday. There is a Land-Rover missing at Narok. Somebody steal it in the night."

"You don't know it was van Delden then?"

He grinned, a white flash of teeth. "You meet him. Nobody take a Land-Rover from the Army, only Tembo do a thing like that."

"And where's Narok?"

"That's the point," Abe said. "Narok is almost due west of here, about sixty miles." He swung the map round so that I could see, his finger pointing. "The scale is about thirty-six miles to the inch, so that puts him almost a hundred miles north of the Lodge." From Narok a gravel road ran north to Nakuru with a main road to Thomson's Falls and Nanyuki to link up with the highway north to Marsabit.

"He's not making for the coast then?"

98

"No, not if it's van Delden."

Our breakfast arrived—bacon and eggs, toast, butter, marmalade, coffee, yellow slices of paw-paw and half a lime, sugar if we wanted it. "No balance-of-payments problem here," Abe said, and Karanja grinned. "All black market for the rich men who run the rackets."

"And that doesn't include you?"

He shook his woolly head. "I am only here when I have guests of the Government. You are guests of the Government this morning. Mr. Kimani's orders."

Abe bowed his acknowledgment. "Most generous of him. And even more generous to spare you to accompany us."

Karanja laughed. "Mr. Kimani has his reasons."

Abe's eyebrows lifted, but he didn't say anything, and Karanja went on, "Those pictures at the Conference, some people think I engineer the whole thing."

"Is that what Kimani thinks?"

"I don't know. Maybe. But is good excuse sending me with you." And he suddenly burst out laughing for no reason that I could see except perhaps to cover embarrassment. "He don't want me here in Nairobi."

I think Abe had the same feeling as myself, that Karanja was in a very excitable state, his nerves on edge, for he quickly changed the subject. "That Land-Rover, how much gas was in it, do you know?"

"Nobody tell me." He was no longer laughing, his voice sulky.

"Could he get gas at Nakuru?"

"For petrol he must have a permit."

"What about the black market?"

"Maybe."

"At Nakuru?"

Karanja shook his head. "At Nakuru the police watch for that Land-Rover. At all towns, and there are Army patrols on the highway. I think he keep to the small roads." His finger traced a thin red line on the survey map running north from Narok to link with a network of tracks west of Nakuru. "Maybe some farmer sell him petrol to get to Baringo. But after Lake Baringo . . ." He shook his head.

"What about us?" I asked. "Where do we fill up?"

"At Samburu. That is Northern Army Headquarters now." He turned the map over, indicating a green patch just north of Isiolo. It was marked Samburu Game Reserve.

"And beyond Samburu?" Abe asked.

Karanja shook his head. "I don't know. Maybe they have some soldiers at Maralal or Baragoi. Is more probable Baragoi. You see Horr Valley between the mountains—there." He jabbed with his knife. "Is only way for trucks coming south from Ethiopia, that track and the highway through Marsabit. And where there are soldiers is petrol." He nodded emphatically. "We ask at Samburu."

I stared down at the map. Lake Baringo was at 3,300 feet with mountains towering all round it and only a single track running north, soon petering out into a broken red thread in the vast emptiness of the Rift Valley as it sloped down to Lake Rudolf. If he made it to Baringo, then he would have no alternative but to take the track eastwards into the mountains, and if he were heading for Marsabit, that meant swinging north through Maralal, Baragoi, and the Horr Valley. "Have you read von Höhlen's account of Teleki's expedition to Lake Rudolf?" I asked Abe.

He shook his head.

"Well, I have, and unless he can find enough petrol I don't see how he can make it, not to Marsabit, through the mountains and across the desert."

"Okay, so you've read about it. But he's lived there, remember. It's his country." He pushed his plate away and reached for the coffee. "What do you say, Karanja? You know the area."

"If he don't have fuel for the Land-Rover . . ." Karanja paused, his forehead creased in thought. "Very bad now for foot safari. Very bad drought, no water in Balesa Kulal." He pointed to a thin line on the map at the foot of the mountain's eastern slope. "And if Kalama waterhole also dry . . ." He shrugged.

100

"Maybe there is some rain now." But he said it without conviction. "Maybe Samburu don't eat all their camels. With camels it is not more than two, three days from Horr Valley to Marsabit."

"And there's water in the Horr Valley?" Abe asked.

"Yes, at South Horr. Always water at South Horr." He looked up as a soldier came to our table. They talked for a moment, and then he said, "The bus is here." He produced an envelope from his pocket and handed it to me. "You sign please and I leave it for Mr. Kimani at the desk."

It was a typewritten letter authorising the American Consul to hand over to the Minister of Lands the package containing my film, provided we had been transported to Lake Rudolf and returned safely to Nairobi. I looked across at Abe, but he was lighting a cigarette, avoiding my gaze. Outside on the road I could see a minibus drawn up in the shade, its dusty body still showing the zebra stripes of tourist days, but faded now and streaked with rust. Karanja was holding out a pen for me. "If you don't sign, then maybe Mr. Kimani think I engineer that too." And again he burst into laughter that was high pitched and without any humour.

I was still reluctant, but all the delegates had gone now, the time for refusal past. I took the pen and signed it, and Karanja went off with it to the reception desk. "I thought for a moment you were going to back-pedal." Abe was smiling, I think with relief.

"What would have happened if I had?"

He shrugged. "I guess we'd have been in trouble, both of us. Kimani's taking a bit of a risk as it is. The area we're going into is an Army responsibility."

I nodded, feeling the sun hot on my back, a flutter of nerves in my stomach. "I'd better get my things then and check out." Nothing else I could do now, and he smiled and said, "See you in the bus."

In the foyer I found Karanja still at the desk, chatting up the pretty little African receptionist, and when I asked her for my bill, he said it was all settled. "You and Mr. Finkel are the guests of the Government now.

101

I show you what we do for our people, how the Government is helping them. Also very interesting country. Not many white men go where we are going and you get better film, very much better film, with shots of the lake and El Molo people." He said something to the girl, his teeth shining in a broad smile, and then he picked up my suitcase, leaving me to carry my camera, and we went out to the minibus.

Abe was already sitting in front beside the driver, two guns and a water bag beside him, cartons of ammunition at his feet. "We'll take it in turns," he said as I climbed past him. The body of the vehicle was a jumble of camping gear, sacks, and cardboard boxes, with jerricans ranged along each side and two soldiers sitting on the heap of stores, clutching their rifles, their heads almost touching the roof. Karanja joined me on the transverse seat, sliding the door to behind him. "Is more comfortable the minibus," he said, but without much conviction, and I was thinking a Land-Rover would have been better.

We drove out through the centre of Nairobi and took the road northeast to Thika, climbing steadily into old settler country of citrus fruit and tea plantations, jacaranda everywhere and the Cape chestnut trees in flower. There were plantation houses set well in the shade of the trees, but they looked tired and neglected, their verandahs peeling paint, the gardens overgrown and littered with huts and rubbish, African children everywhere. The road was almost empty of traffic, its macadam surface pitted with holes loosely filled with gravel that rattled against the chassis.

Beyond Thika we began to catch glimpses of Mt. Kenya, its summit like a great medieval fortress, black rock against the crystal of perpetual snow and the hard blue of the sky. We were into more open country then, the Aberdares closing in to our left, and just before midday we passed the turning to Nyeri. There was a signpost there that still said Treetops, but when Abe asked Karanja whether there was any game left around this old tourist haunt, he said he didn't know. "The Outspan Hotel, where tourists stop for lunch, is now administration office for resettlement of Aberdare mountain region."

"And Treetops is abandoned?"

"Not abandoned. Is camp for hunters working with the Ministry."

"Your Ministry, eh?"

Karanja nodded.

Abe turned to me. "I was at Treetops once." His eyes gleamed behind his glasses. "I had been attending the UNCTAD meeting here in Nairobi, a United Nations conference to work out how the rich nations could best assist in the development of the Third World. Very boring, and after it was over I decided to take a break and get a glimpse of this wildlife people talked about. You ever been to Treetops?" He didn't wait for me to answer, but went on talking in that fast monotone of his that was sometimes hard to follow because it came in one continuous flow. "There was a white hunter with a rifle to meet our bus from the Outspan and we covered the last five hundred yards on foot with warnings not to talk and if we met a dangerous animal to slip into one of the hides provided. Good tourist stuff! I guess I was in one of my cynical moods. And then suddenly there was this rhinoceros less than two hundred yards away with a horn on him like a spike about two feet long, sniffing the air, his little ears cocked, and peering myopically in our direction."

He grinned. "I wasn't so sure about the tourist stuff then, but we made it to the stairs without him charging us and then we were back to the flush-toilet world we all knew. Treetops was no longer the original glorified hide in a tree, it was a comfortable hotel built on piles with a circular pool of muddy water in front of it and salt thrown down to attract the game. But nothing came, the rhino had disappeared and we had to be content with filming the baboons scampering about on the roof like clowns in a circus. At dusk some buffalo appeared, looking about as wild as a herd of black cattle; two of them had a wallow and that was just about the highlight. I was bored as hell."

103

"You got nothing out of Treetops then." I was wondering if that was the point of the story.

"Oh, but I did," he murmured. "That was the extraordinary thing. I got something so beautiful. . . ." He hesitated, staring at the road ahead, the long slope of the mountain, then turning to me again and asking whether I was a balletomane. He shook his head at my reply. "Then I'm not sure you'll understand, but I'm quite close to Lincoln Center—I live on West End and I see a lot of ballet. I love it, I really do." He shook his head, smiling. "It's difficult to explain if you don't appreciate the beauty of movement. We were still at dinner when somebody said, 'There's an elephant out there.' The long dining table emptied in a flash and there was this elephant, grey-white in the flood-lights, surrounded by buffaloes. She just stood there, moving the tip of her trunk delicately over the ground until she finally fastened on the particular bit of salt she fancied. I'm sure it was a young female, she was so feminine, so dainty in all her movements, and the buffaloes stood glowering at her, disputing the ground. She shook her head at them, fanning her ears and taking a few tentative steps as though about to charge. Then she wheeled abruptly and tripped off-stage like a ballerina who finds herself crowded by a bunch of yokels."

He twisted further round, gripping my arm. "You know, Colin, she was just about the prettiest thing I ever saw. No, that's not the word. I guess you can't describe an animal that big as pretty, but she was beautiful—so light on her feet, so graceful." He shook his head, laughing at himself, then reached into the pocket of his bush jacket and brought out his wallet. "I've always wondered whether I'd see her again, and when I got this assignment—" He produced the faded photograph and passed it to me. "I was shooting in black and white, of course, and that size I guess it doesn't look all that much. But the big blow-up I've got at home is really something. I shot three reels of her, so I had plenty to choose from."

It showed an elephant limned in light and ghostly

white, the ears spread out like the wings of a butterfly, the trunk curled up, and it appeared to be dancing, one foot raised, the body twisted slightly as though caught in the moment of pirouetting, and to the left of the picture was a rhino pawing the ground in a scuff of dust, the head lowered so that the long horn was like a spear. It was a fantastic shot, every detail clear and and whole picture so perfectly balanced it was like an artist's impression.

"Nice, isn't it?" he said. "You know, I'm really proud of that picture. Compensation for all the dreary stuff I've shot in years of travelling around for the media." He leaned over, his finger pointing at the animal's left ear. "See that hole there. In the blow-up you can see it very clearly. It's a great tear shaped like a duck on the wing. That's how they recognise elephants. It's like a tag."

"What caused it?"

"The horn of a rhino probably. That's what I'm told, anyway. And she'll carry that mark to the end of her days."

"And you shot three reels in that one brief sighting?"

"Oh, no. I was up watching her half the night. She came back, you see. About midnight. There were rhinos then as well as buffs. And one of the rhinos began snorting and mock charging her. It was always the same place, the same bit of salt, and she'd just stand her ground, flapping her ears and laughing at him. In the end she'd shrug and stroll away as though she wasn't really interested, make a slow, stately circuit of the waterhole, and come back to the same spot. Then the whole ridiculous pantomime would start up again, the rhino snorting and Sally—" He looked at me, a solemn, sad look in his eyes. "That's what I called her —Sally. My wife's name, you see. She was in the Corps de Ballet when I met her, such beautiful balance, and so dainty." He was silent for a moment, the smile gone. Then he gave a quick little shrug. "Well anyway, this elephant, she'd flap her ears at the rhino, standing tall and stately—just like Sally—her front legs close together so that she was slender and neat and statuesque. Yeah, that's the word—statuesque. Then she'd drift out silently for another circuit of the waterhole, moving like a shadow in and out of the trees until she'd disappeared. And after a while, suddenly, she'd be standing there like a ghost again, absolutely still, waiting to make her entrance." He reached out and took the photograph from me, replacing it in his wallet. "All that patience, all that quiet determination over a little bit of salt, it was a lesson in animal behaviour and in deportment. The rhino, too, all that snorting and pawing and mock charging, it wasn't real aggression. He wasn't spoiling for a fight. He was just saying, 'For Christ's sake give me a little more room.' And though Sally could have picked him up in her trunk, all two tons of him, and slammed his body on the ground and knelt on it, all she did again and again was take a wander round the pool."

He had turned away and was looking out the window towards the mountains, where wisps of smoke showed blue against the dark of forest green. "That's what Treetops meant to me—the tolerance and beauty of big game animals. Also," he added in a whisper, "it gave me the urge to spend a few moments of my life in the company of elephants." He nodded towards the fires and the gashes where the trees had been felled. "There's going to be soil erosion there." He twisted round and faced Karanja. "Why doesn't your Ministry stop it? As well as soil erosion you'll have a drop in rainfall. Don't you ever think about the future? Or is that all our civilisation has taught you—rape the land, grab what you can, and to hell with tomorrow?" He stared at the puzzled Karanja, then looked at me, that sardonic little smile, lifting the corners of his lips. "A long time ago now," he said, "since your Queen heard of her succession up there in that Treetops lookout. A lot has happened, the world gone sourer on the human race and everything more complicated." He said it sadly, then lit a cigarette and relapsed into silence.

We were just north of the equator then, close under the western slopes of Mt. Kenya. A white cloud had formed over its top and our talk was desultory, the heat increasing. At Nanyuki the broad main street was almost deserted, its shops all boarded up. We stopped outside one of them. Faded lettering announced it as The Settlers' Store. "Maybe he have some beer," Karanja said. "Is only place till we get to Samburu." He remembered it as an Indian shop where safaris stocked up with wine and liquor, fresh vegetables and tinned goods, but it had been Africanised long ago and now the shelves were largely bare, only local produce sold, sacks of maize flour they called posho, melons over-ripe and crawling with flies, root vegetables I had never seen before. The beer was warm and flat from an old plastic container. We bought oranges and on Karanjas' advice a bagful of local cigarettes, then we drove on.

I had changed places with Abe, but it was hotter in front and no more comfortable as we climbed into open country on the northern slopes of the mountain. "Much resettlement here," Karanja said, indicating the dried-up vistas of grassland below us. It was dotted with groups of huts and patches of abandoned cultivation. "After the settlers go the land is given to the Meru people and the Samburu." But there was no sign of life there, no people, no cattle, no game.

"Where are they now?" I asked, and I had to shout above the noise of the labouring engine and the rattle of gravel against the mudguards.

He looked unhappy and shrugged his shoulders. "Drought very bad."

He came to the high point of the road and suddenly we were on the brink of the northern frontier region, a burned brown plain reaching out to desert in which towering buttes of pale red rock stood like castles shattered by wind and sand. The survey map showed that we were at 6,390 feet, the road snaking down from the shoulder of Mt. Kenya and running out into an infinity of sand and rock. Dust devils whirled and there was no horizon, the deadness of the country losing itself in haze, land and sky the same opaque sun-blistered white, and away to our left the blurred shape

107

of mountains rising like ghosts on the edge of visibility. It was appalling, breathtaking. Abe leaned forward, his voice in my ear. "The promised land!" He turned to Karanja. "You reckon elephants can cross that and reach the mountains?"

"Oh yes." He nodded. "Is not desert like the Chalbi. You look, you see trees, plenty of dry scrub, and they know where water is."

We coasted down into the oven heat of lower altitude, swinging north where the road from Meru came in, everything shimmering now, acacias lifting their flat tops above a glazed heat mirror, thorn trees standing on their heads, wisps of brittle scrub floating in the water mirages and butte tops trembling in the distance. The little township of Isiolo appeared as a glint of corrugated iron winking in the sun. The road passed it by and the macadam stopped abruptly. We were on to gravel then, the noise deafening and dust streaming out behind us, and that was where we saw our first sign of animal life, two giraffe standing by a thorn tree, their necks leaning sideways and a quizzical expression on their faces as they stared at us absolutely motionless.

It was the driver who saw them and he braked, shouting excitedly and pointing. The soldiers in the back reached for their rifles. The giraffe were barely a hundred yards away, but by the time we had stopped they were already on the move, galloping off with that stiff yet graceful gait that enables them to keep their heads at a constant elevation. "They are reticulated giraffe," Karanja said as though he were courier to a group of tourists. "Is a species belonging to the north here."

"It's good to see something that's survived," Abe said sourly, his eyes on the two soldiers, whose disappointment showed in their faces as we drove on.

"Very difficult to shoot giraffe," Karanja said, as though he shared the soldiers' disappointment.

I was looking at the country now with a new interest, but we saw nothing else, only some ostrich, and ten miles further on we forked left on to a track that led to some round thatched huts that had once been the entrance to the Samburu Game Reserve. Now it was a military post. Karanja showed his pass and we were waved on, past some scout cars with their crews asleep in the shade of the armour, the track running out into open savannah country, a sort of plateau of sered grass bordered by a fine stand of acacia, dark umbrellas against a burning sky, mountains blue in the distance. The track had been pulverised to a fine grey dust and in the distance the dull green shapes of Army tents floated above the shimmering grass, a windsock hanging limp and the dust of a plane that had just landed lying like a pall of smoke over the improvised runway. Nothing stirred, the sun blazing down, the heat intense. "You want to swim?"

"In the river?" I could see it marked on the map.

"No, not in the river. At Buffalo Springs. He directed the driver at an intersection. "Very good water, very clear. No crocodiles." And he laughed.

"What about game?" Abe asked. "Any game left?"

"I don't know," he said uncertainly. "I think only Army now."

"How long since you've been here?"

"Four years, maybe five."

"And what was here then, when it was a game reserve?"

"Herds of eland, zebra, buffalo, also gazelle and oryx. There were bustards here in the grass, and lion, always some elephant down in the doum palm by the river." And then, brightening, he said, "Here is Buffalo Springs. You swim now."

The driver slowed. Two Army trucks were parked in the shade of some twisted trees. There were shouts and the sound of laughter, and when we stopped we saw the glistening black of naked bodies crowding a small rock pool. "Is very nice the water, very cool." Karanja's voice sounded uncertain, and when neither of us responded, he said abruptly, "Okay. We go straight to lodge now." And he spoke sharply to the driver.

The lodge had been sited close beside the river. It

109

still possessed something of its original charm, but now that the Army had taken over, all but the largest trees had been cut down to make way for vehicles and a sprawl of tents and latrines. At the guard tent we dropped off our two soldiers and a corporal directed us to a stretch of the river bank where four large container trucks were parked. The river was very low, the trees on the further bank drooping in the heat and the head of a crocodile showing green in the sluggish water.

I climbed stiffly out and Abe followed me. "Those look like refrigerator trucks," he said. The grey slabs of their sides were painted with the Federation flag, an elephant on a bright blue background, and underneath in bold lettering were the words: K-S GAME CONTROL COY. A Land-Rover drove into the parking area, stirring the dust.

"We're staying the night, are we?" I asked Karanja.

He shook his head. "We are civilians, not Army. We cannot camp here."

"Then what have we come for?" Abe asked, the heat giving an edge to his voice.

"Is necessary we have military permit, also petrol. And I have business to see about, a matter of communications."

"Okay, and while you're doing that, you might enquire if Major Kirby-Smith is here. Looks like he's made this his base." He walked over to the nearest truck and stood staring up at it. "Game cropping must be quite a profitable operation," he murmured. "Those things aren't cheap."

The truck was much bigger than any of the Army vehicles and it looked fairly new, the design on its side brighter than the tattered flag that had flown over the Wildlife Conference. Flip-flops sounded in the dust behind us and an Irish voice said, "Don't say we got tourists now."

It was the driver of the Land-Rover, a rather shabby little man with sandy hair and a rag of torn silk knotted round his throat. He held a battered briefcase in his hand and his bare toes were grey with dirt.

"That your minibus? I haven't seen one of those in years."

There was a sudden gleam of interest in Abe's eyes as he looked at him. "You must be the pilot of that plane we saw landing."

The other nodded. "How do you like our new flag? Pretty, isn't it?"

"A golden elephant with ivory tusks?" Abe gave a sour laugh. "Very appropriate."

"Would you be a conservationist then?"

"Television," Abe said.

"Well, if you're looking for shots of the drought I can tell you this, there's plenty of material for you north of here, the carcases of dead cattle thick round every dried-up waterhole." His leathery face cracked in a grin. "But that's no reason why we should die of thirst, too. Come and have a drink. My name's Pat Murphy."

We introduced ourselves and Abe said, "You fly reconnaissance, do you?"

"Right. Bill Maddox and me, we take it in turns to watch over the northern frontier."

"And report on any unauthorised movements."

"Our reports cover everything—tribes, animals, the state of the waterholes." He stared at us narrowly, a nerve fluttering the corners of his eyelids. "They're confidential, of course. You here on a story, or just for background shots?"

"Right at this moment I'm looking for Kirby-Smith."

"Then you're out of luck. He's not here."

"These are his refrigerator trucks."

"He left this morning. They'll follow when he gives the word. Now do you want that drink, because I certainly do and we got a truckload of beer in yesterday."

We left the driver in charge of our gear and followed the pilot along the river bank. At the entrance to the lodge, Karanja went off to find the adjutant and Pat Murphy took us through into the old tourist bar. It was now the officers' mess. There were several Africans there, very spruce in clean shirts and neatly creased trousers. He back-slapped his way through

111

them and gave his order to the barman. "Did you come up through Nanyuki and Isiolo, or by way of Baringo?"

Abe did not say anything and when I started to answer, his hand gripped my arm, silencing me, a bright gleam in his eyes.

Murphy had turned back to the bar. He settled for the drinks, then handed us our beer. "Don't reckon you'd make it through Baringo." He laughed. "An old minibus like that, it's hardly the vehicle for the Baringo track."

The beer was ice-cold from the fridge and as we drank Abe said innocently, "You flew out that way this morning, did you? See anything interesting?"

Murphy hesitated, gulping the rest of his beer down and watching us. "Television, you said. We haven't had any television people up here before so you must have been at that Wildlife Conference." He put his glass down and lit a cigarette. "There was an old-timer, Cornelius van Delden, gatecrashed the Conference. That's what I heard. Care to fill me in on the details?"

Abe told him briefly what had happened.

"And now he's disappeared. Pinched an Army Land-Rover and took off into the blue." Murphy hesitated. "Is it Kirby-Smith or van Delden you're interested in?"

"Elephants," Abe said, and the Irishman laughed.

"Sure, and you'll find them, too. But you're here on a story and that means van Delden." He finished his beer and ordered three more. I have been flying bush a long time now. Safaris, oil prospectors, Government officials—I met most people. Not many of them left now. White people, I mean."

"So you know van Delden?"

Murphy nodded. "Sure I know the old devil. I was the one who flew him down from Marsabit after the Enderby affair. You heard about that?"

"Come to the point," Abe said. "You saw the Land-Rover, did you?"

Murphy smiled. "I spotted a Land-Rover, yes."

"On the track from Baringo?"

"Could be." And he added, "Yesterday Bill flew Alex up to look at the South Horr Gap. So today I make my recce to the west along the edge of the Suguta."

"And that's where you saw it?"

"Right."

"Abandoned?"

"Hard to say. Could be just parked." He had dropped his voice so that the African officers couldn't hear. "My report doesn't go in till the morning, if that helps, and I owe van Delden something."

"Could you show us the position on the map?"

He nodded and reached for his briefcase.

II

WE WERE AWAY from the Samburu lodge by late afternoon and camped that night under Lolokwe, a great bald sugar-loaf mountain that stood up out of the plain just north of the cut-off to Maralal. The sheer sides of it were red in the sunset as we pitched our tent, Karanja showing us how the tubular framing fixed in to the canvas fly while the driver got to work with a panga gathering wood. Starlings watched us with inquisitive eyes, their metallic plumage iridescent in the slanting light, and colonies of weaver birds darted noisily in and out of nests clustered like small coconuts in the wait-a-bit thorns. The fire was roaring and the tea made by the time we had our bedding laid out under the rotten canvas.

The dusk was brief, darkness rushing in, Lolokwe a black mass against the stars and only the crackle of the blazing fire. Everything was suddenly very still, no sound of birds now. "Something I've always dreamed of," Abe murmured, his voice a whisper in the night. "Does it worry you, camping out like this in the middle of Africa?"

"No," I said. "No, of course not." But there was a tautness running through me, an awareness of the senses I had never felt before, my ears alert for sound, my eyes straining to pierce the darkness beyond the fire.

A faint breeze was coming off the mountain and Karanja sniffed the air, his face glistening black in the lurid light of the flames. "I think it rain tonight. Is why we sleep under cover." And he added, "You watch for scorpions in the sand here. Scorpions very bad."

"What about snakes?" I asked.

He grinned. "Snakes very bad, too, and we don't have snake kit. But here scorpions more bad than snakes."

The evening meal was posho and tinned stew, and while we were eating it, squatting round the fire, I told Abe about Pieter van Delden's book and the reasons for my wanting to go to Lake Rudolf.

"It seems," he said, "there is a certain dichotomy of purpose. Yours is practical. You want to confirm an archaeological discovery and capture it on film. I just want to absorb the quiet immensity of Africa and see how elephants solve the problem of survival in the hostile world of man." He lit a cigarette. "But for tomorrow I think we're both agreed, aren't we? We go take a look at that Land-Rover."

"I suppose so." I said it reluctantly, thinking of Lake Rudolf. I had a chance now to get to Lake Rudolf and I did not want to be side-tracked. "The pilot didn't say it was abandoned."

"He flew low over it and saw nobody."

"That doesn't mean it's van Delden's vehicle."

"All the more reason why we should take a look at it." He was sitting hunched up, his hands clasped round his knees, and in the firelight I could see the glint of curiosity in his eyes. A newsman on the scent of a story, I thought. And then he looked at me, smiling quietly, and said, "Have you thought about what we're doing here, really thought about it? We have moved back many centuries to a time when man was a part of the animal world. There are no garages here in the desert, and if we run out of gas, then we are as alone and vulnerable as those early men you've been telling me about who fired pottery on the shores of Lake Rudolf and marked it with the design of a pyramid topped by dwelling places. We are primitives now, huddled round a fire for protection, and for the future I can only think of the Arab word Inshallah. If it is God's will, then we shall find van Delden, and if van Delden is with us, then he is your best guide to Lake Rudolf. And for me—" He hesitated, staring into the fire. "He can teach me about elephants and how to live in harmony with this country where death and life are all one, an inevitable process that fascinates me because I've never felt it to be that way before."

"And if we don't find van Delden?"

"Then there's Kirby-Smith at South Horr. If we get a chance to see him at work I guess we'll both of us have a better understanding of Genesis and how the Tree of Knowledge made all creatures afraid of man." He turned and looked at me, smiling again. "This, my friend, is a journey back in time, and if I die as a result, then I shall die with some understanding, my body disintegrating to merge with the dust of the desert where it will give life. . . ."

"For God's sake!" I said. "You're not going to die."

"Of course not. But if I did—" He shrugged, still smiling, and now his smile was melancholy in the firelight. "I've never wanted to lie under the weight of a marble tomb in acres of headstones or have my carcase despatched to the crematorium because there's no room in the graveyards of our over-population. Better my rotting flesh keep a jackal going for another day or contribute to the soaring flight of a vulture, my bones cleaned by ants—"

"What are you—a poet manqué?"

He laughed and shook his head. "I never learned to

115

write that well." He stared into the fire a moment, then added quietly, "All my reading has been in search of knowledge, an attempt to understand. Perhaps here —outside of books, outside of the experience of others —perhaps here, in this solitude, I may discover the meaning of life, the meaning of God even." He shook his head again, smiling and getting abruptly to his feet. "I'm sorry, I talk too much. I'm going to bed now." And I was left with the feeling he was upset at having let his tongue run away with him, revealing an introspective disposition normally concealed from everybody but himself.

I sat on by the fire for a while, smoking a last cigarette and listening to the stillness. And when I followed him to bed, I lay under the fly staring up at the bulk of Lolokwe, unable to sleep. Sometime in the night it began to rain and I woke to the sound of it on the canvas and the drip, drip, drip on the sand beside my camp bed. I remembered stories then of lions sheltering in safari tents and I lay curled up like a foetus, my ears straining for the slightest sound beyond the patter of the rain.

I woke with the dawn and birds were calling. Looking out from under the torn canvas, I saw the rump of a small bird whiter than white against the black of a thorn and far in the distance an eagle nailed like a cross against the sky. The rain had gone, the sky was clear, and in the still-grey light the desert browns had a freshness of colour. Drongos, looking like jet-black flycatchers, flitted from bush to bush in the dry burned scrub and I lay there watching the light grow fast until the sun came up and the bare steep walls of Lolokwe turned blood-red. The driver threw off his blanket, putting sticks on the fire, blowing life into the embers, and Abe came strolling into sight between the thorns, slim and wiry-looking in khaki bush gear, his head bent, his eyes on the ground. I thought he was following the track of some animal, but when I called to him to ask him what it was, he shook his head. "Only birds," he said. "The sand's so soft after the rain the imprint of their feet is everywhere." He

116

came over to me, smiling. "You lazy bastard, you've missed the best of the day."

We broke camp and were away as soon as we had had tea, and by eight-thirty we had passed the turning to Wamba and were on the road to Maralal, driving towards the mountains. It was a dirt road, the going sticky in places, and soon we were climbing in thick bush. Once, where we stopped to relieve ourselves, we saw a pigmy falcon perched like a small brown sentinel on the branch of a tree. The mountains were closing in on us then and shortly afterwards we came across some old elephant droppings. It was wild country, and just below Kisima Lake a track came in from the left and Abe told the driver to take it.

"Is not the way to Maralal," Karanja said.

"No, but we take it all the same."

"Maralal straight on," Karanja insisted.

"I know Maralal is straight on." Abe had the map open on his knees. "But I want to have a look at the escarpment running down into the valley of the Suguta."

"We look over the Suguta Valley from viewpoint beyond Maralal. You see river beds, geysers, volcanoes, everything you want from viewpoint."

The argument went on for several minutes while we sat there motionless, the engine throbbing and the heat trapped in the valley. I took no part in it, watching a bateleur, which I could now recognise by its distinctive cross-like shape against the blue sky. It was planing on the air currents high up where grey crags thrust clear of the dense bush that clothed the slopes of the mountains to our right. In the end Abe had to tell him about the Land-Rover. Karanja was suddenly silent. He was sitting with me on the front seat and there was sweat on his face, his body tense. "Is no good," he murmured. "They send patrol—"

"The pilot doesn't file his report till this morning." Abe leaned forward, gripping Karanja's shoulder. "Are you going to let them pick him up? You worked with him. You were one of his game scouts. You can't just drive on, now that I've told you."

117

"Is Major Kirby-Smith you go to see. That is what you say to me and what I tell Captain Ngaru. Our permit is for Baragoi. Also," he added desperately, "we don't have enough petrol."

"We have eight jerricans in the back."

"They are water."

"Four of them are water, four of them gas, so tell the driver to turn left."

"Let's go on," I said. "It only means trouble if we do find him."

"And suppose it isn't van Delden? Suppose it's some poor devil—"

"It's van Delden all right." It had to be, no patrols out on the Baringo track and nobody but the Army allowed in the area.

"Okay then, it's van Delden. And how do you expect to find your way in the lava wastes round Lake Rudolf without him to guide you? It's what you wanted, isn't it, for him to take you there?"

I shook my head, knowing he had made up his mind and unable to argue with him in the suffocating heat. All I could say was, "I'd rather drive on." I had a deep, instinctive feeling of unease, and it wasn't only because of that strange old man; it was Abe, too. But I couldn't put my feelings into words and with a sense of inevitability I heard him say, "Okay, Karanja, we turn left here."

Something in the way he said it, the quiet certainty in his voice, seemed to settle the matter. Karanja spoke quickly to the driver in Swahili and we turned on to the track that led back in a south-westerly direction into the Ol Keju Osera Valley. It was thick bush all the way, the road steep in places and sticky with the night's rain, and half an hour later we had a puncture. It was hardly surprising, the tyres were almost bald, and while we were helping the driver change the wheel Karanja took the shotgun and went in search of game. He had heard the cackling call of guinea fowl.

"What happens if we do find van Delden?" I said.

"There'll be a patrol out after him now. Karanja's scared of him, and so am I in a way."

We were pulling the spare wheel out of the back and Abe said, "Trouble with you is you think too much. Try taking things as they come. And don't worry about Karanja. A few hours in van Delden's company and I guess he'd be the way he was before ambition and the importance of being a press officer to a minister got hold of him." And then he went on to tell me why the pilot hadn't reported sighting the Land-Rover immediately. A dozen or more years back he had taken off from Loiyangalani airstrip after flying some tourists in for the fishing on Lake Rudolf and had been caught in a hurricane blast of wind from Mt. Kulal. "There's an island in the lake there, South Island, and he crash-landed on the lava slopes and smashed his leg up. Van Delden happened to be at the Mission and he went out at once, paddling across eight miles of water on one of the El Molo log rafts they use for fishing. The wind started up again in the morning and blew for the better part of a week, so if van Delden hadn't paddled out immediately Murphy would have been done for." And he added, "I got it out of him while you were on the terrace looking at that hippo. That's why he gave us time to get down here ahead of the patrol."

We had the spare wheel on and were tightening the nuts when two shots sounded in the distance. A few minutes later Karanja emerged from the bush, grinning and holding up a brace of helmeted guinea fowl. They were plump-looking birds, their dark bodies speckled with white spots, their heads strangely capped with a bony grey horn. He was very pleased with himself as he tossed the birds into the back. "You want we brew some tea, Paul?" The driver nodded, his white shirt dark with sweat, beads of perspiration on his forehead. "Okay, we have brew-up now, then we go find this Land-Rover."

Out here alone in the bush it was somehow comforting to see how quickly they got a fire going. In no time at all the water was boiling and the driver was stirring in tea and sugar. He sat back on his haunches and suddenly his eyes widened. "Ndovu!"

At first I couldn't see them, the bush hazed with heat, the light blinding. Karanja pointed. "See them? Elephants, beyond that big tree." The excitement in his voice vibrated in the air.

I saw the tree, a big euphorbia on a rounded shoulder of the hills, and suddenly a grey shape moved, and then another. I don't know how many there were. I only caught glimpses of them as they glided quietly across a gap in the bush. "Cows," Karanja said. "They have totos with them." They passed across the dirt road, up by the farthest bend, grey ghosts moving north along the contour line, and suddenly they were gone, merged into the shimmering grey-green foliage of the hillside. Abe stood staring after them. "Did you see, Colin? A whole herd of them. Kirby-Smith was right. There are elephants up here."

Karanja handed him a mug of tea and he sat down abruptly. "Meat on the hoof," he muttered, and a cold chill ran through me, the same sort of chill I had felt the day my uncle had taken his life. There had been other times, too. Over-sensitivity, that's what the doctor had said when I had played truant from school because I wouldn't share a desk with a certain other boy. The over-sensitivity of a boy who has lost his natural parents, but I had known something dreadful was going to happen, and a few days later he was found at the bottom of the cliffs. That was when we lived at Peacehaven and I had been on an easy pitch on those same cliffs the week before, prizing fossils out of the chalk.

"There ought to be some way we could communicate," Abe said. "Some language. Then we could warn them. But I guess elephant pidgin requires a deeper rumbling than I can manage on an empty stomach." His hands were clasped round his mug, his head bent as though reading the future in the tea leaves floating on the oily surface. "I wonder if van Delden can make himself understood. He's lived with them so long. . . ." He sipped his drink, his eyes fastening on me, the

120

pupils slightly enlarged by his glasses. "All I know about elephants is what I've read since that visit to Treetops. They communicate by rumbling. But how much they communicate . . . ?" He took the plate Karanja passed him, cold baked beans and some slices of bread, and put it on the ground beside him. "Nobody knows how much they can say to each other, any more than we understand the language of dolphins and whales. For instance, this concentration of game up around Lake Rudolf. You heard what Kirby-Smith said, and he particularly referred to pilots having sighted elephants. I asked Murphy about that, but he doesn't fly to Rudolf. His job is keeping watch on tracks and waterholes. It's daytime flying, anyway, and the only place he's seen elephants is up around South Horr."

He reached for his plate, spooning beans into his mouth and gazing up at the slopes where the elephants had disappeared. "Now if I knew their language I'd go after that bunch and warn them. The way they were headed they'll finish up inside of those refrigerator trucks." He looked across at me, that sardonic little smile at the corners of his mouth. "A hardboiled media man and here I am, squatting beside a dirt track in the middle of nowhere, worrying about a herd of cows and expecting something to happen." His gaze switched back to the heat-hazed mountainside. "It's almost noon. The hottest part of the day. Those elephants should have been under the shade of the trees, fanning their ears to keep themselves cool. Do you realise an elephant can lower its body temperature by as much as sixteen degrees just by flapping its ears?"

"Then I wish I had ears as big as that." His words had made me uneasy again.

The driver rocked with laughter. "Him got big ears." He pointed to Karanja, leaning forward, still laughing, his teeth white. "You flap now, Karanja. Make cool."

"Time we got going," I said.

"No hurry." Abe leaned back, his eyes half closed. "We've been driving since first light."

121

"We can't just sit here on the off chance he'll pass this way." I reached for the map. "We're about fifteen miles from where Pat Murphy saw the Land-Rover abandoned and there's another track running direct to Maralal."

"Sure there's another track, but not suitable for vehicles and van Delden needs transport. He's a long way from Marsabit, and a Land-Rover out of gas is about as much use to him as a load of scrap." He sat up suddenly. "I don't think you quite understand the sort of man he is. He'll have seen that aircraft circling and the patrol when it comes will take this road."

I stared at him. "He can't jump an army patrol."

He shrugged, leaning back and closing his eyes again. Karanja moved uneasily, searching the bush as a dove went clattering through the branches above us. Away to the south, the cackling of guinea fowl came faintly on the still air. The heat was heavy after the night's rain and I felt drowsy, lying back and staring up at white drifts of cloud hanging over the mountains. "I think we go back now," Karanja said. He was getting agitated. "When the patrol come they want to know what we are doing on this road."

"It will be several hours yet before a patrol gets here." Abe shifted on to one elbow, listening as a bird whistled urgently in the bush behind us. A moment later it took flight, a metallic flash of blue. "Starling," Karanja said. "Something disturb him." The guinea fowl had ceased their cackling, everything very still and quiet as though the bush held its breath, waiting. And then suddenly van Delden was there, coming soundlessly out of the undergrowth behind us. Mukunga was with him and they both had rifles. Mtome and a very erect, very good-looking man I hadn't seen before appeared on the opposite side of the track. All of them had old khaki knapsacks, bandoliers stuffed with ammunition, blankets rolled and slung round their shoulders.

"Karanja."

"Ndio, Bwana." He had leapt to his feet, his eyes staring.

"You came to find me?"

Karanja nodded, speechless.

"How did you know where I was?"

"The pilot," Abe said.

Van Delden stood there for a moment, looking down at us. Then he came and sat beside me, placing his rifle carefully on the ground. "I was expecting a patrol."

"The pilot doesn't have to file his report till the morning," Abe said. "He stuck to his routine."

"Didn't he have orders to look out for the Land-Rover?"

"He said he owed you something. His name's Murphy."

"Pat Murphy? Yes, I remember." He nodded. "So we've a little time yet before a patrol comes." He said something to Karanja, who moved quickly to the fire. "And you came looking for me. Why?"

Abe shrugged. "Not sure really. But we have a permit to go as far as Lake Rudolf. Thought you might need a lift."

Van Delden shook his head. "A vehicle, that's all I need." He looked from one to the other of us, his pale eyes watchful. "While tea is brewing maybe you'll tell me how you got hold of an old safari bus and a permit to enter the Military Zone." He gave an order to Mukunga and his three Africans squatted down by the fire, watching us. "And Karanja. What's Karanja doing here?"

"He's on loan to us as guide."

He laughed, that same harsh bark. "You have a way of getting what you want, don't you, Mr. Finkel. So what are you going to film now?"

"That depends on you," Abe said. "If we give you a lift—"

"No."

Abe gave a little shrug. "I guess you don't understand what television can do for you." He hesitated, then changed the subject. "I take it you're headed for Marsabit." Van Delden didn't reply. His eyes had

123

shifted to the slopes above us and Abe said, "You saw those elephants?"

"They winded us."

"Is this their territory, or are they on the move with a definite purpose?"

Van Delden shrugged. "D'you know anything about the migration of elephants?"

"A little."

"Their normal range, for instance?"

"Scientific records suggest the limit is about eighty miles."

"Records—scientific records—" His emphasis on the word *scientific* was contemptuous. "The only official records are for park conditions. Elephants are quick to learn the limits of their protected area."

"And when it's no longer a protected area, what then?"

Van Delden shook his head. "Who knows? There were no so-called scientists recording data when the Cape elephants were wiped out by my father's forbears, or when British hunters eliminated the vast herds of southern Africa, shooting them for their ivory and for the fun of killing. Who's to say that some of those elephants didn't trek north, away from the slaughter area, north into Matabeleland, across the Zambesi? For all any scientist can tell you, man, those elephants you saw up there"—he nodded towards the green-brown slopes—"may be the distant descendants of elephants that came out of Cape Province more than a century and a half ago."

"So they go north, an inherited instinct. Is that what you're saying?"

Van Delden shook his head. "I've lived too long with elephants to be certain of anything. Like man, they're individuals, and, living almost as long, they are unpredictable, each according to his experience, some charging on sight, others fairly tolerant. At Marsabit they had a very restricted range. Just the mountain and its forest area and the grass of the slopes which they shared with the Rendile. They came down into the grasslands at night when the cattle

124

weren't grazing. But there were others that came and went, bulls mainly, trekking from the Tana River, even from this area here. That was what the Boran said. But a scientist wouldn't accept that. He'd need to bug the beast with a bleep transmitter and follow it in an aircraft before he'd believe anything a tribesman told him."

Karanja handed him a mug of tea and he sat there, sipping at it noisily and frowning. "You've got your cameras with you?" Abe nodded. "And you're planning to film Alex Kirby-Smith with his gang of scientific exterminators."

"That wasn't the object," I protested.

But he was looking at Abe. "How did you get Kimani to agree to that?" And when Abe had explained, his eyes fastened angrily on me. "So you traded the film you got with me for the chance of an archaeological find." His voice was hard and unforgiving, the stare of those pale eyes almost baleful. "Mary was right. She said you had no feeling for animals." He turned to Abe again. "Where's Kirby-Smith now?"

"At Baragoi."

He nodded as though he had expected that. "He'll take them as they come out of the South Horr Gap into the near-desert country beyond." And then he was looking at me again. "You'll need a cold heart and a strong stomach, boy. There'll be totos of all ages, from new-born up to a dozen years, all with their mothers, and all led by an old matriarch, a complete family unit, anything from five to fifty strong. He'll bunch them by buzzing them with an aircraft, or maybe he'll use trucks and Land-Rovers to drive them on to his sharp shooters. The matriarch will be shot first, fifty, maybe sixty years of life cut down in a flash, the whole group wiped out in minutes, every cow, every calf." He turned back to Abe. "That way there's no survivor to pass the knowledge of fear and pain and death on to others coming through the mountains, no warning to the next unsuspecting family. Something for your captive TV audience to gloat

125

over." He slung his empty mug at Karanja and got to his feet. "I'm taking your vehicle."

"Does it occur to you," Abe said quietly, "that the captive audience may feel the way you do, that the sight of such whole-sale slaughter will sicken . . ."

"There won't be any slaughter if I can help it." He spoke quickly to Mtome, who began getting our bags out of the minibus. "And if you were able to film it, do you think you'd be allowed to take that film out of the country?"

"Maybe not. But with your help we could smuggle it out." Abe got to his feet.

"Stay where you are." He was moving towards the minibus. "Dima." He motioned the tall African into the back. Mtome followed him, Mukunga standing beside the door, his rifle cradled on his arm.

"You're making a mistake," Abe said. "We come along with you now, we could film it all from your point of view. A great story. I could really make something of it."

"You'd make a lot of money. That's what you mean, isn't it? Like Alex, you're not thinking of the elephants, only of money."

"You're wrong. That's not why I'm here." Abe moved towards him. "What about it, van Delden? I'm offering you a world audience, the chance to make them understand the nature of elephants and what's happening to them in Africa."

But he shook his head. "What I have to do . . . I don't want anybody else involved." He had the door open and reached inside. "But you can have your cameras." He dumped the cases on the ground beside our bags.

I scrambled to my feet. "You can't just leave us here. We only turned down this track because we knew you were in trouble."

"Relax," Abe said. "He's not going to take us and the patrol will be here in a few hours."

Van Delden was moving round to the driver's seat and Karanja started forward, a tense, urgent look on his face. I thought for a moment he was going to try something desperate. So did Mukunga, but he was too late. Karanja was already on the far side of the vehicle talking urgently to van Delden. He seemed to be pleading with him. Then van Delden did a strange thing. He put his arm across Karanja's shoulder, a gesture of affection almost.

They were like that for a moment, Karanja staring up at the other with a rapt expression, then he was nodding and van Delden got into the driving seat. He nosed the minibus into the bush, backed and turned it. "Karanja." He leaned out of the window, speaking quicky in Swahili. Karanja nodded, sweat on his face and his eyes wide. Mukunga climbed in and the bus moved off, a thick cloud of dust hanging in the air as it disappeared round the bend where the elephants had crossed the road.

I turned to Karanja. "What were you telling him?"

He shook his head, his eyes still on the dust cloud. "Is nothing."

"What was it?" I insisted.

"I offered to go with him." He turned away then, adding angrily. "But he don't want me."

"There was something else," Abe said. "Something about Kirby-Smith. I distinctly heard him mention the major's name."

"Is a message, that's all."

"What was the message?"

Karanja hesitated, then he shrugged. "I am to tell him if he kills elephants his men will die."

"Did he mean it?"

Karanja nodded unhappily. "He always mean what he say."

Abe looked at me, his dark eyes sombre. "There's a line: *Now he is treading that dark road. . . .*" He shook his head, the corners of his mouth turned down. "It isn't just a civilian outfit he's up against. Kirby-Smith has the support of the Army and in every African unit there'll be men who've been hunters or trackers all their lives." He turned to Karanja. "You going to pass that message on to Major Kirby-Smith?"

"Yes. I tell him." His eyes rolled, the whites showing. "You know I have to explain how we lose our vehicle and everything in it."

We went on talking about van Delden for a while, but gradually the heat overcame us and we lay there waiting as the sun slid down the brazen sky and the shadows lengthened. There was no wind, nothing stirring, no sound except the sleepy murmuring of doves. I was dozing when the patrol arrived.

They came in a truck, the driver slamming on his brakes at the sight of us, soldiers tumbling out of the dust cloud, deploying with their guns at the ready. They looked tough, battle-trained men, their camouflage green merging into the bush. Karanja called to them, stepping out into the road and walking towards the stationary truck where a corporal stood waiting. He talked to him for a moment, then orders were shouted, the soldiers climbing back into the truck, and it came on to stop beside us. "You get in now," Karanja said. "When we find the Land-Rover I talk with the corporal about transport."

"That Land-Rover would do us fine," I said.

But Karanja shook his head. "Is Army vehicle."

We slung our gear into the back of the truck and clambered up, the soldiers making room for us. "Looks like our only hope is Kirby-Smith," Abe said doubtfully. The black faces around us were covered in dust, watchful and unsmiling. About three miles down the road we rounded a rock outcrop and ran slap into a barricade of thorn, the truck slamming to a halt, enveloping us in dust. It was the ideal place for an ambush, the road blocked and rocks all round. Under a wild fig we found the blackened embers of a fire, the stripped remains of a dik-dik carcase lying on the ground beside it. The thorn barrier took some time to clear, so that it was dark when we reached the Land-Rover. The embers of another, larger fire, some blankets thick with dust, and two empty jerricans lying on the ground.

It was cooler now, the soldiers more friendly as a fire was lit and food prepared, the empty tank of the Land-Rover filled with petrol. Over the meal Karanja

128

talked to the corporal, trying to persuade him to let us go on to Baragoi in the Land-Rover. I don't know whether it was the military permit or the need to radio a report of van Delden's movements that finally decided him, but shortly after eight we got into the Land-Rover and started back up the track, the corporal driving us.

It was a clear moonlit night and he drove fast. At Maralal he stopped at the old safari lodge, now a military post, to radio his report back to headquarters. The town itself was off the main road, but all round the junction leading to it rough shelters sprawled over the grass, a great concentration of tribesmen driven into the mountains in search of food and water. Beyond Maralal the road climbed steeply through a forest of trees and it became quite cold. "Soon we come to viewpoint," Karanja said. "Maybe we stop there."

The trees were a black arch in the headlights, their branches blotched with some growth that was pale like lichen. And then they ceased and we were out on to the top, in a burned brown scrub of moorland. Far away to our right the shadow of the Mathews Range stood against the sky and to our left the land dropped steeply down into the Rift and the valley of the Suguta. The moon was clouded now and we did not stop, driving on and on through desolate country, the dirt road gradually losing height as we wound our way down towards Baragoi. I slept fitfully, my head lolling as the Land-Rover bucked and jolted over the uneven surface, and then suddenly we were there, driving slowly down a street of grey dirt flanked by dukas, the village shops that had been built by Asians long ago. It was a dilapidated miserable place, the wood and daub buildings falling into ruin and sleeping bodies lying in the dust.

The military post was a huddle of tents and trucks on the edge of a landing field east of Baragoi. We stopped at the guard tent and while the corporal and Karanja explained themselves, Abe and I stretched our legs. The night was clear again, the moon set, and all around us, at every point of the compass, the jagged outline of mountains reared up like cut-outs against the stars. Abe nodded towards the north, where the Horr Valley showed as a black V. "I wonder if he made it through the gap there."

I thought he probably had, but dawn would find him exposed on the semi-desert land beyond, and right beside us was a Cessna. It was the only plane on the field, and if it was serviceable, one quick sweep northwards would be enough, the dust stream of the minibus visible for miles. "How far do you reckon he'll have got by sunrise?"

Abe glanced at his watch. "Five hours from now, and he's about six hours ahead of us—that's eleven hours motoring from Baragoi." He shook his head. "He'll have run out of gas long before then."

"So he won't make Marsabit?"

"Not a hope." He looked at me, a sidelong glance. "Was he ever going there?"

"Where then?"

He shrugged, and I felt a sudden prickle of uneasiness. We were on the threshold now of country that van Delden knew better than anyone else. Karanja returned to say that Major Kirby-Smith was now camped about five miles beyond South Horr and the question of transport would have to wait until the morning.

We spent the rest of that night in the Land-Rover and woke in the dawn to the sound of voices and the movement of men as the camp came alive. I had never been in a military post before and my chief recollection of it is the open latrines with African soldiers squatting and jabbering, dung-brown beetles crawling in human excrement, and the wood smoke smell of cook fires hanging in the still air. There must have been over a hundred Africans there including hangers-on and when the officer in command saw us shortly after seven he had already been in contact with Kirby-Smith's outfit and established that a vehicle had crossed the lugga near their camp about ten-thirty the previous evening. Captain Kioko was still interrogating us through Karanja when an orderly came in to say that Major Kirby-Smith was on his way to Baragoi.

He arrived about half an hour later. I was sitting in the shade of one of the trucks rereading von Höhlen's account of the Teleki expedition's first sighting of Lake Rudolf when the open Land-Rover roared into the camp. There were two of them in it, the windscreen folded flat and both of them wearing goggles. He stopped by the Cessna to have a word with the pilot, who was working on the engine, then he drove on to the command tent. Karanja was waiting for him there and when they had ducked inside the flap I returned to my book. We were so near to Lake Rudolf now that reading about it gave me the illusion that I had leapt the intervening miles of desert and lava and was already there.

I was reading again the passage that begins: "Almost at our last gasp, we hastened towards the slightly rippled sheet of water" when a shadow came into my line of vision and a husky voice said, "So it is you. Where is he, do you know?"

I looked up, recognising her voice, and for a moment I was too surprised to say anything. She was wearing the same faded safari jacket, the bush hat pulled down over her eyes. The book slipped from my hands as I scrambled to my feet, pleasure at seeing her again overcoming the sense of shock that she really was with Kirby-Smith. "I didn't realise it was you—in that Land-Rover."

"Where was he going?" she demanded, her face set, and no sign of greeting. "Was it Marsabit?"

"He didn't say."

"He must have told you something when he took your vehicle. What was it, a minibus? That's what we were told over the radio."

I nodded, conscious of the tightness of her lips, the strained look in her eyes.

131

"Was there enough petrol on board for him to reach Marsabit?"

"No, I don't think so."

"Just as well," she murmured. "Marsabit is no place for him now. Alex says there's hardly anything left of his sanctuary. It's been agronomised, most of the forest cut down to make way for shambas." She was staring at me, her eyes wide. "Why the hell didn't he make for the coast?"

"Perhaps if you'd been with him—"

"It wouldn't have made any difference." She bent quickly down, picking up my book and glancing at the title. "Still thinking about Lake Rudolf?"

I laughed. "Not far now, but it seems the last part is the most difficult. I need transport."

"I'll talk to Alex. Maybe he can help. You shouldn't have let him get away with your minibus."

"We had no alternative."

She nodded. "No, of course not. Did he say anything about Kulal?"

I shook my head.

"Some years back he tried very hard to have the rain forest on top of the mountain made into a game reserve. He was very friendly with John Mallinson at the Mission there. Do you think he was making for Kulal?"

"No."

She was silent for a moment, her head turned to the north. "So he's somewhere out there, waiting." And she added almost in a whisper, "God! If only he'd got out while he had the chance."

I had a feeling then that it wasn't her father she was worrying about, and the question that had been at the back of my mind from the moment I had seen her burst from my lips. I asked her why she had gone off with a man whose business was to kill the animals that had been her father's whole life. "I don't understand," I said. "I searched the hotel. . . ."

"You don't understand?" Her eyes blazed suddenly in the sunlight. "You saw what he did to that elephant.

132

You were there. You saw Mukunga and Mtome drive it, with the snare still round its leg and the foot so rotten it was almost falling off. . . . Anyway, it's none of your business what I do." And she added fiercely, "At least Alex kills cleanly."

These words, the way she defended him . . . I stood there, staring at her dumbly, knowing now that it wasn't just for the story she was here. It was something else and I didn't want to think about it, remembering what she had said about his charm. And at that moment the Cessna's engine burst into life. I could see the pilot sitting at his controls, running through his checks. "Is that an Army plane?" I asked, glad of the excuse to break the awkward silence between us.

"No, it's ours—part of the outfit."

"And it's being sent up to look for him?"

She nodded.

"Can't you do something?" I was thinking of the tough, wild African soldiers I had seen in the camp here and what would happen when the pilot reported seeing the minibus.

But all she said was, "If he'd seen what I've seen these last two days . . . the effect of this drought. As soon as you're clear of the mountains, all to the north . . ." The Cessna was moving now and a stream of dust enveloped us as it turned and began taxiing out to the end of the dirt runway. "There's been no rain up there, no rain at all. Every well, every water-hole is dry." And she added, as though to justify her acquiescence in the search, "If we don't find him, that's something he'll discover for himself. There's no water out there."

"He has four jerricans full."

"That won't last him long in that heat." She turned to face me again. "How many are with him now?"

"Three," I said.

"Mukunga and Mtome. Who else?"

"A man called Dima."

She nodded. "Another ex-poacher. A Boran. All his best shots, except Karanja."

The plane's engine note increased. It had reached the runway end and we watched in silence as it moved towards us, rapidly growing larger. The wheels lifted clear of the ground and it banked slightly, roaring low over our heads as it turned northwards. In a moment it was no more than a speck flying towards the mountains that formed the south Horr Gap. "You should have stopped it," I murmured.

She shook her head, still staring after the plane. "Alex is afraid he'll try and do something stupid."

"And when that plane finds him and they send the Army in—what happens then?"

She turned on me angrily. "Do you suppose I haven't thought about that? But he's got to be stopped, somehow. He could have made for the coast. Instead he came up here, and I think Alex is right."

It was incredible, his own daughter. "You really want him caught."

She gave a little shrug. "Somebody's got to make him see reason, and the sooner they get him out of here—"

"You don't care what happens to him, do you?" I think I wanted to hurt her then. "You're not worrying about your father, only about Kirby-Smith."

"How dare you!" she breathed. "You know nothing about him, or about me. Nothing about either of them."

I could see Karanja waiting in the sun outside the command hut and I told her the message he had been given. "So you'd better make up your mind whose side you're on."

She was staring at me, an appalled look in her eyes. "So Alex was right."

"If Kirby-Smith starts killing elephants . . ." I hesitated, but what the hell? How else could I get through to her, through the thick skin of her apparent hero-worship of the man she was camped with? "When that recce plane gets back," I said, "you'd better arrange it

134

so that you can talk to him. Talk to them both, or somebody's going to get killed."

She stood there for a moment, still with that shocked look in her eyes. I think she was near to tears, her lips trembling, her nostrils flared. But then she turned abruptly and walked away, back towards the open Land-Rover. I watched her go, feeling wretched, her figure tall and graceful in the blazing sun, and knowing the things I had said were better unsaid. I was still worrying about that when Abe appeared round the back of the truck. "What did your girl friend have to say?"

"Nothing," I snapped, angry at the glint of laughter in his eyes.

Kirby-Smith had come out of the command tent. The captain was with him and they were talking to Karanja. "She must have said something," Abe murmured. "You were talking with her long enough."

"She said the plane that just took off belongs to Kirby-Smith and is flying a search."

He nodded. "That was to be expected." He was looking at me curiously as he went on, "But they won't find him, that's for sure. He's too old a hand, and the zebra stripes on that vehicle are designed for sunlight and shade. "Did she tell you why she'd gone off with Kirby-Smith?"

I shook my head, not wanting to talk about it.

"She could be half in love with him." That sardonic smile and the dark eyes laughing at me behind the glasses. "You want some advice?"

"No."

He laughed. "I'll give it to you anyway. Lay her if you can, but don't get involved. She's a man-eater and you're too young for a girl who's half Italian and thoroughly Africanised." He patted my shoulder and turned away as Kirby-Smith came towards us, his face hard and his jaw set, the muscles tight behind the cheekbones.

"Is it true what Karanja says about my men being at risk when we start culling?" He was looking at Abe. "Is that what he said?"

135

Abe nodded. "Karanja was to give you the message."

"Do you think he meant it? Or was it just an empty threat?"

"No, he meant it."

"Then we'll have to find him. A man like that at large, he's dangerous." His shoulders straightened, his face loosening in that boyish smile. "Well, it shouldn't take long." He turned to the captain. "Once he's located, it'll be up to our boys. But no bloodshed. Get him surrounded so that he gives himself up."

Abe started to protest, but Kirby-Smith shook his head. "They're bush trained. They know their job. Now about your transport problem. You want to join me in my camp at South Horr, Karanja tells me." He paused, his eyes on Abe's face as though trying to gauge his motives. "I don't object to TV coverage of the way I operate, so long as it isn't slanted. We can talk about that later, but it'll be on my terms. Understood?"

"Naturally," Abe said.

His gaze switched to me. "And you?"

I nodded.

"Okay then. Get your gear into my Land-Rover. I'll be leaving just as soon as an Army plane arrives and I've had a word with the pilot."

About half an hour later we heard the sound of it diving down out of the sun, and then it was coming in from the south-east, a twin-engined monoplane with its undercarriage down. It landed in a cloud of dust and when the pilot got out I saw that it was a stranger. I had hoped it would be Murphy.

Kirby-Smith did not wait to see the plane take off and we were halfway to Baragoi when it passed over us heading north. It was a windy hair-raising drive, the wheels skidding on gravel, half floating in patches of sand, nobody speaking. Karanja had dropped his role of courier. Beside us in the back his flat broadnosed features had a solemn, dejected look. Doubtless the captain had given him hell for turning on to the Baringo track and making van Delden a present of his

136

vehicle, and I was quite certain Kirby-Smith had made him responsible for every foot of film we shot at his camp.

There were mountains on either side of us now, the country thickening as we entered the restricted gap of the Horr Valley. We were between the Nyiru and Ol Doinya Mara ranges then, towering pinnacles of jagged rock glimpsed through the branches of trees, and shortly after ten we ran into the dusty little village of South Horr. Mary turned to Abe. "This is the last village. North of here there's nothing, just desert till you get to Ethiopia." It was the first time she had spoken and by making the observation directly to Abe she made it clear she was still angry with me and not prepared to recognise my presence.

The village, which was little more than a single street, was packed with tribesmen, some of them armed with slender spears, their ear lobes hanging in loops, and many of their women had necks, arms, and ankles encased in rings of copper wire. They pressed so close around us that the Land-Rover was reduced to a crawl, the ring of dark faces thrust close, hands reaching out to pluck at us and their speech importunate. Some of the younger men with elaborate hairstyles shook their spears at us, older men thrust cowrie shells into our hands.

"It's all right," Kirby-Smith said over his shoulder. He was talking to them all the time in their own language. "They want food, that's all." An old man, one of the elders, barred our way and we stopped while Kirby-Smith talked with him, everybody, even the young men, listening, silent. These were young warriors—the moran, Kirby-Smith called them—and they stood out like peacocks, slender, arrogant, almost naked, except for those with red blankets they wore like capes, and besides their spears, many of them carried a neck rest in the other hand so that they could lie down without disturbing the ochre plastering of their hair. Their elaborate hairstyles varied, some wearing it twisted in tiny plaits, long and swept back over the head, some in a fringe in front and falling

137

halfway down the back, others in a bun or in two long pigtails, and all of them decked out with necklaces and headbands of seeds or shells.

Finally a way was opened for us and we drove on, and a moment later we were clear of the village, back in the emptiness of the valley. "It's this damned drought," Kirby-Smith said. "They'd never beg like that normally. That old man was telling me again how they'd lost all their cattle and their camels. They've trekked in from the desert on foot, depending on their moran for food, and those showy young men have just about killed everything that moves, except for the big game. That's the effect of hunger. They're an indolent lot normally." He laughed, a surprisingly high sound. "All the same, you don't want to tangle with them. They're a bit like the Masai, very proud, and they can be tricky."

The track snaked between thickets of bush, the trees mainly euphorbia and acacia, some leathery leaved evergreens and wild olives, all laced with the parasitic growth of rope-thick lianas. The air was hot and aromatic, and there were sunbirds flickering darts of colour. About five miles out of South Horr we dropped to a lugga where half-naked women were filling large earthenware pots and old kerosene tins. Clouds of insects that looked like mosquitos hung over the muddy stream. The Land-Rover ground up the further slope, and after a few hundred yards we turned off to the right into a stand of giant acacia, where half a dozen tents were scattered round a clearing. Smoke drifted up from an open fire.

This was the base camp, a site, Kirby-Smith said, much favoured by safaris in the old days. "And by elephants," he added, indicating the trunks of the acacias, which all had polished bosses where the animals had rubbed themselves. He handed us over to a tall, very proud-looking African with a brightly coloured kikoi wrapped round his loins. "Eddie is boss-boy here. He'll look after you. The others are all preparing the airstrip. Don't let the girls bother you." He nodded to a little huddle of women squatting at the

138

edge of the clearing. "See you later." And he and Mary Delden drove off, leaving us standing there beside our bags.

Abe looked at me, smiling. "If I've got my geography right, we're now within about thirty miles of your precious lake. And we're still in thick bush, trees all round us and a stream of fresh water close at hand."

"That thirty miles could be as far as the moon if the road is blocked and we've no transport." I wasn't prepared to let him read the typescript of Pieter van Delden's book, but I got volume II of Teleki's expedition out of my grip and handed it to him. "I've marked the passages. Read it and perhaps you'll understand."

Karanja called to us, "You like tea now?" He indicated some canvas chairs grouped around a table under the fly of a tent. "You sit there and I bring you tea." He came with three tin mugs as we were moving our gear into the shade of the tent. "That boy is Masai. I don't like Masai. They are very stupid people."

It was during the day we spent alone in that camp, with nothing to do but read and sit talking about the lake to the north, the lava waste that surrounded it, and about van Delden, that I first began to be really scared about how it would end, a sense of premonition that I tried to pretend was due to the heat and the strangeness of the place. Karanja had cut himself an arbour of shade under a bush and sat there like an animal in its lair, motionless, with his eyes staring at nothing, his face expressionless. The women had gone, driven off by their menfolk, and only the Masai made his presence felt, moving gracefully and doing little, sometimes standing, still as an ebony carving, watching us. The trees towered breathless, their leaves shimmering in the sun's glare, and occasionally, just occasionally, I caught a flicker of a bird. It was hot as an oven with the door open, releasing scents I had never experienced before. It was a heady, overpowering atmosphere and I would not have been surprised if some strange beast out of the past had presented itself before us or an early ape-figure masquerading as man.

Once Abe looked up from von Höhlen's book and said, "That typescript of yours, does it deal with Kulal in detail?"

"Yes, but he was attacked by the men of the rain forest, the Wandrobo. He never got to the top."

"Our friend von Höhlen says it presents '*a terrible chaos of yawning chasms and 'ravines, with perpendicular brownish-black precipices, the general character and trend of which*'—he's not exactly my favourite travel writer—'*led us to suppose this to be a continuation of the same fissure as that in which our progress had been arrested during our march along the western face of Mt. Nyiro.*' That, I take it, is the dark fang of a mountain hanging over us now. If so, he says, then this fissure must extend for some forty miles." He let the book fall on his lap, staring at me sleepily. "Sounds pretty rough going. How do you propose getting to the top of it?"

"There'll be a track of some sort. Mary mentioned a mission."

"Okay, so you get to the top, and it's forest something like we're in now. How the hell do you figure on making an archaeological discovery buried under five or six thousand years of decayed tropical vegetation?"

I shook my head. I hadn't really thought about it. I had been relying on van Delden. But when I told him this he laughed. "Van Delden has other fish to fry and his own safety to consider. He's not going to waste his time searching for pieces of pottery and the remains of an ancient civilisation." He picked up the book again. "Better give some thought to what you plan to do, now you're within striking distance of the lake. And save your film." A bird began a monotonous piping whistle from across the clearing as though calling for rain. *Wet-wet-wet,* it cried, trailing a long tail from one acacia to the next, where it sat on a branch watching us, its black wings folded, its tail

140

hanging down and a large horned beak, bright red with an ivory tip.

I leaned back and closed my eyes, thinking about what he had said, wondering whether to show him the typescript. And still that feeling that it wasn't just Rudolph that was very close, but something more personal, more frightening. It would have been easy to convince myself that it was no more than the strangeness of my surroundings if I had not experienced this feeling before. Through my closed lids the sun shone red on my eyes, sweat on my chest, and that bird, which I later learned was a Van der Decken's hornbill, piping away, the murmur of insects, everything drowsy in the midday heat. I knew Abe was right. Van Delden wasn't interested in archaeological remains. I almost wished that they'd find him and ship him out. But I knew they wouldn't, and as I dozed off I saw his face as he had stood looking at the remains of that wooden lodge at the edge of the Serengeti, tears in his eyes.

Dusk had fallen before Kirby-Smith returned, the Land-Rover leading in two trucks full of Africans, its headlights cutting a swathe through the trees. They had shot a duiker, and while the carcase of the little antelope was roasting over the fire, we sat drinking warm beer with a pressure lamp hissing behind us and the night full of stars. The plane had been unable to make contact by radio, but the pilot had dropped a message over the nearly completed runway. No sign of the minibus. He had swept an area from the Suguta up as far as Loiyangalani and east across the slopes of Mt. Kulal. "From here to the lake, it's all open country," Kirby-Smith said. "Desert and lava, a few isolated trees. Nowhere he could hide a vehicle except at Loiyangalani among the doum palms. But Jeff says he flew low over the oasis several times. If the vehicle had been there I think he would have seen it. So it must be Kulal."

"The oasis or Kulal, what does it matter?" Mary said in a tight, controlled voice. "He's well clear of your operation."

141

Kirby-Smith hesitated, his cigarette glowing in the dark. "I'd still like to know," he said quietly. "I've a radio call—"

"Leave him alone, can't you." She got suddenly to her feet, paused a moment as though about to say something more, then turned abruptly and went to her tent.

Kirby-Smith sighed. "She's like her mother," he murmured. "Very emotional, and her mood changing from moment to moment."

"You knew her mother well?" Abe asked.

"Of course." He said it tersely, resisting any intrusion into that part of his life, and switched the conversation back to Kulal. "He may have made it into the gorge on the eastern side. If he's attempted to reach the top, then there's only one track and it goes past the Mission."

The radio contact was for 2030 hours, but when he had spoken with Northern Army Headquarters he came back, shaking his head. "Their plane had no better luck than mine. Maddox flew from Loiyangalani across Kulal and halfway to Marsabit. Not a sign of him. No tracks visible, nothing." He sat down again and picked up his beer. "So that settles it, he's in the gorge on the eastern side of Kulal. Even Cornelius wouldn't risk foot-slogging it through the Chalbi in a drought."

But later, when Abe had joined me under the fly of the tent we had been allocated, he said, "If you were van Delden, what would you do—in a hijacked vehicle short of gas?"

I had turned in immediately after we had fed and was lying precariously balanced on the seat cushions of one of the trucks, watching a satellite move steadily through the stardust of the Milky Way, enjoying the solitude and thinking of Lake Rudolf, the acacias like a cathedral arch above me and the fire glowing in the night.

"Are you awake?"

"Yes."

He was standing over me rubbing at his teeth

thoughtfully with the end of a green sliver cut from the bush the Samburu use to get the brilliant whiteness of their teeth. The toothbrush bush, Mary had called it. "Well, what would you do?" he repeated.

I shook my head. I didn't want to think about van Delden. I just wanted to lie there, pursuing my fantasy of an archaeological find that would be the talk of the academic world.

"Kirby-Smith starts culling tomorrow." He had stayed up talking to him, and now, as he prepared for bed, he was determined to pass on the information he had gleaned. A born newsman, I thought, as he said, "So this is where the action is. If I were van Delden, I know what I'd do. I wouldn't risk that vehicle out in open country. I'd drive it into the bush here and hide up within striking distance of the culling area."

"Too many tribesmen around," I murmured sleepily.

"Yes, but all of them close by the stream." He wrapped himself in a blanket and lay down on the truck seat they had given him.

"What happened to that hand of his? I bet you asked him."

"Sure I did."

"Well how did it happen?"

"Snake bite." He smiled at me and I wasn't certain whether he was serious. "He was playing around with a mamba. It was when he was a kid and he thought he could handle it like Ionides. So you watch out for yourself." And then he suddenly asked me, "How much film have you got?"

"Not sure. Seven or eight mags. Why?"

"Take my advice. Don't be carried away with the excitement of the kill. Save your film for when van Delden comes on the scene."

"You think he'll carry out his threat?"

"I don't know. But if he does, you'll regret every foot you've wasted."

"Kirby-Smith expects us to film the culling. So does Karanja."

143

"So long as you've got a mag on your camera and they can hear it running, they won't know whether you're taking pictures or not. I've got about the same number as you, so maybe we'd better take it in turns. You want to save some for Rudolf—if you ever get there." He reached out, rummaging in his grip. "You taken your anti-malarial tablet?"

"I took it last Sunday. You only have to take them once a week."

"I'm told it's safer to take the daily dose." Something moved in the bush behind me. There was a snort, and then all hell broke loose, the crash of branches, the padded thud of rushing feet and a body like a tank hurtling past me. It was so close I felt the wind of it, smelled the musky smell of it, and then I saw it wheeling in the firelight, head lowered as it charged one of the tents, its long horn ripping the canvas, tossing it in shreds over its back. Suddenly the camp erupted, yells and shouts as the Africans tumbled out of sleep, and Kirby-Smith was there, a gun in his hand. But by then the rhinoceros had disappeared, leaving the wreckage of the tent scattered on the ground.

Karanja appeared, looking scared. Somewhere a man was screaming, a thin sound like an injured rabbit. "Lord Jesus Christ!" Karanja sniffed the air, the whites of his eyes gleaming in the starlight. "I never know that only once before."

"When was that?" Mary was suddenly there and her voice was shaky.

But Karanja shook his head. "Long time back," he muttered, and went to join Kirby-Smith by the remains of the ripped-up tent. Flames leapt as branches were dragged on to the fire, black bodies in silhouette. The screaming died away. "There's a breeze coming from behind us, off the mountain," Mary said as we moved to follow Karanja. "The camp was downwind of the beast, so it wasn't us that panicked that rhino."

Kirby-Smith was straightening up, a hypodermic in his hands. "Flattened," he said. "Not much I can do for the poor bastard." He was staring past us at the

144

dark shape of the mountain, black against the rising moon. "One of my best trackers, too." He looked at Abe, his face set. "Did you hear anything? You were close to where it came out of the bush."

Abe shook his head, and I said, "There was a crashing in the undergrowth, and then suddenly it was going past me like—"

"But before that. Did you hear anybody shout, any sound of voices in the bush?"

"No, nothing."

He turned to the ring of black faces crowding round us, questioning his men in Swahili. But they shook their heads, jabbering excitedly, their voices high in anger or fear—I wasn't certain which. In the end he posted sentries and went back to his tent. The camp gradually settled down again, but it was a long time before I got to sleep, and when I did I seemed to be woken almost immediately by the voice of the nearest sentry talking to his relief. The two Africans were sharp and clear in a shaft of moonlight. It was almost five and I lay awake until dawn began to steal over the mountains to the accompaniment of the chatter of some vervet monkeys and a rising chorus of birds. It was the dawn of a terrible day.

III

THE DAWN WAS COOL, a freshness in the air, the mountains dark above the trees. I wanted to sleep now, but the camp had already come alive, full of the sound of African voices. Abe appeared, shaved and dressed, handing me a mug of tea. "Better get moving. We'll be off in a few minutes."

Two crows eyed me from a branch as I sat drinking my tea on the cushions to which I had clung during the night. "It's barely light," I muttered. "Do we have to start this early?"

"Elephants are sensible beasts. When the sun's up they move into deep shade."

"You got some sleep, did you?"

"Now and then, when you weren't snoring." He cocked his head, listening. "Sounds like the Army," he said, and I heard the drone of an engine coming from the direction of South Horr. "They're sending a patrol out with trackers."

"What for?"

"What do you think? Rhinos don't normally charge into a camp like that."

The truck's note changed as it ground through the lugga and Kirby-Smith came into my line of vision, neat in freshly laundered slacks and bush shirt, all khaki except for the bright splash of silk at his neck. Two Africans were with him, both with rifles.

"There was a man injured, wasn't there?" The whole episode was vague, like a dream.

"He's dead. Died almost immediately."

I remembered the hypodermic, the look of anger on Kirby-Smith's face. The truck bumped its way into the camp and came to a stop, spilling soldiers. A sergeant jumped out of the cab, went up to Kirby-Smith, saluting. Heads lifted to a roar of sound and a plane swept low over the tops of the acacias, heading north.

"Get dressed," Abe said, "or you'll be left behind."

The tea was thick and sweet. I gulped it down and reached for my clothes. "What's the plane for?"

"Spotter. The pilot is Kirby-Smith's partner. Name of Jeff Saunders."

Karanja appeared with two plates as I was pulling on my trousers. "Ten minutes," he said. "Okay? You take good pictures today." Two eggs each, some sausages, and a hunk of bread. I ate quickly, then went out into the bush rather than use the Africans' latrine. Squatting, with my trousers down, I thought of the night and that rhinoceros, feeling vulnerable despite the movement in the camp. Engines were being started up and through the leaves of a toothbrush bush I saw the patrol move off towards the mountains behind us, a tracker leading them. By the time I had finished, men were climbing into the vehicles. There were four trucks, all 15 cwt. J4s, open-sided with wire mesh guards over the radiators and handbars at the back of the cab. Kirby-Smith led the convoy out in his Land-Rover, Mary beside him and two Africans in the back.

We were in the last truck, and as we pulled out, the sergeant was posting guards round the camp. Karanja, standing beside me, gripping the handbar, pointed to a mound of freshly dug earth, the grave of the man who had been killed in the night. "One time that man serve with me as game scout. Tembo van Delden very hard man."

"What do you mean?"

But all he said was, "He is a Turkana same as Mtome. Abdoul and Mtome, the best trackers Tembo ever had." He shook his head. "Very hard man," he said again as we turned on to the main track and roared north into the choking dust of the convoy. The mountains fell away from us on either side, dim in that cold early light, and the thick bush dwindled, the only colour the flame of a shrub that was bright as a rose against the arid brown patches of sand. We crossed a deep-sided lugga, clinging tightly as the truck nosed down into the dry gravel bed, lifting its metal snout to the further side, gears grinding and the engine roaring.

It was then we saw our first manyata, a complete village of pigmy huts like up-ended wicker baskets. But no humans there. It was deserted, the boma surrounding it a withered tracery of thorn, thinned out by wind and sand so that it looked like dannert wire. The sand increased, the mountains dwindling away to nothing behind us, lost in the thorn scrub, and ahead, over the lip of the horizon, a lump began to take shape. A rock, a mountain? It was hard to tell in that pale light with nothing to measure it by, only the stunted trees, the stiff dried scrub.

147

"Kulal," Karanja said. "Kulal is where upepo is born. Upepo is the great wind that sweeps the lake."

"Have you been there?" I asked.

But he shook his head. "Only Marsabit. Kulal is very much bigger than Marsabit Mountain."

The dust cloud ahead of us thinned as the convoy turned off the track, driving fast over open scrub to where the Cessna stood parked beside a tent, a windsock hanging limp like an elephant's trunk. We came to a halt, the four trucks in line as though paraded for inspection, the drivers leaving their engines running and hurrying to the Land-Rover. The pilot, a younger man, black-haired with glasses and a pale blue shirt, his arm pointing back across the lugga as he leaned over the lowered windscreen, was talking to Kirby-Smith. He made a circling movement, nodding, and then he hurried off to his plane.

From where we stood in the back of our truck we could see the flat expanse of the makeshift airstrip, scrub and boulders piled along the line of its single runway, and beyond it the thicker bush that marked the line of the lugga, acacias with flattened tops, and further still the greener growth spilling from the low arms of the mountains, the Horr Valley a sharp gash between cedar-dark slopes and the sky beginning to take on colour, the first rose tints of the rising sun. The Cessna's engine burst into life, streaming dust as it turned, the drivers running back from their briefing, everybody in a hurry and no time wasted.

The Land-Rover moved off, turning and coming alongside us. "Well, this is what you came for," Kirby-Smith yelled, his mouth stretched in a tight hard grin, goggles pushed up on his forehead, his left hand glinting silver in the sun, a metal split grip instead of the glove and the junction with the flesh of his forearm plainly visible now that he was in a short-sleeved shirt. "Watch your cameras and keep your heads down. I don't want anybody hurt and you haven't done this before. Okay?" He snapped the goggles down, gave a signal for the trucks to follow him, and roared off

148

down towards the lugga, driving one-handed and trailing a cloud of dust.

"You see something now," Karanja shouted in my ear. His teeth were white in his black face, his eyes shining. Suddenly I caught his mood and found myself in the grip of a wild appalling excitement, my blood singing as the dust and wind flowed past me. I called something to Abe, but he paid no attention, his eyes on the plane, which was climbing steeply from the strip towards the mountains.

A track had been cut diagonally across the lugga and we took it at speed, wheels thumping the mudguards, and then we were into scrub, bashing our way through the thorn bushes, branches whipping across us and the dust choking. The plane was ahead of us now, circling and diving into a green patch of trees, its wings brushing their tops as it banked. The bush thickened until we were jinking between trees in second gear. And then we were in a clearing and Kirby-Smith was out of the Land-Rover, the lead truck stopped and men with rifles running to take up their positions. The second truck peeled off to the left. The one ahead of us turned right and we followed it. The stout stems of a toothbrush bush reared up over the radiator and I ducked to the crash of branches and the strong scent of its shredded leaves and pulped stems. When I looked again we were on our own and driving slower, the man riding beside the driver standing now, holding something in his hand. A glint of silver and the plane passed over us, leaving behind the roar of its engines. A short sharp bang like a backfire was followed by a squeal and then a trumpeting sound. And suddenly I saw them, grey humps through the bushes, huddled close, and the driver slammed on the brakes as one of the humps swung round, changing in an instant to a menacing spread of ears, the trunk swinging forward.

I saw the small eyes glaring, heard the thin squeal of rage as it charged, charged like lightning, and without hesitation. The driver had the truck in reverse. We were crashing backwards through the bushes, and the man beside him was swinging his arm in a wild forward movement. Something sailed through the air, the elephant looming large, dust rising from its feet. There was a flash, the crack of an explosion, and the elephant stopped, bewildered. The driver stood on the horn. Karanja was yelling, we were all yelling, and the man who had thrown the thunderflash was pounding on the door panel. The truck was stationary now, the engine ticking over, and the great beast shook its head and turned, moving off to rejoin the others. The driver took his hand off the horn and said something to the man beside him, who nodded.

"They say it is the leader." Karanja's voice trembled with excitement. "They're all cows, cows with totos. You see, they begin to move now."

We sat there, waiting, listening to the others shouting and banging on the sides of their trucks. Then we were off again, swinging back on our tracks, moving slowly and glimpsing the grey shapes through the leafy screen of the bushes. We were riding the edge of the herd, ready to halt them if they broke our way. But they kept straight on, moving like ghosts, silently and fast in an attempt to get away from the smell and din of the trucks' engines behind them. And all the time the plane kept circling overhead. Suddenly we were on the edge of the clearing and my ribs rammed against the handbar as we stopped with a jerk, the engine killed. The elephants had stopped, too. I said something, I don't know what, and the driver hissed at me. "Please. No talk."

I counted five fully grown elephants, two with very small calves under their bellies. There were seven youngsters in all, some of them half grown. A total of twelve. The largest elephant was in the rear of the herd and she paused as though unhappy about the clearing, not sure which way to go. She turned and faced us, her ears spread wide, her trunk raised like a periscope, feeling the air. The sun was over the mountains, shining full on her, and I knew it was the one that had charged us. The trunk moved to and fro, testing and probing. There was a small breeze stirring the leaves above my head.

The whole herd had faced about, the cows' trunks waving, all of them undecided. There was no sound from the trucks now, but that breeze must have carried the taint of petrol fumes for the leader suddenly shook her head, turning and slapping one of the babies with her trunk, nudging it back under its mother. She laid her trunk for a moment across the other's neck as though to comfort her, then moved round into the lead and the whole herd started for the far side of the clearing, moving fast.

That was when Kirby-Smith shot her. The sharp sound of his gun was merged with the thunk of the heavy bullet smashing hide and bone. I saw the great beast check, watched the head sag, the ears folding back, and before she had fallen there were shots slamming in from all around the clearing. Three adults were down, another threshing wildly, then the little ones were falling in a cacophony of shots and squeals and trumpeted roars of pain.

In less than two minutes it was over, and all was quiet, only the great mounds of inanimate elephants lying like giant boulders in the slanting sunlight and the hunters coming out into the open, moving slackly like men who have drunk too much, their rifles across their shoulders and still smouldering with the kill.

The truck's engine sparked into life. We were moving out into the open and when we stopped Kirby-Smith was looking up at us, the goggles pushed up on his forehead, his eyes sparkling bright, his teeth showing between his lips. "Now you know about culling—short and sweet, not a lingering death like that poor beast at the Lodge."

He didn't have to give his men orders. They knew their business and they were already out of the trucks, axes in their hands, chopping away at the heads of the five adults, cutting out the tusks. The hunters exchanged rifles for knives, ripping into the hides, exposing the still-warm flesh. Kirby-Smith was back at the Land-Rover with the long antenna of an aerial up, the mike close to his lips. The cook-boy was scattering diesel from an old jerrican onto a pile of branches and in an instant a fire blazed at the edge of the clearing.

I had climbed out of the truck and was leaning against it, the excitement drained out of me, my mouth dry and my legs trembling. Abe was already crouched in front of the fallen leader, his camera levelled as the two Africans pulled one of the tusks from the axed socket. It came out, red at the root, and they stood it on its tip, laughing and talking as they measured it with their eyes, passing it from hand to hand to test its weight. Abe had straightened up and was standing quite still, surveying the scene, arms limp and the camera hanging at his side. He called to me and beckoned. They were working to loosen the other tusk now and I went over and joined him, gazing down at the great head lying still, the limp trunk with the gaping hole below the glazed orb of the eye, surprised to see that the lid had lashes of fine hair.

"Guns are like power saws," he said, speaking slowly. "I once filmed a redwood being felled. Four hundred years old, they said. Four hundred years to grow and it was cut down in minutes. Have you reckoned up the years of animal growth lying dead around us?"

I shook my head, staring fascinated as the second tusk was worked back and forth to loosen it from its socket. It gave suddenly and the two men tugging at it fell on their backs laughing.

"Twelve elephants. Could be a total of two hundred and fifty to three hundred years cut down in less than that number of seconds. That's progress for you, the march of civilised man. Enough meat to keep a hundred humans alive for another week. Maybe more, I don't know, but—" He gave a shrug. "So little gain for so much destroyed." He turned and looked at me, his glasses glinting in the sun. "You didn't take any pictures."

"No."

"Your blood was up and you were yelling. Did you know you were yelling?"

I didn't answer, remembering the exhilaration of the hunt, feeling ashamed. He smiled, patting my arm. "It's the Saxon blood, I guess. You're a barbarian at heart."

"And you?" I asked. "Didn't you feel any excitement?"

"No. We're an older, more sensitive race. City dwellers with a long history. I felt as though it were myself out there, as though I were this poor beast trying to lead my people away from the guns and persecution."

A voice behind us said, "We'll start with this one. How old would you say she is?" It was Kirby-Smith, and Mary was beside him, notebook open in her hand, her dark face streaked with dust and sweat, the mark of goggles still around her eyes.

"I don't know," she said. "But she was the leader, so she'll be on her last set."

"I wonder how far they've come. They're not in very good shape." Kirby-Smith bent down, tugging at the rubbery lip in an attempt to get the mouth open. The two Africans came to help, pulling the trunk clear and prising the jaw open with their axe handles. "New molars coming forward, but the eight in use well worn." His head was almost inside the gaping cavity of the mouth. "Say forty years approximate. List her as SH.1. I'll have one of the molars extracted for microscopic analysis." He gave an order to the two Africans, still feeling around the inside of the jaw. He straightened up, wiping his hand on his trousers. "A cross-section of the root gives us the age," he said, looking at us. "The layers of dentine can be counted, rather like rings on the stump of a tree. There's a study being made now of the age at which cow elephants become herd matriarchs. This one I think is younger than average. She may have just taken over as leader, possibly breaking away from a larger group, or perhaps the old leader was killed. It's an interesting

153

field for study." And he moved off to the next adult, lying collapsed on its side, a gaunt grey mound.

"All done in the interests of science," Abe murmured. But I was looking at Mary Delden, standing notebook in hand and watching as Kirby-Smith worked to prise open the jaws, the gaping tusk wounds oozing blood. She hadn't said a word to me, hadn't even looked at me.

"For your information," Abe said, grasping my arm, "an elephant has six teeth on each of the upper and lower jaws, only two in use at any time, and these are replaced by new molars moving forward from the back of the jaw. In the full span of its life it goes through a total of six sets of teeth. You're not listening."

"Six sets," I said, staring at Mary's neat straight back and thinking of her father, wondering whether some tribesman would inform him of the death of these elephants. "Can't see how it helps to know their age." Could van Delden really carry out his threat—would he dare, against an organisation as efficient as this?

"Science, my friend. A lot of elephants have been killed over the years to prove this method of ageing them. We mustn't belittle the sacred cow of science."

Karanja called to us, coming from the fire with mugs in his hand, and I was suddenly conscious of my thirst. Work stopped, the place like a factory pausing for its tea-break, and, as we stood around drinking, the first of the meat trucks came in from our South Horr camp, the back of it full of Samburu tribesmen. They rushed at the carcases and had to be driven off at gunpoint. Guards were then posted and each man allowed to cut about a kilo from the flesh of one of the smaller elephants. More trucks were coming in, one of them so crowded with tribesmen they were clinging to the back of it like a swarm of bees. Others were beginning to arrive on foot and soon the clearing was a mass of half-naked Africans, all with long sheath knives of bright honed steel, their hide-covered handles worn

154

with use. In an instant, it seemed, three of the carcasses had been stripped to the bone.

Kirby-Smith had obviously experienced this sort of thing before. He was out there, standing guard with his men on the other carcases. He had a shotgun in his hand and when the first wild rush was spent he picked on a young warrior, red with ochre and splashed with blood, who was cutting out a huge chunk. He shouted at him, and when the man ignored his order, he raised his gun and fired into the ground at his feet. The moran screamed with pain, falling back and scrabbling at his legs, which were blasted more by sand than shot. The whole ant-like mass of Africans was suddenly frozen into stillness. He called the elders out then, and with their co-operation some semblance of order was established, so that each man got his share, and those who were willing to work for more helped load the trucks.

It was the sort of scene camermen dream about, nomadic tribesmen, hunters with guns, and elephants being hacked to pieces, blood everywhere. Close-ups of men, half naked, armed with spears and knives, dark skins stretched over staring rib cages, faces drawn and shrivelled-looking, of dead elephants, of tusks and meat, of Kirby-Smith, the great white hunter, firing at a warrior with his red cloak flung back, his sleek ochred hair coming loose in coils like snakes and his knife flashing. "Africa in Drought." I even had the title. But I had no build-up shots of cattle dead around the waterholes, of the Samburu abandoning their manyatas, and the scene in isolation would make no sense. But I knew I was only making excuses. I had missed the opportunity.

And then Abe said, "So you're taking my advice and saving your film. Funny thing," he added, "when it's an interview, just one guy and perhaps deadly dull, you've got a full unit every time. But get a subject like this, when you could throw the works at it, and you're lucky if you've got a single camera that's working, let alone a crew." He watched as the first truck moved off, loaded with meat and trailing a cloud of flies. "I guess we'll have to make a show of filming this evening."

Flies hung thick over the other trucks, crawling on the carcases. There was a smell of urine and a fainter, sweeter smell, the sun already high and blazing down, into the clearing, the blue sky turning white with heat. "This evening?" I murmured.

"This evening there'll be another drive. There's a herd stalled in thick bush up on the slopes there and Kirby-Smith suggested we stay with the hunters this time, show the world how neat and clean he does it. We got to earn our keep."

A second truck went grinding past. The loading was almost complete, the carcases stripped to skeletal remains that gleamed white and red in the sun. The Samburu were beginning to drift away, clasping their bloody packages of meat wrapped in leaves. "The parable of the fishes, African style. You'll get hardened to it, and so will I, until it becomes just an operation—monotonous." The two last trucks pulled out and work stopped, the hunters drifting towards the fire, the cook-boy pouring out mugs of tea from a huge blackened kettle, and the men drank, their arms and bodies caked with dried blood, the smell of it sour on the shimmering windless air.

A Land-Rover had brought in Kirby-Smith's partner from the airstrip and the two of them were deep in consultation. Mary was sitting alone under the shade of a thorn bush, the branches above her hung with the nests of weaver birds. I had just made up my mind to go over and talk to her when the driver of the truck returned on foot. He was bogged down in the lugga and we all piled in to one of the hunting vehicles.

The track through the lugga was now so badly churned and rutted that it was almost impassable. Trying to avoid the deep ruts of other vehicles, he had hit a soft patch of sand and was bellied down axle-deep. It took the better part of an hour to dig the vehicle clear, then winch it out backwards, and they still had to get it across the lugga. In the end they had to unload it, get it across empty, and then walk the meat across by hand and reload it on the far side. It was almost two-thirty by the time we were back at the clearing and being issued elephant steaks, fire blackened on the outside, raw inside. I was ravenously hungry, but by then I had had my fill of bloody bundles of meat crawling with flies and my stomach rebelled.

Mary was talking to Karanja and I saw her glance in my direction. She was holding a steak in her hand, tearing at it with her white teeth. She came over. "You're a carnivore, remember." She was smiling, a dribble of fat on her chin, and her fingers clasping the charred steak were streaked red. "Eat up or you'll run out of energy by the end of the day." Her eyes, shaded by the safari hat, were gazing towards the distant mountains. "You didn't film any of it this morning."

"No."

"Why not?"

"I didn't know what to expect."

"The light may not be so good this evening."

"It can't be helped."

"And that scene with the Samburu streaming in, hacking at the carcases. You won't get a repeat of that."

"Christ! A sickening sight like that. Do you think I want to see that again?"

She laughed. "You're all strung up still. But you'll get used to it, and it's what the public wants, isn't it? Plenty of blood, plenty of violence."

"I don't make that sort of film."

"Of course. I forgot. You like it to be remote, discursive, and only long shots of sea creatures dying of pollution."

"Elephants aren't the same as fish," I said. "They're mammals, and no viewer wants to see—"

"Dolphins are mammals, too. And whales." Her eyes glowed brightly, her face still flushed. "But here, it's different. Africa isn't remote like the sea. You're in the thick of it. That's the difference, isn't it?"

"Maybe." And I added angrily, "You're in no position to read me a lecture. What the hell are you doing here?"

Her gaze went back to the mountains and she was silent for a long time. We were both of us silent, eating slowly. "God knows," she breathed. "Something I've asked myself." And she added, "Hunting is in my blood, I guess."

"Elephant cows with young," I said. "Is that what you call hunting?"

She sighed. "Perhaps not. But it's all I'll get." And then, her voice suddenly practical, "Have you got enough film? Alex asked me to find out. He's always refused permission for cameramen to tag along. But now you're here, he's very anxious to have a proper record made of his culling methods. There'll be a truck going into Nairobi tomorrow. With a good supply of film you wouldn't have to be so careful of it."

"There's no film to be had in Nairobi," I said. "At least, that's what Karanja told us."

"The truck will be carrying ivory. If you're trading in ivory you can get anything in Nairobi." She looked at me questioningly. "Well?"

"I'll have a word with Abe," I murmured.

"Surely you're old enough to make up your own mind. There'll be no charge to you. He asked me to make that clear." She hesitated, then she said, "Alex is English, remember. It's the BBC he's interested in, a BBC 2 programme." She shrugged. "Talk it over with Mr. Finkel if you must, but let me know as soon as we get back to camp. I'll need a note of the make of film you require. Okay?"

When I told Abe of the offer, he smiled and shook his head. "Strings," he said. "He gets the film and pays for it, and then he has a say in what you shoot." He sighed. "I came here for the ride, to see a little more of Africa, and what happens?—I'm being pressured back into the business. I don't want to make a film for Alex Kirby-Smith. I don't want to be professionally involved. If I film anything, it's the solitude and the beauty I want to film, not bloody massacres, however well intentioned."

"You took pictures of the tusks being cut out."

"Yes, ivory. I may need that." He stared at me, his

brown eyes sad. "You do what you like, Colin. It's a question of motivation. I know what I'm doing here. But do you?" And he added, "Better give it some thought. For all the chance you'll have of getting to Rudolf it might just as well be a thousand miles away."

The fire was already being put out. Orders were shouted and within minutes we were embarked and headed towards the mountains. We were the lead vehicle this time, the Land-Rover close behind us, the back of it piled with tusks and Kirby-Smith pointing the way by signalling with that gleaming metal hand of his as he navigated by compass. Whenever we were halted by a patch of bush so dense that we could not bash our way through, everybody would be out with pangas cutting and slashing.

It was almost five by the time we reached the edge of a dried-up stream bed. The Land-Rover went on ahead, feeling its way up the middle of the lugga, over banks of sand and round gravel beds full of rocks and boulders, until finally the lugga broadened out in a wide curve towards the mountains, which were sharp now against the westering sun. It was then that I used my camera for the first time, filming as Kirby-Smith stood on the seat of the Land-Rover briefing his hunters. Seen through the viewfinder, it was like a picture I had seen of Rommel in that desert war so many years ago, his face burned and creased with the sun, his goggles snapped over the brim of his safari cap. But this was a man briefing African hunters equipped with .458 magazine rifles which they carried carelessly slung over their shoulders, not German panzer troops, and he was speaking Swahili.

A final gesture of the hand and then my camera was swinging as the Africans ran to their trucks and back again to Kirby-Smith, sitting now with the aerial up, talking into the mike. "So you're going to play along." How long Abe had been at my side I don't know.

"What else?" I asked, and he smiled and shrugged.

"The light's going to be tricky. Some cloud forming and it'll soon be dusk. If I were you I'd open up a stop."

"I know what I'm doing," I told him, my words half drowned in the roar of the Cessna as it passed over. It was so low I was able to trigger off a quick shot at it, its wheels almost brushing the trees on the opposite bank, its nose up as it began to climb. The engine note faded, to be replaced by the sound of the J4s as they fanned out, grinding and slashing through the bush.

"Four cows and about three calves." Kirby-Smith's voice was close beside me, high and sharp. "And Jeff says there's a young bull tagging along." He gripped my arm, his hand tight on my bare flesh. "Keep close to me and you'll be able to film the action as though you were seeing it over the sights of my rifle. I always fire the first shot. That's the signal—when I drop the leader. Got it?"

I nodded and he let go of me, moving quickly to the Land-Rover and backing it into a thicket of evergreens. Then he came back to the lip of the bank, carrying his rifle, a pair of binoculars swung round his neck. The rifle was a Rigby .416 with telescopic sights. He dropped to the ground, snapped the split grip that was his left hand on to the stock, settling himself comfortably on his elbows and slowly raising the gun to his shoulder. It was steady as a rock in the grip of that metal hand. He checked for wind, adjusting the sights, then his face became set in concentration as he swung the barrel across the broad open sweep of the lugga.

He must have heard the hum of my camera as I took a close-up, for he turned on me almost irritably and said, "You can do the personal shots tomorrow. For the moment just keep your mind and your camera on what's going to happen down there in the open curve of the stream bed. You missed a great opportunity this morning. I'm told you didn't take any film at all. In my outfit everybody has to pull his weight." He signalled to the others to get down under cover, then settled himself deeper into the hard sandy ground, took several deep breaths, and relaxed.

The plane swung against the clouds piling up over the mountains, a glint of wings in the slanting sun as it dived. The sound of its engine came to us faintly, and we could hear the trucks still grinding up the slopes as they manoeuvred into position for the drive. "About ten minutes," Kirby-Smith said, and motioned Karanja to move further back. "But it could be sooner—you never know. Elephants move fast when they've a mind to." He turned to Mary. "Take the time from the first thunderflash. And then again from my shot to the last beast down. You've got the stop watch?"

She nodded, lying prone beside me. We were all of us lying stretched out on the ground, and after that nobody spoke, the only sound the monotonous call of a dove somewhere behind us. I checked my film. More than a hundred feet to go, almost three minutes' shooting. It should be plenty and I glanced at my watch. Five twenty-seven and the shadows lengthened every moment. The sun was only just above the trees, a bank of cloud below it to the west. If it went into the cloud . . . I was trying to decide what the setting should be if I lost the sun and then the first thunderflash went off. The sound of it was insubstantial, a distant bang. The birds heard it, the grey-headed social weavers setting up a squeaky chatter in a tree behind us that was festooned with their nests. A starling was chattering and whistling on the ground nearby. But the dove was suddenly silent. Far away across the lugga we heard the note of the trucks' engines change as they revved up. There was a faint breeze blowing towards us from the mountains, carrying the sound of shouts, and the Cessna was diving, closer this time. The drive had begun.

"Wind's right and the light's still good." Kirby-Smith's voice was quiet and controlled, no tension at all. "Just relax," he whispered, "and concentrate on the centre of the bank. See that sandbank with the shadow of a tree across it? I shall take the leader about there. The whole bunch will be out in the open then."

I saw the spot and checked the focus, the camera cradled on my arm. I glanced at Abe, his camera showing above Mary's shoulder as he lay stretched beside her, and I wondered whether he was going to film the kill after all. Five twenty-nine and the lower edge

161

of the sun almost lipping the clouds. But the trucks were coming fast, the sound of their engines growing, and when next the plane dived it was less than a mile away. Another thunderflash, followed by squeals, and the sound of trumpeting and of men yelling and beating on the sides of their trucks, the engines coming nearer.

"Very soon now," Kirby-Smith breathed, his eyes fixed on the far side of the lugga, the heavy rifle pushed slightly forward, his good hand on the butt close by the breech. It was a big strong capable hand, the back of it sun-mottled and the hairs on his bare arms bleached almost white. A truck appeared on the far bank and stopped abruptly, the two men in it sitting motionless, watching. The plane came back, flying low, its engine drowning the noise of the other three trucks, and suddenly a grey shape appeared far up the lugga, moving fast. Out of the tail of my eye I saw Kirby-Smith raise the rifle, snugging it into his shoulder. The grey shape paused on the lip of the bank, trunk raised, scenting the open space of the lugga. All was quiet, even the birds, a breathless hush. Then the elephant started down the bank, moving slowly now, and behind it the backs of others, ears spread, trunks waving.

It was at that moment that somebody fired. It wasn't Kirby-Smith. The shot came from up the lugga. There was a piercing squeal and the leader wheeled so fast I could hardly follow her as she plunged back up the bank. I saw the others turn, all trumpeting and squealing, and then Kirby-Smith fired, the crash of his rifle so loud my ears sang with the noise of it. But the leader did not check and in an instant the grey shapes had vanished from sight. More shots, the roar of engines starting up, and suddenly a burst of flames from far up the lugga. It was there for a moment, a great blossom of fire, and then it died to be replaced by a pall of smoke, rising and drifting, thick and heavy in the breeze.

"Christ!" Kirby-Smith had dropped his rifle, the binoculars gripped in one hand, levelled at the smoke.

162

"It's one of the trucks." He leapt up, seizing his rifle and running for the Land-Rover. I squeezed the trigger of my camera, taking a wild sweeping shot as I jumped to my feet and followed him, the others piling in beside me as he started the engine and we went bucketing down the bank and roared off up the lugga towards the dense pall of smoke still billowing over the bush ahead.

It was the far flank truck and as we rounded the bend we could see it out in the open on a sandbank in the lugga, a blackened hulk half hidden in an oily cloud. All four tyres were alight and burning furiously, and when we reached it the heat was so intense we could not get near. Nothing we could do anyway. No water, no fire extinguisher. We just stood there helpless and watched it burn.

We couldn't even drag the bodies out. There were two of them in front. We caught a glimpse of their charred remains as the smoke from the burning tyres rolled over them. "Why didn't they jump clear?" Mary's voice was taut above the crackle of the flames. "Surely to God they could have jumped." And Kirby-Smith, close beside her, said, "Wario could have been trapped by the steering wheel." He was tight-lipped and frowning. "But Jilo—he was a youngster, very quick, nothing to stop him jumping clear."

And Abe's voice, whispering in my ear, "Unless he was dead before the petrol tank caught fire."

I turned, saw the look in his eyes, and was suddenly appalled. "For Christ's sake," I breathed.

"There were shots, several shots." And he added, still speaking so low the others could not hear, "I started life as a newspaper reporter. Seen a lot of accidents and in cases of fire I never saw anybody burn to death without at least some evidence they had tried to get out. And this was an open truck." He nodded at Kirby-Smith, watching him. "Karanja warned him. And he's a hunter. He'll soon work it out."

Mary was staring, her eyes wide, her face pale under the brown skin. Abruptly she turned away, sickened at the sight. The stench of burning rubber hung on the air, and with it the smell of hot metal and blistering paint, the sizzling stink of roasting flesh. Nobody said anything more, even the Africans were silent. I didn't know what to think, unwilling to accept Abe's observations, shutting my mind to the implication.

Gradually we all drifted away. Nothing we could do except leave the truck to burn itself out. The elephants were gone, the hunt over, and nobody wanted to talk about it, all of us, white and black, locked in on ourselves, silent. Surely to God it must have been an accident.

A voice spoke sharply in Swahili. It was Kirby-Smith ordering the men back to their vehicles. The sun had set, the short African dusk closing in on the lugga. Only Abe remained by the burning truck, taking stills with a tiny miniature camera. Then he, too, turned away. But he did not join me. He went over to where Mary sat alone on a boulder, her head bowed as though in prayer, her face devoid of any expression. He sat on the sand beside her, not saying anything, just sitting there as though sensing that she had a need for the silent companionship of another human being.

I wished then that I had his emotional perception. Kirby-Smith was against the Land-Rover with the aerial up and the microphone in his hand, his African driver, with Karanja, squatting on the ground nearby. One by one the engines of the three remaining trucks started up, the sound of them gradually fading as they headed back to camp. Nobody else but ourselves now in the open curve of the lugga, the dusk deepening and the first stars showing, everything silent.

I was standing on my own, feeling isolated in the utter stillness. There was no sound, not even the call of a bird. Nothing moved, only wisps of smoke from the still smouldering tyres, and my thoughts in turmoil as I tried to come to terms with the possibility that somewhere, out there in the gathering darkness ... But my mind shuddered away from the prospect.

And then I heard Kirby-Smith's voice: "Could be

just the heat friction of a bullet passing through the tank." He and his driver were moving slowly towards me, a powerful torch beamed on the ground, and Abe was with them. "Or maybe he was using tracer. Did you notice what sort of rifles his Africans had?"

"I know nothing about guns." Abe's voice was a disembodied whisper in the night. "But he had a double-barrelled rifle. I remember that."

"A Rigby .470, that's what he always used. He must have had it stashed away somewhere." Silence for a moment, two figures bending down, searching the ground, and then Kirby-Smith straightened up and switched off the torch. "Looking for a spent bullet in the gravel here, it's hopeless." He was staring off into the darkness beyond the truck. "An old Lee Enfield firing tracer, that's my guess."

"Where the hell would they get tracer bullets?" Abe asked.

"Same place as the rifles. From the old battle areas. A lot of the game I've seen killed in the last year was shot with .303 and there's still plenty of ammunition lying around if you know where to look."

They were moving off towards the Land-Rover and Abe said, "You saw the driver's skull?"

"Of course."

They came back with a pick, shovel, and crowbar, and we set about digging a grave. We dug it on the top of the bank, working in the light of the Land-Rover's headlights, and by the time we had finished the truck was no longer even smouldering, the metal just cool enough for us to drag the remains of the two Africans out. It was a messy, unpleasant job, a roasted smell still clinging to the shrivelled tatters of flesh, the bones brittle from the heat. Karanja pointed to the driver's head, which had a hole drilled in the blackened bone just above the remains of the right ear, another larger hole on the other side. "This man shot dead." His voice was high and excited, trembling in the hot, stinking air.

"His gun must have gone off by itself," Mary said quickly. "The heat . . ." But she stopped then, knowing it wasn't that, for Kirby-Smith's torch was beamed on the rifle still clipped to its bracket.

Nobody said anything after that and we laid the bodies on a groundsheet and carried them to the grave in silence. When we had shovelled back the earth and built a small cairn of boulders over the mound, Kirby-Smith drove us back to camp. He drove fast, crashing through the bush, swerving between the trees, tearing over the uneven ground, as though in fighting the wheel one-handed his powerful body found an outlet for the anger that showed in his face.

That night the tension in the camp was something almost tangible. Presumably Kirby-Smith had told his driver not to talk, but in a close-knit group of men it is impossible to conceal a thing like that entirely. It was in the air, a feeling of menace. And the patrol was back. They had found the tracks of humans mixed with those of the rhinoceros and further back the remains of a camp. Kirby-Smith's tracker and two of the patrol, who were also expert trackers, were agreed that the camp had been used the previous night. They had followed fresh tracks northwards in the direction of the morning cull, but had lost them where the intruders had waded through the waters of the stream. They had failed to pick up any tracks on the further bank, but the information they brought back had convinced every African in the camp that the rhinoceros had been cleverly manoeuvered into charging our tents, and that somebody, ivory poachers probably with a vested interest in preventing an official cull of their source of supply, had been responsible for firing on the truck.

All this we heard from Karanja as we sat by the fire eating a mess of posho and elephant meat. And something else. The patrol had also back-tracked the intruders on the approach to the site of their night camp. Again they had lost the tracks in the stream, but the approach had been made from the east, down the slopes of the Mara Range. "Many years ago," Karanja said, "when I first work for Tembo and he is game warden of this area, we capture a very bad

166

poacher who is hiding in a secret hole in the rocks up there on the Mara."

The cook-boy was issuing cans of beer, one to each man, and the patrol sergeant threw another branch on the fire. The flames rose, flickering on the black faces, everybody huddled in groups, talking, their voices hushed. And close beside me, Abe said, "Do you think he's up there, holed out in the same place?"

"Maybe." Karanja hesitated. "Maybe he is somewhere else now, but is good place to hide. When we capture that poacher, if we do not have an informer with us who know the place, we never find it." And he added, "Also, there is only two ways to approach. We can climb up, or we can climb down, and if we don't surprise him we are all dead. He was bad man and he had a gun with him."

"And what happens in the morning?" Abe asked. "Is the patrol going out again?"

Karanja nodded. "They will leave at dawn."

"Which direction?"

"Up on to the Mara."

"To search the other side of the stream for tracks?"

Karanja shrugged, his eyes shifting in the firelight, his hands gripped tight around his can of beer.

"Do you think they'll find any tracks?"

"Maybe."

There was something in Karanja's manner that worried me. He seemed nervous and very tense, unwilling to continue the conversation. Abe snapped the ring-opener of his can, threw it into the fire, and drank. "Anybody else know of this hideout?" It was said innocently enough, but I saw he was watching him out of the corners of his eyes.

Karanja didn't answer, and when Abe repeated the question, he shook his head. "I sleep now." He started to get to his feet, but Abe pulled him back, his hand on his arm, holding him.

"I have told you what I know," Karanja said.

"Why?" Abe asked. "Why did you tell us about this hideout?"

Karanja shook his head again, the whites of his eyes

167

gleaming in the flickering firelight. "Maybe you, or Mr. Tait, go with the patrol."

"You told Major Kirby-Smith about it."

"No, not Kirby-Smith."

"The patrol sergeant then."

Karanja was silent. Then suddenly he said, "There is a man in the patrol who is with the police when we bring that poacher in. He knows we caught him up in the Mara, but he don't know where."

"So you told them."

Karanja hesitated, then nodded slowly. "What can I do? If I don't co-operate—" He spread his hands in a gesture of helplessness, then caught hold of Abe's arm. "Why did he do it? Is crazy, to shoot men because they are killing elephants."

"You're certain it was van Delden then?"

"Who else? Who else but Tembo van Delden do a crazy thing like that?" And he added, "Once before, when we were at Marsabit—" He was suddenly silent, shaking his head. "But now it is different. Now, if he's taken by the Army . . ." He was staring at Abe and his eyes in the twilight seemed to be pleading.

"You don't want his death on your conscience, is that it?"

Karanja hesitated, then nodded, a reluctant, barely perceptible movement of the head. "If you were with the patrol—a newsman representing CBS—then I think they are more careful." And after a moment he said hopefully, "Then it is all right? I can fix it?" And he sat there, staring urgently at Abe, who didn't say anything for a long time, sitting hunched over his beer, sipping at it occasionally, lost in thought.

Finally he seemed to make up his mind. "I have a better idea." He finished his drink and got to his feet, dragging Karanja with him. "We'll take a walk, see where the night guards are posted." He turned to me. "You stay here. I'll tell you what's in my mind later." And, still gripping the unwilling Karanja by the arm, he led him out of the circle of the firelight. I watched them until they were no more than shadows against

168

the bright gleam of pressure lamps hung outside the tents.

I leaned back and closed my eyes. The night was full of sound, the crackle of the fire, the whisper of voices, the incessant, strident cacophony of cicadas. Somewhere an owl was hooting, the first I had heard, a mournful, monotonous sound, and down by the lugga a nightjar was over-riding the croak of frogs with a shrill churring. I thought how wonderful it would be, camped here under the mountains, if this were just a photographic safari, no killing, no sense of something hanging over me. There was a shout, the click of a rifle bolt, and I opened my eyes, staring into the night. Abe and Karanja had been challenged by one of the guards. I could see a torch shining on their faces and I lay back again, watching a satellite, bright as a planet, moving steadily across the velvet sky.

Out of the tail of my eye I saw a figure move, flop down beside me, and Mary's voice said, "What does Abe Finkel think?"

"About what?" I sat up, leaning on one elbow. The fire was dying and I could not see the expression in her eyes.

"About what happened, who did it. God, you're slow. What else?" The husky voice trembled on the night air and I felt sorry for her. She knew there was only one man who could have done it and silence was the only answer I could give her. "You think I should have gone with him, don't you? You think I'm to blame. But it wouldn't have made any difference. He never listened to me." Her hands were clasped tight together, the fingers locked. "Well, say something, can't you?"

"What is there to say? You're here, and that's all there is to it."

"You don't understand, do you?". .

"No, I don't," I said. "If you'd been with your father, if you'd gone with him——"

"He's not my father."

I stared at her, shocked as much by the tone of her

169

voice, the emotional violence of it, as by the denial. "But when we were at the Lodge . . ."

"He gave me a name, brought me up—but he's not my father. Surely you must have guessed." And when I shook my head, she said, "Alex is my father. Now do you understand?" She seemed to expect some comment, but when I didn't say anything, she said angrily, "Well, don't just sit there staring at me. He's my natural father and I don't know what to do. A situation like this—I need help." She was staring at me, her eyes unnaturally bright. "Well, Christ! Can't you say something?" And then she laughed, a trembling note near to hysteria. "No, of course. Keep your mouth shut, don't get involved. Don't even bloody well think about it." Her eyes shifted to the forest. "All very well for you. But that man out there—you don't know him like I do."

She was silent for a moment, and then, in a quiet voice tinged with bitterness: "I thought—at that Conference—I really thought a confrontation would get it out of his system. I thought if they argued it out, the two of them, in public, before all those delegates—that would be the end of it. I thought he'd be satisfied then, feel he'd done all he could. But I was wrong. Instead, it seemed to fuel again all the old resentment, all the basic fundamental differences. The two of them, they're like two sides of the same coin, both of them obsessed with the rightness of what they're doing." The rush of words ceased abruptly, her voice trembling into silence. "But not this," she breathed, her nerves strung taut and a note of hopelessness. "Nothing can justify this." She was silent for a while, her fingers moving, clasping and unclasping. Then suddenly she rounded on me and said, "You've got to stop it—somehow."

"Me?" I stared at her, wondering what the hell she expected me to do about it.

"You and that American," she said, her eyes staring at me, large and wild in the dimming firelight.

"You've got to do something. You're the only men here who can come between them."

I sat there, silent, not knowing what to say. There was no comfort I could give her. And then Abe came out of the shadows, Karanja beside him, both of them subdued. "The guards are on their toes," he said. "We were challenged twice." He glanced at Mary, then sat himself on the far side of her. "I think you could help." He stared at her, then said hesitatingly, "That is, if you're willing. Karanja here knows of an old poacher's hideout—"

"I know about that," she said quickly. "The patrol leaves at first light."

He nodded. "Then it's a question of whether you're prepared to let your father be cornered up there without warning him."

"It doesn't worry you that he's killed two men?"

He smiled and shook his head. "I've seen too much bloodshed, too many people killed. . . ." He gave a little shrug. "Too many of us in the world anyway."

She turned to Karanja, speaking to him rapidly in his own tongue. And when he had answered her questions, she said, "He may not be there, of course."

Abe nodded. "Then we come back. But if he is . . ." He paused, facing her. "You realise they'll shoot him."

"I was hoping," she said, "that I could persuade you . . ." She glanced at me. "That's why I came to talk to you." Kirby-Smith called to her and she said she was coming. "He wants to dictate some notes."

"Will you create a diversion for us so that we can slip away unnoticed?"

She nodded slowly. "I—suppose so. Yes, of course. It's what I wanted—for him to be warned. But on one condition, that you make him realise it's useless to interfere. More troops will be arriving in the morning. He won't stop the culling and if he tries to attack the outfit again, then there'll only be one end to it. They'll track him down and kill him. Tell him that please, if you find him, and make him promise to head for the coast. It's his only hope."

Quickly they arranged the details between them. Just after midnight Mary would approach one of the guards, tell him she had an upset stomach, and go into the bush. She would stay there long enough for them to become anxious, then she would scream and start to run. After the rhinoceros episode of the night before, it would be sufficient to reduce the whole camp to instant turmoil. She got up. "That's settled then." She hesitated, suddenly bending down to Abe and kissing him on the forehead. "You're a very strange man. Thank you." And she turned and went quickly to the tent where Kirby-Smith sat at a table, his face lit by the bright light of a pressure lamp clouded with insects.

"Well." Abe had shifted his position. He was close beside me now. "What are you going to do—come with us or stay and film tomorrow's cull?"

I stared at him, thinking what it would be like climbing up through the forest in the dark, up the densely covered slopes of the Mara. A night march like that, God knows what we would meet—elephant, rhino, and Kirby-Smith had said there were lions. And if we made it, if we found the poacher's hideout and van Delden there . . . What then? Would he do what Mary asked. "You really think you'll find him?"

He shrugged. "It's worth a try."

"So you'll go, tonight?"

He nodded. "Karanja says there's a track goes up from the South Horr side of the stream."

"And he'll guide you?"

"He thinks he can remember it."

I looked across at Karanja, sitting cross-legged, his hands clasping his knees, his face sombre. I didn't understand why the man was prepared to risk his life, his whole career, and when I asked him he simply said, "I must." His eyes shifted, staring at me, a helpless look. "If I don't then I am Judas." And he added, his voice soft in the night, "Many years and I almost forget how I love that man."

I thought of van Delden, trying to understand what

172

there was in him that could engender such a bond of loyalty and affection. But it was outside of my experience, something beyond my comprehension. And Abe —what made him take such a chance for a man he hardly knew? "Why are you doing it?" I asked. But he only smiled that infuriating little secret smile of his. "Do not ask," he murmured, "such knowledge is not for us."

"What do you mean by that?"

"Only that I don't know. You should read your Horace. He puts things very well. Probably better in Latin, but I was never taught Latin or Greek at school. I hadn't that sort of education." His eyes stared past me into the ember-glow of the fire. "If we find van Delden I don't think he'll do what Mary asks. He'll be warned, that's all, and shift his base. In which case I'll see something I've never seen before, a man in total defence of another species. To film that, so the viewer sees it all through his eyes—the elephants, the trucks gathering for the drive, the hunters waiting for the kill, the long barrel of the rifle, the sights coming up on to their target, and the target not an elephant, but a man, and then the truck a blaze of fire . . . But that was today." He smiled and shook his head. "I missed a great opportunity today."

"You'd have filmed it?"

"Sure I would. I won't get a chance like that again. Next time it will be different."

"There won't be a next time," I said. "Or if he tries it, then the Army will get him."

"Oh, I don't know. I guess he knows this country better than the Army." He laughed. "Anyway, I want to be with him when they start culling again. I don't want to be with the hunters. I'm on the side of the elephants, you see."

"You'll be in real trouble then." I was really concerned about him. I couldn't help it. I'd grown fond of Abe and to go off into the Mara seeking the company of a man who had put himself in such a terrible position seemed dangerous in the extreme. But when

173

I tried to explain this to him he only laughed. "I may not find him anyway."

"No, but the patrol sergeant will know you were trying to warn him."

"So?" He looked at me, a strange expression in his eyes. "Does it matter?" And he added, "I don't mind all that much what happens to me, not now." His gaze had wandered back to the fire, and after a while he said, "I know what you're thinking, that van Delden has killed two men. But that's not the point." He paused for a moment, then he was looking at me and smiling again. "That shocks you, I suppose? But it shouldn't, not when you consider it in the context of all the senseless killings that go on in the world. You see, he believes passionately in what he is doing. To him it is justified." He stretched out his hand and gripped my knee. "I guess you're too new at this game to grasp what it is we've got here. This man is no ordinary man. He's something unique. He has so identified himself with the elephants that they are in a sense his own people."

"He didn't need to kill those men," I said obstinately.

"Didn't he? How else was he to stop the slaughter? How else protect them from extermination?"

"He'd only to turn the leader."

"That was today, but what about tomorrow and the next day and the next, the refrigerator trucks standing by, that freezer plant empty, and the word running like wildfire through South Horr to Baragoi and Maralal—all those tribesmen waiting to get their hands on the meat. One man against a bunch of professional hunters backed up by the Army." He was staring off into the fire again. "It's a damned odd story, the oddest I've ever come across."

It was stupid of me, but I thought then it was the story, not the elephants or van Delden's safety, that was driving him to this crazy idea of a night journey up the Mara. But when I put my thoughts into words, he turned on me angrily. "You fool! How can you understand my motives when I don't understand them

174

myself? All I know is I'm going. There's nothing for me here. Kirby-Smith can't give me what I'm seeking here in Africa. But this man van Delden, I think he can." He got to his feet. "I'm going to get some sleep now. Whether you come or not—that's up to you."

Part Three

THE LAST
REFUGE

I

THE MOON WAS WELL UP, but its light barely penetrated the leaf canopy. Evergreens and patches of thick impenetrable bush, the boles of tall trees, twisted ropes of lianas, and my heart pounding as we climbed, following the beam of Karanja's torch. We had been climbing for two hours without a break. I could hear Abe's breath coming in gasps, occasionally he stumbled. We were neither of us fit, but he kept going and I followed him, the camera and my grip becoming heavier, my shoulders aching. I no longer thought about the possibility of coming face to face with some nocturnal animal or even why I was here and not sleeping down at the camp. We had left it in a scrambling chaos of men shouting, but whenever we paused to listen, half expecting the sound of pursuit, we heard nothing, only the rustlings of the night, the occasional clatter of tree fruit falling or a nut.

We came at last to a stream, the same little river the road forded below South Horr. Now it was narrower, more of a mountain stream running fast over smooth boulders, a dark tunnel winding up through thick undergrowth. We waded up it, moving slowly, feeling for foot holes, moonlight glinting on water and on the barrel of the rifle Karanja had taken from one of the hunters, everything black in shadow and monkeys restless in the trees, sharp barks of defiance. Something moved on the bank and we checked as it went crashing away through a thicket. "Nyati," Karanja said. "Buffalo." There was less bush now, the cedar beginning, and we left the stream, clambering straight up. We were no longer in the foothills. We were on the Mara itself. Exhausted, we reached the trail again. It was wider here and damp under the trees, the firm-packed earth marked with the footprints of elephants.

Abe flopped to the ground. "How much further?" he gasped.

"I carry your bag now," Karanja suggested.

But Abe shook his head. "You keep your hands free in case we meet something. All I want to know is how far from here?"

"An hour, two hours. Is long time since I am here."

"You haven't forgotten, have you? You know where it is?"

"Ndio."

"And this trail leads to the hideout?"

But all Karanja said was, "We go now. Maybe patrol wait for dawn, maybe is behind us." He reached down and picked up Abe's bag, and then we were on our feet again, following the trail as it climbed up through the cedar forest, clinging to the face of the mountain, winding round outcrops, the ground falling away below us.

It was not all cedar. There were patches of green-leaved trees and shrubs, but these were now like clearings in the forest, the broken stems sticking up out of a trampled litter of branches, and only the largest trees left standing. For the first time I was seeing the role elephants play in the natural order of African ecology, but stumbling over broken branches with my feet slipping on the soft mush of elephant turds, and coming suddenly out into the first of these clearings, I was suprised to see the effect of such big animals browsing on forest growth.

Karanja had stopped. "Many elephants come this way," he said, looking cautiously about him.

"How long ago?" Abe asked.

He picked up one of the droppings and sniffed at it. "That is old. But this—" He put his foot on a smaller, softer ball. "This dung ball is fresh."

"How fresh?"

He bent down to smell it, then shook his head.

"Maybe tonight. Maybe last night. I am not like Mukunga. Mukunga could say to an hour how old this is." He straightened up, staring across the clearing again. "Many elephants," he said again, his voice sounding uneasy. And then abruptly: "We go quickly now please. Is not far."

We went on then, across the broken litter of branches into the forest again, our eyes searching ahead in the gloom, expecting any moment to see the dim shape of an elephant loom up through the trees. More areas of green-leaved devastation, and then we were under a wall of rock and Karanja had checked. The moon was low in the west, the light of it shining full on the mountain, jagged peaks pale against the stars and just ahead of us another clearing thick with a tangle of torn-off branches and trampled bushes. I saw leaves moving, heard the snap of a stem, a low rumbling sound, and Karanja was backing away, searching the cliff face. "Ndovu," he whispered. "Is best we climb into the rock." There was a crevice and as we scrambled up, the rumbling was nearer. There was a thin squeal and the crash of branches, then silence.

We waited, crouched in the gulley, listening. More rumblings, nearer now, and then suddenly a grey shape moved below us. Tusks glinted pale in the moonlight, a trunk lifted high, sniffing the air. The elephant had stopped and I realised it was a cow, for she had two calves following close behind her, one half grown, but the other so tiny it looked no bigger than a Shetland pony. It had a branch gripped in its miniature trunk and was trying to manoeuvre the leaves into its mouth, a puzzled, concentrated look on its small face. The cow turned, her ears spread in alarm, her stomach rumbling. She was so close I could see the way the top edge of her ears folded back, a sort of rubbery fringe, the bony outline of the huge head and the deep creases in her waving trunk.

The baby had caught the note of alarm now. It dropped the branch and vanished from my sight. She was guiding it under her belly with her foot and the

179

older one was pushing past her. There was a shrill squeal as the trunk came down, slapping it into position against her gaunt flank. They stood like that for a moment, mother and child together and her trunk raised again, the prehensile tip of it feeling the air as though sensing our presence so close among the rocks, while behind her the rest of the family group came into view. They were cows with two or three half-grown calves bunched close around them as they stood filling the trail, alarmed and restless, their trunks moving from side to side, their feet scuffing the ground.

Karanja gave a short sharp whistle and stood up, clutching a sapling growing out of the crevice. Silence then and the grey tide of heads and hunched backs flowing past us. In an instant the trail below us was clear and not a sound anywhere. "Did you see it?" Abe breathed, his voice trembling on a note of surprise and wonder. "When she stopped right below us, her ears spread?"

"See what?" I asked, still thinking of that baby elephant, the only tiny one in the group, the impression they had given of a family fleeing through the night, and wondering how far they had come, where they were going.

"I guess it was just a trick of the light," he murmured. But as we scrambled down on to the empty trail I heard him ask Karanja how far we were from the Aberdares, and Karanja answered shortly, "A long way." He was moving out ahead of us, rifle gripped in his hand, head thrust forward, peering down the trail.

We passed the rock face and came in sight of the clearing again, Abe beside me saying, "She had two calves, and that little one, it couldn't have been more than a few months old. Did you see it?" He seemed to have an urgent need to talk, not caring that there might be more elephants ahead of us. "A baby calf like that, could it come all that way? And they were heading north. Do you reckon they were the same elephants we saw from the Baringo track?" And when I didn't answer him, my eyes fixed nervously on the far side of the clearing, he said, "Van Delden seemed to

180

think it was some sort of inherited instinct. But north from here it's desert. Hey, Karanja!" And he caught him up. "All those tracks we've seen, they're all heading north, isn't that right?"

"Yes, all going north."

"So where do they go?"

"The major thinks Ethiopia, the Omo River maybe." We had come into the clearing and he was walking slowly, his eyes searching the forest on the far side. It was difficult to see ahead, for there was more bush here. Close beside us was a tree festooned with strips of torn bark like pale streamers in the moonlight.

"They can't cross the desert. They looked shagged-out already, and they've got calves with them. Those calves—"

Karanja silenced him with a sharp hiss. He had stopped and was staring intently ahead. We stood in a bunch, listening, but there was no sound, everything very still, the air breathless in the moonlight and the trail running ahead of us, across the clearing into the dark of the cedars. And then we saw it, on the far side of the clearing, a dim shape coming towards us. No time to get back to the gulley and the bush thick on either side.

Karanja dropped Abe's bag, gripping his rifle. I heard the click of the bolt as he cocked it. The elephant heard it, too, its ears suddenly spread wide, the trunk curling upwards. It was out in the open now and I could see it quite clearly. It had stopped and was feeling the air, its trunk moving snake-like above its head.

Whether the elephant winded us or whether it actually saw us, I don't know, but its left eye was glinting in the moonlight and I had a sudden feeling it was focussed on me personally. My heart was thudding, my mouth dry, and as though he sensed what was in my mind Karanja hissed, "Stay still! Even if he charge, don't move." He took a few steps forward and stopped, the rifle gripped in his hands ready. The elephant was less than a hundred yards away.

181

I think it saw Karanja move, for it suddenly curled its trunk and let out a wild trumpeting that echoed and re-echoed from the rock walls above us. Silence then and the grey bulk coming towards us, slowly, almost hesitantly, so that I was reminded of that elephant at the Lodge, weak from starvation. It stopped again, its front feet on a log, its head up and its ears spread wide. It looked enormous in the moonlight, my gaze so concentrated upon it that I had the distinct impression that it filled the clearing. "Is bluffing," Karanja whispered. But his voice trembled and I didn't believe him. The beast was swinging its right forefoot back and forth, scattering leaves and broken bits of branch, its body rocking from side to side and its trunk coiling and uncoiling.

"I've read about this," Abe whispered. "I never thought I'd see it." He sounded excited rather than scared, and then the elephant tucked its trunk up under its tusks and charged. It was a slow, lumbering movement, yet it covered the ground all too quickly, and incredibly there was scarcely a sound.

I thought Karanja would fire then, and I stood rooted to the spot expecting any moment the sound of the shot. But instead he jumped on to a fallen log and just stood there, the rifle high above his head, both arms raised, facing the elephant. And when it was barely ten yards from him, the huge bony head, with the ears spread like sails seeming to fill the sky and the tusks pointing straight at us, it suddenly skidded to a halt, shaking its head furiously and scattering brushwood with its flailing trunk. Then for a moment it was still, its trunk uncurled and hanging down, its head lifted until it seemed as though it were standing on tiptoe to look at something behind us. Again that shattering trumpet sound, and then it seemed to grow smaller, the skin of its flanks hanging in folds and its bones showing, its ears folding back, the trunk hanging down again. It shook its head as though disgusted at its failure to make us give ground, turning slowly and shambling off, head and tail up,

182

sliding like a ghost into the tangled thicket of broken bush, going downhill and making scarcely a sound.

Karanja let out his breath in an audible sigh of relief, and I knew he hadn't been as sure of himself as he had pretended. "Long time since I see elephant behave like that. Tembo call it—" He frowned, laughing nervously. "I don't remember what he call it."

"Good for you." Abe was laughing and clapping him on the back. "But how did you know we weren't going to be trampled to death?"

Karanja shrugged, pleased with himself now and beaming all over his face. "Is a bull," he said, "and not certain of himself. You see him swing his foot and sway, and then trumpeting and making to stand big. Not often bulls make real charge. Cows, yes, 'specially when they have young. Not bulls."

"It is what they call a threat display then?"

"Ndio." Karanja nodded eagerly. "Threat display."

"Let's get on," I said, annoyed that Abe could stand there, quietly discussing the behaviour of the beast, while my legs were still trembling and weak from the shock of that charge. He seemed entirely unaffected, as though what he had seen at Treetops God knows how many years ago had convinced him all animals are innocent of any real hostility. I picked up his bag and went on across the clearing, wanting to get off that trail as quickly as possible, my mind still full of the memory of that great bulk skidding to a halt and the big domed head and the great ears blotting out the stars.

Behind me I heard Karanja say, "Is the word Tembo van Delden use—threat display. Where you learn it, eh?"

"Something I read."

"In a book?"

"Yeah. In a book."

Karanja shook his head. "Is difficult for me. I don't have enough books—no books like that." The cedars closed over our heads and we moved cautiously, the trail climbing steeply up through the forest. A lot of elephants had come that way, the trail marked

183

by their great footprints, their droppings everywhere and a debris of leaves and discarded saplings. Once we disturbed a bird that went flapping past us silent as an owl. "Mountain eagle," Karanja said. "Mountain eagle very common on Marsabit." We were passing under a towering crag, almost a cliff, the face of it showing above the trees. "We go up into the rocks soon." We were on the level here, the going easier. I had got my second wind and I began thinking about the future, remembering the map and all the miles of semi-desert surrounding this range of mountains. The canopy thinned and I saw Abe's face looking drawn, his thin shoulders bowed and his breath coming in quick shallow gasps. "You all right?" I asked him.

"Fine," he said, and managed a smile. "Not as young as you, that's all, and CBS never gave us time off for physical training."

We were round the base of the cliff, the rock curving away to a dark cleft, and there was the sound of water. It came from the thin trickle of a stream falling over green-slimed rocks to a pool edged with ferns that elephants had trampled, the marks of their feet everywhere and lumps of dung. We waded into the pool, drinking the water as it came fresh down the rocks. It was clear and beautifully cool, and when we had finished drinking we splashed it over our faces, cleaning off the dried salt crust of our sweat.

Karanja drank only sparingly, then began searching the ground with his torch.

"Any sign of them?" Abe asked.

He shook his head and straightened up. "Too many elephants."

"How far now?"

"Not far."

"And you still think he's holed up on the mountain here?" Abe's voice sounded doubtful. "It's a hell of a way to the lugga where he stopped the cull."

"Eight miles maybe. Is nothing." Karanja was beside us, the rifle slung, his hands reaching for a grip on the slimy rocks. "We go up now." He began to climb, feeling for footholds. The rocks formed a slippery staircase that went up at an angle of about forty-five degrees. Burdened with cameras and our bags, it took us a long time to gain the top, where it flattened out after about two hundred feet to a series of shallow rock pools in a steep-sided gulley. It was almost dark, the moon hidden by a black pinnacle of rock, the gulley narrowing to a cleft and the thin whisper of water falling. All round us were the shapes of fallen rocks, everything dark and no breath of wind.

Karanja, probing with his torch, suddenly bent down. "Angalia!" He was pointing, and though he had spoken quietly the whisper of his voice came back to us from the surrounding cliffs, an eerie echo in the gloom. It was difficult to make out what he was exclaiming over. "That stone—is dislodged. See the mark of his heel. There—is a toe." It required a good deal of imagination to interpret those faint marks in the gravel, but Karanja seemed satisfied. "One man wearing boots, another with bare feet. Now we know he has been here."

I stared round the jumble of fallen rocks, remembering how Mtome had materialised out of the bush the first time I had visited van Delden. Just over a week ago. It seemed an age, and Mtome had moved so silently. "Where?" I whispered, the hairs crawling on the back of my neck at the thought of a shot crashing into us from the shadows. "Where's the hide-out?"

Karanja shook his head. "Is difficult," he breathed, staring off into the darkness. High above us a pinnacle of rock gleamed white against the stars and the moon-pale sky. But the cleft was a black abyss, shut in and full of the whisper of water as it fell down some hidden rock face. "Is higher, I think. When we capture that poacher we approach it from above."

"That's quite a climb," Abe said, staring up to where the V of the cleft showed on the skyline high above us.

Karanja nodded.

"But you brought him out this way."

"Ndio." He hesitated, then said, "You stay here please." And he left us, moving deeper into the cleft, his shadowy outline merging into the rocks until suddenly I couldn't see him any more. A moment later he called softly, the murmur of his voice whispering among the rocks, giving his name and ours too. I think he spoke in two different languages, for he repeated the names. After that there was a long silence.

"He's not there," Abe said wearily.

"Well, if he's not there," I said, "there's no point in our whispering like a bunch of conspirators." The place was getting on my nerves and only one way to settle it. "Mr. van Delden!" I shouted, and the cliffs were still repeating Delden as I announced who we were and why we had come. "There's a patrol coming to get you in the morning. We came to warn you. Mary asked us to." The echo of my words died away, then silence, only the sound of water. There was no reply.

"Pity," Abe murmured, disappointment in his voice. "If we could have gone with him—" A boulder moved in the stream bed behind us and I turned, my eyes straining into darkness. But nothing moved. A hand gripped my arm and Karanja said, "You make too much noise. Is dangerous if patrol is close behind us."

"What's it matter?" I said. "He's not here."

"For you, no. Is no matter. But for me . . ." The uncertainty in his voice and the shifting movement of his eyes in that dim light made me realise how much he had risked leading us up here. Abe realised it, too. "I'm sorry," he said. "You were hoping to join him, weren't you?"

Karanja nodded.

"And now?"

There was a long silence. Then Karanja said, "Now I must try to find him." And he added in a whisper, "Is nothing else for me to do."

"Where do you reckon he is then?"

He hesitated. "I think maybe he is waiting for tomorrow's hunt, out in the desert towards Kulal."

"That's quite a way." Abe sounded doubtful. "Perhaps if we rest here, get some sleep—"

Karanja shook his head. "Is necessary I go fast. In the morning there is more Army, more patrols. Is impossible for you."

Abe put his camera down beside his grip and sat himself on the rocks. "Okay, so you leave us here and go on alone. Is that it?"

He nodded, standing there, hesitant, staring up at the black V of the cleft. "Is what I must do." He said it reluctantly, unwilling to accept that van Delden had left and he had committed himself to no purpose. Then he turned to us again. "You will be safe here. In the morning, when the patrol come, tell the sergeant please I go back to Nairobi."

"Will he believe that?" I asked.

"Maybe." He sounded doubtful. "But tell him please." And then he said. "I go now. Goodbye, Mr. Finkel. Happy to have met you."

"I could say that I insisted on your guiding us here," Abe murmured.

"Is no good, not after I lose the minibus."

"That was my fault."

But he shook his head. "They do not believe that." He gripped Abe's hand, then mine, and a moment later he was gone. The flicker of his torch showed for an instant as he searched for the first footholds leading down over the lip of the watercourse, then it disappeared and we were alone. "Poor devil!" Abe murmured. "All those years with van Delden . . ." He shook his head. "And if he finds him, what then? What's the future for a man who abandons the position he has reached in the hierarchy of this new régime in Africa?"

His words reminded me of that night journey to the Serengeti, how scared Karanja had been. And now he was on his own, trying to make his way alone across a desert in search of the man who had been a sort of god to him long ago in another age. "Why do you think he's doing it?" I asked. "Burning his boats like that. It doesn't make sense."

Abe laughed. "You always want to know why."

"Don't you?" I asked irritably. "You're a reporter. You must be curious."

"Oh sure. But logic and emotion . . ." He smiled and shook his head. "Man is a crazy, mixed-up creature and I have long since given up trying to rationalise his behaviour. D'you think he'll make it?" he asked. "On his own, and no water?"

"How the hell do I know?"

"You've read up on this country. You should have some idea. Have you brought that book with you?"

"Yes."

"I'd like to have another look at it when it's light."

"You'll wait here for the patrol then?"

"What else?"

"We'll be sent back under escort to Nairobi."

"Probably."

I sat there, feeling angry with myself. If I had stayed down there in the camp I could have been filming this morning. Something I could have sold, and like a bloody fool . . .

"Mr. Finkel." The voice, coming to us out of the darkness, was so quiet it was barely audible above the thin sound of water. "You're alone now, is that right?" A shadow moved, coming towards us. "Cornelius van Delden," it said.

The outline of his head was in silhouette against the stars, the beard and the long flowing hair showing white, the barrels of his rifle gleaming dully. He called softly into the darkness, giving instructions. "Now we must go out by a different route, and that will take longer." He glanced at his watch. "I was intending to leave at three and it's already past that." He hesitated and Abe got to his feet, facing him.

"Where were you planning to go?"

"There's a family of elephants must be kept moving or they'll be caught in the culling area. We ran into them at dusk browsing on some wild fig on the north shoulder of the Mara."

"And we met another bunch on the way up here," Abe said. "But there's nothing you can do about it now. You've killed two Africans and the Army is sending more troops."

But all van Delden said was, "Where did you meet this new lot?"

"Coming past the first outcrop about half a mile back."

"How many?"

"We didn't count."

"We've sighted thirty-seven so far. Three family groups with a few odd bulls tagging along. All going north. Were yours going north?"

Abe nodded. "And the tracks we've seen, they're all going north, too. But this is no time for you to be worrying about elephants. Your only hope is to get out of here." And he added, his voice suddenly urgent, "Make for the coast. That's the message Mary sent you."

Van Delden shook his head. "I've no intention of leaving now. Those elephants need me and I want to know where they're going. If I can keep them moving, get them clear of the culling area by dawn and then follow them . . ." He turned abruptly away, calling softly to Mukunga. And when the man appeared like a shadow at his side, fully equipped with rifle and bandolier, he spoke to him softly in his own language. The word *simba* was repeated several times, Mukunga nodding, a gleam of white teeth in the darkness. Then he had gone, disappearing down the rocks we had climbed, silent as a cat and moving fast. "Mukunga imitates a lion very well," van Delden said. "Bulls don't mind so much. But cows accompanied by their calves will keep away from lions. He'll get them moving, and he'll do it better on his own."

"And suppose he meets the patrol?" Abe's voice was suddenly angry. "Risking your own life, that's one thing, but sending a man out—"

"I know what I'm doing," van Delden said sharply. "It's you who are risking lives, coming here. . . . Why? Why did you come?"

"I told you, Mary asked us—"

"She's a fool, sending two men up here who know

189

nothing about Africa. And Karanja, why did he come?"

"God knows, since you let him believe you weren't here. But he said something about remembering the love he had for you, and because he'd told the patrol sergeant about this poacher's hideout—"

"Said that, did he?" Van Delden laughed softly to himself, adding harshly, "Silly bugger. He's Kimani's man now." He called to Mtome. "We'll get moving now, if you're ready. I'm afraid you'll find it pretty hard going. And we're out of grub. Have you got any food with you?"

Abe shook his head. "But you'll take us with you, will you?" There was a note of surprise in his voice.

"I can't very well leave you to tell the patrol Karanja was right. They're bound to have a good tracker with them." He started to move, but then hesitated, turning again to Abe. "About those elephants you ran into. They were cows, I take it?"

"I guess so. They had some young with them. But there was a lone bull following behind, a big gaunt-looking fellow." And Abe told him how Karanja had stood his ground when the bull charged.

"Damn fool thing." There was a grudging respect in his voice. "You could have been killed, all of you."

"I don't think so," Abe murmured. "He seemed to know what he was doing, and the bull wasn't sure of himself."

"You were lucky, that's all. At Marsabit, when I was there, you could do a thing like that and not much danger. The elephants were safe and they knew it. But here, after all that's happened—" He shook his head. "Here all the elephants are driven by a desperate urge to get away from man. I've been charged three times already. You were damned lucky." He paused, and then, as though merely voicing his thoughts: "A bull, you say. There were bulls hanging around the family group we saw at dusk, another with the herd we stopped them culling." He seemed about to say something more, but then he turned. "Wait here." He went back into the rocks, calling softly to Mtome again and issuing orders.

I looked at Abe. "You going with him?"

He nodded, and I caught a gleam of excitement in his eyes. "It's what I came for."

"But if he attacks Kirby-Smith's outfit again . . ." I was thinking of the elephant at the Lodge. He could use us, as I suspected he was using Karanja. "You realise it was deliberate. He deliberately waited until Karanja had left on his own."

"Sure. What else do you expect after you'd shot your mouth off like that?"

"How do you mean?"

"You shouted it all round this gulley, that the patrol was on its way, and he knew at once there was only one man who could have told them about his poacher's hideout."

"So I'm to blame—is that what you're saying? It's my fault if Karanja gets killed."

"It doesn't matter." He had sat down again, leaning back, gazing up at the stars. "Heading north," he murmured. "The only migration I've read about was between the Tana River and what used to be Tanzania. That was years ago when there were big herds. But whether it was just the bulls—bulls range wider than cows. . . ." He seemed lost then in contemplation of an enigma that had no bearing on our situation.

"You don't seem to care that you're risking your life." The echo of my words sounded high and uneasy.

He smiled at me. "Scared?"

"Yes, but you're not. That's what I don't understand."

"No, that's right. I don't care very much." He turned slowly towards me, leaning on one elbow. "You can still go down that watercourse, back the way we came until you meet up with the patrol. So maybe I ought to tell you. My wife died, just over a year ago. It was a long, slow, painful end, and we were very close. After that—well, I guess, my view of life changed. You've never been in love, have you?"

"Of course I have."

"But not with one woman, over many years." His voice trailed off into silence.

"Haven't you any children?" I asked.

"No. And if we had, I don't know that it would have made any difference. They'd have been grown up by now. That's how long we were together." He leaned back again. "Well, there you are—that's as near as I can get to explaining why I'm here, why I'll go on with van Delden. You do what you like."

But then van Delden reappeared, Mtome beside him, and I no longer had any choice. "Time we left." He picked up Abe's bag, feeling the weight of it. "What's in it, film?"

Abe nodded. "Some clothes, too."

"Shirt, spare trousers, socks, towel, pullover, that's all you'll need."

"My camera is no good without film."

"We're travelling light."

"I guess that settles it then," Abe murmured, still sitting there on the rock and his voice obstinate. "I'm not leaving without my camera."

Van Delden stared at him a moment, then pushed my bag with his foot. "More film?" And when I told him what was in it, he added, "All right then. One camera and one bag with as much film as you think you can carry." He was turning away, but then he paused. "Didn't that Austrian count hunt elephant on the shores of Lake Rudolf? When was that? I can't remember."

"March 1888," I said.

"Just cows, or were there bulls, too?"

"Bulls and cows."

He nodded. "Interesting, providing he knew the difference. It's a long time since I read von Höhlen's account of that expedition. If it isn't too heavy bring it along. And the map, too." He went back into the rocks then, leaving Mtome standing over us while we packed everything into the one bag.

"Which camera?" Abe asked me. "I've never used a Beaulieu before, but I think it's lighter so maybe we should take that."

"Whichever you like." I think he was being kind, knowing the Beaulieu belonged to me personally, but at that moment I didn't care. I was in a gloomy mood now, convinced that we would never have the opportunity of filming anything. How could we, in the company of a man waging a sort of guerrilla war? We would be lucky if we got away with our lives. And yet he had agreed to our taking a camera. First Kirby-Smith, now van Delden—it was extraordinary how publicity-conscious these men were. Each seemed to have a need for his activities to be recorded.

We left Abe's Bolex, and a bag with our discarded clothing, hidden under some stones in a crevice. Then we went up into the rocks, to a niche above the poacher's cave where van Delden and Dima were busy obliterating all sign of footprints. And when they had swept the ground clean with a leafy branch, we left, clambering up a rock face that brought us out above the thin trickle of the waterfall. The time by my wrist-watch was just after three-thirty and the moon was lost behind the mountains across the valley.

It was all rock, the cliffs and peaks black above us, and we travelled fast, only the stars to light us, stumbling for footholds in the dark. The bag I was carrying became a leaden weight dragging at my shoulders. Once van Delden dropped back. "Want one of my men to carry it for you?" But I shook my head. They were already burdened with packs, blanket cloaks, water bottles, ammunition belts, and rifles.

"I'll be all right," I said, knowing that if we were going to make a film I would just have to get used to it. Abe, with only the camera to carry, was finding the going difficult enough.

Shortly after that we began to descend and soon we were clear of rock and into the cedars again, following some sort of a game trail. It was very dark, the descent steep as we dropped down on to the northern shoulder of the range. Here van Delden left us, taking Mtome with him. He gave no explanation, merely saying, "Dima will look after you now. He knows where to go." The forest swallowed them and we were alone with Dima, who said urgently, "We go quick now. In little time is day."

"Where are we going?" I asked him.

But he walked on, not answering, and Abe, beside me, said, "The question is, where's van Delden gone?"

"To join Mukunga, I imagine."

But he seemed doubtful. "If it was that, why didn't he go with him at the start?"

Dima hissed at us to be quiet and we stumbled on through the dark in silence. Gradually the forest thinned, gave way to a mixed growth that dwindled into bush as the first glimmer of light showed in the east. It was over half an hour since van Delden had left us and as the ground became easier Dima increased the pace. For a while I was barely conscious of the improving visibility, then dawn came in a rush and we could see the whole sweep of the Nyiru Range rearing peaks of bare rock on the far side of the Horr Valley. Ahead of us the land sloped to the desert brown of sand and gravel, and far ahead, where the horizon merged with the milk-pale sky, I thought I could see the top of Kulal.

We came off the shoulder of the mountain into dry scrub country dotted with thorn and acacia, and here we saw a zebra the moran had failed to kill. It was a Grévy's zebra, the type peculiar to this arid northern territory. It had a large head and neck, and the stripes were closer. It stood watching us curiously until we came within its flight range, then it cantered off, pausing occasionally to look back at us. There was a sparkle in the air now and a freshness I had not felt since arriving in Africa.

We crossed a lugga fringed with trees and shrubs, their leaves drooping from lack of moisture. Probably the same lugga we had been in the night before, but further east. Dima had lengthened his stride, the going good over hard sandy gravel, and no sound except a few bird calls. We passed the thorn skeleton of an old manyata and I wondered what van Delden was up to and whether Mukunga would get those elephants past the culling area in time. Kirby-Smith would be leaving camp now and soon the plane would be in the air. "We should be able to see the plane when it takes off," I said.

Abe turned, looking back at me. "If we can see it, then the pilot will be able to see us." His face looked drawn and tired, dark shadows under his eyes.

"Maybe that's what van Delden wants."

He gave me a wan smile. "Maybe." And we pushed on, silent again, walking in a pale, cool light that was the interregnum between night and day. But it was brightening all the time and then suddenly the sun pushed a great shield of burnished red up into the eastern sky, and instantly the land flared with colour. From the flat sepia of desert gravel it turned to a dried blood hue in which everything glistened with light, scrub and thorn and skittering birds all brilliant with the great red glow of heat to come. It was fantastic, breathtaking, and all because I was seeing it on foot, not riding in the dust cloud of a line of trucks. And it was in that fantastic sunrise flare that I saw the neck of a giraffe stuck up like a post and peering at us over wait-a-bit thorn. I wanted to stop then, enjoy this moment of startling beauty, but Dima hurried on.

The giraffe moved, became four, thin long necks and sloping bodies shining in panels of rich dark red separated by variegated lines of white as though a wide-meshed net had been flung over them. They stood in a bunch watching us, then trotted off with a rolling, camel-like gait that changed for a moment into a supremely graceful gallop that disturbed a family of ostrich. "Reticulata," Abe breathed as though making a mental note. He paused for a moment to stare after them, then trudged wearily on, his shoulders bent.

We were climbing now, the land sloping gently upward, the heat increasing rapidly. Blood pounding in my ears and both of us tired, walking on and on in a daze, gravel and sand glaring in the sun and dust devils beginning to form. And then, from the top of a rise, we had our first sight of the lava that lay ahead,

195

a great wall of it like a railway embankment, black in shadow with not a tree or a shrub, nothing growing. Beyond it, bright in the sunlight, were what appeared to be slag heaps and old mining tips. "Is where we go," Dima said, pointing to the formidable embankment of lava. "We find spring there."

"It'll be dry," Abe told him, and the African nodded. "Dry." He paused, his face glistening black and frowning as he stared northwards. "One day it rain again." He said it hopefully, but without conviction. "After rain desert very good."

The humped back of Kulal lay on the horizon like a stranded whale and in the clarity of that early light the green of forest showed a glint of emerald below the pink-white cloud suspended over the summit.

It was while we were still standing there, staring at the desolation ahead, that, faint on the morning stillness, came the sound of a shot. It came from our left, a sharp thin sound, followed by another and another. And then a wisp of smoke curled up as though somebody far to the west of us had lit a bonfire. I looked at Abe. "What is it, another truck?" Surely to God the man wouldn't have tried the same thing twice.

"Not a truck," Abe said quietly. "The plane, I think."

Dima seized hold of the bag, wrenching it from me. "We go quick." He said it urgently, shouldering the bag and breaking into a long loping stride.

"It has—to be—the plane," Abe grunted. "Those elephant . . ." But he was trotting now and had no breath for talk. I took the camera from him and as we went down the northward slope first Kulal and then the lava ridge dropped from view, our horizon closing in. Ten minutes later we encountered the first of the lava, an area of crumbled, perforated rock that forced us to a walk, picking our way and balancing precariously on shifting lumps of volcanic magma. More gravel interspersed with lava incursions, then the gravel became isolated patches and soon we were into nothing but lava, an incredible brown waste, all rounded boulders, through which we moved laboriously, the embankment black in shadow and rising up ahead of us like a slice of the industrial revolution painted by a madman.

Never in my life had I seen such a country, a hellish misery of moonscape rubble that looked as though great slabs of chocolate had been put through a grinder, then flung with wild abandon by giant hands across the face of the earth. And the embankment, when we finally reached it, was a crumbling wall of shattered metallic rock, so shot through with holes that it had the appearance of a fire-blackened row of office blocks badly shelled and falling into ruin. We moved slowly along the petrified base of it, feeling our way like crabs along the edge of a reef, and though we were in shadow the heat was overpowering. Twice Abe fell and it was only the fact that he had his hands free that saved him; the second time he grazed a knee, tearing a hole in his trousers. We were half an hour covering less than a mile, the shadows hardening as the sun struck with growing fierceness on the lava field to produce a blinding glare that hurt the eyes. Dima was well ahead of us then. I stumbled, just saving myself, and when I looked up again he had vanished. Far away to our left a stunted thorn tree stood on its head, the first mirage of the day's heat. He was nowhere to be seen and I had a sudden crazy feeling that the lava had swallowed him up. Then he was there again, beckoning us on, and he no longer had the bag in his hand, only his rifle.

It was a great cleft in the lava cliff and he was waiting for us at the entrance. "Stay now till Tembo come." The cleft was deep, a dark gash in the fault line, and at the back of it brown grit like a very coarse sand overlaid the crumbled rock. It was cool by comparison with the temperature outside. Abe flung himself down, his thin chest heaving, his mouth open, panting with exhaustion.

"Where's the water?" I asked Dima.

"Dry now. All dry. He pointed to where he had dug with his hands in the grit. The hollow was cool to my touch, but bone dry.

197

"So what do we do now? Where do we get water?"

"Sleep now," he said.

I felt the dryness of my lips with my tongue, staring at the water bottle at his belt. But when I asked him to give us some, he shook his head. "No drink. When Tembo come—"

"We want a drink now."

"No drink," he repeated obstinately. I stared at the bottle thirstily, knowing it was no good. He had his orders and that could only mean van Delden knew bloody well there wasn't any water now between here and Rudolf.

"How far to the lake?"

He shrugged. "For this man—" He nodded to Abe, who was lying back, his eyes closed. "Too far, I think."

I sat down and leaned my back against the rough metallic surface of the rock. A wave of tiredness swept over me. And if I was tired . . . "You all right?" I asked Abe. There was no reply and I saw he had fallen asleep, his mouth open and his tongue showing dark and rough. I closed my eyes and in an instant I too was asleep.

I woke to the moan of wind and a gritty sifting of sand in the cleft. Dima was squatting in the entrance, his rifle wrapped in his cloak and his eyes slitted. Beyond him the lava glare was subdued, nothing visible, a sepia haze of windblown sand. The moaning died, the glare increasing as the sand subsided until the walls of the cleft framed an eye-searing glimpse of heat-hazed rubble. No shade now, the sun striking down almost vertically and my body parched. I glanced at my watch, surprised to find that it was already past eleven. I had slept for almost two hours.

The moaning started up again, but distant now like the far-away roar of an express train. "That damned wind," Abe murmured.

"How long has it been going on?" I asked.

"About an hour, I guess. It comes and goes."

I nodded, seeing his cracked lips, feeling dehydrated myself. God, the sun was hot!

"What's happened to van Delden?"

198

He shook his head, a minuscule movement as though even that were too much of an effort. I leaned back against the rock, trying to visualise what it would be like driving wild elephants into the teeth of a sand-storm, remembering von Höhlen's description of hur-ricane winds roaring down off Kulal. If only it would rain. I closed my eyes against the glare, hearing the murmur of his voice as he said, "In two hours we'll have shade again."

"You think he'll come?"

Abe didn't answer and when I looked at him again he had his towel over his head to keep off the sun. Through narrowed eyes I looked out across the field of lava to where the wind was spiralling sand high into the air. "This evening," I said, "when it's cooler and no wind, we'll have to try and make it to Sirima. There's a waterhole there."

"How far?"

But it wasn't a question of distance. I tried to ex-plain the sort of terrain we would have to cross, but I couldn't remember how long Teleki had taken. Four hours, a whole day? I couldn't remember and I hadn't the energy to get the book out and look it up. "There's a moon," I murmured. "A night's march—"

"Forget it," he said. "It'll be dry like this place."

"There's always the lake."

"Forget it, I tell you." His voice had risen to a sharper pitch. "No elephants can live in this sort of country and I am not going where there are no ele-phants."

"There were elephants on Lake Rudolf when Teleki was there, lots of them."

"Bugger Teleki," he snapped. "You're always quot-ing Teleki. It's nearly a hundred years ago. The cli-mate has changed. Everything has changed. And if van Delden doesn't come I'm going back."

I looked at Dima. "Are there elephants on the shores of Lake Rudolf?" I asked him.

He shook his head, frowning, and I didn't know whether it was because he didn't understand or whether he was saying there were no elephants. "We'll decide when it gets cooler," I muttered.

"Do what you like," Abe said petulantly, and hid his head in his towel again as another moaning holocaust of wind drove sand into the cleft.

I must have dozed off, for when I opened my eyes again it was with a jerk and the instant knowledge that Dima was gone from his watchdog post. I forced myself up and went to the entrance. No wind and the sun directly overhead. The reflected glare of the lava was worse than any studio's arc lights. It was eye-blinding and for a moment I could see nothing except sand moving a long way off and carrying with it the faint murmur of the wind. No sign of Kulal. It was hidden in a sepia haze. I shaded my eyes, straining south to where something shimmered in the heat. Bushes, trees—or were they moving? I wasn't sure. They merged and became one, separated into three—no five—all blurred, and then they started to run.

It took me a moment to realise they were ostrich, longer to work out that something had disturbed them. They were at least a mile and a half away, out beyond the lava where the first of the scrub showed as a wavering reed-like fringe. A man appeared, clear and sharp, and the shape of him was instantly shattered by the heat, a sand devil twisting up at the very spot where I had seen him.

"What is it?"

I turned to find Abe coming out into the entrance and when I looked again the sand devil was gone and there were two men, not one. "Van Delden," I said. "At least, I think it is. Dima has gone to meet him." I had seen Dima now, standing motionless at the far end of the lava wall, the dark of his body merged with the rock. A brown haze of airborne sand was flowing to the west of us and the sun bore down like a furnace.

"I wonder what he's done with those elephants," Abe murmured.

The figures moved in slow motion, crawling across the shimmering edge of visibility towards Dima and the lava wall. A breeze touched my face, the sand haze moving closer, the sound of it rising, and we went back into the torrid sun-trapped heat of the cleft, wrapping our towels round our faces. But this time it did not reach us, and when we went out into the entrance again I could see them quite clearly, Dima hurrying back ahead of them.

He was panting when he reached us, sweat glistening on his forehead. "Tembo say you go in." And he pushed us back into the cleft. A few minutes later van Delden arrived, Mtome close behind him. They flopped down, both of them exhausted, and I was shocked to see how deep the lines of van Delden's face showed under his beard. "What happened?" I asked.

He didn't answer for a moment, wiping his face on the sleeve of his bush jacket. Then he leaned back against the rock and closed his eyes, a pair of binoculars still slung round his neck, his rifle propped up beside him. "There was a guard on the plane, of course, and the damned fool had sat himself in the cockpit. Gone to sleep there and he didn't get out until he heard the Land-Rover coming in from the South Horr camp. It was Alex's partner, Jeff Suanders, and he had four soldiers with him." His voice was thick, almost a croak. "Didn't give us much time. We hit the plane and ran. We had to backtrack as far as the stream and wade up it. Only way I could be sure of shaking them off. A hell of a trek."

"Why wait for the guard to get out?" Abe asked.

Van Delden's eyes flicked open. "He might have been killed, that's why. The poor devil wasn't there because he liked it. He was a soldier, not a hunter."

Abe shook his head, smiling at such a fine distinction. "Where's Mukunga?" he asked.

"Still on the shoulder of the Mara with those elephants."

"Will they be all right?"

"I think so. With no plane it will take time to locate them. Too late to set up a proper cull. And if they do catch up with them it'll be dangerous stalking.

Those elephants had Mukunga making lion noises at them all night. They'll be thoroughly roused and in an angry mood." He closed his eyes again, breathing deeply, his belly moving in and out in a controlled exercise of the diaphragm.

"There's no water here," Abe said.

"No. I hardly expected there would be."

"So what do we do now?"

"Wait for Mukunga. He knows where to join us."

"Yes, but what then? Where do we go from here?"

"Sirima, the lake, Balesa Kulal—wherever those elephants are going." He looked across at me. "Have you got that book? I'd like to check what von Höhlen says about the elephants they shot on the shores of Lake Rudolf. It was the east shore, wasn't it?"

"Yes, but when they discovered the lake, they were approaching it from the Nyiru Range, not from where we are now." I got the book out of the bag and handed it to him. "If I remember rightly they found two herds of elephants just south of the lake, then nothing till they were north of Mt. Longondoti."

He nodded. "Elephants would never move into the lava country under Kulal."

Then how would they get up to the Longondoti area?"

"They would have come south along the lake shore from Abyssinia. But if they were going north, like the ones we've been following, then they've either got to cross Kulal or else follow the bed of the Balesa Kulal up the east side of the mountain. There's usually water there under the surface, but I don't think there'll be any now, not after the drought." He had opened the book and I watched him as he pulled a pair of steel-rimmed half-glasses from his haversack, marvelling at the man's stamina. He had been on the go most of the night and half the day and he still had the energy to check on von Höhlen's book.

The wind sound rose, sand driving against the lava edges of the cleft, and we lay curled up, our heads covered. This time it kept on blowing for a long time and even when the sound of it finally subsided I remained where I was, locked tight inside myself, wondering what the night would bring, where we would be tomorrow. I didn't dare think further ahead than that, committed now to the company of this old man and his strange obsession. Once, when I pushed the towel away from my face, I saw him still propped up against the rock, but his eyes were closed, book and glasses lying on the ground beside him. The others were asleep, too, and I dozed off to memories of Battersea Park in summertime and the shade of trees.

Surfacing at last, I found the sun had shifted, striking obliquely across the cleft, so that we were in shadow. Van Delden had the book in his hands again and was making notes. He looked across at me over his glasses. "You were right," he said. "Two herds of elephant just south of the lake on the edge of the lava country. After that, nothing till Longondoti, and then it was a young bull he encountered." He searched back through the pages. "That was March 17. Five days later Teleki refrained from shooting a herd of—'*six females with five little ones of different ages . . . the Count brought down a rhinoceros and we heard lions roaring in the night.*' That's on the shore of Alia Bay. Later the same day Teleki bags five elephants. He was firing so furiously he ran out of ammunition and had to send to camp for more. Two herds were involved, one of six cows with young, the other five full-grown bulls. As you said, bulls and cows, and both on the shore and in the water." He leaned back. "I can't remember ever hearing before of elephants browsing on seaweed."

I had shifted my position, for I found it difficult to follow him, tiredness accentuating his peculiar accent. "There was a bull browsing on weed," I murmured. "It smashed the canoe they'd carried up from the coast."

"He doesn't say it was a bull, and he doesn't say it was eating the stuff." He looked down at the book again. "He just says it was *quietly rooting up seaweed*'—he means lakeweed, of course. Later—" He searched the next few pages. "Later he meets up with

203

'a great many elephants—first two, then four gigantic beasts with huge tusks; then a herd of twelve bulls, four of which were very old; then three young bulls, with tusks reaching to the ground; and lastly, a herd of fourteen animals bigger than any we had yet met with.' And the only comment he makes at a sight like that is to tot up the value of the ivory!" He gave that strange laugh of his, half bark, half grunt, then turned the page and said: "Ah, this is what I was looking for: Wednesday, March 28—'During the afternoon a herd of female elephants with young ones went down into the lake near the camp, and remained for a long time standing still with water up to their bellies, rooting up seaweed with their trunks, from which they shook the water before eating it.'" He closed the book with a snap. "The man's too dull a writer to have made it up." And he added wearily, "But there's no weed in this part of the lake and Alia Bay is almost a hundred miles to the north beyond Mt. Longondoti and Jarigole."

"There's Loiyangalani," I said. "That's marked on the map as an oasis."

He nodded. "There's always water there. It comes down from Mt. Kulal, down the great gorge. There's a track runs from the Horr Valley to Loiyangalani built by the missionaries. But even if it has survived the war, and hasn't been destroyed by earth tremors, it's still no good to elephants. They wouldn't like it. Goes through the most Godforsaken country, nothing but lava and old volcanic vents." He stared out into the blinding glare. "No, my guess is they're going to pass Kulal to the east. They'll make for the dry bed of the Balesa Kulal and if they can't find water there, then the only hope is to try and drive them towards the track that leads up the shoulder of Kulal, past the Mission and into the forest." He shook his head. "Not easy, but we'll have to try it. Alex can't cull there, too far and the forest too thick. At least, it used to be thick. I dont know what it's like now."

"It's still green on top," I said. "You can see it."

He was silent for a while, then he looked at his

204

watch. "Nearly two. Better try and sleep now. We'll have food and water in three hours' time, start moving again at five-thirty. See if we can find Mukunga before it's dark." He put his glasses away, laid the book on top of our bag, and, stretching himself out, was instantly asleep.

I sat there for a while, thinking about what he had said and gradually resigning myself to the certainty that I would never get to the great rock pyramid of Porr. So near. I picked up von Höhlen's book, unfolding the flimsy map at the end with their route marked in red and the dates of each camp. The closest they had come to where we were now holed up was March 5 and it was March 13 before they had been skirting the lake under Mt. Porr. I folded the map up again and threw the book down in disgust. A big expedition with a herd of cattle for food and it had taken them over a week to cover less than fifty miles.

I lay down then and the next thing I knew there were voices and Mukunga was there, squatting beside van Delden, talking urgently. The words *ndovu* and *askari* were repeated several times. "What's happened?" I asked. Van Delden shook his head impatiently and they went on talking. Finally Mukunga moistened his mouth from his water bottle, curled up, and went to sleep. Abe stirred and asked for water. "Lie still," van Delden said, "and you won't need it."

"Mukunga's had water."

"He's been on the run, that's why. The patrol that was sent out after you picked up the elephant tracks and if they hadn't been diverted by their desire for meat they'd have got him. They shot a full-grown calf and are camped beside the carcase."

We left at the time he had said, having had a sip of water. The wind had died, the sun low in the west. Behind us Mt. Kulal was a great reddening sprawl, the forest on its top showing green, the cloudcap gone. Everything was very clear in that evening light. There was a family of ostrich waiting for us as we came off the last of the lava into scrub. Ten minutes later we came upon the tracks of a vehicle.

The sun was setting in a red glow behind us, colour flooding the desolate landscape, lighting up the face of the lava embankment away to our left so that it was brilliant with purples and greens and sulphurous streaks of yellow. Faint on the evening stillness came the sound of an engine revving. Van Delden said something to Mukunga and he went on ahead, loping up a rise topped by the ragged shape of a thorn. When we reached the thorn tree he was far down the further slope, running for the cover of a thorn thicket, and in the plain beyond a Land-Rover was raising a cloud of dust and a group of elephants was milling around in confusion.

There was no doubt what the Land-Rover was doing, as it turned, then turned again. It was trying to head the elephants off by driving back and forth across their line of march. Van Delden had halted, standing with his head thrust forward, staring angrily. "Too late," he muttered. "Another hour and they—" He stopped there, his body suddenly rigid. "Who's that?" A figure had emerged from the thicket, a man no bigger than a speck in the immensity of the rolling gravel plain. But even at that distance I could see that he was an African, and he carried a rifle in his hand. He was running—running towards the elephants. "Who is it?" van Delden said again, and raised his binoculars to his eyes.

I turned to Abe, a sudden thought in my mind. He had the camera to his face and was looking through the eyepiece. "Can you see?" I asked him, but he shook his head.

"Can't be one of the hunters," van Delden murmured. "They'd never risk their lives on foot, not with all those elephants, and they're thoroughly roused now."

The Land-Rover had turned again, the sound of it overlaid by squeals and trumpeting. Then suddenly there was only the sound of the Land-Rover. The elephants had closed up in a tight bunch, several calves in the centre so that they were completely lost to view in the packed mass of grey backs and wide-spread

206

ears. They were all facing the Land-Rover, and behind them the African was approaching them, trotting now and moving out to the flank.

The grip was suddenly wrenched from my hand and Abe zipped it open, burrowing around to produce the telescopic lens. "Light's not good, but worth a try." He was tense with excitement, his hands trembling as he changed the lenses. And at that moment the shot came, the sound of it clear in the sudden stillness, the silent, frightened herd, standing like sculptured figures, motionless. Mukunga was only halfway to the thicket, standing now, his rifle still slung across his shoulder, staring at the tight-packed elephants and the Land-Rover's dust stream. It could only be the unknown African who had fired, but I couldn't see him. It was as though the desert had swallowed him up. There was not a tree, not even any scrub in which he could have hidden himself.

Another shot, and then another, and suddenly the Land-Rover was swerving, half out of control.

The elephants had all swung round, trunks weaving, seeking the new source of danger. No trumpeting now, everything silent, even the Land-Rover stopped. I saw him then, lying prone, the rifle out in front of him, his body merged into the sunset red of the desert gravel. In that stillness we could just hear the Land-Rover's engine ticking over. The elephants heard it, too, and it distracted them from the lone figure lying so close to them. They turned, the sound of the engine drawing them like a magnet, and suddenly one of them moved out ahead of the herd, trumpeting loudly. The next instant the dust was flying from its feet and it was charging with its head up and its trunk curled below its tusks. I heard the soft whirr of the camera and then it was lost in the revving of the Land-Rover's engine as it began to move, heading in our direction, but slowly, jerkily, its wheels spinning and throwing up streamers of red dust. The elephant was gaining on it fast, and it wasn't a mock charge. It was the real thing. "What the hell's wrong?" I breathed, and Abe close

207

beside me answered through clenched teeth, "They've got a flat."

The Land-Rover stopped, I think to engage four-wheel drive, and Abe still had the camera turning when the elephant reached it, lowering its head and ramming its tusks into the rear of the vehicle. It pushed it forward perhaps twenty yards, head down and flanks heaving, the man in the passenger seat struggling to turn round, a rifle in his hand. The elephant lifted its head, tearing its tusks free, slamming them into it again and trumpeting in a fury of rage. Then it got a grip and was lifting the Land-Rover up off its back wheels, heaving and growling at it. For a moment I thought it would toss the whole thing over on to its nose, but the man with the gun at last managed to turn into a kneeling position and the crack of the shot seemed to stop everything dead, the animal standing there and the Land-Rover still up-ended, engine roaring and rear wheels spinning. Then the ears folded slowly back, the head and shoulders sagged, and as the elephant sank to its knees, the wheels got a grip and with a rending of metal the Land-Rover jerked forward.

The driver must have seen us now, for the vehicle was heading straight up the rise towards us, grinding slowly in four-wheel drive and bumping over loose stones, riding on the rim of a flat rear wheel. Through the haze of its dust I could see the dead elephant lying motionless like a great grey rock, and beyond it, the rest of the herd, half hidden in their own dust cloud, milled around, the sound of their squealing and growling coming to us as a distant, confused din, like the roar of a panicking crowd.

The Land-Rover topped the rise and in the last of the sun I saw Mary driving, and Kirby-Smith, beside her, with his hand on the wheel, trying to turn it away from us. Then it stopped, the engine gently ticking over, everything silent, even the elephants quiet. Nobody said anything, Kirby-Smith sitting there, his face caked in dust and sweat, and van Delden standing with his head thrust forward, staring.

"Leave your rifle and get out." Van Delden started to move slowly forward, Mary and Kirby-Smith still sitting there, watching him as though stunned. Her face was drained of blood and white under the tan. She pushed her goggles up, glancing at the man beside her, eyes wide and scared-looking. Her lips moved and in answer to the whisper of her words he shook his head, climbing slowly out and standing there, facing van Delden, his gun left on the seat behind him.

Slowly he pulled off his goggles, staring at van Delden, the white of his teeth showing in a smile, a conscious effort to appear casual. "You might have killed us."

"Maybe I will next time," van Delden said quietly, "But it wasn't any of my men fired those shots."

"Who was it then?"

Van Delden shrugged. He had reached the Land-Rover, his eyes on Mary sitting there behind the wheel. "After all I've taught you!" His voice was thick and angry. "Get out of there."

She shook her head, staring at him dumbly.

I thought for a moment he was going to tear her bodily out of the driving seat. "Get out," he said again, and it was obvious from the tone of his voice that he couldn't bear the sight of her sitting there in Kirby-Smith's Land-Rover. "Stop playing the fool with this man."

Her mouth opened, her eyes suddenly wide and appalled. "You think that? You think because my mother—"

"Shut up!"

The harshness of his voice was like a slap on the face, and she shrank back, her hands clenched on the steering wheel, her body rigid, the two of them staring at each other. Then he turned to Kirby-Smith. "I brought her up to respect life." He moved a few paces forward then, till they stood face to face. "Now I'm warning you, Alex," he said, speaking slowly. "I'll do anything, anything at all. . . ."

"You've done quite enough already." Kirby-Smith's voice was high and angry. "Yesterday it was a truck and two men dead. This morning you shoot up my plane. That can't go on."

"Why not? Do you think I'll give up." And then he leaned his great head forward, his voice gentler, almost reasonable. "Even you must have realised there is something strange about this movement of elephants northwards. You must have noticed their condition. I've seen two of them dying on their feet. And though they're exhausted, they don't stop. Even you and your hunters don't turn them back. They keep on coming, in family groups that are small and unbalanced. Haven't you noticed? Cows and bulls all mixed up. They've lost most of the very old and the very young. Only a few calves left. It's a pitiable sight. I've been following them now for three days, observing them. They're all converging here, so that I have the feeling this is some sort of a gateway to a place they know about. Is that your observation? You've had planes flying. You must know far more about their movements than I do." He paused, staring at Kirby-Smith. "Well? Am I right? Are these the last sad remnants coming together in their effort to find a place of safety?"

Kirby-Smith hesitated, and I got the impression he was trying to work out in his mind how best to meet this long outburst. "They certainly seem to be converging—"

"Little groups from all over this part of Africa. All that's left."

"I wouldn't say that." And he added quickly, trying hard to maintain a casual reasonable air, "Really, you know, it's quite impossible to be sure of the exact distribution and numbers of the elephant population. There may be more left than you think."

Van Delden nodded, fingering his beard. "It's a nice, comforting thought. I'd like to think you're right. But I've lived in the company of elephants long enough to sense when something unusual is happening, and I tell you, Alex, what you're witnessing here is a quite extraordinary migration. It may be this is the last time these great animals will move over the face

210

of Africa in large enough numbers for them to make a pattern." And he added, still speaking quietly and with great intensity, "They were nearly wiped out once before. It took the fall of the Roman Empire to save them that time—because the trade routes that took the ivory to the East were cut. Almost as though the country closed in to protect its own. But this time—".

"I think you exaggerate."

"I hope I do. But when the last of the bisons stood before the hunters, they didn't know it was the last."

"I assure you I have no intention of shooting them all. I made that clear at the Conference. I've always stuck to my quota—"

"Your quota!" Van Delden gave that harsh laugh. "You'll do what Kimani tells you and if I know that little man it's ivory he's interested in. Like you, he's a businessman, and when there's no more ivory, no more elephants, then you'll start in on any other profitable species that hasn't been wiped out, until one day you'll be down to a quota for warthogs." He stared at him for a moment, then said quietly, "You've a long walk ahead of you, so better get going."

It took a moment for Kirby-Smith to realise what he meant. Then his gaze shifted to the Land-Rover. I could see him measuring the distance, considering the time it would take him to jump in and get clear. Van Delden saw it, too. "Just stay where you are, Alex. I need a vehicle, so I'm borrowing yours. And I'm taking Mary with me."

"That's for her to decide." His eyes were still on the Land-Rover. "Taking my Land-Rover won't get you far," he said. "As for the culling, you can't stop me. I've got a Government contract and the support of the Army. You can't take on the Army."

"Up here I can do anything." Van Delden said it slowly in a tone of absolute conviction. "I know this country. You don't." He turned then, calling to Dima to get the wheel changed, and then he reached into the Land-Rover, picked up the discarded rifle, emptying it of ammunition and throwing it into the back. He came back then to face Kirby-Smith again, saying

211

quietly, almost conversationally, "I've nothing to lose, you know. Nothing at all. I don't set great store by my life in the Seychelles. I only went there when they kicked me out of Africa because it was handy, not because I liked it. But you . . . you've always managed your life so much more cleverly than I have. You've got plenty to lose, haven't you? Everything you've built up over the years."

Kirby-Smith gave a little shrug, and after that they didn't say anything, the two of them standing facing each other while Dima got the jack out of the back of the Land-Rover and slid it under the rear axle. The sun had set and down in the darkening plain the elephants had gone. Nothing stirred and there was no sign of the African who had fired those shots.

"Give Dima a hand, will you," van Delden said to me, not shifting his gaze from Kirby-Smith, and I got to work on jacking up the vehicle, glad of something to do. Mary was still sitting there, a lost, frozen look on her face. But in the end she got out and helped me get the spare wheel down. I think she felt the need of something to occupy her mind.

Dima had obviously done this many times before. It didn't take us long to get the wheel off, darkness already closing in as I hefted it up on to the bracket at the rear. Its rim was badly dented, the outer case cut to shreds. Behind me I heard Kirby-Smith talking to Abe, trying to persuade him to get van Delden to see sense. "More troops arrived in camp this morning and the Army now has two patrols out. They've already found the minibus and it's only a matter of time—"

"You could stop the cull," Abe said mildly.

"You saw what he did yesterday. Two men killed."

"I'm just a newsman."

"You saw it. You're a witness."

"They were shot, yes. I saw that. But I didn't see who shot them."

"I shot them," van Delden growled.

Kirby-Smith started to say something, then checked himself, turning to Abe again. "Tomorrow the Army are sending up another plane. He hasn't a hope—"

212

"Oh, sure," Abe said. "He hasn't a hope, as you say. But he'll do it, just the same."

"Then stop him. You heard what he just said. You're a witness to that."

Abe shook his head, smiling. "I didn't hear anything. You see, Major, I don't go along with what you're doing, so don't expect me to hold your hand."

We were tightening the wheel nuts and Mary was standing close beside me, just standing there, watching them, her eyes staring, the pale oval of her face devoid of expression, her body tense. I could guess what she was feeling, all hell let loose inside her in a conflicting tide of loyalties and emotions. From the rear of the Land-Rover came the scrape of metal as Dima pulled the jack clear. Kirby-Smith heard it, too. "Be sensible, Cornelius. All this part of the Federation is under Brigadier Osman and his Army Brigade." He was making a conscious effort to appear reasonable. "The old days are gone. They're gone for good. Taking my Land-Rover—" He hesitated, then said, "Tell you what I'll do. I shouldn't, but for old times' sake I'll tank up with fuel and drive you through to Marsabit. From there you should have a chance of reaching the coast."

"And what about the elephants?" Van Delden laughed. "No. You want a deal, you know my terms."

"I told you, I'm under contract. I can't break that."

"You mean you don't want to. That's understandable, since I hear you worked very hard to get it." He thrust his great white-maned head forward. "But it's a contract you can't fulfil. You tell them that." He stood like that for a moment with his head thrust out, and then he said, "I don't give a damn about my life. I've told you that. Or yours either. All I care about now is to see that enough of those elephants get through to wherever it is they're going. Then they'll be able to rest up, recover, breed, begin the long slow cycle all over again, building up their numbers. That's what's important, all I care about."

Kirby-Smith shook his head. "Your trouble is you've lived on your own too long. It's not what you want.

213

Not any more." His voice had risen, the need for self-justification very evident as he said, "It's what the people want now. The people and the Government of this new Federation . . ."

But van Delden had turned his back on him. "Dima." He jerked his head towards the driving seat, and as the African slid behind the wheel and started the engine, he came over to Mary and said, "Get in the back."

She shook her head, her eyes unnaturally bright. "I'm not coming."

"Get in."

"I'm not coming, I tell you." Her hands clenched tight on the clips that secured the bonnet, and when he reached out and took hold of her arm, she flung him off. "I'm not. I'm not." Her voice was high, on the edge of hysteria. "I wish to God I'd never asked them to warn you."

To my surprise he turned to me. "Get her in the back and keep her there." His voice was surprisingly gentle. He looked at Abe. "I take it you're coming with us."

"Sure I'm coming with you."

"Then get in. It'll be difficult to see their tracks soon."

The first stars were already showing in the night sky. I tried to take hold of Mary's arm, but she drew back from me, half turning towards her father, staring at him as he stood there. The others were already clambering into the Land-Rover and I thought I was going to have trouble, but then she suddenly turned and walked to the back of it with her head up and her face set, climbing in and seating herself close by the tailboard. As I joined her I heard Kirby-Smith say, "What about my gun? I'm not leaving without my gun."

Van Delden lookel at him. "Your gun. Of course." He reached into the back and picked it up by the barrel; then, standing back, he swung it up and brought the stock crashing down against the hub of the spare wheel. He handed it to him then without a word and got into the seat beside Dima.

214

I didn't hear what Kirby-Smith said, his words lost in the revving of the engine and the slam of the gears as we began to move. The lights came on and for a second he was outlined in the red glow of the tail lights, a solitary figure standing with the broken rifle in his hand. Then he was gone, lost in darkness and the dust thrown up by our wheels. "He didn't have to do that," Mary breathed, her voice barely audible and a shiver running through her. "He'll never forgive that."

No point in reminding her there were evidently things van Delden could never forgive. The man's pride had been injured, and I pictured him in the morning limping wearily into camp with that broken rifle. To lose face in front of his African hunters, in front of the Army, too—she was right, he'd never forgive van Delden for that. I reached out and took her hand. It was hot to the touch and I could feel her trembling. She let it rest there for a moment, her hand in mine quite passive, then suddenly her fingers tightened, gripping hold of me as though she were desperate for somebody to cling to. She stayed like that, tense and rigid, as we went roaring down the slope and into the flat land below. Then gradually her fingers relaxed their grip and she let go of my hand.

The gravel plain was a narrow strip barely half a mile wide. Black outcrops of lava loomed away to our left. The southern cross showed faintly above the outline of the mountains to our right. We turned eastwards, lurching and bucketing as Dima swerved to avoid wind-bared rock. And then we slowed, searching the sand with our headlights dipped for the tracks left by the elephants.

II

IT SEEMED A LONG TIME before we finally found those tracks. We had been casting back and forth over a wide area, driving slowly with Mukunga and van Delden standing up in the front of the Land-Rover. It was Dima who spotted the broken branch on the small acacia and after that Mukunga went ahead on foot, tracking them by the light of our headlights. It was slow work and the moon was just rising when we sighted them, dark shapes all motionless in silhouette. Dima cut the engine and switched off our lights. Darkness enveloped us, the moon like a half of an orange on the hard black line of the horizon.

Abe leaned forward. "Where do you think they're going?" And when van Delden didn't answer, he added, "They can't survive in this waterless desert."

"Don't talk. Just watch."

We sat there in silence as the moon lifted clear of the horizon, its flattened orb changing from dull orange to white, its brilliance lighting the desert, resolving the shapes of the elephants. We could see several half-grown calves huddled against their mothers, and ahead and a little to the left of them, a group composed entirely of adults moving restlessly. "Bulls." Van Delden had the binoculars to his eyes. "Strange to see half a dozen bulls herding with cows and their young." There was no wind, the air completely still. Faint rumblings made a ghostly sound in the stillness. Gradually their ears were laid back against their massive shoulders and the trunks stopped testing the air; first one of the bulls, then another, turned their backs on us, and in a moment the whole herd was on the move, and we were

216

following them, driving slowly through a pale white desiccated landscape with the moon hanging over the bonnet of the Land-Rover like a great lantern in the sky. Far ahead of us the elephants lumbered towards it as though drawn by its light.

Suddenly the Land-Rover stopped, van Delden reaching for his binoculars again, staring fixedly at the pale distant shapes. One of the elephants had paused, its trunk nuzzling at something on the ground, pushing at it with a forefoot. "Toto," Mukunga muttered, and van Delden nodded. All the elephants had stopped now, the cows bunching to present a solid front as they faced towards us, their ears spread, their trunks moving. They were about two hundred yards away, and I thought for a moment they were going to charge, they looked so menacing. The bulls, too, were restless, milling around, an impression of confusion and hostility.

"Have they winded us?" Abe asked, but van Delden shook his head. "It's the Land-Rover they don't like. That means they've already had experience of being hunted from vehicles."

Two of the cows detached themselves from the bunched family group, moving slowly back to join the distracted mother. She had got the calf to its feet and it was standing there, head dropped, ears flat against its shoulders, the little trunk hanging straight down. The three elephants were close around it now, their trunks moving over its body as though to give it confidence, urging it forward. "Can't be more than a few months old." Van Delden sounded surprised. "That's the only toto we've seen. In fact, we've seen very few calves and most of those have been nearly full grown."

"Is that because of the drought?" Abe asked.

"That and the fact that calves are vulnerable to predators and man."

"And this is the only baby elephant you've seen. Strange that hers should have survived."

"She's probably the matriarch of this group. That might explain it." He shook his head. "Doesn't look as though it will last much longer though."

We had lost sight of it now, all three elephants close

around it and moving slowly to rejoin the others. It was the signal for the whole group to begin moving again, but as Dima reached to start the engine, van Delden held up his hand. The mother had stopped again, and a moment later I caught a glimpse of the calf between her front legs and there was a bigger calf beside her, pressing against her flanks. She pushed the baby away, and Mary said in an appalled voice, "She's got no milk." The calf tottered to one of the other cows, pushed between her forelegs, attempting to suckle, then wobbled to one side and collapsed on the pale sand. Again the three elephants gatherd round it the older calf hovering in a restless, distracted manner, and the whole herd watching uneasily. This time the little calf did not rise and even at that distance I could sense the emotional disturbance affecting the whole herd, their distress obvious from their movements, some of them coming back to stand over the small bundle lying collapsed on the ground, moving their trunks over its body, the others either milling around or just standing distractedly, shifting their feet and swinging their heads.

Abe had found a pair of binoculars in the back and he had them glued to his eyes, leaning forward intently. Once I heard him mutter something about it being the same one, but he was only talking to himself and after that he was silent. We were there the best part of an hour while the little group round the fallen calf gradually broke up, leaving just the mother and two other cows trying to nudge it to its feet or lift it with their tusks. "Once at Marsabit," van Delden said, "one of my cows was wandering around three or four days carrying a dead calf in her tusks. But I don't think they'll be long now."

It was the bulls who moved first and I realised they had not the same close-knit family association. As soon as they had disappeared over the horizon the cows became very agitated, finally beginning to move off, uncertainly and looking back every now and then, sometimes half turning as though still unwilling to leave. Then the two remaining cows followed and only the mother was left, scuffing irresolutely at the ground, the older calf close against her as she continued to move her trunk over the body of her baby as though to fix it in her memory. Finally she abandoned it, turning and moving hesitantly after the others, rumbling and growling her distress, occasionally laying her trunk across the older calf's head and back. Abe let the binoculars fall. "She's very gaunt, quite different—she must be half starved."

Van Delden nodded. "They're none of them in good shape. Looks like they've come a long way, travelling fast."

"It's the same herd we saw last night." Abe was still staring after the retreating elephants. "They've come a very long way." He shook his head, his eyes strangely bright behind his glasses. Dima started the engine and beside me Mary's voice high and urgent, cried, "You can't leave it—not like that."

"Why not?" van Delden asked. "It's not our job to interfere with nature, or have you forgotten?"

"But suppose it's still alive? You can't—"

"If you've got bitten by the silly sentimentality of the cities, forget it. As long as you're with me—"

"I didn't ask to come with you."

He nodded. "No, you didn't. But you're here, so don't argue." And he told Dima to get moving again while she sat there staring sullenly at the back of his head. "You could have shot it," she muttered. "If it had been Alex .. ." But Abe turned on her angrily, almost shouting: "Isn't it enough just to have watched it? No need for a post-mortem."

The body of the calf was already merging into the moon-white landscape, the mother moving after the rest of the herd, the half-grown youngster still beside her. But her movements were slow and she kept on turning her head and looking back as though still expecting the calf to get to its feet and follow her. Finally she stopped beside a stunted acacia and began tearing at a branch. We stopped too, Abe picking up the glasses again and watching her intently as she wrenched the branch off and then went all the way back to lay it

219

over the inert bundle lying in the sand. She remained there for some time, her head bent and her trunk constantly moving over it, then suddenly she turned and went lumbering off after the others already disappearing over a ridge dotted with a few thorns. Her feet made no sound and though she seemed to be moving slowly she covered the ground at surprising speed. We waited until she had disappeared, then followed, and when we sighted her again she was back with the rest of her group and they were bunched together with the bulls out ahead and moving quickly.

Gradually the moon shifted its position. From being over the bonnet it swung slowly to our right until it was above Abe's head. The elephants had changed direction. They were headed north now, and away to our left Kulal loomed, a pale cloud-capped sprawl.

I leaned across Mary, calling to van Delden. "They're making for the Balesa Kulal, aren't they?"

"Probably. The river bed isn't far now."

"Hey, but that's a dry watercourse." Abe seized my arm. "Didn't you say it was dry? Somebody said it was dry."

The Land-Rover slid to a halt. The elephants were standing in a huddle, so close they seemed to be in conference. I grabbed the binoculars lying by Abe's feet, thinking another calf was in trouble.

"How much water do they need? I read somewhere it's thirty gallons a day. Right?"

"That's about the normal intake for a full-grown adult," van Delden said.

"Hell! There must be twenty, thirty elephants there." He turned to me. "Are they clear enough to count? How many are there?"

Through the glasses I could see them quite clearly, all standing in a line as though they had come to some sort of fence. "I make it seventeen," I said, "But it's difficult to be certain. There are several big calves and they're keeping very close to their mothers."

"That's almost five hundred gallons a day. A lot of water, and in country as dry as this only a man like Aaron—"

220

Van Delden told him to be quiet. The elephants were moving again and he signalled Dima to drive on. But we were too close now and at the sound of the engine starting up several elephants whirled about, ears spread as though about to charge, and the mother who had lost her calf moved out in front, swinging her trunk and throwing sand in the air. Van Delden leaned forward quickly and switched off the ignition. In the sudden silence we could hear them, a low rumble of sound. They stood there watching us for perhaps a minute, but with the light breeze off the mountain blowing towards us, the Land-Rover still and no sound, they gradually relaxed, finally losing interest and going off after the others. Occasionally one of them looked back.

"Would she have charged us if we'd gone closer?" Abe asked as we got moving again.

Van Delden nodded. "Probably. She's very distressed. The others certainly would. They're just about at the end of their tether, but cows in defence of their calves wouldn't hesitate."

We could just see them now, heading north-east, and a few minutes later we discovered what it was that had stopped them. It was a track that still showed the faint treadmarks of vehicles, its edges bordered by stones. Van Delden said it led through the Chalbi Desert to Kargi and on to Marsabit. "In two or three miles they'll come to a crossroads. There's a well just to the west of it."

"They can't draw water from a well," Abe murmured.

"It will be dry anyway."

"Can they make it across the Chalbi?"

"The bulls might. But not the cows with their young."

Sitting there, being driven through the stark beauty of that moonlit night, the desert flowing white to the pale horizon and Mt. Kulal towering high above us, I had a sense of unreality, as though it were all a dream, the death of that little calf, the distress of its mother and her family group, the whole macabre scene vivid

221

in my mind, and yet everything strangely remote. And the elephants out ahead of us, dim ghostly shapes moving steadily towards a hostile desert. Looking at that desiccated scene, knowing that worse lay ahead of us if the herd tried to cross the Chalbi, I was suddenly very conscious of the dryness of my mouth. There was only a single jerrican in the back of the Land-Rover, presumably petrol, and nothing that looked as though it contained food. It was twenty-four hours now since we had fed. "How far to the well?" I asked, hoping he was wrong and there would be water in it. Mary laughed, her teeth white in the oval of her face. "Haven't you ever been thirsty before?"

I shook my head, not answering her. We had left the track and there was scrub now, occasional thorn trees. We were heading across country in a more northerly direction, our speed gradually increasing, patches of soft sand, the scrub thicker and more trees. Then suddenly we had stopped, the engine switched off. In the stillness we could hear the elephants rumbling to one another. We were closer than we had been before, but they ignored us, standing shoulder to shoulder in a ring.

They had found the well.

They remained like that, in a tight huddle, for several minutes. Two of the younger calves showed signs of exhaustion. One was sitting all alone on its haunches with its ears drooping like a dejected bloodhound. The other kept moving in on its mother, searching for a teat and being constantly thrust back by her trunk or a foot. And there were one or two almost fully grown who just stood waiting patiently, occasionally scuffing at the ground or feeling it with their trunks.

It was the cows that broke away first, drawn by the plaintive sounds of their young. They spread out uncertainly, searching the ground with their trunks and digging into it with slicing movements of their front legs, the toenails acting like a spade. One cow went on digging with her forefeet until she must have been down three or four feet. Two younger females came to help her, using the tightly curled tips of their trunks to scoop the loose sand out. But though they could smell water, they could not reach it.

The bulls began milling around, their trunks waving, their bellies rumbling. They were unsure of themselves and in a testy mood, the larger animals turning on the others if they got in their way. Finally one of them moved off. Others began to follow him, their backs towards us, a baggy-trousered shambling walk, the cows watching, some still digging at the soft sand. They took no notice of us, rumbling amongst themselves, and then, with much squealing and growling, the few young were marshalled and led away, out of the dry bed of the Balesa Kulal towards the great volcanic heap that towered above us in the moonlight.

Van Delden leaned back, lighting his pipe, the smell of his tobacco strong in the dry air. "There's a gorge," he said, "runs right back, almost splitting the mountain in two. Looks like they're making for that."

"Any water?" Abe asked.

"No. Not in a drought like this. Least I don't think so. But there's shade and enough greenstuff for them to browse on." He sat there for a while, smoking and not saying anything while the elephants disappeared from view over a rise that seemed to be a part of a long shoulder running up towards Kulal. "Well, we know where they're headed now, so no point in wasting good meat." He gave an order to Dima and we turned and started back on our tracks. We drove back until we reached the fallen heap of baby elephant. I don't know whether it was actually dead, but it made no movement as Mtome plunged his knife into it and began carving out chunks of flesh. Blood was darkening the sand as I joined Dima in the Land-Rover to go in search of wood for a fire.

It was a strange, eerie meal, squatting there beside the carcase of the little elephant, the desert white in the moonlight and flames flickering from thorn tree branches hacked off with a panga that was part of the Land-Rover's equipment. At first Abe refused to touch the blackened meat, but when Mary said, "For

God's sake, be practical," and began feeding him bits of her own steak, he overcame his revulsion. She watched to make certain he ate it, then asked me, "What happened to Karanja? Where is he?" And when I told her how he had left us the previous night, she nodded. "So it was Karanja." She turned to van Delden. "It was Karanja who fired on us, wasn't it?"

He was squatting on his hunkers between Mukunga and Dima, gnawing at a rib bone. "Could be," he said, working round the bone with his teeth.

"But why? I don't understand why."

He looked at her, holding the bone like a corn-cob. "Because he's back in a different world now, and in his way he's fond of elephants."

Abe shook his head. "If it was Karanja, then why did he disappear like that? He must have seen you standing there."

"He knows I don't trust him."

"But he wanted to join you."

"Maybe." He tossed the bone away and reached into the embers for a piece of meat. "He's an ex-Mission boy, you know. Clever as a vervet."

"And handsome," Mary whispered to me with an odd look on her face.

"After all the years I've known him I wouldn't like to say what goes on in his head. He's cunning and he never does anything without a reason. He's a bit of a showman, too."

"But a shot like that," Abe murmured. "Hitting the tyre on a moving vehicle. He wouldn't have risked that with Mary driving."

"He didn't know it was Mary, and there was no risk. He's a first-class shot. You know, when he left the Mission to join the Game Department he wasn't good for anything but office work. Most of my boys made fun of him, so he set out to become a better shot than any of them. I've seen him go into a thicket after a wounded lioness, no hesitation and grinning all over his face. Bravado, you'd say, but not quite that. He knew what he was doing, how sudden it would be. You see, a lioness doesn't growl a warning like a lion,

224

the growl is instantaneous with the spring. I had a touch of malaria at the time, so I didn't dare risk it myself, too shaky. I let him have my .470 and he dropped the animal dead, right at his feet, with a single shot." He wiped his hands on his beard. "So long as he's got an audience . . . He must have an audience." He turned to Mtome. "Chai. Brew up some chai, and then we'll get going." And he added, "We'll drop Dima off to keep track of those elephants, then drive up to the mountain. I've got a feeling that's where they're headed. There's always water on Kulal."

There was a goatskin waterbag I hadn't noticed before, a chargul hung on the side of the Land-Rover. Mtome produced a blackened tin from the back and in no time at all we were passing round an enamel mug of hot tea.

The moon was high in the sky when we finally left the white-boned carcase with a pile of red meat bloodying the back of the Land-Rover. We crossed the track again and stopped at the well, dropping the bucket on its frayed rope into the hole. There was no splash, no drop of water in it when we wound it up on the cumbersome wooden roller. Dima left us here, filling his waterbottle from the chargul and taking some meat with him. "Kambi ya mawingo," van Delden said as he got into the driving seat, and Dima, slinging his rifle over his shoulder, waved a hand in acknowledgment as he set off after the elephants.

Van Delden sat there for a moment, watching until the lone figure had disappeared from sight. Then he started the engine. "Kambi ya mawingo—that means the camp in the clouds. If we can get through to it, we'll stop the night there. I want to take a look into the western gorge." We moved off then, heading westward up the track that climbed the long shoulder of the mountain, and I sat there, feeling the hot air rushing past, thinking that at least I was going to get part of what I wanted. I was going up on to the great volcanic mountain that Pieter van Delden had written about with such awe.

It was a rough ride, and it got rougher as we

climbed, the surface deteriorating until we were grinding up in low gear round hairpin bends flanked by crumbling banks of earth, the disused track falling away in places to the moon-white desert far below. High up on the shoulder, we rounded a bend and, suddenly, we were out on the lip of the world, looking down into a yawning chasm with the pale glimmer of cliffs and buttresses rising sheer on the far side. Ahead of us, the great bulk of the mountain filled the sky, half obscured by cloud, the gorge running back into it and lost in shadow.

We stopped there, all of us getting out to stand on a flat rock platform that seemed to hang in space. The bottom of the gorge was a good two thousand feet below and deep in moonshadow. Van Delden was scanning it through his glasses, Mukunga lying flat on the rock, his woolly head over the edge, peering down. "Fantastic!" Abe murmured, sucking in his breath at the sight of the world falling away into darkness below us. "Just fantastic! It must have been one hell of an earthquake to split the mountain open like this." He was staring down into the depths and he added sadly, "No way they could climb up out of that. No way at all."

"The Wandrobo had a way," van Delden said.

"You've been into that gorge, have you?"

"Once, but not right to the end."

"Then how do you know?"

"Jack Mallinson. He was the missionary here and he said the people of the forest used to come and go between this gorge and the one leading down to the lake."

Abe shook his head. "Mountain people maybe. But not elephants. They'll be trapped down there." The way he said it conjured a picture in my mind of elephants backed up against sheer buttresses of rock and the ring of hunters closing in.

Van Delden let his glasses fall, looking at him curiously. "Nothing we can do about that."

"And tomorrow, when Alex goes in after them—where will you be?" Mary's voice was a hoarse whisper, barely audible. "And there's Karanja. Karanja never liked Alex, and if he's down there—"

"You think he'd shoot him?"

She hesitated, staring at him. "There was that man Enderby." She said it slowly, almost reluctantly. "There was only you and Karanja at Marsabit when it happened. I know that now, so it was either—"

"You know nothing about it. You weren't there." He had gripped hold of her arm, silencing her. They stood like that for a moment, facing each other. Then he let go of her, leaning down and tapping Mukunga on the shoulder. "See anything?"

"Hapana, Tembo. Is too dark." He got to his feet.

Van Delden nodded, turning back to the track. "We'll get moving then."

"They won't have a chance," Abe murmured.

"Dima will tell us what happens."

Abe was silent then and my gaze shifted to the mountain, remembering the older van Delden, who had climbed Kulal, alone and on foot, all those years ago. But not from this direction. He had gone up from Lake Rudolf, spending six days exploring the mountain, finally driven down by starvation and the damp chill of the clouds. He'd found no traces of any civilisation, only the small black people who lived in the rain forest, the Wandrobo, and they had proved hostile. Now, looking up at the huge mass of the mountain, I felt it was hopeless, like searching for a needle in a slag heap. What possible chance was there of my stumbling on some vestige of the culture that had prompted a design on pottery that might be five, ten thousand years old? This was all part of the Rift Valley, shattered by volcanic upheavels; so much could have happened in that time.

The engine of the Land-Rover started up and I turned to find van Delden already at the wheel. "Hurry up. We need some sleep and we've still got quite a way to go."

The two Africans were getting into the back. Mary lingered a moment, gazing down into the gorge, her face pale in the moonlight. Then she turned abruptly and I followed her. Only Abe remained, a slight, lone figure standing on the lip of the gorge.

"Mr. Finkel."

He turned as though in a dream. "I'm not coming," he said. "I'm going back." He spoke slowly, hesitantly, and I could see by the look on his face he was appalled at his own decision. "That gorge is nothing but a great rock trap. If somebody doesn't shift them out—"

"Don't be a fool, man," van Delden said sharply. "You go down into that gorge, you won't shift them out—more likely you'll get trampled to death."

"I can at least try." It was crazy, and he knew it. To go back down the track and into that gorge, no gun, no food, and nobody with him. It would be the first time he had been on his own in Africa.

Van Delden shrugged. "Please yourself."

It was then that I started to climb out. I didn't want to, but I couldn't just leave him to go off on his own. Mary caught hold of my arm. "Don't be silly," she hissed. But it was van Delden who stopped me, leaning out of the driving seat and speaking quietly. "You scare them out of that gorge and tomorrow Alex will be able to run circles round them with his trucks. And if Alex doesn't kill them, then the heat will. It's hot like a furnace down there in the heat of the day. Now, for God sake, man, get in. Those elephants need time to recover themselves. Dima will tell us where they are when we pick him up in the morning."

There was a long silence, Abe standing there, irresolute, a small figure dwarfed by the immense bulk of the mountain behind him. Slowly he turned his head, looking back down into the gorge. "What is it?" Mary whispered. "Why is he so concerned?" But I couldn't tell her. I wasn't sure myself. It could be the ghost of his dead wife he saw trapped down there. Anything seemed possible in that weird light, and when van Delden turned to me and said sharply, "Go and get him," I shook my head. He revved the engine then, and the sound of it shattering the stillness seemed to break Abe's reverie. He looked round, his shoulders sagging, and as though still in a dream came slowly down off the rock and got into the Land-Rover without a word.

There were only a few more bends, then the track straightened out and we were approaching the Mission. Mary, close beside me, whispered, "All my life I've wanted to come up here, but he wouldn't let me."

"Why not?"

She shrugged and the movement of her body so close against me was disturbing. "I was fifteen then." She gave a little giggle. "Perhaps he didn't trust me. It was a two-day journey from Marsabit to Kulal. It meant camping out in the desert. He sent me to school at Nairobi instead."

We had come out on an open stretch of grassland, the clouds low and casting a dark shadow ahead. There was no wind and nothing stirred as we turned off the track, driving out on to the shoulder of the mountain where a rock outcrop stood black against the moon like a ruined castle. Below it was a waterhole that had once been used by the Mission cattle. It was fed by a pipe and there was still a steady trickle of water running out of it, but there were no cattle now. Instead, the ground was marked by the feet of elephants, the dry sered grass trampled bare and the waterhole itself a muddy wallow. "So there is water here," Abe said, and van Delden nodded.

"It's the forest and the proximity of the lake," he said. "At this height the combination of the two tends to produce cloud."

"You knew that, and yet you let them go into that gorge when they could have come straight up the track." Abe was staring at him accusingly. "You could have herded them on to the track and up to the water here."

"Maybe." But he sounded doubtful. "Those elephants weren't in a mood to be driven. And I didn't know what we'd find here."

"But you said there's always water on Kulal."

Van Delden turned on him angrily. "Look, man, a lot has happened in this part of Africa during the last

229

few years and Mallinson's been gone a long time. What they did to Marsabit they could have done here. As soon as I left Marsabit the bloody missionary there let the Rendile and Samburu move into the forest. Dima was there about a year ago and he says the whole mountain was bare, nothing but shambas, the lake we called Paradise dried up, most of the water-holes too. And not an elephant to be seen." He turned to Mukunga, who was bent down, studying the ground round the pipe. "Any totos, Mukunga?"

"Ndio. Ndovu na watoto yao walikuwa hapa."

"He says cows with calves have been here." Van Delden sounded puzzled. "I never saw any cows here before. Either they're staging through on their way north, or else some of my elephants have moved in from Marsabit."

"I thought you said they couldn't cross the Chalbi."

"Not now they couldn't. But once in a while it rains. They could have crossed then."

Mtome had started to fill the goatskin bag from the pure clear water running out of the pipe and I was thinking of all those tribesmen we had seen, their cattle and their camels dead. "Why didn't the tribes move up here?" I asked him.

"They're desert people and Kulal is cold and damp. Most of them are afraid of the mountain anyway."

"But the Mission had cattle."

"The Mission was closed at the start of the African war." Mtome had finished filling the waterbag and van Delden went over to the pipe, drinking from it in his cupped hands, then sluicing it over his face and neck, and Abe, standing beside him and waiting his turn, said, "Would you recognize your elephants if you saw them now?"

"Of course."

"After more than two years? It's at least two years since you had to leave."

"Nearer three. But I'd still know them. And they'd know me."

"I'm told you can talk to them."

Van Delden straightened up, smiling. "You don't

want to believe all you hear, Mr. Finkel. I can imitate some of their rumblings, but the vocabulary, if you can call it that, is limited. I wouldn't be able to enquire of a cow how she'd got here, for instance." He turned back to the Land-Rover. "Leave it at that, shall we? We'll know soon enough."

Abe followed him, his voice persistent. "And if they were yours, how would you know? By earmarkings, or have you some other method?"

"Sometimes by the way they move, the tone of their rumblings, squeals and growls. But earmarks are the most reliable method."

"Those could have changed in three years."

"More rents and tears, yes. But the old marks still remain."

We were all back in the Land-Rover then and he had started the engine. Abe leaned forward, his voice urgent. "So if there were a big, very recognisable tear, you don't reckon it would have changed?"

"No, I don't." Van Delden glanced back at him, a gleam of interest in his eyes. "You've seen one of those elephants we were following before, is that it?"

Abe hesitated, then nodded reluctantly.

"Where?" van Delden asked him.

"At Treetops. It was a long time ago."

Van Delden looked at him a moment, then smiled. "So that's why you didn't want to eat from that calf. It was the mother, was it?" And as he let in the clutch, heading back to the track, he said, "That rent won't have changed much. Point her out to me if we come across her again."

The Mission was set on a rise above the track. The sprawl of wooden single-storey buildings had a dramatic appearance in the changing light, the moon coming and going as outlying veils of the cloudcap shifted. There was foliage growing through the roofs, no paint anywhere, and the verandah of one building almost completely collapsed. Where the track bent round to the right, towards some store-sheds, van Delden stopped to sit gazing at what was obviously a staff cottage. It had been a pretty place at one time, but

231

now the roof was sagging and all of one end of it had collapsed inwards. "Elephant," he murmured. Then turning to Abe, he said, "That was Jack Mallinson's place. He and the man before him were very conscious of the ecological importance of the forest. If the forest were cut down, then there would be no cloud over Kulal, no rain, just wind erosion, the sort of thing that's happened at Marsabit, at Meru and the Aberdares, all over the country. That's why the water is piped, so the cattle had no excuse to invade the forest. It was quite a job for a Mission to undertake, out on a limb here with supplies a major problem."

"And there weren't any elephants here then?" Abe asked.

"The odd bull, that's all Jack and I ever saw. I used to come regularly at one time to check on the greater kudu. It's a good place for kudus. But this mountain isn't like Marsabit. The altitude there is much lower and no storms." He turned his head away, staring at the black impenetrable shadow ahead of us. "Now we go into the forest. It's about six miles and if elephants have taken up permanent residence it may be slow going with a lot of tree shifting." He flicked the headlights to high beam and put the Land-Rover in four-wheel drive as we ploughed left through the remains of a gate and down a vague track surfaced with the soft mould of forest humus, the moon suddenly obscured by the leaf canopy that had closed over us.

At first it was easy going, but in less than a mile we were bashing our way through a close thicket of reed-like stems. "Like driving through corn," Abe said as we crouched low to avoid the springing stems and flying debris. Twice Mtome got out to hack a way through with the panga, but after we had ploughed through the swamp of a stream bed, the track climbed again and we were slipping and sliding on mud-covered boulders. It was like that for perhaps another mile, our progress slow but steady, then quite suddenly we were into an area of forest that had obviously been browsed over by elephants. Their droppings were

232

everywhere and as we laboured up the track, mud to our knees, clearing the fallen trees ahead of the Land-Rover, we became covered with mud and dung slime. Fortunately it was all fairly small timber we had to shift, but by the time we were through the area and back on to almost-clear track again, I was feeling utterly exhausted. Mary, who had been working just as hard as any of us, simply went to sleep.

Shortly after that we joined another track, turning left and climbing steadily along what seemed to be the crest of the mountain. The trees were taller now, the going firmer, less mud and no boulders, only elephant turds that sometimes looked like small boulders in the headlights. We stayed in four-wheel drive, but moving fast, for there were no trees across the track, just the brash of stripped and broken branches. It was very dark here in this high forest, dark and dank and no sign of the moon. We were into the cloud now and contrast between this and the dry desert country far below was such that I had a feeling of intense antici-pation. I don't know what I expected, but my tiredness was gone as I leaned forward, straining to see beyond the headlights, feeling that if I watched closely some marvelous revelation would leap into view.

I think perhaps I was a little lightheaded. The only thing of note we saw was one of the sacred trees. It was a giant of tremendous girth, and van Delden, pointing it out to us, said that the people of the forest believed that if ever those trees were destroyed it would be the end of the world. "It's a taboo that Jack Mallinson always respected. The Wandrobo would never survive the destruction of this forest."

"Have you ever met them?" I asked him, thinking that if I were to find the needle of that old civilisation it could only be through the people whose home this was.

But he shook his head. "Jack knew them, of course. He was always walking the forest alone. He loved it. Occasionally one of the few safaris that made it to the top of Kulal would report food or clothing missing, but they never caught sight of the thieves. The Wandrobo know their forest and they move like shadows in the mist. They're a very secretive—"

The brakes slammed on, throwing us forward. And then we were roaring backwards, two grey shapes in the headlights, their heads up and their trunks tucked underneath their tusks as they charged us. They were gaining, the two of them shoulder to shoulder and filling the track. I could see their feet moving, but there was no sound, no trumpeting, only the noise of the engine. Rotting undergrowth cracked under our wheels and suddenly we were flung to the floor as the back of the Land-Rover smacked into the bole of a tree. We stopped dead, the engine stalled. Van Delden switched the lights off, everything black and no sound.

I didn't know what was going to happen and I just lay there, not daring to move. And then they trumpeted. The sound of it was startling in the stillness and very close, the most terrifying sound I thought I had ever heard. The lights came on and over my shoulder I could see the pair of them standing on the track with their trunks curled upwards and the eyes in their great domed heads glinting as they stared into the headlights. The starter whined, the engine came to life, and then we were driving straight at them, the horn blaring and van Delden swinging the wheel over as we hit the track. I had a glimpse of the two heads towering over us, the bright ivory of their tusks and their trunks writhing, then we were past them and driving furiously along the track.

Nobody spoke as we sorted ourselves out. I could see the black outline of Mukunga in the front, still with his rifle gripped ready in his hands. Van Delden turned his head and laughed. "All right in the back? You all right, Toto?"

"I'm okay, Tembo. We're all okay." She was laughing, too, as she gripped my arm and said, "You're trembling like a leaf. Wait till the engine doesn't start and they're leaning over you, ramming their tusks into the bodywork." Her grip was hard, her eyes glinting with excitement, and close beside me Abe's voice asked, "What were they, bulls or cows?"

"Cows," van Delden said.

"From Marsabit? Could you recognise them?"

"In that light and with them charging us?" He laughed. "Not a chance." And he added, "Cows don't usually charge like that, without any warning at all. Wonder where it was they got such a bellyful of man that it changed their nature." He was driving slower and both he and Mukunga were peering cautiously ahead. Once he stopped and switched off the engine, but there was no sound, the forest wrapped in its shroud of mist.

A little further on the trees fell away and we were into a clearing that was like a meadow climbing steeply up to the left of the track. Shadows moved in the mist and we stopped again. Beside us a pool of water had been trampled into mud and above it the grass of the slope was beaten flat. "Kambi ya mawingo," van Delden said. "But no good to us. It's already occupied." Vague shapes loomed beyond the headlights, their outlines blurred by the light drizzle that was falling. "We'll have to camp on the open slopes." The engine roared again and we shot across the clearing and into the dark tunnel of the trees on the far side, elephants moving like shadows and the track littered with broken branches so that we were crashing through a sea of half-dead foliage.

Gradually the debris thinned until finally the track was almost clear, the forest normal again and only the football-sized heaps of dung indicating that it had been used by elephants. The trees were smaller now and thinning out. Suddenly we were at the end of the track, a deep trench running across it. Van Delden backed the Land-Rover into the undergrowth and switched off the engine. Darkness enveloped us and a great stillness, only the faint sound of moisture dripping from the leaves. "What now?" Abe asked, and there was a tenseness in his voice.

Van Delden got out. "We go on foot now. A few hundred yards, that's all. Put on all the clothes you've got. It will be a cold night."

It was a relief to get into our sweaters, for we were

235

already chilled by the drive. Mary wrapped herself in a blanket he found for her under the front seat and then we skirted the trench, climbing through a tracery of thin-stemmed growth. It was, as he had said, about two hundred yards, and suddenly we were out in the open and there was grass beneath our feet. The cloud cover was thinner here, the moon's light filtering through. Just clear of the forest we cut branches and lit a fire, huddling close to it, grateful for the warmth and drinking scalding hot tea from a single tin mug passed from hand to hand. Incredibly, it was still only just after midnight. We seemed to have been travelling for hours.

But tiredness did not seem to have damped Abe's curiosity. "How long can the forest support that number of elephants?" he asked.

Van Delden shook his head. "To answer that requires a proper count, and we don't know how much of the forage is suitable. Not all of it, I suspect. Like I told you, Kulal has never been a natural habitat for elephants."

"It's a staging post on their way north, is that what you're saying?"

"Possibly." Van Delden took out his pipe and began to fill it. "That's what I need to know."

"And if they're just passing through, then they must have a way up and a way down. Isn't that right?"

"It's logical. But animals are directed by instinct, not logic."

"Are you sure? Would instinct alone be directing them north? It's a time of crisis for them and you said yourself they could be heading north because of some deep-seated knowledge. That's not instinct. That's something passed on from generation to generation. Or maybe it's imprinted in their genes."

"It's all speculation." A match flared, the hook-nosed, bearded face momentarily lit as he put it to his pipe. The tobacco smoke was comfortingly normal in the strangeness of that place. "There was an elephant at Marsabit—Ahmed. The biggest tusker anyone has ever seen. He was under the protection of Jomo

236

Kenyatta. The one elephant whose ivory was safe. That was before the war, when Kenya was still a separate country. He was reckoned to be more than seventy years old when he died. That's a lot longer than most of them live. The average is about fifty years. But even fifty years, you go back three generations and you're back before the South African war, before Rhodes and the main drive of the English settlers." He was silent for a moment, drawing on his pipe. Then he said, "They can communicate, that I know. But what they can communicate is a different matter. The knowledge of safe territory is very abstract information, compared with danger warnings, behavioural instructions, food satisfaction."

Abe nodded, taking out a packet of cigarettes and staring at it thoughtfully. It was his last packet and there were only three left. He put it away, sniffing the smoke from van Delden's pipe. "How many conversational sounds have you identified?" he asked.

"About forty."

"And they're all concerned with ordinary everyday things like food and behaviour?"

"Those I have identified, yes."

"What about extra-sensory perception?"

"I'm not an animal psychiatrist."

"Meaning you don't believe in it?"

"I stick to what I know, that's all. Things like telepathy . . ." He was staring into the fire, fingering his beard. "I just don't know. Anybody who's lived close to animals has observed patterns of behaviour they can't explain."

"So you've no idea why they're moving north, why there's this concentration of them up here?"

He puffed out a stream of smoke and shook his head. "Any observation I made now would only be guesswork. It could be that roaming bulls remember Marsabit as a safe area, nothing more complicated than that. But to switch to Kulal would mean they also know that Marsabit can no longer support them." He shook his head, silent then and gazing thoughtfully into the fire. "Inherited memory, a built-in survival

237

instinct. I don't know what makes them head north, but that's what they're doing. And if there's a way up out of that gorge——" He tapped his pipe and got to his feet. "We'll see what Dima has to tell us in the morning." He said something about having used a lot of fuel on the way up, but by then I was so drowsy I could no longer keep my eyes open. Mary was already asleep, curled up in her blanket, and in the glow of the embers Mukunga lay on his back with his mouth open, snoring gently.

I stretched out on the grass, already half asleep, firelight flickering on my eyelids as Mtome added more branches. The sound of voices came to me as a vague murmur, but I was lost to the world and no longer heard what they said.

Maybe I dreamed. But I don't think so. I was too tired to dream. I woke with a piercing scream still ringing in my ears. My heart was pounding in my throat and I was shivering. The fire was glowing faintly, but there was no warmth in it. A breeze was stirring in the trees behind and it was cold, a damp chill. I knew instantly where I was, who the bodies were stretched out around me. Nobody else had stirred. No sound anywhere now and stars showing through a ragged gap in the clouds above. Something moved in the shadow of the trees. The light from the moon momentarily increased and I thought I saw a figure standing erect and covered with hair. I sat up, fear clutching at me, my mind leaping from the Wandrobo to yetis and all the stories I had read of wild primitives found on mountains. Again that piercing cry, a scream of rage and fear that made the hair crawl on my neck. The figure had vanished.

I sat there, shivering and staring at the forest. But the gap in the clouds had closed and all was dark again. "Baboon." The voice so close beside me was quietly reassuring. In the glow of the embers I could just see his bearded face, one eye open and his teeth showing in a smile. "I should have warned you."

"It looked so big," I murmured.

238

"Yes, they're very big up here. They live in the gorge."

"I thought we'd left the gorge miles away."

"Kulal is full of gorges." The eye closed and I lay down again.

The next thing I knew dawn had broken and Mtome was trying to rekindle the fire with wet branches cut from the undergrowth close by. It was a grey dawn shrouded in mist, the grass beaded with moisture and falling away from us in a smooth downland sweep that vanished into a veil of cloud. I lay there clinging to the last vestiges of sleep, too cold to move. Somewhere the sun was shining, our opaque world beginning to glimmer with a strange iridescence.

Mary came out of the bushes looking like a squaw with the blanket draped round her shoulders and her black hair hanging damp and straight. "There's a breeze," she said.

I could feel it on my face then. Flames flickered in the piled-up branches and overhead the mist swirled, the sun's iridescent glow coming and going. Away to our right a phantom pile of rock appeared in the sky. It was there for a moment, a disembodied peak hanging in space, then it was swallowed up again in the slow gyration of the clouds. Van Delden sat up, beard and hair glistening with moisture. "What's the time?"

"Past eight." The mist had lifted and she was standing looking out across the grassy slopes to where they ended abruptly at a fringe of small rock outcrops. "I want to see the lake," she said. "We'd be able to see it from here, wouldn't we?"

"If the cloud shifts," van Delden said.

"It's shifting now and it's only thin stuff. The sun will soon burn it off."

"Maybe, but Kulal is unpredictable, and it's the gorge I came to see."

Abe sat up abruptly. "You think those elephants could have made it across into this gorge?"

"It leads down to the lake, and if we get a breeze—" Van Delden glanced up at the thin layer of mist covering the sun. "Dima will be at the Mission

239

now, but he can wait. We'll breakfast here and see if it lifts."

I got up then and went into the bushes. Abe followed me. "I didn't sleep much, did you?" His face looked thin and drawn.

"The baboon woke me."

"What baboon? I didn't hear any baboon."

"You were dead to the world. It practically screamed in your ear."

He laughed. "I guess I did get some sleep then. But I don't feel as though I did. I was worrying about those elephants, and about Karanja. You think it was Karanja fired those shots?"

"Van Delden seems to think so." A pale shaft of sunlight came through the branches. "Dima may be able to tell us something." And I went quickly out into the open again. It was warmer now, patches of blue sky and the mist blowing in the wind. The others were all standing by the fire, gazing down the grass slopes to where they ran out over the lip of a gorge. More and more of those grass slopes were slowly unveiled, the gash of the gorge smoking with mist, pinnacles of rock appearing and disappearing. Then suddenly the veil of humidity was swept aside and far below us Lake Rudolf emerged, a great expanse of water running north and south, bright in sunlight. There was an island, brown and bare, all lava, and the far shore just visible as a line of cliffs. The lake itself was pale blue and flecked with white.

"The Jade Sea," Mary murmured. "But it's blue, not green."

Van Delden nodded. "It's blowing like hell down there."

It was like that for a moment, an astounding, unbelievable revelation. Then the mist closed in again and it was gone, the glimpse so brief I could scarcely believe that what I had seen was real, clouds swirling over the sun.

"How far below us?" Her voice was still entranced.

"About six thousand feet," he said.

"Kulal is higher than that."

240

"The peak lies north-east of us, the other side of the gorge. We're a good bit lower here."

"And the gorge runs down to Loiyangalani?"

"It's the water from that gorge that makes it an oasis."

She turned, staring rapt at the mist rolling along the lip of it. "I'm going to have a look."

He nodded absently, fingering his pipe. The brew tin was boiling and Mtome, sitting cross-legged in front of the fire like a black priest at some primitive rite, threw in a handful of tea. Baby elephant steaks sizzled on their sticks, the embers blazing momentarily as the mist came down again so that Mary became a ghostly figure walking into an opaque void. "Last night," van Delden murmured, sucking at his empty pipe and looking sideways at Abe. "I was thinking. No elephant droppings on the track up the mountain. Did you notice any droppings?"

"Not till we got to the Mission." A sudden gleam of interest showed on Abe's face. "You mean there is a way up out of that eastern gorge?"

"A lot of elephants have been through the forest here and they didn't come up the Mission road." He nodded. "Yes, that's what I was thinking. This must be the route they're taking, all of them." He stared into the fire a moment, then slapped his hand against his side, turning to Abe again, the great head thrust forward, the pale eyes gleaming. "If that's the case, then elephants have a built-in survival sense that draws on the experience of previous generations. Exactly what you were talking about last night. I've never seen elephants on the shores of Lake Rudolf. There haven't been any there in my lifteime. But, according to von Höhlen, Teleki was shooting at them in the water there and they were feeding on the lakeweed. How could animals far to the south of here know there was weed in that lake, or even that Rudolf existed?"

"They couldn't," Abe said. "It's either intuition or inherited memory."

"Or else the sounds they make are capable of expressing more than I had thought. Some wandering bull . . ." Mtome handed him the tin mug full of tea and he passed it on to Abe. "A form of telepathy?" He shook his head. "That's getting close to your extrasensory perception."

"I guess we have to accept," Abe said slowly, blowing on the tea, "that there are some forms of communication unknown to us. Or perhaps forgotten by us in our civilised materialism."

Van Delden grunted sceptically, his eyes shifting towards the gorge. The mist had closed right down on us, no sign of Mary, nothing but the damp green of the coarse grass. He called to Mukunga, who was dragging some more branches towards the fire, and he dropped them and hurried off into the mist. I followed him, hoping the mist would lift again. I don't think I would have risked it on my own, but I wanted to see down into that gorge. Behind me I heard Abe say, "Birds and migration, elvers, the young salmon —I guess we don't know so very much after all." But when I glanced back over my shoulder the two of them had been swallowed up and only the glow of the embers showed dull red through the thick cloud blanket that enveloped the mountain. From somewhere far away there came a faint cry. It fell away into echoing cries smothered by distance and humidity. "Nyani," Mukunga said, the wizened face grinning at me. But he moved faster after that, so that I was almost trotting. The grass ended, rock emerging, and he stopped abruptly, the ground falling away in a series of ledges and outcrops. The cry of the baboons was louder now, echoing up from below.

"Where is she?"

He raised his hand, listening, and then Mary's voice, away to the left: "Is that you, Colin?"

She appeared suddenly, her figure taking on substance as she climbed up out of a fold in the gorge edge. "Phlumps," she said, her eyes sparkling, her face fresh with exertion and the moisture in the air. "I'm sure I saw phlumps, then the bloody cloud clamped down."

242

A breeze touched my face, the opaque void at my feet shifting, the greyness glimmering. She pushed her damp hair back from her face. "They were on a sort of island, a mile, maybe two miles down the gorge. It was there for a moment only, floating in the mist and bright green in a shaft of sunlight. They were on the slopes, just grey lumps like rocks. But I saw them move—I'm sure they moved."

"Then there must be a way down." Or did this gorge link with the one we had seen last night? "Are you sure they were elephants, not baboons?"

"Don't be silly. I was brought up with them and I'm long-sighted." Her face was suddenly clouded. "Do you think they were the ones we were following? If it's all one great gorge, the mountain slashed in two—" I knew what she was thinking, that if the elephants could get through then so could the hunters. She lifted her head. "Look! The sun." And she turned to me, laughter lighting her face. "Now, at this moment, all I care about is that the world is beautiful. This mist, the gorge, everything—" She hesitated, looking at the mist flowing now like a river down the gorge. "Strange," she murmured. "Back down where we've come from it's all heat, sand, and lava, the harshness of life—reality. And up here—" She turned to me again, smiling. "Let's forget about reality, shall we? Just enjoy this moment."

I nodded, not sure what she expected, conscious of the mist flowing past us, brightening as the washed-out orb of the sun scintillated on a myriad of airborne droplets, feeling my blood respond to the vitality that emanated from her. "Look!" She was pointing up the gorge and I turned to see the peak I had glimpsed earlier floating again, disembodied, high against a pastel blue sky. But this time it did not disappear.

The wind was strong now. I could feel the weight of it against my body, could see it blowing her dark hair back from her face. A shaft of sunlight swept across the grass, the slopes spreading further and further, a downward sweep of incredible, brilliant green. Mukunga moved, craning forward. He said something and then went scrambling down the rocks, sure-footed as a goat, to stand on a final outcrop, peering down.

"He thinks he saw somebody."

"A man?"

"He's not sure. Maybe a baboon." She had turned away from me, staring down the gorge, watching as the sun burned the clouds up and the wind tore them into fragments. "There!" Her island had appeared, a jagged pinnacle of rock and grass swimming in a white sea of cottonwool. "See them?" She was pointing. "Pity we didn't bring the glasses."

Grey shapes dotted the emerging slopes, but whether elephants or rocks I could not be sure. I was too busy searching the summit, where exposed rock topped the whole green pyramid like a castle or small walled city. But it was too far away to make out whether there were any vestiges of human habitation. The gorge was opening out further and further, the clouds breaking up into isolated wisps, the glimmer of the distant lake beginning to show through. Mukunga called to us, scrambling back up the rocks. "What's he say?" I asked.

She shook her head. "I couldn't hear."

Behind us van Delden's voice said, "So there are elephants down there." He had his glasses to his eyes and was chewing on a piece of meat. "Half a dozen at least, one or two half grown. What's Mukunga up to?"

"I think he's seen something," she said.

"Better get some grub," he told her. "Time we were moving."

The baboons were quiet now. No sound except the blowing of the wind, and the lake becoming clearer, a gleaming sheet of bright water on the edge of visibility. I could feel the sun now, grateful for the warmth of it. "Can I have a look through the glasses?"

He handed them to me, but though I searched every rock on the top of that tooth of worn volcanic debris I could see nothing that belonged to man. Two young elephants, bulls I think, were flexing their muscles, bodies straining to the thrust of head and tusk, locked in mock battle, and close beside them a cow

244

suckled a half-grown calf. It was all very peaceful, a relief to watch after what I had seen near South Horr, and behind me I heard Mukunga talking quickly, explaining something in his own tongue. "He thinks he saw two men climbing up out of the gorge." And van Delden added, "Could be Wandrobo, or perhaps Samburu. The Samburu used to graze their cattle on the lower slopes." He turned to Mukunga, questioning him. The word *nyani* passed between them, and in the end he shrugged. "It could have been baboons. He's not certain. There was a lot of foliage and he only caught a glimpse." He turned to Mary. "Your tea will be getting stewed."

She nodded, staring down the gorge. But the wind was dying as fast as it had risen, clouds like wreaths of smoke eddying around the green sloped pinnacle, the elephants lost to view. We started back then, the sun already half obscured and the top of Kulal disappearing in a bank of cloud. "It was down there in that gorge," I said to van Delden, "that your father made some of his pottery finds."

"Where exactly?" But I could tell by the tone of his voice he wasn't really interested.

"I can show you on the map," I said. "It gives the position of all his finds." He didn't say anything and I asked him whether he could talk to the Wandrobo, if they had been Wandrobo down there in the gorge.

"I think Dima could. He's a Boran and familiar with the people of this area. But I certainly can't, nor can Mukunga." He strode ahead then, calling to Mtome, and Mary said quietly, "Pottery doesn't interest him and he hated his father."

"Then why did he ask me to lug the typescript and the map with me?"

She shrugged. "Perhaps he thought it could tell him something about Kulal, or Lake Rudolf—something he doesn't know."

"Such as?"

"Elephants," she said, grinning at me. "Or water. Some spring he doesn't know about, and elephants do."

We reached the fire just as the mist drove down over us again, thicker than ever, and I sat there drinking tea and chewing on a great hunk of meat, wondering why I hadn't the guts to walk off into the mist. There must be a way down into that gorge, and if I could meet up with the people of the forest who knew the mountain . . . I pictured myself being taken by little dark men to a peak of rock, the mist lifting like a veil to reveal some strange primeval stone wall, the sort of wall the Incas built. But it was just fantasy. I was daydreaming, knowing very well I would never survive without van Delden and his Africans. And so, when they started packing up and moving along the edge of the forest, back towards the Land-Rover, I went with them, carrying the bag with the film and the typescript in it.

"Why didn't you go and see what you could find in the gorge?" There was laughter in her eyes, a glint of mockery. She guessed what I had been thinking.

"How did you know?"

"What else could you be thinking about with such a lost, dreamy look on your face? Well, why didn't you?"

"Because I don't have that sort of nerve," I said angrily.

"Suppose I got hold of a rifle?"

"And came with me?"

She nodded, her eyes bright, and I didn't know whether she was serious or just fooling. "I'm a pretty good shot. At least I used to be."

But we were into the forest now, slithering down the muddy game trail in single file. Through the small-stemmed trees I could see the trench. It was deeper than I had realised, a vertical-sided gash with a water pipe still visible at the bottom, the same pipe that served the Mission. Beyond it the bonnet of the Land-Rover gleamed wet behind its screen of leaves. We piled into it and got going, but we were hardly out on to the track when the engine coughed and died. The fuel gauge showed the tank empty and I asked van

Delden what the reading had been when he had taken it over.

"More than half full, say ten gallons. He's sure to have had an extra tank fitted in place of the tool box."

We could hardly have used that much, and while Mtome unclipped the spare jerrican, I jumped out and crawled underneath, cleaning the mud off the tank with my bare hands. There was some rusting, but it was a dent in the side welding at the base of the tank that produced a reek of petrol on my fingers. "We snagged it on a branch or a piece of rock," I called up.

"I was afraid of that," van Delden said. "We were using too much on the way up." And he added, "More likely one of those bullets ricochetted."

We found some electrical tape in a toolbox in the back and bound it up as best we could. But I didn't think it would last and the spare jerrican was barely two-thirds full, so we had only about three gallons. At kambi ya mawingo we had to wait for a big-tusked bull to finish showering himself at the spring. The sun was shining then, the grass slope glistening with moisture, steaming in the heat, and there were yellow swallow-tailed butterflies sunning themselves on the broken bushes close beside us.

It was very quiet as we sat watching the elephant syphoning the water up with his trunk and squirting it over his head and back, everything done in slow motion and time standing still. "Look! A touraco," Mary whispered. It was staring down at us from the branch of a tree, its body bright green with a splash of red on its wing, the black head cocked. Below it a sunbird flashed a brilliant emerald, its curved beak darting. It was a place of extraordinary peace. But then the bull began to move, ambling silently up the slope, and we drove on into the dark of tall timber beyond the spring.

Where the track forked, and we came off the spine of the mountain, it was all downhill and we made it to the Mission in about half an hour, thrashing our way through the debris of broken branches without any hold-up. There was no sign of Dima, the Mission

247

deserted and nobody answering the blare of our horn. "Have a look at that tank," van Delden said, and he and his two Africans started up the slope to the Mission buildings.

The tape hung in tatters and I could smell the leak before I had even touched it with my finger. Mukunga was hollooing up the slope, and above me Abe said, "Maybe he went up to that clearing." I called to Mary to pass me a rag and the remains of the tape, and I was still lying there under the chassis, cleaning the mud off the fuel tank, when I thought I heard the sound of something far away. Mukunga had stopped calling, everything quiet again except for a distant bee-like drone. "Can you hear anything?" I asked.

There was silence, then Mary said, "Sounds like an engine."

"Coming up the road?"

"No. No, it seems to be above us."

I finished the taping, and when I crawled out from under the Land-Rover I could hear it quite clearly, the drone of an engine high up on the mountain. "Must be a plane," Abe said. Van Delden had heard it, too. He was standing by the broken verandah, staring up at the sky. "There!" Mary was pointing and I saw it then, coming low over the forested slopes, its wings tilted slightly as it banked and headed straight for us, the sound of it growing until the roar of it was sweeping over us. It was so low I felt the rush of it through the air, saw the Federation markings and the face of the pilot looking down at us.

It was a twin-engined monoplane and as it zoomed over the Mission buildings, it tipped over on to one wing, sliding round in a tight turn. "Was that Murphy?" Abe was staring up, shading his eyes with his hands. "It was an Army plane and I thought . . ." His words were drowned in the noise of it passing low over the Mission. It climbed steadily above the forest, dwindling until it was a bright metallic speck glinting in the sun. "I'm sure it was Murphy."

And then van Delden was back. "Mary, and you, Mr. Finkel—quick, get out. I'm leaving you here, all three of you." He turned to me. "How's that leak?" And when I told him, he said, "It doesn't matter. It's all downhill now and what's left in the tank wouldn't get me back up again."

The plane was coming back, drifting down with its nose up almost at the point of stall, its engines throttled right back. And as it glided over us something white fluttered down from the open cockpit window and I saw Pat Murphy wave to us. Then he boosted the engines and went zooming up, turning and heading away down the line of the gorge. What he had dropped was his handkerchief, and tied into one corner of it was a message: *K-S plus Army support moving Kulal E gorge. Advise proceed Marsabit fastest. Radioing report abandoned Land-Rover Kulal Mission. Good luck. Pat. (Destroy)*

Van Delden read it out to us, then put a match to it. "I'll come with you," Abe said. He knew—we all knew—he was going down into the gorge. But he shook his head. Mtome was already unloading the remains of the meat, Mukunga checking the rifles and ammunition. "You'll stay here, the three of you. I don't know what's happened to Dima, but when he turns up tell him to wait for me here." He was already moving round to the driver's seat. "Get that meat cooked right away, then take it into the forest with you and hide up. They're bound to send a patrol."

"What are you going to do?" Mary was still sitting in the back of the Land-Rover, and the tone of her voice, the frozen look on her face, the way she sat, bolt upright, her body tense, her hands clenched—I knew what she was thinking. "Please," she said. "Go back into the forest. Go back, before it's too late."

He stood there, looking at her a moment, his big head hunched into the massive shoulders, the grey hairs of his chest showing in the gap of his half-unbuttoned bush jacket. "I've never run away from anything in my life."

"But you can't do anything." The words came desperately, as though trying to break the barrier of his

249

obstinacy with the strength of her own emotions. "Please. For my sake."

He shook his head, a slow, angry movement. "When he stops killing elephants, then I'll go. Not before."

"I'll come with you. I'll talk to him."

Again he shook his head. Then, in a surprisingly gentle voice, he said, "Nothing you can do. We are all of us born the way we are." He smiled, the smile creasing his eyes, lightening the hard lines of his face. "You stay and wait for me here. I'll be back by nightfall. Now get out, there's a good girl."

"I'm coming with you."

"No." He reached out, gripping hold of her arm, his voice harder now: "I'm in a hurry."

She shook her head dumbly, her eyes wide, her body straining back from the grip of his hand. "No. You're going to kill him."

"Not if I can stop him some other way." He was staring at her, knowing now that it was her father she was thinking of, not him, his pale eyes hardening, the softness gone from his voice as he said, "You'll do as you're told, wait here—and if I don't come back, then you can join him and hunt down the fleeing remnants of East Africa's elephants." He leaned forward, taking hold of her with both hands and lifting her bodily out of the Land-Rover. And when her feet were on the ground, he put his arm round her shoulders the way he had done with Karanja on the Baringo track and said gently, "It's not your fault, Toto. Just wait here, and pray for us. Pray for both of us." He bent his head down and kissed her forehead. "Whatever happens, you mustn't feel you're to blame."

He let go of her then, calling to Mtome and Mukunga and climbing in behind the wheel. The engine started, the two Africans piling in. "Deal with that meat now," he shouted. "Then watch for the patrol. And keep hidden." He gunned the engine and the Land-Rover went roaring off down the track, trailing a cloud of dust. She stood there, not saying anything, not moving, just watching as he disappeared round the first bend. She stayed there until the dust had settled, then turned slowly as though in a dream, her face pale and drawn, and in a small, vague voice she said, "It's always been like that, all my life." And I knew she was referring to van Delden going off and leaving her to wait.

"He'll get those elephants out of the gorge somehow," Abe said. It was meant to soothe her fears, but the lack of conviction in his voice only increased them.

"How?"

He shrugged, smiling vaguely. "I guess he'll find a way."

"And the Army? What about the Army?" She was still staring at us, her fingers twining nervously. And then she laughed, a high, uncertain sound, and she smiled wistfully. "The trouble is I love him. With all his faults, his obsession, his stupid, bloody obstinacy, his ruthless disregard for other people—I can't help it, I love him." She sighed. "Something he'll never know." And she added bitterly, "Even if he did, he'd never understand."

There was nothing Abe or I could say, no comfort we could give her, the three of us just standing there in silence. "Well, I guess he can look after himself," Abe said awkwardly.

"Oh yes, he can do that all right." She gave a false, bright little laugh. "He's over sixty and never suffered anything worse than a few knife wounds and his shoulder mauled by a man-eater, so why worry about him, or about Alex? What is written is written." She seemed to come to life then, moving quickly towards us, and in a firm practical voice she said, "Come on, better get that meat over a fire before it's crawling with maggots."

III

THERE WAS a strange atmosphere about the Mission, the wood of the buildings eaten away by termites and the forest moving in, the marks of animals and their droppings everywhere. As at the Lodge during the Conference, we were interlopers in a complex that had been built for a specific purpose, but here the sense of abandonment was overwhelming, our footsteps resounding in an emptiness that was full of the ghostly relics of a community dedicated to Christianity. And the disintegration of the fabric was not the result of war; it was time and the silent invasion of nature that had left its mark, so that I felt no sense of violation. But the sadness of all that hopeful endeavour wasted made it a strangely depressing place and I think we were all glad to get away from it, to the edge of the forest where we had a view of the road and the water-hole, and the Mission buildings were out of sight.

We got a fire going, and while Mary was dealing with the remains of the meat, I walked across the open grassland to fill the plastic water container we had found in the abandoned kitchens. The area round the pipe was so thick with mud and the slime of animal droppings that before wading into it I removed my boots and socks and rolled up my trousers. It was hot in the sunshine, and when I had filled the container I stripped off my shirt and ducked my head under the pipe, sluicing the clear cool water on to the stubble of my face, letting it run over my back, thinking how marvellous it was that there should be water up here on Kulal when all this Northern Region was dying of drought. And afterwards I ran barefoot up the slope to the ridge above. Crouched among the rocks, I had a clear view of the road running in hairpins down the ochre-coloured shoulder of the mountain to the plain below.

I lay there for quite a time, the sun drying my bare back and all that empty, desert-yellow country hazed with heat, the mountains of the Mara shimmering in the distance. But though I strained my eyes against the glare, there was nothing visible, no movement except here and there the dancing whirl of a sand devil. It was all emptiness, no stir of dust from a moving vehicle, the road up the mountain empty, too. And having satisfied myself of that, I relaxed, enjoying the solitude, the feeling of being raised up on a pinnacle of unbelievable remoteness, a world apart, untouched by man. And behind me, the mountain with its primeval forest, the source of water and of the storms that lashed the lake. Lying there, I felt I didn't care if I never returned to civilisation.

It was only gradually, and with a sense of reluctance, that I acknowledged the sound of distant shouting and turned my head. A small herd of buffaloes, black in the sunlight, stood motionless halfway between the forest and the waterpoint, their heads all facing towards the haze of smoke hanging over our fire.

I got to my feet, then sat down abruptly, conscious that I was alone and unarmed, cut off from the others. The calls had ceased, but the buffaloes remained with their heads up, all staring at the still figures by the fire. There was no suggestion of hostility, only an intent watchfulness, and they looked so ordinary, like long-horned cattle.

At last they moved, flowing in a black tide to surround the waterpoint, trampling the mud under their hooves as they jostled one another to get at the source of the water. There was nothing I could do except sit there and wait for them to go. One of them, having drunk its fill, moved on to where I had left the container, sniffing at it with a wet nose, nuzzling my boots. Something moved on the edge of the forest, a muddy shape pushing through the leaves, and an elephant emerged, moving slowly with that soft, silent tread that seemed to cover the ground without contact. It saw the buffaloes and paused, fanning its ears, its trunk exploring the grass irresolutely. Then it glided slowly forward, and with much snorting and backing the buffaloes made room for it. The scene reminded me of Abe describing the salt lick at Treetops, for though both the buffaloes and the elephant demonstrated, there was nothing positively aggressive in their behaviour. The elephant was putting the tip of its trunk to the pipe, sucking at the water, and then transferring it to its mouth, and when it had drunk its fill, it began spraying water over its head and ears until all the mud was gone and the fore part of its body glistened darkly in the sun.

It was while I was idly trying to count the buffaloes, wondering how long it would be before I could retrieve my gear, that I seemed to remember more than two figures standing by the fire. But when I looked again the fire was almost out, only a faint flicker of flame from the pile of dead ash, and no sign of Abe or Mary, or of anybody else. I tried to recall exactly what I had seen on turning my head at the sound of their calls, but all I could remember clearly was the shock of the dark herd standing there.

My gaze switched to the buffaloes again. They were on the move at last, drifting back towards the forest. But the elephant remained. It was kneeling now, a picture of innocent enjoyment, sucking at the pipe, and each time it curled its trunk up over its head the prismatic colours of a rainbow showed momentarily in the sprayed water.

The fire died and nothing stirred, the sun burning my bare shoulders. At last the elephant finished its ablutions and got to its feet. It had one last drink from the pipe, then turned and ambled slowly off. The moment it had disappeared among the trees I ran down the slope, put on my boots and shirt, grabbed the water container, and made for the fire. The leafy fringe of the forest hung trembling in the heat, no animal emerged to face me, no sign of Abe or Mary when I reached the burned-out embers.

I stood for a moment, feeling deserted, but with the shelter of the trees to give me confidence I called to them, my voice loud in the burning stillness. There was an answering call from the direction of the Mission and then Mary appeared on the track, waving and walking casually towards me. "Where have you been?" I asked her. "Why didn't you wait for me?"

"We didn't know how long you'd be." She was laughing. "That bull might have stayed there all morning and we wanted to look at a map of Kulal made by the Reverend Mallinson. It's in the house back there." She took hold of one of the handles of the container, easing the weight of it as we walked down the slope to the track. "Karanja turned up while you were enjoying the view."

"Karanja?"

She nodded. "Karanja and Dima, they both arrived together." Her eyes were on the track leading down the shoulder of the mountain. "If we'd known about that map . . ." She turned to me. "You see, there is a way up out of that gorge. It's shown on the map, a game trail. Those elephants are safe on the mountain now."

So there had been no point in van Delden going back down into the plain.

"You must have had a good view up on those rocks. Did you see any vehicle moving?"

"No, nothing."

She shifted her grip on the container. "Well, I hope to God he finds out in time. . . . If he thought those elephants were still there and Alex was going in to get them . . ." Her voice trailed away. "Are you sure you didn't see anything? No sign of the Land-Rover? Most of the track we came up must have been visible—"

"I told you, nothing." I was still angry at having been left to fend for myself. "Where's Abe? Why didn't he wait for me?"

"As soon as Dima mentioned this map he insisted

255

on seeing it right away. Now, of course, he wants to go off into the forest and have a closer look at those elephants." And she added, smiling, "You were in no danger from that phlump and I was keeping an eye out for you."

I asked about Karanja then. He and Dima had apparently stumbled into each other in the moonlight, following the elephants along a narrow game trail that snaked up the almost vertical side of the gorge. "Did Karanja say why he was following them?"

"I didn't ask him."

"But surely you must have—"

"He's rather full of himself at the moment."

We had reached the track and she turned left, walking towards the missionary's house, her head bent, lost in her own thoughts.

"Didn't you ask him why he'd shot up your Land-Rover?"

"It wasn't my Land-Rover and he didn't know I was driving it."

"What the hell's that got to do with it?" I said irritably. It didn't explain his motive, or why he had tried to stop the Land-Rover from turning those elephants. But when I said it was important to know what was going on in his mind, she turned on me angrily. "So you don't care that I might have been killed."

"Oh, for God's sake!" I wrenched the container from her grasp and transferred it to my other hand. "All I want to know is why he did it. If the Army catches up with him he stands a good chance of being shot."

"They could make him Minister in place of Kimani."

I glanced at her, thinking she was joking. But she wasn't. "You're serious, are you? His motive was political, a gesture to draw attention to himself. Is that what you mean?"

"Anything to do with game in this country is political. I told you that before."

"But he's an African, a Government employee. It's

256

one thing for van Delden to take the law into his own hands—"

"Is it? He's killed two blacks and he's South African born. They'll never let him get away with that."

"And what about Karanja? Going off to warn van Delden, shooting at Kirby-Smith—"

"Karanja's one of them and Alex is a white hunter. In opposing him he'll have the support of all those who believe in Africanisation."

"But surely—"

"Oh, it's impossible," she cried, "talking to you about Africa." We had reached the gate of the missionary's house and she turned in quickly. "Ask Karanja," she said. "Maybe he can explain it to you."

The door of the half-ruined house was open and I could hear the sound of voices. They were in the room to the left, Abe and Dima standing in front of a map pinned to the wall. Karanja was seated at the missionary's desk, his rifle propped against the wooden arm of the chair, and as we entered he said, "No. I don't go from here until I talk with Tembo." There was a decisiveness in his voice, his manner indefinably different—more confident, almost authoritative. "Is important I talk with him." He saw us and swung round in his chair. "You, Mr. Tait, tell your American friend is dangerous for him to go into the forest alone."

"No danger, Karanja, if you come with me," Abe said. "You know almost as much about elephants—"

"I tell you, I not coming. I stay here and wait for Tembo." And he ordered Dima to the door to keep an eye on the track.

Abe turned to me. "Come and have a look at this map. And you, Mary. Right now this is where we are." He jabbed his finger on the paper. It was yellowed with sun and damp, the ink faded, but I could just make out the shape of the buildings and the track snaking up the mountain. All the gorges were marked, the tracks and game trails showing faintly, the broken line of the waterpipe, and right in the centre the peak itself, its height in feet written beside it. "The elephants came up out of the gorge on this trail." He traced the zig-zag line with his finger, and then he was pointing to a position due north of the Mission. "That's where Dima and Karanja left them. The scale is an inch to the mile, so it's only just over three miles away. Say we make it in two hours, that's nine hours since they left them. They won't have moved far."

"Perhaps they come down here for water," Karanja said. "In that case you see them without need to go into the forest."

"There's water at kambi ya mawingo," Mary said. "There'll be other places, too."

"Well, what do you say?" Abe asked me. "If we find the Wandrobo then maybe you'll get your archaeological mystery solved."

I shook my head, thinking of the elephant at the waterpipe and the two that had charged us the night before. "Van Delden asked us to wait for him here."

"He may not come."

"If Tembo say he come, he come," Karanja said.

Abe shrugged. "Okay, Colin, you and Mary stay here with Karanja, I'll take Dima—"

"No." Mary shook her head vehemently. "I'm not staying here while you go off exploring the mountain."

"It will only be for a few hours."

"I want to see those elephants, too, and now Karanja is with us—" She looked at me, her eyes sullen. "If Abe is willing to go into the forest on foot . . ." She hesitated, then said angrily, "What are you scared of? Dima will have a rifle with him."

I hesitated, unable to explain to her the sense of uneasiness the mountain gave me, or tell her about Abe's wife and the feeling I had that his addiction to danger was very close to a death wish. But in the end I agreed. "All right," I said. "I'll come."

Karanja got to his feet. "Is not good for us to split up."

We might have wasted more time arguing, but Dima suddenly poked his head round the door. "Patrol," he hissed, and in the sudden silence we could hear the sound of a vehicle coming up the track. By

258

the time we had gathered up our things and reached the gate it had stopped and a dozen or more African soldiers were running up the slope towards the Mission buildings. Abe darted back inside the house, and when he joined us on the track leading into the forest, he had the map of Kulal stuffed into the front of his bush jacket.

We went down the track as far as the swampy stream with its thick cane growth and there Karanja left us, going back to check on the movements of the patrol. "You said there were no vehicles down on the plain," Mary whispered accusingly. "Nothing on the road."

"They must have been hidden by the shoulder of the mountain."

A few minutes later Karanja came running with the news that the patrol was close behind us, following the track into the forest. He had us moving fast then, along a narrow game trail that climbed steadily upwards through the trees. It was the same trail that he and Dima had followed on their way down to the Mission and shortly after noon we reached the spot where they had left the elephants. There was no sign of them now, only bushes and saplings freshly browsed and droppings that were warm to the touch.

Karanja paused for a moment, listening intently. But the forest was silent, a cathedral stillness, and he hurried us on, following the big footprints of elephants through a litter of broken branches that he hoped would make it more difficult for the patrol to follow us.

The trail broadened, the footprints increasing in number. And then the ground levelled out and suddenly we were in hot sun. It was a little glade full of butterflies and the quick darting of sunbirds, the grass falling steeply away, and across the green of foliage below we had a view eastwards into the Chalbi, the sand of the desert glimmering white like a great salt-pan to the blue horizon hazed with heat. The tracks kept to the high ground and after that we were in thick forest again, amongst wild olive and other tall

259

trees laced together with a liana tracery of rope-like strands.

"Where do you reckon we are now?" Abe stood with the map unfolded in his hand, holding it out for Karanja, who stared at it and shook his head. "We come to gorge soon," he muttered.

"And then?"

Karanja had his head cocked to one side, listening. "Maybe if we climb down into that gorge nobody follow us there."

"There's a game trail marked, but it zig-zags all the way, so I guess it's steep. Could elephants make it down a trail like that?" His mind was still on the elephants, not on the Army patrol following us.

Karanja shrugged. "We go on," he said tersely. "Not far now."

The trees became smaller, the forest thinning as we climbed, and suddenly there was light ahead, white and blinding. And then we were out of the undergrowth and on to a green strip of coarse African grass that went rolling down a shoulder of the mountain, cascading over rock outcrops towards the distant blur of Rudolf. Directly ahead of us it ended, vanishing abruptly into space, and, across the void beyond, a great peak of rock, all greys and greens and the black of shadows, rose naked against a blue-white background of cloudless sky. An eagle skimmed across the face of it, poised like a speck of dirt on a colour slide, and in the foreground, on that green grass sward, round elephant turds lay like footballs on an empty soccer field. The eagle swooped and was gone. Something died with a distant cry and we started out across the grass to the edge of that gorge.

God knows how deep it was. Two thousand, three thousand feet? It was impossible to gauge, for there was nothing to measure height or distance by as we stood on a rock platform staring down to terraces of grass and undergrowth falling away into clefts of shadow, the bottom of the gorge invisible. Abe shook his head. "No elephant could possibly—" But Karanja was pointing away to our right where a tumbled ter-

260

race of rocks had the brown earth of a beaten track through it. "Game trail," he said. And then he was staring up at the peak opposite, his eyes slitted against the glare. "Is there a trail marked up the far side?"

Abe pulled the map out. "No. There's a trail running along the bottom of the gorge, that's all."

"Maybe it go up the gorge and round the other side of Kulal."

Abe shook his head. "Up the gorge it crosses the height of land, then down along the shoulder of the mountain eastwards." He looked up at the peak. "That's no place for elephants."

"I am not thinking of elephants, Mr. Finkel."

"What then—that we've got to go down and up the far side? Do you really think that patrol would follow us down into the gorge? It will be dark in a few hours."

Karanja didn't say anything and Mary murmured, "I wish Tembo were here. He's no way of knowing where we are." She was staring at the far side of the gorge. "Unless—" She turned to Karanja. "Do you think he'd see a fire if we lit it high up, near the peak? There's no cloud. It would be visible for miles."

Karanja looked doubtful. "Is how we signal before we have walkie-talkie," he admitted. "But is dangerous." Whether he was referring to the patrol or to the mountain itself I wasn't sure, but I could sense a deep uneasiness.

"It's volcanic, so the rock will be bad in places." Mary was staring up at the peak again, her hat pulled down to shade her eyes. "I'm not certain about the last pitch, but up to that rock band just below the summit . . ." She turned back to Karanja. "Do you think he'd see it?"

"Maybe cloud later."

"Then hurry." She was suddenly urgent. "We'll find a way up. And if he sees the fire, then maybe it's not too late." Her voice trailed away, his reluctance becoming apparent to her. "At least there's a chance," she said. "If he's out on the shoulder of the mountain,

261

clear of the forest." And Karanja nodded uncertainly, his eyes troubled.

We started down then, into a tumbled litter of rocks, the trail falling steeply, twisting and turning down the buttressed face of the first of a number of ledges, and there were the slide marks of heavy bodies that had come this way before us. As we wound our way down deeper into the gorge it became hotter, occasional thickets of undergrowth hung drooping leaves in the windless air and there was an increasing sense of being shut in. A squeal from the shadowed bottom of the gorge stopped us momentarily, but we could see no sign of any elephants and nothing moved. A few moments later, coming out of a thicket below a sheer buttress of rock, we had a view right down the gorge with the same "island" of rock we had seen the previous morning rising up out of the bottom, and the green of the steep meadow slopes was dotted with moving figures. Dima grinned. "Nyani." And as I focussed my eyes in the sunglare, I could see they were baboons, crouched and moving on all fours, and there were young ones clinging to their mothers' fur.

The island looked nearer than it was, for we were now more than halfway down and my impression was of a great rock and grass plug blocking the gorge. Mary was searching the opposite face, which now seemed to rise up almost sheer, the peak of Kulal hidden by obtruding bands of rock. "There's sure to be a game trail there."

"Not for elephants," Karanja said firmly.

"No, for kudu."

He nodded. "Is good place for greater kudu."

"To hell with kudu," Abe said. "You find me those elephants." And as if in response to his words a thin squeal came up from below us.

"Ndovu." Dima nodded. But the squeal was not repeated, everything hushed and still in the lifeless air, only the coughing grunt of baboons made faint by distance.

It took us another half hour to reach the bottom, but though we could occasionally hear elephants, we never saw them. There was water in the bottom, actual running water that flowed in a channel that was deep in shade and twisted like a tiny canyon among cliffs and buttresses, and there were sudden expansion chambers that were flat and full of the debris of lush growth. The humidity was very high and the sweat poured off us. Karanja sent Dima on ahead, then stood staring up at the precipitous trail we had descended. Abe and I followed Mary's example, took our safari boots off and dabbled our bare feet in a pool. Small birds flitted in and out of the rock face. There was no sign of any patrol and the only sounds were the faint rumblings of elephants and the snap of branches, from far down the ravine.

Dima came back after about ten minutes, his black splayed feet carefully treading the middle of the stream. He reported a well-used game trail with elephants on it, but not the elephants they had been following during the night. This was a small group of three cows and two almost fully grown calves, and he said there were more further down the gorge—he had heard them, but he had not seen them.

Abe wanted to go on, but Karanja had taken charge of us now and he was still worried about the patrol. The only way to be certain they were not following us down into the gorge was to climb to a vantage point on the opposite side. We sat there, chewing on some of the leathery elephant meat and drinking all the water we could absorb while we discussed it. The ascent looked difficult, sheer cliffs of rock interspersed with clefts full of boulders and tangled vegetation, and Abe had the sense to realise it was beyond him. In the end it was Karanja who made the decision. Dima would remain with Abe and the two of them would head downstream, keeping to the water all the time. Mary and I would go with Karanja and try to scale the side of the gorge. If the patrol did catch up with us, then ours would be the only tracks for them to follow, and by then we should be well above them.

I left my bag and all the film with Abe and as we started up the gorge he called to me, "If you find an

263

old city perched on the top, send word and I'll come and film it for you."

"If it has pearly gates," I shouted back to him, "I'll have them opened so you can ride your elephant through." It was a silly remark, nothing more, but I was to remember it later.

He was splashing down the stream bed behind Dima. I saw him wave acknowledgment, then he was lost to view behind a buttress and we began casting along the north face, searching for a route up. But every cleft we tried proved impenetrable, all of them choked with fallen rock and vegetation. In the end it was the remains of stale kudu droppings that guided us. Mary spotted them, barely visible on a pile of detritus below a cliff overhang. The spill of rock and rubble led up behind the overhang, and after a few minutes' steep, almost vertical climbing from rock to rock we were out on a grass ledge with a melee of rock outcrops towering above us. It looked as though a demolition gang of giants had been at work on the mountain and if it hadn't been for the rare antelope that grazed there we would never have found a way. Their droppings were like signposts and both Karanja and Mary seemed to have an uncanny instinct that enabled them to follow the trail from one pale, dry-straw feces to the next.

We were in the sun's full glare, the climbing hard and exhausting, so that I was glad of the frequent pauses Karanja made to scan the far side of the gorge. Each time we stopped a new section of the trail we had descended became visible until at last we could see the lip of the gorge itself, a jagged line against the sun's glare. All this time we had seen no sign of movement anywhere on the trail.

The slope became easier for a while, our way winding through smooth battlements of rock, and when we paused again the sun was much lower and all the far side of the gorge was in deep shadow. Suddenly Karanja whispered hoarsely, "Soldiers. Don't anybody move." He would never have seen them if they had been on the trail, but they were on the skyline on the very edge of the gorge, figures moving in silhouette, climbing the rock outcrops and peering down.

We stood there, all three of us absolutely still, nakedly exposed in the slanting sunlight and very conscious that the gorge was so narrow we were in range of their rifles. Then Mary, who was standing only just above me, leaned cautiously down and gripped my shoulder. "See them?" she whispered. "Just starting down the trail."

"Of course I see them." They were leaping down the rocks, crawling out on to ledges, searching the trail.

"Not the soldiers, elephants—in the green of that first terrace." Her face was close to mine, the voice husky with excitement. "That's what they're all looking down at."

"Ssh," Karanja hissed from above us. "Don't talk, don't move."

I didn't see them at first. The sun was in my eyes and with the sides of the gorge all dark in shadow it was difficult even to detect the line of the trail.

"Almost level with us," she breathed, and slipped her hand over my shoulder, pointing.

I saw them then, on the trail we had come down, where it twisted among the rocks, dropping steeply into the gorge—brown-grey shapes plastered with mud, moving cautiously. A trunk waved above a low thicket, a great head thrown back, and there was an elephant sitting on its haunches as though performing some ridiculous act at a circus. It was sliding on its rump, two great leg stumps thrust out ahead. It checked on the lip of a sheer drop. Behind it, a youngster squealing miserably with another squatting adult holding on to it with its trunk.

We stood there transfixed, incredulous as the whole herd—seventeen of them—made that precarious descent to the sheer drop, made it safely and disappeared behind a buttress to lose themselves in a patch of forest thicket that clothed the next terrace. "I wouldn't have thought it possible," she breathed. "Tembo has talked about them going up and down

265

steep mountain paths, in the Aberdares and the Ngorongoro, but I never saw it so I never really believed it." She was chuckling quietly to herself. "The patrol hasn't a hope of getting down into the gorge now, not with that herd blocking the trail. They'll have covered our tracks beautifully." The elephants had started to browse now and she whispered in my ear, "You counted, did you?"

I nodded, wishing to God I had my camera with me. If the sun had been behind us and that bloody patrol weren't watching, what a picture it would have made—something unique, something I couldn't remember ever having seen on film before.

"I made the count exactly the same as last night."

I nodded. "Looks like Abe may meet up with his elephant after all."

"I hope not," she breathed. "They'll be frightened and exhausted, and when they see there's water there—"

Karanja hissed at us for silence again and after that we didn't talk, just stood there watching the African soldiers on the lip of the gorge and the elephants slowly moving down the trail. I was thinking of Abe, imagining him relaxed by the side of some pool with his trousers rolled up and his feet in the water and those elephants suddenly looming up in the last of the light. I wasn't seriously worried. He had Dima with him.

We were stuck there on the side of the mountain for almost half an hour. Then at last the patrol gathered together in a group and headed back into the forest. But even when they had all disappeared Karanja insisted on our remaining absolutely still until he was convinced they really were returning to the Mission for the night. At last he moved, coming down to join us. "Is getting late." There was an urgency in his voice as he stared at the lengthening shadows in the rocks that surrounded us.

"We've got to get higher," Mary said. "High enough for Tembo to see it. And the sky is clear. There'll be a moon later. We can come down by moonlight."

266

They stayed arguing for a while, Mary pointing out that the fire would not be visible from the Mission and Karanja still reluctant even though he was no longer in danger from the patrol. He was standing irresolutely, staring across the gorge at the trail opposite where the elephants were on the move again, performing their extraordinary circus act on the deep drop from one terrace to the next. Then he nodded abruptly, turning to face the mountain again, stocky black figure clawing his way up. Following close behind him, I sensed his reluctance, the tension building up in him, and I knew he was afraid. The sight we had just witnessed was in no way remarkable to him. His imagination operated on a different plane, the old superstitions of his race more deeply felt than any miracle of animal behaviour. And as we climbed higher and higher, the world dropped away below us, the gorge, the long grass shoulders of the mountain, the dark green cap of the rain forest that lay like a mantle across its broad back, all visible like a topographical map rolled out now that we were nearing the peak itself.

"Bad place," he muttered as I scrambled up to join him on a pinnacle of rock.

"How do you know? You've never been here before." My voice came breathless, the altitude pressing on my lungs.

"No. But is what everybody say. Nobody like Kulal. Cloud. Storm. Wind." His eyes rolled heavenward as though at any moment he expected a hurricane to hurl itself at us out of the cloudless sky. "Even Tembo don't like Kulal. Very dangerous mountain."

The sun was falling into the west, lighting the surface of Lake Rudolf to a deep jade green, the cliffs of the distant Turkana shore a faded line of brown, and no breath of wind. Another hundred feet and we reached a broad ledge close under the rock band. There were clefts and deep gulleys choked with vegetation and the stunted growth of trees. We rested for a moment, watching the sun grow in size and the sky turn to an incredible, brilliant green as the red disc dropped below the earth's rim. The long flat mountain ranges beyond the lake were turning black, puffs of white cloud over the Mara suddenly taking fire, the sky deepening to purple as we began searching the gulleys for dry wood, piling it on the ledge.

Stars were showing before we had finished, and when it was too dark to gather any more wood, Karanja settled down to the task of getting the heap to burn. At first all he achieved was smoke, for the wood was green and damp, but gradually the pile warmed through and flickers of flame appeared. We had less than two hours before the moon rose and we sat there feeding it sticks, nursing those feeble flickers until at last the whole pile suddenly caught.

It went up with a roar then, showers of sparks lifting into the velvet darkness, the glow of it lighting the rock face. Shadows danced and flickered, our faces red in the flames. Karanja had fashioned a long branch into a sort of pitchfork with the panga, and when the whole pile was alight and blazing red, he began to spread the embers westward along the ledge so that from a distance it would have the shape of an arrow pointing down the gorge towards the lake. I never saw the stars go out one by one over the Mara. I was like a kid on Guy Fawkes night, intent on the bonfire we had created, watching the sparks riding the heat upwards into the night, the red blaze warming the rock behind us, our shadows looming large. It was exciting, wildly exhilarating—a roaring fire on the top of a mountain peak where perhaps nobody had been before us.

And then it was done, the signal arrow made in glowing embers that must look from the distance like the red of lava flowing from a newly opened volcanic vent, and we sat there, the three of us, watching it, feeling the heat of it on our bodies, enjoying a spurious primeval sense of power, the mountain conquered, ourselves the masters sending out our message to the world. I can remember Mary's face bright with flame, her dark hair falling to her shoulders, her slim hands held to the blaze, sitting there, cross-legged, the firelight dancing in her eyes. And Karanja with his white teeth showing in a grin, and his face, with its broad flat nose, no longer black, but a dark bronze red.

"You think he'll see it?" she asked him.

"If he is looking towards Kulal."

"He must see it."

Far to the east the desert began to reveal itself in a soft light like the loom of a distant city. There were no flames now, only the charcoal hot red of burning embers, so that we saw the moon quite clearly as it came up over the edge of the Chalbi, a huge great Hallowe'en lantern, its slightly lopsided pumpkin face glowing orange as though lit from within. Karanja went to gather more wood. The moon was an African moon and he was an African, taking it for granted, but to me it was a strange unearthly sight as it rose up out of the desert like some ghostly phoenix to turn the far off sands the colour of dried blood. Mary saw it differently, sitting there beside me, hugging her knees and staring entranced. "It's beautiful," she breathed, and I thought I felt the mountain shiver as though with laughter. A spark flew and I heard the sound of the panga slashing wood deep in the cleft behind us. "I wish he were here," she murmured.

"Who? Your father?"

"If you like."

It was on the tip of my tongue to ask which one, but I knew—knew also in that moment that she didn't think of him as her father. The heat of the fire that warmed our bodies was not for van Delden's safety, but only to draw him away from Kirby-Smith. I left her then and went into the cleft to help Karanja. There was something I had to ask him. And as we hauled at the branches of a half-dead tree, standing shoulder to shoulder in the dark of the cleft, I said, "You don't like the mountain, do you?"

"No."

"What are you scared of—devils?"

He looked at me and laughed, his eyes gleaming white. "Not devils, Mr. Tait. Only this mountain that is a volcano has exploded many times."

"Then why are you here?"

He turned, the panga hanging loose in his hand. "I don't want the Army to trap him in that gorge, and if he kill Major Kirby-Smith . . . either way is bad politically." He shook his head. "Is better I am with him."

"What can you do?"

He shrugged, the lift of his shoulders barely visible in the shadowed glow of the fire. "Maybe nothing. I don't know." He stood there, a dim shape, very still, and he was frowning, his thoughts turned inwards. "Is difficult for me. I am African and no influence outside of my country. I cannot write about elephants. But now that I have seen what is happening here, how they climb up out of that gorge, all together on this mountain and heading for Lake Rudolf . . ." He paused. "He and I, we think alike now, and I have friends in Government. When they know I am also trying to stop this killing—" He was staring out to the darkness of the gorge and after a moment he said, "Is part of our heritage and one day, maybe, I live to see those same elephants crossing Kulal again, but going the other way, going south into the lands they live in when I am young man, going to protected areas where the world can see them again. Quiet, dignified elephants living in peace and rearing their calves. Not fleeing half-starved and in terror, charging everything." He shook his head, smiling to himself. "Is a dream maybe, but that is what I hope."

I didn't say anything for a moment, surprised at his depth of feeling, the way his words echoed van Delden's. But it was one thing to declare himself against the killing of elephants up here in the fastnesses of Kulal, quite another to put it into practice, and if he started shooting at Kirby-Smith again . . . "You'll get yourself killed," I said. "You may have political friends, but they're a long way away."

"Okay, then I am killed." And he laughed, his teeth shining white. "But if I am killed, then it is reported in the press and everybody know that Karanja dies because he is opposed to the policy of extermination."

270

He was still laughing, as though death were of no account, and when he saw I was shocked by his acceptance of it, he slapped me on the back. "No need to be afraid." He didn't realise that what appalled me was the harshness of this foreign world where everybody seemed to walk with death looking over their shoulders.

We finished breaking up the tree and dragged the branches to the fire, but the dead wood did not burn and it was the moon now that lit the rocks, its light white and brilliant, the desert turned to snow. "It's bright enough for us to find our way down," I said. But Mary shook her head, huddled close to the fire, staring at the moon. Karanja, too, seemed transfixed by it, and suddenly I realised there was a circle of light around it and the air was colder, a damp breeze blowing. And even as we stared the moon's halo intensified, a great circle filling half the sky. The desert blurred and vanished, the bright moon dulled, and in an instant the halo was gone and the moon itself had vanished, leaving only a vague translucence. A damp cold touched my face and suddenly we were in cloud and everything dark, only the fire glowing red on the eddying curtain of dampness that enveloped us.

"Does that mean we're here for the night?" I asked, and Mary nodded.

A blinding flash forked down the gorge, followed instantly by a crash of thunder that seemed to shake the whole mountain, and then the wind came, blowing out of the desert towards Lake Rudolf, and it began to rain. The rain was heavy for a moment and it was pitch black as we groped our way to the cleft. The noise of the thunder was incessant, flashes of lightning continually illuminating the rocks that sheltered us. Karanja curled himself up like a foetus, lying with his arms over his head, his eyes tight shut, moaning softly. The wind died and the air became charged with electricity. I could feel it tingling on my body as I crouched in the damp recesses of the rock, listening to the storm advancing on us from across the gorge. It was like an artillery barrage, the noise deafening.

271

I crawled to the entrance, lying there with the ground shaking under me, watching through slitted eyes the supercharged currents stabbing at the rocks in sizzling, blinding bolts of brilliant electric blue. And in their reflected glare I saw the black belly of the cloud hanging over the mountain, writhing and contorting. An eye-searing bolt struck just beyond the feeble glow of the fire, the thunder of it mingling with split rock in one gigantic crash. The ground shook and the acrid smell of pulverised rock drifted up on an eddy.

But that was the worst and I lay there, listening, as the core of that electrical storm swept over the peak above us, the noise of it gradually lessening to the grumble of a barrage battering the further slopes. I crept out then to tend the fire, my body chilled by the damp air swirling round us.

Mary joined me just as I had coaxed the embers into a blaze and we sat as close to the fire as we could, watching its glow reflected on the dense cloud mist pouring like smoke up out of the gorge. Lightning stabbed behind the peak above us, the growl of thunder reverberating through the rocks. She rolled over, staring up at me, her eyes wide and luminous in the firelight. "Frightened?"

I didn't answer, suddenly aware of her reaching out, her hand on my arm, pulling me down beside her. "Well, I am," she breathed, her face flushed, her lips parted, and the glow of the embers in her eyes. "Don't you know what to do when a girl is frightened?" There was a bubble of laughter in her throat, the hot glow of her eyes no longer borrowed from the fire, the passion of her nature overflowing. I felt the blood leap in my veins, the sudden appalling ache, and then her shirt was open, breasts bare, and she took my hand in her hands, pulling me down, the open eagerness of her mouth reaching up to me. That kiss was like a flame running through me, the touch of her tongue, the feel of her hands tearing at my clothes, stroking me, and those breasts, the fullness of her flesh pressed against mine. Some residue of puritanical ancestry caused me

272

to withdraw involuntarily, my brain flashing a memory of Abe's warning. "What about Karanja?" I breathed, my lips buried in her hair.

"Karanja?" The laughter bubbled again. "In Africa mating is normal." She suddenly drew back, staring at me. "You are normal, aren't you?"

"Yes."

"Well then—" And after that I didn't care as we sought the comfort and the warmth we needed, the reassurance of our physical existence. It wasn't love. It was something wild, primeval, totally primitive, our two bodies swept away by natural forces beyond control, and in the urge to imprint upon each other the fact of our survival we seemed charged with the same stabbing electrical currents as the air we breathed. It was as though the storm had entered into us. With passion we reincarnated the fury of it, and when we had spent ourselves and were lying on our backs, naked to the fire, there were stars overhead and the thunder was a faraway grumble fading into the distance.

For a brief moment the moon smiled down on us from a ragged gap in the clouds, but then it was gone and we were enveloped once more in a blanket of mist. I slept fitfully and woke with the dawn. There was a damp chill in the air, both of us lying fully clothed so close to the burned-out embers of the fire that the shoulder of my sweater was scorched brown. There was no wind and the mist hanging thick round our ledge made it seem as though we were imprisoned in an empty void, nothing visible except the rock behind us reaching up into clouds. I was lying there, my eyes searching the rock face, wondering what lay hidden behind that veil of mist, when Mary asked, "Did Pieter van Delden ever make it to the top of Kulal?"

"No," I said. "He never came to this side of the gorge."

"Well, now's your chance." She jumped to her feet, tossing droplets of moisture from her lank hair, her arms hugged around her, staring upwards. But then Karanja said, "We go down now." Sometime during

273

the night he had come out of the dark womb of the cleft seeking the warmth of the fire. Now he was huddled close to the dead embers, shivering with only a thin shirt, his black skin blue with cold, and all he wanted was to get back down into the gorge. "You go on," Mary told him. "We'll follow."

He shook his head, arguing that we had better go down while we could. But there were currents of air swirling the mist around us, a faint glimmer of sunshine. "The cloud will clear soon," she said. He seemed to accept that, so we left him there, trying to get the fire going again, and climbed up the side of the cleft where erosions had fashioned footholds in the rocks. It was easier than I had expected and above the rock band the slope was gentler, a chaos of mist-enveloped outcrops and boulders, the shattered debris of a mountain shaken by volcanic disturbance. The cloud thickened as we climbed and in the end neither of us was certain that we had stood on the actual summit of the mountain, for it was a nightmare of rock castles and gulleys all dimly seen through a thick grey miasma of moving cloud.

"So where's your ancient city?" Mary stood laughing at me, with her hair blowing in the clouds and her face glistening with moisture.

"Well, at least we're on the peak. I've seen it for myself." I turned away, knowing now that no race of early men would be fool enough to build in such an area of instability. And since it wasn't Kulal, then it had to be Porr. It was the only other notable peak, and as we started down I was wondering whether I would ever get to that lone pyramid of a mountain halfway up Lake Rudolf. My mind on that, I lost all sense of direction. The cloudcap over the mountain had brightened now to a white translucent fog. It began to drizzle and we both of us stopped, realising suddenly that there was nothing to guide us in that tumult of dim-seen rock shapes. The only certainty was that we were on the slope leading down into the gorge, and so we went on, until suddenly we found ourselves on the edge of a void. We had reached

274

the rock band, a vertical drop falling into nothingness. We stood there, calling to Karanja, our shouts lost in cloud and no echo of an answer. Then, but a hundred yards or so to our left beyond a pinnacle of shattered rock, we heard the sound of an answering call.

It was only when we reached the fire that we realised we were both of us shivering with cold. "Better we go down now," Karanja said, "before the mist clears." He was thinking of the patrol, which might well have started out from the Mission again at first light, but when I looked up at him and saw into his eyes there was a sudden flash of understanding between us. It wasn't just the patrol; we were both of us filled with the same urge—to get off that bloody mountain before it brewed another storm.

I think Mary felt the same, for she was on her feet at once, following close behind Karanja as she began the descent from that ledge. He moved fast, following unerringly the route we had climbed, and when we were about halfway down a breeze touched our faces, the mist lifting and brightening until it was a white intensity of trapped sunlight that was almost blinding. The far side of the gorge emerged first as a dark shadow, then as something visible but blurred. A moment later the mist vanished like smoke. The sun shone down on us and it was suddenly hot.

The abruptness of that transformation was startling, everything clean and fresh with moisture, and brilliantly clear as though we were looking at it under slight magnification. But the sun burned in a sky that was white, not blue, and it had a great circle of light around it. An ice halo, Mary thought. She had seen it once on Kilimanjaro.

We reached the bottom and turned downstream; no sign of any human having been on the trail before us, only the tracks of elephants. We caught glimpses of that island of rock and grass coming gradually nearer until it seemed to block the gorge ahead, and every now and then the hot stillness was pierced with the cry of a baboon. We were right under that island with the wind on our back when there was a sudden roaring

275

and squealing of elephants, a cry of pain, and then the crash of bodies in thick bush. Silence, and Karanja moving cautiously, his rifle ready in his hand. "What was it—baboon?" I asked.

He shook his head. "No, not baboon."

And Mary said, "It sounded human."

Outcrops of rock now, the trail narrowing and everything suddenly very still, the heat oppressive. Karanja called softly—"Dima! Dima!" We rounded a bend, the trail opening out again, a thicket of bushes on both sides of the stream, and suddenly there was Dima half hidden behind a rock, his rifle pointed at us. He stood up at the sight of us, calling urgently, and when we reached him there was Abe lying at his feet, his face ashen, blood streaming from a gash in his head and his right hand at a grotesque angle. His eyes were open, a glazed look, so that for a moment I thought he was dead. But then his lips moved in a whisper: "Is the camera all right, Colin?" He didn't seem to realise he still had it gripped in his other hand, cradling it on his stomach. And when I told him, he said, "Take it, will you. There's about a minute and a half exposed, all close-ups." He had closed his eyes, the sweat standing in beads on his face.

Mary came back from the stream, her neckerchief soaked in water. She bathed his head, then gently began rolling up the sleeve of his shirt. His arm looked as though it had been hit by a sledgehammer, the flesh all bruised, the bone broken just above the wrist. She straightened it with a deft, quick movement, the bone grating and his mouth opening in a thin scream. "We'll have to splint it." He had fainted and she looked up at Dima. "What happened, for God's sake?"

The explanation came in a flood of Swahili and when he stopped she said to Karanja, "He could have shot it."

Dima shook his head obstinately. "Patrol come quick if they hear gun."

"Bugger the patrol," she said angrily. "He might

276

have been killed. And that patrol, wherever it is, is out of earshot."

"He don't know that," Karanja reminded her. "And if we are not coming down the gorge—"

"The calf winded us, is that what you mean?"

Karanja nodded unhappily and I said, "What's this about a calf? A calf couldn't have done that."

"No? Even at one year old they weigh about twelve hundred pounds, and that big calf of hers must be at least five; that's the average gap between births."

"But what happened?"

She stared at me, exasperated that I hadn't understood a word of what Dima had said. "It was the elephant he called Sally. They were holded up in the rocks there, waiting for us, and then this herd arrived and she was in the lead. She was right there in that open glade and he couldn't resist the opportunity. He crept down out of the rocks with his camera. . . ." She turned to Karanja and asked him to cut some sticks to use as splints. "Dima says he tried to stop him, but Abe wouldn't listen. The cow came right down to the water and the odd thing was she didn't seem to mind him. He was right there in front of her as she started drinking and then spraying water over herself. There was just the stream between them and he was crouched there, filming her when it happened. Her ears suddenly spread out, her head lifted, she swung quickly round, facing up the gorge and trumpeting. That was when the calf came out of the thicket there, right behind him. It was obeying its mother's orders, trying to get back to her, and Abe was in the way. It sent him flying with a sweep of its trunk, ploughed through the stream, and in an instant the whole herd was crashing away down the gorge."

"It was my fault." Abe's eyes were open again, his voice urgent as he struggled up on his left elbow. "I was between the calf and its mother. I should have realised . . ." He sank back, exhausted, his lips bared with pain. "I forgot—she still had a calf." And he added in a whisper, "She was so quiet, so relaxed—until she scented danger. She seemed to understand I

277

meant no harm, that I was unarmed." He closed his eyes against the glare. "I'm glad Dima didn't shoot," he murmured. "You can't blame the calf." He reached out and gripped Mary's arm. "Will it hurt much—when you splint it? I'm an awful coward."

"You'll be all right," she said cheerfully. "It will hurt for a moment, that's all."

But it took much longer than a moment, the three of us holding him down while he screamed and screamed. Then, thank God, he passed out and she was able to finish the job without him struggling all the time. She was covered with sweat as she sat back on her heels, staring down at the splint bandaged with strips of towelling. "I hope it's all right. I've only done that with animals before, and usually we had an anaesthetic." She looked round vaguely. "How far is it to Loiyangalani? There's an airstrip there, and if a plane came over . . . Where's that map?"

I found it in our bag. The oasis camp of Loiyangalani was a good six miles away. "He can't walk that."

"He'll have to. Or else we carry him. He has to be got to a hospital somehow."

We started as soon as Abe recovered consciousness. I wanted to abandon all our gear, but Abe wouldn't hear of it and Karanja clung to the camera and films as though they were more precious than the plastic water container. Because of the elephants we were forced up on to a shoulder of the mountain, clear of the gorge, which gradually petered out below us. We moved slowly with many pauses, Abe lightheaded and in pain, but doggedly staying on his feet, the heat increasing as the day wore on and the lake drawing gradually nearer.

Coming down off the lower slopes was the worst. It took us over an hour to cross an old lava field, the black rocks jagged and broken, the late afternoon sun beating down at us, dust blowing and the temperature in the high nineties. After that it was sand, long rolling dunes of it with isolated patches of thorn and furze. By then we had finished our meat and almost all the water, and Abe was barely conscious, stumbling along

278

with two of us supporting him. But we could see the broken palms of the oasis now, the fire-blackened roofless buildings of the tourist camp, and the remains of the Catholic Mission that Dima said had been run by Italians. And across the flat land beyond the palms, the lake stretched flat as a steel sheet to the jagged volcanic outline of South Island, the Turkana shore dim in the distance. There was not a breath of wind and nothing stirred along the lake's edge, no elephants, not even any sign of life around the huddle of cone-like dwellings that had been the manyata of the El Molo.

All the way down we had reckoned on the El Molo supplying us with fish, for this small lakeshore tribe had existed for centuries on the teeming marine life of the lake, particularly tilapia and the huge Nile perch. Now instead we would have to catch our own fish and Dima went on ahead with Karanja, the two of them rapidly lost to view as they loped off across the sands. We had glimpses of them later, after we had reached the shelter of the doum palms. Abe had fallen into a deep sleep, utterly exhausted, and Mary and I stood on top of the shallow escarpment on which the palms grew, looking out across the flats towards the sunset. Below us was the airstrip, the frayed windsock still hanging from its pole, limp in the breathless air, and the green line of a ditch carrying a trickle of oasis water out towards the deserted village, and beyond the manyata two tiny figures were hurrying towards the flat burnished circle of the port. And when they had disappeared from sight behind the jetty, there was nothing moving at all except birds flying in dark rafts close above the surface of the water.

The sun had set, everything very still, the sky a violent purple, and out across the pale, almost luminous waters of the lake, South Island stood black against the sky, a hideous, piled-up melee of volcanic vents and old lava flows. Years ago, I remembered, a British expedition had landed two men there and they had never been seen again. When I mentioned this to Mary she named them—Martin and Dyson. "Fuchs was leader of the expedition." And she added, "Tembo has been over there several times, once on an El Molo fishing raft. There's a herd of goats there and the largest crocs he's ever seen. He says it's just about the most desolate place on earth."

Night fell and with the stars came the mosquitos. We dozed intermittently, bitten to hell. A wind got up, rattling the palm fronds overhead, the moon leering down at us, more lopsided than ever, and then at last there were shouts and the two Africans were back with an old fishing net full of tilapia, all gutted and cleaned. We got a fire going and cooked them on sticks of thorn, holding them by the fins that fringed their flat bodies, and it was while we were squatting there in front of the blaze, sucking the flesh of the tilapia and trying to fend off the mosquitos, that a dark figure suddenly emerged from the palms. Karanja grabbed his rifle and we all leapt to our feet.

It was Mukunga and he held something out to us, wrapped in a palm leaf and all bloody. "Tembo send you present."

"What is it? Where is he?" Mary asked.

It was crocodile meat and van Delden was camped about seven miles to the north of us in what Mukunga called El Molo Bay. I remembered it from the map, a shallow inlet opposite the small El Molo Islands. "Me watch from hill of the dead. See smoke here." He had a 15 cwt truck with him. "You eat meat, then go with me. Loiyangalani no good—upepo now."

The moon had gone, black clouds overhead, and the wind in the palms was like the roar of the surf breaking on a reef. Gusts blattered at the fire, the meat sizzling and Mukunga talking fast in Swahili, gesturing and laughing. He was telling the story of how they had got hold of the truck, and I sat there, listening to the roar of the wind and thinking of van Delden. At one point Abe said urgently to Mary, "Ask him if he's seen any elephants along the lake shore."

"Ndovu?" Mukunga nodded, and after listening to him for a moment Mary said, "Yes. There are elephants in El Molo Bay, a whole herd, and more to the north. He says they're feeding on the lakeweed, lots of them wading in the shallows all along the shore."

"Does Kirby-Smith know that?"

She nodded. "Yes. Alex knows." And she added, so quietly I hardly heard her above the shattering blast of another gust, "He's moving the outfit up to Loiyangalani." And she closed her eyes, sitting very still, not saying anything until finally Karanja dowsed the fire with sand and we walked through the palms to the truck.

Part Four

WARDEN OF
THE NORTH

THE MOON WAS GONE, black clouds hanging over the oasis as we headed north on a rough track, our own dust billowing past us in the gusts. We crossed a lugga, the track like the gateway in some ancient earthworks, and after that the wind was less. There was vegetation here, thorn trees mainly, and small birds rose up from under our wheels, skittering away like grasshoppers in the headlights. "Namaqua doves, I think." Mary was leaning forward, her hand on Abe's shoulder. He was in the front seat and he half turned to her. "This is one of the hunters' trucks, isn't it? How did he get hold of it?"

"Hijacked it."

"Yes, but how? Did Mukunga say?"

She nodded, silent for a moment. I don't think she wanted to talk about it. To talk about it meant thinking about what happened now. But in the end she told us what had occurred after van Delden left us at the Mission. He had coasted halfway down the shoulder of the mountain to a point where he had a clear view down into the gorge and could get the Land-Rover off the track into the shelter of some rocks. Below them a party of hunters was moving slowly back to their vehicles parked in the flat scrub country where the cliffs widened out. Later, from a different vantage point, they had watched the vehicles crawl across the plain below, and at the well, where the elephants had dug for water, two of the trucks had turned off and started up the track towards the Mission. The first was the Army three-tonner carrying the patrol. "They let that pass," she said, "then blocked the road with the Land-Rover and ambushed the second vehicle, which was following some way behind to avoid the dust stream."

"What about the men in it—they were Africans, were they?"

"Yes, four of them. He dropped them off by the well."

The moon had come clear of cloud and I could see Abe's face, dead white and frowning. "At least he didn't shoot them."

"What happened to the Land-Rover?" I asked.

"They ran it over the edge into the gorge."

The track had become harder, the shoulder of hill rising black to the left, a glint of water far ahead. Abe was holding himself tight. "So what happens now, Mary? You said something about Kirby-Smith moving to Loiyangalani."

She nodded, that shut look on her face. "They were due to break camp at dawn this morning. At least, that's what the hunters said."

"To move up to Loiyangalani?"

"Yes."

"Then why aren't they here? There's no sign of them and it can't be more than a day's journey."

"The track, probably. Mukunga says it's very bad where it crosses the lava fields by Sirimar. Earth tremors have destroyed several of the concrete ways the missionaries built to get their trucks over the worst of the boulders. Maybe they couldn't make it."

Abe was silent then, knowing it was what she desperately hoped. We were running along the side of the hill now, close above the water, and it was shallow, more a marsh, with countless birds asleep like black stones. The headlights swung, the black stones turning to white, and three pelicans pulled pouched beaks from under their wings in slow motion. A goliath heron, still as a post, lifted its razor-sharp head and there were storks standing one-legged in the mud. On the edge of visibility grey outcrops of rocks moved. "Elephants?" But Mukunga shook his head. "Kiboko."

284

"Hippos," Mary said. And then we had reached the lake shore and the moon was clear so that we could see islands pale beyond the wind-whipped water. The track ceased and we were on the beach, the truck bucking as it ground in low gear up a long promontory dotted with the cairns of ancient burials. "Hill of the dead," Mukunga shouted above the noise of the engine and the breaking waves. Then we stopped and van Delden was standing there like some prophet in a hostile desert of rock, his white hair blowing, and a rifle, gripped by the barrel, lying across his shoulder. "That you, Toto? I was afraid we'd lost you." He spoke gently, a note of fondness in his voice.

"You didn't see our signal then? We climbed to the top of Kulal, lit a fire there." She was nervous, her words coming in a rush.

He shook his head, his eyes fastening on Karanja. "So it *was* you." He didn't ask him why he had fired at Kirby-Smith's Land-Rover and then gone after the elephants, he just stood there, smiling, his teeth showing white in his beard. "You stupid show-off bastard." It was said affectionately, almost admiringly, and he seemed on the point of saying something else, but Mary interrupted him, explaining about Abe's arm. "Has that plane been over here? We need to get him to hospital."

"Army planes have other things to do besides look for me." He went over to Abe, examining the splint. "A good job you did there. Anyway," he added, "nothing can land at Loiyangalani till the upepo dies down."

The truck had a first aid kit and he gave Abe an antibiotic injection. After that we settled down to sleep, building little stone windbreaks for ourselves. The ground was very hard, the noise of the wind and the lake incessant, but I was asleep almost immediately.

I woke with the first of the light to the sound of voices, Mary arguing with van Delden.

"It wouldn't do any good."

"You thought differently the other morning."

"I was afraid you'd kill each other."

"The situation hasn't changed."

There was a long pause. Then on a note of forced cheerfulness she said, "Perhaps he'll have turned back. Mukunga said the road was in bad shape."

"We got through."

"But with this wind blowing . . ."

"The wind won't stop him and he has enough men to rebuild the road where it drops down the lava escarpment to the shore."

"He won't risk those refrigerator trucks on a road like that."

"There's a back route. It was completed for the Mission early in 1973. One way or another he'll be here today."

Silence then. Finally she said, "All right, I'll try. But why is it always other people who must give way, never you?" Her words tumbling over one another, deep-throated and sullen. "It's always been the same. Can't you ever see another man's point of view?"

"No, not in this."

Another long silence, then he said: "You tell him. Tell him to pull his outfit back to the South Horr Gap."

"Why me? Why not talk to him yourself?"

That quick bark of a laugh. "We've nothing more to say."

"If you'd only talk to him reasonably. Not threatening, but trying to agree some limit—"

"You know that wouldn't work."

"Because you hate him."

"We don't speak the same language, that's all."

"You hate him," she repeated, her voice no longer sullen, but high and wild.

"That's enough, Mary."

"No. No, it isn't. You've always hated him, ever since—"

The smack of his hand on her face, her shocked cry brought me to my feet. They saw me then, their dark dawn figures turning away almost guiltily and van Delden calling to me gruffly: "Fetch some water from the lake, will you. I'll get a fire going."

286

I went down the hill, my mind still on that scene, past the heaped rock piles of ancient burials, the light growing all the time and the water glinting pale, wavelets whispering in the wind. Was she right? Was it the hurt pride of a man who had lost his wife to another man? Inland, the shallows of the marsh were a still pale expanse, coots bobbing and waders busy at the edge. The pelicans had all gone, the storks too, but the herons were still there, motionless. And then I was remembering the Serengeti and how he had stood there at the Conference full of a deep anger, and I knew it wasn't that.

The lake shore, when I reached it, was black lava shingle, the water tepid with an alkaline taste. I would have stripped off and waded in, but as I filled the jerrican something big swirled in the moving shadow of a shoal of fish and the surface of the water was whipped to froth, leaping glints of silver. The sky was taking on colour now, a faint blue with thin wisps of cloud drifting like fog patches, but the islands close offshore were still dark silhouettes. I left the can and walked along the shore towards what looked like a dug-out canoe drawn up on a stretch of dark sand. Three logs lay stranded close beside it, but as I approached them they rose up on short legs and went sliding into the water, hissing angrily. The sand was gritty and just beyond the straight furrows scored by the crocodiles were the great rounded pug marks of a hippopotamus. The canoe was a raft of logs lashed together.

The clouds took fire as I climbed back up the hill, the light intense and luminous, a brilliance that was harshly beautiful. A blackened tin of water was already boiling and Mtome was squatting beside the glowing oven of stones, kneading posho into a dough, Mukunga plucking two Egyptian geese shot the previous evening. Van Delden looked up from cleaning his rifle. "When the upepo stops blowing maybe I'll take you out in that raft."

I shook my head. "Don't bother."

"You want to see Porr, don't you? You can't see it from here."

"Not if it means going out into the lake on that thing."

"It's safe enough when there's no wind. The El Molo use them for spearing perch. Have you still got that typescript with you?" And when I told him I'd jettisoned it on the mountain he said, "Pity. I'd like to have read it while we're waiting." He put his rifle down and fished something out of the pocket of his bush jacket. "This might interest you." He held it out to me, a broken piece of pottery, badly pitted, but still showing the dark brown marks of a design.

"Where did you find it?"

"On that first island, in a fissure, and there were marks on the rocks; too faint to make out what they represented. Did Pieter van Delden get out to those islands?"

I shook my head, turning the fragment over in my hand. "Is this part of a pot, do you think?"

"Keep it if you like. Take it along to the British Museum. They'll tell you. And there's more below the fissure, but all small pieces by the look of them. Maybe if you searched the other islands . . ." He stopped at a sudden outburst of bird cries and reached for his rifle.

We all turned, gazing down at the flat sheet of the mere where the birds moved restlessly. Something had disturbed them. Then, round the corner of the hill, an elephant appeared, moving slowly, its trunk exploring the mud and weed at the water's edge. It moved with a quiet, deliberate pachydermal dignity that seemed entirely at one with the primordial setting, and I had a sense of timelessness; I could be back a million, two million years, back further, perhaps, to a time when the first ancestor of man inhabited the shores of this ancient lake.

"A bull," van Delden said quietly.

Its back and head were plastered with mud and the sun, coming up over the hill in a burst of heat that coloured the land a fire-brick yellow, turned the animal from grey to pale ochre so that it merged into the background of sand and rock, barely visible as it shambled along the far edge of the marsh towards the lake shore, an ugly gash across its shoulders. More elephants made their slow weary entrance upon the scene. I counted seven of them, all adults, moving in a stumbling silent rush towards the lake, which was now a brilliant sapphire blue. The islands off the shore were no longer vague humps, but clear and sharp in that bright light, all browns and reds with a frill of white where the wind broke waves against their base. The bull, a distant tide-rock shape standing in the lake, was spraying water, its trunk lifting and falling, its body already glistening black, the wound showing as an open slash of red.

"A lost world," Mary murmured. And van Delden, looking at her sharply, said, "This is their last refuge."

"It can't support them."

"Always some specious argument . . ." He turned abruptly away, talking to Mukunga in his own language and shutting her out as though afraid of losing his temper with her again. We drank our tea and ate our breakfast, and all the time I was conscious of the tension between them. The fragment of pottery van Delden had given me seemed suddenly of no importance beside that little group of tired gaunt leviathans all standing now in the lake and drinking thirstily. How far had they come? I wondered. From the Aberdares where the forest trees were almost all cut down? Or Tsavo perhaps, across several hundred miles of hostile land peopled by man, their young all slaughtered, their numbers reduced? I picked up the piece of pottery and in a mood of sudden disgust I threw it on to one of the burial cairns, where it shattered into fragments. "You'd better show me how to use a rifle," I said to van Delden. "I've never fired one before."

"Later," he said. "If you wish." He was talking to Abe about the lake and its strange colouring, and I lay back, thinking about those elephants, the stones under me burning hot, the wind dying. Skeins of birds flew low over the lake, fish shoals dark like cloud shad-

ows occasionally bursting into frenzied splashes of silver, and van Delden's voice murmuring gently in the
heat: "They say it's the algae. When the surface is
calm, then it really is a jade-green sea, all the mass of
algae coming to the surface, a green skin of plant life.
But with the upepo, it all sinks and the lake becomes
hard and blue. Mostly, when I've been up here, it's
been blue in the early morning, then the wind takes
off and it turns green. You'll see—about noon it'll turn
green."

Mukunga said something, getting to his feet, and
Karanja also rose. "I go with him."

"No. One is enough."

But Karanja shook his head. "Is better I go with
him. When the hunting trucks arrive I think they still
have the support of an Army detachment. Maybe I
know the officer." He shouldered his rifle, and without
waiting for permission he went after Mukunga. The
old man sat there, not saying a word, his eyes on the
truck as it drove off, and I could guess what was in his
mind. This was a different Karanja and he wasn't sure
of him.

The truck disappeared beyond the line of the hill
and he gave a little shrug, then turned to me. "Okay,
if you want to try a few shots, we've spare guns and
plenty of ammunition."

He had me firing at an old tin set on one of the burial mounds, and with the first shots the elephants were
gone, lost to view behind a low rise. Van Delden,
watching them, nodded his head in satisfaction. "The
further north they go the better it will be for them. I'd
like to get them all off that mountain and headed
north." And he added, "They've a long way to go before they get to the Ethiopian border. This lake is all
of 180 miles long."

I fired altogether about a dozen rounds, and with
the last shots I hit the tin twice at a distance of fifty
yards. "Calm," he said. "That's the secret. You have
to keep calm. Whatever's coming at you, just hold
your breath, aim, and fire, bringing the sights up on to

290

the mark, steady and unflustered, just as if you were firing at that tin. Okay?"

The lake was already turning green, and not a breath of wind, the heat heavy and humid. Mary was splashing about in the shallows and I joined her, wading in with my clothes on. Her wet hair clung to her head, making it seem smaller, and I could see her breasts with the nipples poking at the thin wet khaki of her shirt. The water was tepid, the sun on it a blinding glare. Far to the north a toy elephant stood in a posture of levitation, its image raised by the lake's steaming heat. "So now you're a crack shot." She was grinning at me and I dived and grabbed her legs, tipping her up, and we played, laughing in the water till our eyes were sore and our heads burned with the heat.

I went up the hill then to see how Abe was, lying in the shade of the truck's canvas top, which they had rigged up in the lee of a burial mound. "Lucky devil!" he said. "I'd give anything to be in the water." It was airless under the canvas and he was sweating.

"Where's van Delden?" I asked.

"On top of the hill, keeping watch, and he's sent Mtome and Dima to guard the road. I don't think he trusts Karanja."

"How's the arm?"

"Fine. It doesn't hurt too much." He took his glasses off and asked me to wipe them. "What do you reckon is going to happen?"

I shook my head. It was something I didn't want to think about.

"You realise Kirby-Smith has lost a plane, two trucks, and a Land-Rover."

"He can always call on the Army for replacements."

He nodded. "If it wasn't for the Army I'd say van Delden was waging a pretty successful holding operation." I handed him back his glasses and he said, "Sometime during the night he's going to dump me as close as he can to the oasis. Mary will be with me. I think he hopes she can persuade Kirby-Smith to pull his outfit back. A truck, in other words—a sort of

291

modus vivendi. What's Mary think? Is that possible?"

"I doubt it. They were talking about it this morning and she didn't think he'd agree."

"Nor do I." He eased his buttocks on the stones. "With luck I'll get evacuated. What about you? If it's a shoot-out—" He was staring at me and there was real concern in his eyes. "You'll have the camera, but if you've got pictures they consider damaging . . . I don't know; maybe you can trade the film for safe passage out of the country, but I wouldn't bank on it." I thought I heard the sound of an engine, very faint and far away, and I ducked out from under the canvas shelter. The road was empty, but Mary was calling something from the lake shore, and then the 15 cwt came into view with Mukunga driving, nobody else. It stopped beside her, and van Delden, halfway down the slope, called out, "What's happened? Where's Karanja?"

"Gone off on his own," she answered.

When I reached the truck they were still interrogating Mukunga and I had to wait some time before Mary explained that the old oasis touring camp had been occupied by an Army patrol and Karanja had gone down to make contact with the officer in charge. "One of the trucks had a radio aerial and he was very confident the officer in charge would let him contact Army HQ. The last Mukunga saw of him he was holding his rifle up with a handkerchief tied to the barrel and walking straight towards the building that used to be the bar."

"When was this?"

"About ten-thirty, just after Alex's outfit had established themselves in the Mission buildings."

"Mukunga didn't wait for him?"

"Yes, but back at the truck, which was parked in the doum palms. He waited about half an hour, then one of the hunting trucks started down to the harbour and another headed out towards the airstrip. He was afraid of being cut off, so he came straight back."

Van Delden was still talking to Mukunga, both of

them gazing out across the shallow expanse of water to the bare brown slope beyond and the islands shimmering in the heat. Finally he nodded, looked at Mary, and said, "Okay, we'll shift camp. You get your patient ready to move." He called to Mtome, gave instructions to Mukunga, then turned to me. "You want to try paddling an El Molo fishing raft? Take it up along the shore there. We may need it."

The raft, when I launched it, proved more stable than I had expected, but it had almost no freeboard and I hugged the shore, scared of deep water. Also it was difficult to steer until I got the hang of it, kneeling at the centre of balance and using the primitive paddle blade as a steering oar at the end of each stroke. I was almost out of sight of the hill of the dead before the truck began to raise its telltale dust stream. There was no wind now and in the passage between shore and island the water was flat, a dark viscid green. Shoals of fish moved like cloud shadows and when I stood up, balancing myself carefully, I could see, far to the north, a heap of rock glowing white in the sun like the great pyramid of Cheops. And in a little bay about a mile away there were elephants standing in the water.

I began steering for the first of the islands, feeling free and full of a sense of exhilaration now that I was on my own in the immensity of the great lake. But I did not land, for as I glided into the shore long lizard shapes slid soundless and without a splash into the water. I had no rifle, no means of fending off the crocodiles, and I turned the clumsy craft and headed back towards the shore, the heat making the blood pound against my temples.

The hollow in which they had parked the truck was a mixture of sand and rock interspersed with gravel, and it was all the same colour, ochre yellow washed out by the glaring heat haze. From the top of a rise we looked out across the mere with its bobbing coots to the hill where we had spent the night, and half an hour later an open Land-Rover with African soldiers in it appeared in a cloud of dust from the direction of

Loiyangalani. "They'll see our tracks," Mary whispered, and van Delden nodded. "So what happens then?"

"There are only four of them."

Nobody spoke after that, the Land-Rover crawling along below the shoulder of the hill until it came to the lake. It stayed there for a moment, one of the men in it standing and staring up at the hill. He was not in uniform, and van Delden, with his glasses to his eyes, muttered, "Karanja." The figure sat down again and the Land-Rover turned, moving back along the edge of the mere to the point where Mukunga had turned the 15 cwt off the track. It stopped there and we watched in silence as Karanja got out, stood talking to the driver for a moment, then turned and began walking towards us, his rifle gripped by the barrel and swung carelessly across his shoulder. The Land-Rover drove off, its dust gradually settling, nothing now below us but that solitary figure plodding steadily along the water's edge and up the slope, following the 15 cwt's tracks. Van Delden stood up, calling to him, and Karanja waved, coming straight towards us with something of a swagger, his teeth showing white in a broad grin. "So what have you been up to?" van Delden asked. "You look bloody pleased with yourself."

Karanja nodded, still grinning. "I think maybe the Army fly you out." He sat down, rubbing the dust and sweat from his forehead.

"You made contact with the military commander, did you?"

"Ndio. I talked with him by radio. There is report of a band of Shifta moving towards Marsabit, so he don't want any trouble here. But first he must speak with Nairobi."

"And what about Major Kirby-Smith? What about the elephants here on Rudolf? You know I'd never agree to leave without some guarantee they would be left in peace."

Karanja looked at him, not grinning now, just smil-

294

ing quietly. "But if Ileret is made a game reserve, I think you leave then."

Van Delden gave that quick hard laugh. "With you as warden, is that the deal?" And Karanja went into a high peal of laughter.

"Would Kimani agree to that?"

"Kimani? Kimani is finish, I think. After what you do at that Conference." But he wouldn't even hazard a guess at Kimani's successor, still laughing in embarrassment and excusing himself by saying that he was not exactly at the centre of things here on the shores of Lake Rudolf. And though van Delden questioned him closely, his answers were evasive. All he would say was that Pat Murphy was the source of the rumors, having just flown back from Nairobi, and that Major Kirby-Smith was worried that he no longer had full backing for his operation.

"He'll be ordered to stop it, is that what you mean?"

But Karanja shook his head. "That will depend on who is made Minister in place of Kimani." And he added, "Is only talk at the moment, you understand."

He wasn't being devious and his laughter seemed a cover for his own uncertainty rather than any amusement at the situation. His relationship with van Delden was a very strange one now, the old subservience overlaid by a pushful self-confidence, and yet underneath it I sensed that nothing had really changed, the bond between them as strong as ever, so that I wasn't surprised at the deep concern in his voice as he said, "Please, you take my advice. Do nothing. Perhaps tomorrow the major get a new directive."

"In this country," van Delden growled, "things don't happen as fast as that, and tomorrow he may kill enough elephants to fill those meat trucks of his."

Karanja shrugged, as though to indicate there were other, more immediate problems engaging his attention. "Is not the elephants," he muttered.

Van Delden reached out and grabbed him by the arm. "What do you mean by that?"

But Karanja shook his head, wrenching himself free

295

and getting to his feet. "The Army don't want any trouble," he said again. "I am to tell you that and I have told you. They have mortars and machine guns and they know where you are." He turned to Mary. "You talk to him. Maybe he listen to you." And he walked off, down towards to lake shore, a suddenly impressive figure, solitary against the flat immensity of that jade sea.

"He's right." Mary was leaning forward, her dark eyes pleading. "Wait and see what happens."

Van Delden said nothing, sitting there, his rifle across his knees, staring after Karanja, and I wondered what he was thinking. Was he seeing Karanja as I saw him, symbolic of the future here in Africa? Or was he resenting the passage of time, the change in attitudes? And Abe said quietly, "If the cull is called off, then I hope to God he's stopped in time." And I knew he was thinking of that elephant making her way down the gorge.

There was nothing for us to do now but wait, and after we had fed the afternoon passed slowly, a somnolent interlude, the heat intense and the lake a shimmering, blinding glare. We kept watch in turn from a crumbling outcrop, but no vehicle came down the track and nothing moved except the waders probing the mud at the mere's edge. I lay dozing, conscious of dehydration and the burning power of the sun, and all the time that sense of waiting heavy on my mind. At one point I remember studying van Delden through half-closed lids and thinking of Lear—that gnarled face burned brown by the sun, the long white hair lank with sweat. For Lear there had been nothing but disaster, and I wondered, my mind dulled by the heat and full of foreboding as the sun swung slowly across the brazen sky and sank towards the Turkana shore. And still nothing happened.

The sunset that evening was a purple flare like rich blood spilled across a pale blue-green ceiling. The lake turned red, then faded to the dull sheen of beaten metal, and with the dusk the birds came, pelicans, storks, geese, all manner of birds singly and in flights.

Two shots gave us a meal, and while Mtome prepared it, the rest of us laid out the net in the shallows and hauled in more tilapia. On the shore there, looking across to the fading shapes of the islands and thinking of the people who had inhabited this world thousands of years ago, I had a sense of frustration: to have come so far, and in van Delden's company, everything I had planned, and now I knew instinctively that this was the end of the road. Mary, standing barefoot in the water, caught my mood: "You should have explored those islands while you had the chance. I'd have come with you."

"We'll go tomorrow," I said. But I was certain we wouldn't. And so was she. She shook her head, staring out across the lake to where the first star showed in the dying green of the sky. "Tomorrow I'll be at Loiyangalani," she said, her voice a whisper, her face a pale oval against the dark of her hair. And suddenly I knew that deep down inside she was afraid.

"You could refuse to go."

"No." She shook her head, silent for a moment. Then she said, "But there's nothing I can do. Nothing anyone can do." And she turned abruptly away, heading back towards the fire that now glowed brightly in the dark outcrop of the rocks. I stopped to slip on my boots, wondering that she could walk barefoot over stones and gravel, and as I neared the fire I had a picture of dark African faces lit by the flicker of the flames and the old man sitting cross-legged, his great bearded head ruddy in the glow. It was a very Biblical scene, but Old Testament, not New. No man camped on Lake Rudolf could think in anything but Old Testament terms. This was eye-for-an-eye country, intensely primitive.

That night we took it in turns to keep watch and when Dima woke me, just after midnight, the moon was up and the lake was so still it was difficult to tell where sky and water met, the reflection of the stars equally bright. The hill of the dead was almost white in the moonlight and below it the pale shape of the mere was dotted with the paler shapes of birds all fast

297

asleep. It was a dead world, and lying in the hard hollow of the rocks, I had a sense of unreality, a feeling almost of disembodiment. There was no sound, no movement, everything frozen into immobility, no breath of wind and the air hot and heavy. I had time to think then, all the time in the world, but my mind seemed disoriented, incapable of concentration.

Time passed and gradually I became aware that the night was not entirely lifeless. Behind me, down the lake shore, shapes were shifting position almost imperceptibly. A hippo had its snout just clear of the water and there were crocodiles slithering on the dark volcanic sand. And towards the end of my watch several elephants appeared over a rise to my left, pale prehistoric shapes moving soundless through the moonlit landscape. They passed within a few hundred yards of where I lay, moving in a straggling line towards the lake. It was like a slow-motion film with no sound track, and as they disappeared from sight a voice behind me said very quietly, "If this could ever become a safe place you could walk among those elephants as you would among friends."

"Was that how it was at Marsabit?" I asked, looking back at him over my shoulder.

He nodded, his white hair gleaming silver in the moonlight. "I knew them all, and they knew me. Some I could go right up to and they'd touch my face with their trunks." And he added in a hushed voice, "It's a wonderful thing when an animal as big as that, and wild, gives you its confidence. It's like a revelation. Can you understand?"

"Yes, of course."

"Hmm." He sounded dubious. "To understand that is to understand the relationship of man to beast, the need they have of each other." He was silent then, watching as the last of the elephants slowly disappeared into a shallow dip between two pale rock hillocks. "Have you checked your camera?"

"It's okay."

"You realise nobody has ever shot a film of an elephant kill being stopped." He was staring at me, his

298

voice suddenly urgent. "It means a great deal to me, that it should be on record. And the future of these animals could depend upon it."

"I've still got to get it out of the country."

"Yes, well, we'll have to think about that. But after you've got the pictures." And he nodded. "Better get some sleep now. We start at four."

But after what he had said sleep eluded me, my mind on what the day would bring. The world I knew seemed very far away, the harshness of this near-desert country all about me and the memory of those elephants gliding silent through the moonlight very vivid. Elephants. I could hardly remember when I had not been following their big footprints. I tried thinking about the night on Kulal, and romping in the warm waters of the lake, but it was all ephemeral. And that glimpse of Porr, the broken piece of early pottery I had discarded, nothing had any significance now, except this ghostly congregating of elephants. This was the day towards which we had been steadily moving, Abe and I two outsiders, spectators, caught up in a confrontation that was an extension of the arguments we had heard at that Conference. So long ago it seemed with the lake gleaming pale under the stars and Karanja snoring gently, his broad nostrils quivering.

Dozing, I was vaguely conscious of Mtome fanning the embers of the fire, of dark figures moving against the stars. The moon was half across the sky, lighting a bright path from South Island to the shore below us. No sign of dawn yet and I sat up and looked at my watch. Just after four and van Delden sitting on a rock, his beard limned in light, his head bent over an old Lee Enfield rifle, checking the magazine. Below me, Mary was stooping over Abe and I heard her say, "A few hours now and you'll be able to get it properly set."

"I'm okay," he murmured. "It's just stiff, that's all." But his voice sounded tired. "Any elephants passed during the night?"

I didn't say anything, nor did van Delden, and no-

299

body spoke much as we sat there among the rocks, drinking tea. By the time we had finished breakfast and loaded the truck, the first faint glimmer of dawn was showing behind the bulk of Kulal. Flights of birds were circling the mere as we drove round the edge of it, back on to the track, Mukunga at the wheel and van Delden sitting beside him. Karanja leaned across to Abe. "When you see the major, ask him whether Kit Kimani is still Minister. If he does not know . . ." He hesitated, then added firmly, "Is important he does not do anything without authority. Tell him that."

Abe nodded, but his eyes looked glazed and I wasn't certain he had understood. We were driving without lights, the bumps in the track unavoidable, and he was obviously in pain.

It was about six miles to the lugga and as we approached it the truck slowed. Van Delden had the glasses to his eyes, searching the line of drifted sand and rock outcrops. We ground our way through the empty stream bed, past the twin hillocks that formed a natural gateway, and then we were out in the open with the raised line of the doum palms away to our left, and all ahead the land stretching flat like a salt pan to the El Molo manyata and the port. There was grass here, dry wisps overlaying a carpet of fresh growth, and above us the stars were paling, the dawn light growing.

We were about five hundred yards beyond the lugga when the truck slammed to a halt. A light had appeared at the furthest extremity of the palm tree ridge. Mukunga switched off the engine and in the sudden silence we could hear doves calling. A hyena whooped up among the sand slopes we had crossed coming down off Kulal, the sound very faint and changing to an ugly chuckle. There was the snap of branches, something moving on the doum palm escarpment, then we heard the sound of an engine and headlights swung across the shape of the Mission buildings. Van Delden turned to Mary. "Looks like they're on the move, so I'll have to leave you here."

300

"He can't walk that far."

"Then you'll just have to wait for one of their trucks to pick you up." He had the glasses to his eyes, watching the headlights flickering in the palm tree boles. "Hurry now. I can't wait here."

She got out then and Karanja and I gave Abe a hand. His face looked very pale, his glasses owlish as they caught the dawn light. "Okay?" I asked him.

He nodded, standing with his head up and his mouth set. "I'll make it."

A thin squeal sounded from the doum palms and we all turned our heads towards the ridge, but nothing moved and the sound was not repeated. Van Delden leaned out of the truck, his head turned to Mary. "Try to make him see sense. Because if he doesn't . . ." He bit the words off short and told Mukunga to get going. "Goodbye, Toto," he called softly. Her answer was lost in the sound of the engine and all I caught was the emotion in her voice. It was in her eyes, too, staring at him, very wide. Abe, standing beside her, his arm in the sling she had made for him, said something and she darted a quick glance towards the palms. Only then did she look at me, but our wheels were already stirring dust as we swung round to head back the way we had come and she turned away with a casual wave of her hand.

I was still staring after them, wondering why I had not insisted on going too, when Dima shouted something, pounding on Mukunga's shoulder and pointing towards the lake. A box-like object which could only be a truck was moving against the pale glint of the water, and there was another almost hull down beyond it. They were both moving parallel to us, feeling their way slowly without lights. Our speed increased and we scuttled for the protection of the lugga, bucketing across it and swinging sharp right to skid to a halt behind an outcrop. Van Delden jumped out, swearing softly. "Get your camera."

"It's too dark," I said.

But he brushed my words aside, giving orders to the Africans and clambering up into the rocks, his rifle

301

in his hand. "Take them a little time to flush those elephants out of the palms," he said as I joined him, lying in the shadow of an almost perpendicular rock. "Dawn will come fast now and they need the light for accurate shooting."

"You mean they're going to cull—now?" My mouth was suddenly dry.

"Yes, what else? Dawn's a good time."

"What about Mary?"

"I tell you, it takes time to set up a big kill. They'll have reached the Mission before anything happens."

But as the light strengthened and the hunters' trucks began to take shape in the flat country towards the lake, we could just see Mary, with Abe beside her, still standing on the track almost exactly where we had left them. Van Delden nodded towards the dim-seen figures. "What are they waiting for?"

I shook my head, unwilling to tell him what was in my mind.

"Silly little fool," he growled. "They'll be in the way if they don't get moving."

Karanja slid along the rocks towards us. "What you do now?" But at that moment lights blazed behind the escarpment and we heard the roar of engines, head-lights flickering on the tree boles. Trucks were moving on the sand slopes beyond and we heard the distant sound of men yelling, banging on door panels, horns blaring, followed by squeals and trumpeting—a ter-rible hunting-cry noise that ripped the peaceful still-ness of that lakeside dawn to shreds. And down on the flats towards the lake the trucks we had seen mov-ing into place in the half light were closing in, slowly, menacingly, the sound of their engines lost in the up-roar.

For a ghastly moment I thought van Delden was going to do nothing. He lay there, shaking his head as though willing it not to happen, his gaze fixed on the doum palm escarpment. Dark shadows drifted through the tall curved stems, and then they were coming out, a whole herd with calves of various ages, sliding down the escarpment to the flat arid grassland below, not trumpeting, not making any sound, but moving swiftly, almost purposefully, to their appointment with death. And in the lead, as they headed straight for the lake and the waiting hunters, was a large tusked elephant with a single calf beside her, tripping daintily—like a ballet dancer. The words flashed into my mind, Abe's words, and in that instant, my gaze switching to the two figures still standing on the track, I saw him start forward and Mary trying to restrain him. "Oh God!" I breathed aloud. And van Delden, beside me, muttered, "What's he think he's doing?"

But by then Abe's figure had detached itself and was running awkwardly. I thought I heard him shouting but I couldn't be sure, there was so much noise, a thunderflash exploding and the trucks racing for the end of the palms where they could come down into the flat and complete the drive. Abe was still running forward and Mary had almost caught up with him, two tiny figures running in the pale dawn, and the lead elephant had sighted them. She had stopped and was standing, stiff-legged and uncertain, her head moving from side to side, one foot scuffing the ground. The calf moved ahead of her and she laid her trunk across its shoulders, edging it into safety behind her as she faced the two humans hurrying towards her. The rest of the herd were bunching up behind her now, adults presenting a solid front, the calves pushed in behind, all of them alert to danger, thoroughly roused.

I knew what was in Abe's mind. He was remembering what Karanja had done, up there on the Mara, hoping to turn them towards us before the trucks came down off the escarpment and began the final drive to the killing ground. Van Delden knew it, too, and he was already on his feet, running for the truck. And as we piled into it, the engine bursting into life, I had a feeling of panic, a dreadful certainty; Abe knew nothing about elephants, only what he had read in books.

We came out between the twin hillocks, the wheels churning gravel as we hit the dip of the lugga, and van Delden had the Lee Enfield instead of his double-barrelled rifle gripped in his big hands. I was standing in the back, holding on to the hand-bar, the cloud hanging over Kulal glimpsed out of the corner of my eyes, tinged with red, and away to the right the hunters' trucks raising streamers of dust. Abe was motionless now, about fifty yards from the elephants, one arm raised above his head, and Mary had also stopped a little way behind him. I saw it like that, the scene set as in a still, very clear in the rapidly increasing light, everything motionless. And then the two trucks came belting round the end of the palms. There was an eruption of noise, the crack of a shot, flat and hard, the sound of it coming from a Land-Rover moving in from our right, and in the same instant the herd matriarch charged, not trumpeting, not making any sound, just covering the ground at great speed, the dust flying from her dancing feet. And behind her half a dozen others, big beasts with their trunks curled underneath their tusks and their heads high.

I saw Abe flung aside and Mary trying to run, engulfed in a grey mass. Another shot sounded, and another, a whole ripple of fire. One elephant checked, another down, but the rest of them kept going, driving straight for the Land-Rover and the two trucks now stopped and in the direct line of their charge. And it was in that moment I grabbed the camera, a reflex action, the need to do something, to blot out the scene I had witnessed. By the time I had it to my shoulder the elephants were in among the trucks and all was confusion, my impression blurred by the din of shots and the squeals of rage, the camera whirring and everything seen through the eyepiece. Another elephant went down, rifles blazing and drifts of smoke, and one of the trucks backing away, but not fast enough. A thunderflash burst, but the elephants swept on, a grey tide engulfing it and the matriarch's flailing trunk smashing down on the driver's head, splitting his face open like an over-ripe melon. Tusks drove into the body of the vehicle, heads lowered, grey flanks heaving, and then the truck was on its side, with the wheels spinning and spurting sand, men running.

The cows stood there for a moment, bayoneting the

304

truck with their tusks and trumpeting in fury, then broke, roaring and screaming, as the Land-Rover drove in furiously and bullets slammed into their hides. A shot right beside me, deafening, tracer streaming out on a flat trajectory to strike at the Land-Rover. More shots and the Land-Rover stopped, two men jumping out of it as an elephant bore down, raising it with her tusks, and another, a big bull, I think, coming in from the other side, and the men running as it bore down on them. One man was picked up, flung in the air, the elephant suddenly on top of him, kneeling on him, crushing the life out of him, and then it rose, shaking its head at the bloodied pulp on the ground at its feet.

I ran out of film then, standing there dazed and shaking, realising suddenly that we were stationary. Van Delden and Mukunga were firing over the bonnet, shooting lines of tracer, and the others had scattered, lying flat on the ground at either side of us. One of the trucks from the escarpment was on fire, the other backing away with a flat tyre. More thunderflashes went off, but the elephants ignored them. They had regrouped around their young and they passed within a hundred yards of us, taking no notice and moving swiftly northwards towards the lugga. By the time I had changed the magazine in my camera they were gone and only the dead remained, lying like low tide rocks, all still except one, which was thrashing its legs and trying to lift its head. And in the silence I could hear the gurgle of breath coming laboured from its wide-open mouth.

I sat down then on the tailboard edge, my knees shaking, my legs suddenly weak. The cloud over Kulal had thinned and was now a canopy of violent red. The sun was up behind the mountain, the palms a brilliant green, the earth blood-red and the lake blue, all bright, brittle colours in the sunrise, and van Delden walking slowly with bent head towards the curled-up khaki heap lying in the dust ahead of us. Exhausted, and moving like an automaton, I scrambled out and followed him. Mary lay in a fallen heap, her head at

305

an awkward angle, the neck broken. But for that she might have been asleep. All those elephants passing over her and no mark. It was unbelievable, and only the flies clinging to her eyes to show she was dead.

Van Delden knelt down, brushing the flies from her face. "That fool American." He closed the lids with his fingers, his hand quite steady and nothing else said, no expression of grief. It wasn't callousness. I knew that. It was just acceptance. The man who had been a father to her and had never really known her. . . . "You realise she loved you—very deeply?" My voice was hesitant, under compulsion and sounding strange.

He looked up. "What do you know about it? About love and the pain of love?" And he added quietly, "She was very like her mother—tempestuous, hot-blooded, full of vitality and grabbing at life with both hands. Do you think I didn't love her?" He stared at me, no trace of emotion in the pale cold eyes, and his voice hard as he said, "She's dead, and that's that." He got to his feet, his big head turning to watch Kirby-Smith as he came limping towards us, and I saw his hands clenched on the gun he was still holding.

I don't know what he said to him because at that moment I heard a groan and a voice, very faint, calling me. It was Abe. He was about forty yards away, lying twisted against an old antheap. "Is that you, Colin?" The blood bubbled in his lungs as he forced the words out, his eyes staring up at me, glazed and not seeing. His thin chest was so badly damaged he might have been in a road accident, the rib cage stove in, the white of shattered bone protruding through a dark mess of congealing blood that buzzed with flies. "Is she all right?"

"Yes," I said. "She's all right." I knew it wasn't Mary he was thinking of.

"They were shooting."

"She got away."

"It was those trucks, the bastards! She was charging them. Not me." His voice was suddenly strong and he tried to sit up. "Sally. I can't see her. I can't—" He fell back with a gurgling cry, blood frothing in his mouth.

"Just lie still," I said. "Save your strength."

But he didn't hear me, his lips moving, framing his wife's name, but no sound coming. His eyes closed and he gave a bubbling groan, his mouth spilling more blood. I think he died in that moment, but I couldn't be sure, never having seen anybody die before, and I called to van Delden. But he didn't hear me, his mind shut to everything else but the man facing him with one trouser leg ripped open at the knee and a lacerated arm. ". . . your own child. God help me, I can't shoot you in cold blood—"

"You dumped them there deliberately."

"Don't be a fool, man. Finkel had busted his arm."

"You were using them."

"He was injured, I tell you."

"But Mary—to leave Mary there. Right where I was going to cull. You knew what was going to happen. You knew." His voice was high, almost out of control, the two of them facing each other, ablaze with anger, the body at their feet forgotten, and van Delden saying, "You could have stopped it." His voice was hard and full of menace. "Instead, you fired. You fired at the lead elephant."

"To turn them."

"No. To start the cull."

"If I hadn't had to shoot from a moving vehicle—"

"You'd have killed that cow, but it wouldn't have stopped the others. Don't you understand what those beasts have been through? They're so desperate now they'll charge any vehicle on sight."

"We'd have stopped them if you hadn't interfered. Firing on our vehicles—"

I saw the gun come up, the flash of the barrel in the sun, and I shouted something. But Mukunga was already there, his hand on van Delden's arm, and the old man suddenly came to his senses, turning angrily away. "Get out of my sight," he growled, shaking his head like a big bull uncertain what to do next. "Christ Almighty! I should have killed you long ago." He glanced briefly at Mary and his eyes passed on as

307

though she were nothing now, his gaze fastening on a truck raising a cloud of dust as it came down the track from the Mission. It was an open 15 cwt. Kirby-Smith had seen it, too. His Land-Rover had been righted and one of his men drove it up to him, rubber flapping from the front tyres, which had both been ripped open by the thrusting tusks. Mukunga was talking urgently to van Delden, Mtome and Dima gripping their rifles, eyes watching nervously as the Army truck approached. The hunting vehicles were sorting themselves out, one of them already under tow, and overhead the red of the sky was beginning to fade.

The Army truck slowed as it approached Mary's body, a young black officer standing up beside the driver, holding on to the windscreen. It stopped and he stayed there for a moment, his gaze switching from the dead girl to Abe's body lying at my feet, and involuntarily I thought of Fortinbras, expecting him at any moment to make a speech. Instead, he shook his head, at a loss what to do in a situation like this. Slowly he stepped down from his vehicle, turning to Kirby-Smith as though seeking a lead. He said something in Swahili and Kirby-Smith nodded. Then suddenly they were all talking and Kirby-Smith's partner, Jeff Saunders, drove up in one of the hunting trucks to join in the angry exchange. Everybody was talking at once, all except van Delden, who stood there, not saying a word, just waiting.

Finally the officer turned to him. "Where is Karanja?" he asked in English.

It was only then that I realised Karanja was not there, that he had not been with us in the truck when we had driven out from the lugga in our abortive attempt to head the elephants off. Van Delden shook his head, turning and looking back. The others also turned and following their gaze I saw a lone dark figure halfway along the track from the lugga, walking steadily towards us.

The officer got back into his truck and went to pick him up. When it returned Karanja got out. "Very bad

308

business," he said, addressing Kirby-Smith, his voice high and trembling slightly, either with tension or suppressed excitement, I wasn't certain which. "There will be no more culling please and you will withdraw your outfit to South Horr to await further instructions." And when Kirby-Smith started to argue, Karanja cut him short. "Those are the orders of the Military Commander." And the officer beside him nodded.

It was Saunders who said quickly, "Brigadier Osman doesn't control this operation. It's a political matter and Kit Kimani has given us—"

"Mt. Kimani is not any longer Minister. There is a new Minister of Resources, Mr. Abbas. That is what Lieutenant Elmi has just told me." And he turned to the officer beside him, who nodded his head again and said, "Ndio."

"So you don't shoot any more elephants, not until I have spoken on the radio with Headquarters." He turned to van Delden. "I suggest you go back now to your old camp beside the lake and wait there. I will make endeavour to arrange safe passage for you out of the country. Okay?" And he added, "I am sorry— about this." He made a gesture that embraced the two sprawled bodies, then indicated the truck. "This detachment is leaving now in support of the Army post at Marsabit. Maybe I arrange for you to go with them." He turned to me. "You took some film. I would like it please." He was looking straight at me, his tone commanding, and when I hesitated, he said, "Is not good that what happens here is shown in the West, so you will hand it to me please."

I glanced at van Delden, but he didn't say anything, his gaze turned inwards, his eyes blank. And as I turned away to get the film I heard Kirby-Smith say, "Abbas. There was a Tanzanian called Simon Abbas, took over Tsavo East just before the Ugandan Army moved across the frontier. Is that the man?" And Karanja nodded. "Is why I tell you there will be no more culling without his authority. He has great interest in elephants."

I got the film and when I came back with it Kirby-

309

Smith was talking urgently with his partner. "If they won't loan us a plane, then see if you can persuade Brigadier Osman to have Pat Murphy fly me to Nairobi. The sooner I talk to Abbas . . ." They were already moving away and van Delden, still standing by Mary's body, suddenly lifted his head and called out, "Alex!" And when the other paused and turned to face him he said quietly, "Where are you planning to bury her—here or in Nairobi?"

"How the hell can we bury her in Nairobi?"

"You could fly her down."

"There isn't room in a Cessna."

"Use one of your refrigerator trucks then."

"No." The suggestion seemed to upset him.

"All right then. Where?"

"It's nothing to do with me."

"She's your child."

"I tell you, it's not my responsibility. You brought her up. You caused her death. You bury her."

Van Delden stared at him for a long moment, then he nodded his head slowly. "All right. If that's the way you feel."

We loaded both bodies into the 15 cwt and drove back to the hill of the dead. We buried them there on the stony slope that looked out over the little bay to the El Molo Islands. ". . . ashes to ashes, dust to dust . . ." Van Delden knew the relevant passages of the burial service by heart, and seeing him standing there, white-headed and bearded, intoning the words of committal, I knew he had done this many times before. The dust we tossed into the shallow graves was volcanic dust, and the sun shone out of a clear sky, the heat blistering.

It took us the rest of the day, working with wet towels over our heads, to build the two cairns, and in the evening, when it was done, we sat over a brew of tea, watching the birds fly in to roost on the mere below us, the sun falling below the Turkana mountains and the first stars showing pale in the rapidly darkening sky. Nobody spoke, van Delden sitting silent and withdrawn, the three Africans squatting round the embers, a stillness settling on the land, and I found myself remembering Abe's thin, sallow face, the dark wordly eyes, and the little twisted smile. I hadn't been brought up to believe in anything very much, but now, in this wild place with the stone cairns shadowy above me, I knew there must be something—something to reach out for. He had possessed an inner strength. He had talked of love, and suddenly I envied him, his peace, the certainty of his beliefs.

Sometime during the night Karanja arrived. He and van Delden were talking for a long time, but I couldn't hear what was said, only the murmur of their voices. I went to sleep again, and when I woke it was dawn and van Delden had gone.

I got to my feet, looking wildly round, realising I was alone, the two cairns outlined against the sun rising behind Kulal. And then I saw them, four dark figures splashing through the shallows of the mere, and north along the shore a solitary figure kneeling on a log raft and paddling it across the still, calm surface of the lake towards a small group of elephants standing up to their bellies in the water. I stood there for a moment, staring at the white of his hair shining in the early morning light, the paddle flashing drips of water and fish breaking the surface ahead of him in glints of silver. It was something I shall always remember, that lone figure on the El Molo fishing raft paddling slowly up the shore of Lake Rudolf, heading north like the elephants.

By the time I had reached the bottom of the hill the four Africans were waiting beside a Land-Rover parked on the track above the mere. Karanja came to meet me, smiling and with something of a swagger in his walk. "You sleep very deep, Mr. Tait." And on his shoulder he carried van Delden's double-barrelled rifle.

The sight of it, with the picture of that lone figure still vivid in my mind, shocked me. "You let him go—unarmed."

He shrugged. "Plenty of fish. He live like the El Molo now." And he added, "He is Tembo van Delden

311

and he is back with his own people. With the elephants." Then, with something of a flourish, he said, "The new Minister has appointed me Warden of the North. I look after all game in this region now. That is what I came to tell him, that he and his elephants are safe."

Six hours later Pat Murphy landed me at Wilson Airport, Nairobi, and that same evening I boarded a flight for London. Since then I have been scripting a documentary, *The Building of the Canals,* and in my spare time writing this account of the fortnight I spent in Africa. I have had no news of Cornelius van Delden, though I have written twice to Karanja, once in care of his Minister, and have made enquiries at the E.A.F. Embassy. I have, therefore, no certain information as to his present whereabouts, or even whether he is still alive. But in my mind I see him still as I last saw him, paddling alone along the shores of Lake Rudolf against a background of elephants belly-deep in the water. My guess is he will remain there till he dies, a forgotten man, lost to anything but the world he knows and understands better than any other human being.

Author's Note

MY FASCINATION with Lake Rudolf is of long standing —a first meeting with Joy Adamson in 1960 at which she gave me a detailed description of this most extraordinary lake, which is part of the great volcanic fault of the Rift Valley. At that time politics predominated, and I felt very strongly that if I was to set a novel in that area, I wanted to write about the underlying, enduring Africa that had survived the political winds of change. By 1972, however, friends I had met initially through my publisher, Sir William Collins, who has produced so many of the books on African wildlife, were warning me that if I wanted to see the last great game herds I had best come soon, before the pressure of population destroyed them.

The journeys my wife, Dorothy, and I made in Africa in 1972–73 began with Joy and George Adamson and Christmas spent at George's lion camp on the Tana River. His brother Terence was there, and Ken Smith, the Game Warden, so that I could not have had a better introduction to animal behaviour. And our understanding grew as we journeyed north, a safari of our own under the guidance of Jonny Baxendale that covered a considerable area of the N.F.D., including the southern part of Lake Rudolf and camp established close to the summit of Mt. Kulal. Later Richard Leakey flew us up to the northern part of the lake to visit his discovery site of the skull that put the origins of man back a million and a half years. Later still, we went south into the Serengeti, catching the migration in full swing, visiting Mary Leakey in Olduvai Gorge, Hugo van Lawick in the Ngorongoro Crater, and then out into the plains with Hugo and Jane Goodall to follow their Ghengis pack as the wild dogs hunted down a baby wildebeest.

To all these people, and many others, including Ian

Player and Nick Steele in other parts of Africa, I am greatly indebted—for the time they gave to us, and for their advice, assitance, and the great fund of knowledge they imparted. And since this is a story about elephants, I must pay tribute to the work of Iain Douglas-Hamilton in the Manyara Reserve. During our travels in Africa we had the opportunity of observing the behaviour of these remarkable animals over long periods and at close quarters. But the proper interpretation and understanding of that behaviour would not have been possible without constant reference to *Among the Elephants,* the fascinating book written by Iain and his wife, Oria.

For those readers who have a scientific interest in animal behaviour I feel I should make it clear that, like the characters, the central theme of *The Big Footprints* is purely imaginary. I discussed it with Iain Douglas-Hamilton, but the circumstances of total disaster I have described are as yet outside anyone's experience. Nobody can say whether elephants have an inherited knowledge of safe areas, or whether, given the circumstances, they would undertake such a desperate migration. As to the presence of elephants on Lake Rudolf, though I saw none myself, and Ken Smith states positively there are none at the present time, they were certainly there in considerable numbers less than a century ago when Count Teleki discovered the lake. They were not only watering there, but also subsisting partly on the weed available in the shallows.

To what degree I have taken liberties with my subject only time will tell. And time is fast running out. There are believed to be not more than 120,000 elephants left in this part of Africa and the rate of killing has risen to some 20,000 a year. This appalling toll is mainly due to the rapid rise in the price of ivory, and I would beg my readers to remember that the purchaser of any ivory object is directly responsible for the protracted, lingering death of another elephant. No purchasers, no poachers—it is as simple as that.